HOLIDAY GRIND

"Other honorable mentions for new holiday booking . . .
Holiday Grind by Cleo Coyle, a new addition to the coffeehouse mystery series that . . . adds in jolts of souped-up coffee,
sweet cooking . . . and super-sleuthing to deliver a fun and
gripping fa-la-la-la-latte surprise." —*The Huffington Post*

"The charming eighth coffeehouse mystery . . . will keep readers guessing until the end, while the drink and accompanying
treat recipes will send anyone to the kitchen in search of a
candy cane brownie and a caffe mocha latte."
—*Publishers Weekly*

"Gives readers . . . many holiday recipes while throwing in
a good plot and an in-your-face look at life in the Big Apple
for good measure. Fans of culinary cozies by Joanne Fluke and
JoAnna Carl will want this." —*Library Journal*

"Coyle's greatest strength is writing characters that feel real.
Clare and company are some of the most vibrant characters
I've ever read . . . Coyle also is a master of misdirection and
red herrings. I challenge any reader to figure out whodunit
before Coyle reveals all." —*Mystery Scene Magazine*

"Coffeehouse manger Clare Cosi and her band of her merry
men lead readers on a wild and hilarious ride to find out who
killed her Santa in this witty and intelligent cozy. Readers
will be enthralled as the mystery unravels and the surprise
killer is revealed." —*Romantic Times*

continued . . .

ESPRESSO SHOT

"Coyle's Coffeehouse books are superb examples of the cozy genre because of their intelligent cast of characters, their subtle wit, and their knowledge of the coffee industry used to add depth and flavor to the stories. Highly recommended for all mystery collections."   —*Library Journal* (starred review)

"Clare visits underground restaurants, temples to high fashion, and the hotel room of a seductive Italian sculptor in her attempts to keep the bride alive . . . A realistic depiction of New York City high and low life. The smattering of recipes, romance, and caffeine-fueled detection add up to a lively tale."   —*Kirkus Reviews*

"Enjoyable . . . This mellow-paced cozy includes some surprises . . . Recipes and coffee tips are a bonus." —*Publishers Weekly*

"Cleo Coyle's Coffeehouse Mysteries, which are among my favorites, can be counted on for great characters, smooth plotting and pacing that keeps readers engaged . . . *Espresso Shot* is seventh in the series and, in my opinion, it's the best one yet."   —*Mystery News*

"Oh, *Espresso Shot* is a fun read! I kept turning the pages long after I should have turned off the light." —*Armchair Interviews*

FRENCH PRESSED

#1 Paperback Bestseller
Independent Mystery Booksellers Association

"Engaging . . . Keeps the reader in suspense to the very end, *French Pressed* is well worth reading."   —*New Mystery Reader*

"Once again, Cleo Coyle has written an enjoyable, fast-paced mystery that features a perky heroine who has gone from single mother to savvy business owner . . . Readers may be stumped until the very end."   —*The Mystery Reader*

"I love Cleo Coyle's Coffeehouse Mysteries and *French Pressed* is the best yet."
—*Cozy Library*

"I have read all the Coffeehouse Mysteries and enjoyed them thoroughly. Cleo Coyle has written a wonderful series."
—*I Love A Mystery*

"Coyle again entertains, informs, and challenges the reader... The clues are there in the open, but we must put them together."
—*Gumshoe Review*

DECAFFEINATED CORPSE

#1 Paperback Bestseller
Independent Mystery Booksellers Association

"Great characters, smooth plotting, and top-notch writing, it's no wonder these books are bestsellers."
—*Cozy Library*

"Author Coyle displays a deep understanding, not only of coffee . . . but also of coffee shop culture. She treats espresso shop work as an honorable profession . . . Coyle knows her coffee so well that even I have learned new coffee bits by reading her books. If you have not yet discovered the Coffeehouse Mystery series by Cleo Coyle, you should . . . I heartily recommend them."
—Eric S. Chen, *BARISTO.net*

MURDER MOST FROTHY

"Exciting, delicious fun, with coffee trivia, recipes, a vicarious adventure for those of us at home reading of things we'd rather not face ourselves but understanding Clare Cosi's motives and morals."
—*Gumshoe Review*

LATTE TROUBLE

"Anyone who loves coffee and a good mystery will love this story. Rating: Outstanding."
—*Mysterious Corner*

THROUGH THE GRINDER

"Coffee lovers & mystery buffs will savor the latest addition to this mystery series . . . Fast-paced action, coffee lore, and incredible culinary recipes . . . All hail the goddess Caffina!"
—*The Best Reviews*

ON WHAT GROUNDS

#1 Paperback Bestseller
Independent Mystery Booksellers Association

"A great beginning to a new series . . . *On What Grounds* will convert even the most fervent tea drinker into a coffee lover in the time it takes to draw an espresso."   —*The Mystery Reader*

"A hilarious blend of amateur detecting with some romance thrown in the mix . . . I personally adored this book, and can't wait to read the rest of the series!"   —*Cozy Library*

Visit Cleo Coyle's virtual Village Blend at
www.CoffeehouseMystery.com,
where coffee and crime are always brewing.

HOLIDAY GRIND

CLEO COYLE

BERKLEY PRIME CRIME, NEW YORK

THE BERKLEY PUBLISHING GROUP
Published by the Penguin Group
Penguin Group (USA) Inc.
375 Hudson Street, New York, New York 10014, USA
Penguin Group (Canada), 90 Eglinton Avenue East, Suite 700, Toronto, Ontario M4P 2Y3, Canada
(a division of Pearson Penguin Canada Inc.)
Penguin Books Ltd., 80 Strand, London WC2R 0RL, England
Penguin Group Ireland, 25 St. Stephen's Green, Dublin 2, Ireland (a division of Penguin Books Ltd.)
Penguin Group (Australia), 250 Camberwell Road, Camberwell, Victoria 3124, Australia
(a division of Pearson Australia Group Pty. Ltd.)
Penguin Books India Pvt. Ltd., 11 Community Centre, Panchsheel Park, New Delhi—110 017, India
Penguin Group (NZ), 67 Apollo Drive, Rosedale, North Shore 0632, New Zealand
(a division of Pearson New Zealand Ltd.)
Penguin Books (South Africa) (Pty.) Ltd., 24 Sturdee Avenue, Rosebank, Johannesburg 2196,
South Africa

Penguin Books Ltd., Registered Offices: 80 Strand, London WC2R 0RL, England

This is a work of fiction. Names, characters, places, and incidents either are the product of the author's imagination or are used fictitiously, and any resemblance to actual persons, living or dead, business establishments, events, or locales is entirely coincidental. The publisher does not have any control over and does not assume any responsibility for author or third-party websites or their content.

PUBLISHER'S NOTE: The recipes contained in this book are to be followed exactly as written. The publisher is not responsible for your specific health or allergy needs that may require medical supervision. The publisher is not responsible for any adverse reaction to the recipes contained in this book.

HOLIDAY GRIND

A Berkley Prime Crime Book / published by arrangement with author

PRINTING HISTORY
Berkley Prime Crime hardcover edition / November 2009
Berkley Prime Crime mass-market edition / November 2010

Copyright © 2009 by Penguin Group (USA) Inc.
Cover illustration by Cathy Gendron.
Cover design and logo by Rita Frangie.
Interior text design by Kristin del Rosario.

ISBN: 978-0-425-23788-5

BERKLEY® PRIME CRIME
Berkley Prime Crime Books are published by The Berkley Publishing Group,
a division of Penguin Group (USA) Inc.,
375 Hudson Street, New York, New York 10014.
BERKLEY® PRIME CRIME and the PRIME CRIME logo are trademarks of Penguin Group (USA) Inc.
A COFFEEHOUSE MYSTERY is a registered trademark of Penguin Group (USA) Inc.

PRINTED IN THE UNITED STATES OF AMERICA

10 9 8 7 6 5

To Alex, Andrew, and Tia
Never stop believing in goodness.

ACKNOWLEDGMENTS

I'm often asked what coffeehouses helped inspire me to create the Village Blend. Joe is always at the top of my list—Joe, the Art of Coffee, that is, whose flagship store is located in the heart of Greenwich Village. Joe's visionary founder, Jonathan Rubinstein, and his sister Gabriella run Joe's with the same dedication to quality and the community that I imagine Clare Cosi does.

I'd also like to recognize Joe's coffee director, Amanda Byron, whose fun and informative coffee classes helped educate me on the romance of the bean as well as the culinary expertise of the barista. Since I began writing the Coffeehouse Mysteries, Joe has expanded to several locations in New York—and kudos to them for being named by *Food & Wine* magazine as one of the top coffee bars in the country. For more information, you can visit their online home at www.joetheartofcoffee.com.

No book goes from laptop to printed page without the help of an intrepid posse of publishing professionals, and the people at Berkley Prime Crime are among the best in the business. I'd especially like to thank Executive Editor Wendy McCurdy for her editorial ingenuity and generosity of spirit. A shout-out also goes to Allison Brandau and Katherine Pelz for their good cheer and hard work.

As always, I thank my husband, Marc, who—as many of you already know—is my partner in writing not only this Coffeehouse Mystery series but also our Haunted Bookshop Mysteries. (A better partner a girl couldn't ask for.)

For his consistent professionalism, I thank my agent John Talbot. For advice on matters medical, Dr. Grace Alfonsi is my angel—if literary license is taken in this area, the blame is mine. A tip of the hat also goes to Sammy L. for his tips on Jamaican slang and cuisine.

A sincere salute must be given to the dedicated officers of the Sixth Precinct, which serves and protects Greenwich Village. As these are light works of amateur sleuth fiction, I sometimes take liberties with police procedure, but be assured that my respect for the men and women of the NYPD knows no bounds.

Given the premise of this fictional story, I'd also like to recognize two very real and worthy holiday charities. Operation Santa Claus, run by the employees of the U.S. Postal Service, allows the general public to answer letters to Santa from needy children and families. The dedicated bell ringers of the Salvation Army also aid families in need with the donations they collect via their street-corner kettles. If you'd like to learn more about these two charities, just turn to the afterword of this book.

Finally, I'd like to send good cheer to all of *you* Santa Clauses out there. In an age when anxiety and cynicism keep far too many hands firmly clenched inside pockets, you represent the true spirit of the holidays. Thank you for understanding what joy there is in the simple act of giving.

Yours sincerely,
Cleo Coyle

I have always thought of Christmas time . . . as a good time; a kind, forgiving, charitable, pleasant time; the only time I know of, in the long calendar of the year, when men and women . . . open their shut-up hearts freely and think of people below them as if they really were fellow passengers to the grave . . .

—Charles Dickens, *A Christmas Carol*

PROLOGUE

~~~~~~

SANTA'D been naughty . . .

He also had a pattern, and the shooter was counting on it.

Out the door at noon, then a bus downtown. By one, the white-bearded wanderer was checking in at the depot near Union Square, picking up his green plastic "sleigh," starting his six-hour shift.

Slowly Santa made his way down Sixth, ringing his annoying bells, collecting his precious change. At close to three, he turned west. On Hudson, he parked his little wheeled cart and disappeared inside that Village Blend coffee shop. One interminable latte break later, the wannabe saint was back on the street, ho-ho-hoing his chubby heart out.

Step by agonizing step, the shooter watched while ducking into doorways, hugging dirty buildings, keeping humanity at a chilly distance. When twilight descended, snow began to fall, the temperature dropping with it, and the watching got harder.

At least the bulky overcoat was thick and warm, *the shooter thought. Ratty, too, because it came from a thrift store, but it would soon be trashed, along with the hat, the scarf, the eyeglasses, and other pieces of the disguise.*

Before long, the wasted hours would finally pay off. Santa's wayward travels led him down a stretch of deserted cobblestones. The street was quiet, secluded, frozen over in white. Everything was set now, except for the gloves.

Thick with insulation, the gloves had provided warmth to spare on this long, cold slog, but now they posed a problem. Any padding between trigger and guard could make life difficult—or death, in this case.

So off came the right glove. A bit of anxious sweat on the fingertips slickened the surface of the pocketed weapon. The seasonal weather swiftly solved that glitch.

Icy metal. My new best friend . . .

Impatient now, the shooter moved to finish the job. Then this ridiculous getup could be discarded, replaced with personal outerwear—garments now sitting inside the newly purchased gym bag, which would also be tossed.

Next the gun would be wiped clean and carefully placed. Finally, the alibi would be established, an appearance at a public place, one previously frequented. A register receipt would confirm date and time.

And speaking of time . . .

The shooter's big boots crunched firmly through the sidewalk snow. The air was cold but blood turned colder when stiff fingers tightened around frosty metal.

It's time to end this problem, *the shooter thought.* Time to silence forever the rest of Santa's nights . . .

One

"**WHAT** does Christmas *taste* like?"

That was the question I'd posed to my top baristas the night I discovered Alf Glockner's body. Until I stumbled over the man's remains, however, I hadn't been thinking about murder or corpses or crime-scene evidence. My mood hadn't plummeted; my worries hadn't started; my buoyant holiday spirits hadn't crashed through the floor.

I, Clare Cosi—single mother of a grown daughter and manager of the landmark Village Blend—still believed this was a season for celebrating. Which was why, on that particular December evening, my mind was *not* focused on clues or suspects or the riskier aspects of defying a cocky NYPD sergeant, but on the much simpler problem of my shop's bottom line. Hence the question to my staff—

What does Christmas taste like?

"Well, nutmeg's a must," Tucker replied.

An itinerate actor-playwright and my most reliable employee, Tucker Burton was lanky as a floor lamp, his lean form topped by a defining shock of floppy brown hair. Sitting across from me in our empty coffeehouse, he tossed back the signature hair and added—

"Cloves. And cinnamon. *Definitely* cinnamon."

"Festive spices all," I agreed. "But we've got them covered—" Turning in my chair, I tipped my pen toward the chalkboard behind the espresso bar. "Our Eggnog Latte's got the nutmeg; the Caramel Apple Pie is loaded with cinnamon; the Pumpkin Spice includes all three—"

And that was the problem.

Those drinks had been on the Village Blend's seasonal menu for years now, and they were starting to feel tired. With the sluggish economy taking its toll on everyone's wallets (mine included), I needed to accelerate the ringing of our registers before we rang in the New Year. And, *yes*, I had a strategy.

Later tonight, I was holding a private latte-tasting party; and first thing tomorrow I planned to place a new menu of tempting holiday coffee drinks on a sidewalk chalkboard in front of the coffeehouse. I even had an Excel spreadsheet ready to go. Come January, after the halls were no longer decked and Santa had sent his red velvet suit to the cleaners, I'd start analyzing our sales results to get a handle on the better-selling flavors for next year.

"What *else* tastes like Christmas?" I repeated. "Come on, people, think back to your childhoods!"

My own foodie memories were as treasured as that overused reference to Proust's madeleine—from my grandmother's anisette-flavored biscotti to the candied orange peels in her panettone. And, of course, there was her traditional *struffoli*: I could still see those cellophane-wrapped plates lined up in Nonna's little Pennsylvania grocery, the golden balls of honey-drenched dough mounded into tiny Italian Christmas trees (just waiting to help make me the chunky monkey I'd been until my midteens).

Unfortunately for me, *Fried Dough Latte* just didn't sound like a winning menu item.

"What I remember is the pralines," Tucker said.

"*Pecan* pralines?" I assumed, because he'd been raised in Louisiana.

"Of course. Every year, our next-door neighbor made them from scratch and gave them out as presents. Another woman on the block was German, and she made up these delicious gift tins of frosted gingerbread cookies—"

"*Pfeffernüsse?*" I asked. "*Lebkuchen?*"

"*Gesundheit.*" Tucker replied. "Of course, my *own* mama, being a former Hollywood film extra, was obsessed with Bing Crosby and *White Christmas*, so we had all that traditional Yankee Yule stuff—fruitcake, candy canes, sugar cookies. And, of course, bourbon."

I smiled. "With my dad it was Sambuca shots."

He poured them like water for the army of factory guys who dropped by to place bets during the Christmas season. (Among other things, my father ran a sports book in the back room of his mother's grocery. I'm fairly sure the "other" things weren't legal, either.)

"In my house, it was rum," Gardner offered.

With a voice as smooth as his jazz playlists, Gardner Evans had the kind of mellow attitude any New York retail manager would value—and I did. No amount of customer crush could frazzle the young, African-American jazz musician, who seemed able to calm our most wired customers (especially the female variety) with little more than a wink.

"Rum?" Tucker said.

Gardner nodded. "Oh, yeah. If you're talking *taste* of Christmas, you've got to have rum."

Esther Best—zaftig grad student, local slam poetess, and latte artist extraordinaire—peered at Gardner through a pair of black rectangular frames. "What do you mean, rum? Like the stuff pirates drink?"

"Like hot buttered rum," Gardner said, stroking his trimmed goatee. "Like the rum in mulled cider and spiked eggnog. Like the Jamaican rum in my auntie's bread pudding and black cake. Ever have Caribbean black cake, Best Girl?"

"Haven't had the pleasure."

"Well, it's a lot like you."

"Like me?"

"Yeah." Gardner's smile flashed white against his mocha skin. "It's dark and dense with powerful *flav-ah*."

Narrowing her perpetually critical gaze, Esther replied, "I am *not* dense."

"But you *are* dark," Tucker pointed out. "Besides, the man said *dense* with *flavor*. Or are you too dense to understand Gardner's derisive gangsta-rap inflection?"

"Bite me, Broadway Boy. My boyfriend's the *top* Russian rapper in Brighton Beach. I think I can recognize the mocking of urban street slang when I hear it—" Esther held a palm up to Gardner. "And *do not* give me another musicology lecture. I *know* you've got a major grudge against gangsta rap."

Gardner folded his arms, leaned back in his chair, and shrugged. "Whatever."

"Anyway—" Esther turned to face me. "We can't put *rum* in a latte. Right, boss? Rum is alcohol. And unless I missed the memo, you haven't gotten a liquor license for this place, have you?"

"No *duh*," said Tucker. "We can use rum *syrup*. Why do you think I used peppermint syrup for my Candy Cane Cappuccino? I would have used actual crème de menthe if it were legal!"

"Now that you've brought it up," Esther said, "I think we should eighty-six Tucker's Christmas Cap." She held up one of the many paper cups holding the evening's first round of samples. "His Candy Cane Cappuccino's *way* too sweet. If we put this on the holiday menu, I guarantee two out of three customers will complain to have it remade—or just spew it back out."

"A lovely holiday image," Dante Silva called from behind the espresso bar. With his sleeves rolled up to show off his self-designed tattoos, the shaved-headed fine arts painter had just begun frothing up a fresh pitcher of milk.

"Are you *serious*?" Esther shouted from our table. "Or is that steam wand drowning out your sarcasm?"

"I can see it now," Dante replied with a straight face, "a cobblestone street in the historic West Village, snow falling lightly on shingled rooftops, primary colors twinkling around the trunks of bared elms, and our customers spewing Tucker's Candy Cane Cap all over their Ugg boots."

Tucker smirked. "Now all Dante has to do is paint it for us. Hey, Dante! Why don't you make it into a stencil for latte toppings? Or better yet, just tattoo it to your billiard-ball head!"

Dante's reply was a hand gesture.

I sighed, wondering what the heck had happened to our holiday spirit. An hour earlier, when we'd been decorating the shop, things had gone so well I thought I'd been painted into a Currier and Ives print.

After closing early, my staff helped me pick out a New York white pine from the sidewalk vendor on Jane Street. As Tucker's basso crooned "O Tannenbaum," Dante and Gardner carried the tree back on their shoulders. Then I helped them set it up in the corner, we cut the bundling wires, and the tree's springy branches unfurled, filling the entire first floor with the fresh, sharp smell of an evergreen forest.

Esther (actually cheerful for once) began affixing bright red ribbons to the deep green boughs, and I dug out the lovingly packed boxes of antique miniature coffee cups and tin pots that Madame—the Village Blend's elderly owner—had collected over the years. Then Tucker replaced our shop dinger with jingle bells, and Dante laid out the big red and green welcome mat I'd purchased the week before—the one that said *Merry Christmas* in a dozen languages along with *Happy Holidays! Happy Chanukah!* and *Happy Kwanzaa!*

(Living in a city with as many cultural and religious differences as New York meant you were probably violating someone's belief system just by breathing. Lofty words like *diversity* and *understanding* were often bandied about in hopes of fostering open-mindedness, but after living in this roiling mini-UN for the past two decades, I was convinced that the way to universal harmony lay in a more practical philosophy. A diversity of cultures meant a diversity of foods. *Eat with tolerance*, I say.)

For a full hour, we continued decorating the coffeehouse, stringing white lights around the French doors, hanging fresh spruce wreaths against the casement windows. Finally, we put up quilted stockings over the hearth's stone mantel, where one of Madame's silver menorahs already stood, waiting for the Festival of Lights to begin.

Peace on earth had *actually* been in play, until we all began judging each other's coffee creations . . .

Now, checking my watch, I tensed. Our guests would be arriving soon to sample our new holiday coffee drinks, and we were nowhere near ready.

"Okay, that's it!" I announced in a tone I hadn't used since my daughter was in grade school. "No more bickering! Everyone behind the espresso bar! I want Christmas in a cup, and I want it ASAP!"

FORTY-FIVE minutes later, two dozen bottles of sweet syrups were lined up on our blue marble espresso bar; stainless steel milk-frothing pitchers stood on the work counter behind it; and I was reviewing our hastily scribbled tasting menu.

Tucker's offerings included Butter Pecan Praline, Candy Cane (easy on the syrup), Iced Gingersnap, and Old-Fashioned Sugar Cookie. Dante's flavors were Eggnog Cheesecake, Spiked Fruitcake, White Chocolate Tiramisu, and Toasted Marshmallow Snowflake. Gardner's Christmas memories brought us Rum Raisin, Mocha-Coconut Macaroon, and Caribbean Black Cake. And from my own beloved Nonna's Christmases: Candied Orange Panettone, Maple-Kissed Gingerbread, and Glazed Roasted Chestnut.

Esther also had contributions: Apricot-Cinnamon Rugelach and Raspberry Jelly Doughnut because, as she quite rightly put it, "Chanukah has its own flavors." For Esther, this also included Key Lime Pie because, as she noted, "Every December my family fled to Florida."

The invited guests of our latte tasting were now mingling near the crackling logs of the store's hearth, waiting for us to whip up the samples.

Tucker was entertaining his current boyfriend, a Hispanic Broadway dancer who went by the single name Punch. Gardner was playing host to Theo, Ronny, and Chick, the three other members of his jazz ensemble Four on the Floor. And Dante had invited his two aspiring-artist roommates: a pierced platinum-blond pixie named Kiki and a raven-haired girl of East Indian heritage named Banhi.

Checking my watch, I decided to give our missing guests another ten minutes to show. Esther's boyfriend—Boris the assistant-baker-slash-Russian-rapper—was performing at a Brooklyn club tonight. Since he couldn't make it, she'd invited another taster, a friend named Vicki Glockner.

Earlier in the year, Vicki had worked as a barista for me. She'd loved experimenting with our Italian syrups, and I knew she'd make a good taster, but I had mixed feelings about seeing her again because she and I hadn't parted on the best of terms.

My friend was late, too—although he'd phoned to apologize and warn that he might not make it at all. I couldn't blame him. Since I began seeing Mike Quinn, I'd had to accept that a NYPD detective's work was never done.

My other tasting party guinea pig was now smacking his knuckles against the beveled glass of the Blend's front door. I moved to unlock it and realized the night had grown colder and the snow higher. Fat flakes had been falling steadily for the last hour. Now they layered the sidewalk and street with several inches of crystalline frosting. As I pulled the door wide, the newly installed jingle bells sounded above, and a chilly wind gust sent a flurry of ice diamonds into my dark brown hair.

"You actually made it?" I said with a shiver as Matteo Allegro stepped inside.

Two

~~~~~~~~~~~~~~~~~~~~~~~~~~~~~~~~

SKIN still lightly bronzed from the Central American sun, Matteo stamped the wet snow off his boots—and (happily) *not* onto the shop's restored wood-plank floor, thanks to my brilliant managerial decision to buy the multicultural *Happy Holidays* welcome mat.

"You sound surprised to see me," said my ex-husband, unzipping his Italian leather jacket.

"True. I didn't think you'd show." I shut the door on the snowy night. "You only got back from Guatemala—*what*? Six hours ago?"

"Five."

"And I know how you feel about Fa-la-la-la Lattes." I smiled at the catchy term. I hadn't invented it. Alfred Glockner, our local charity Santa, had coined it. In truth, the whole Taste of Christmas idea had been Alf's.

Matt shrugged. "What can I say? When it comes to coffee, I'm a purist."

As an international coffee broker as well as our coffee buyer, Matt was also a coffee snob, but justifiably so. The lattes and cappuccinos were a big draw to the Blend and a healthy contributor to our bottom line. But they weren't his area of the business; they were mine—and my staff of baristas who mixed them to order.

While I roasted and served the beans, Matt was responsible for sourcing them. And because harvest quality could change from season to season, Matt was essentially a java-centric Magellan, regularly exploring the world's coffee belt—a band of mountainous slopes that circled the globe between the Tropics of Capricorn and Cancer, where sunny, frost-free, moderately wet conditions allowed for the cultivation of the very best arabica beans.

"Good thing your Holiday Blend's a winner this year," I said, knowing that our single-origin coffees, seasonal blends, and straight espressos were what lit Matt up. (No artificial oils, no sugar syrups, just his top-quality beans with natural, exotic spice notes, which I regularly roasted in small batches in our shop's basement.)

"So where's Breanne?" I asked, glancing through the front door's glass. Snow fluttered down through the light of the streetlamps, but the curb was empty. No limo. No hired car. No yellow cab with an open door sprouting an endless, designer-draped leg.

"She was supposed to meet me *here*." Matt scanned the tasting group gathered around the fire. "She hasn't shown yet?"

"No. Is she working late again?"

Matt's reply was a muttered, "When isn't she?"

"I'll bet the snow held her up," I said. "You know it's murder getting a cab in weather like this."

Matt didn't nod or agree, just pulled off his black knit cap, ran a hand over his short, dark Caesar, and looked away.

He and Breanne had gotten married in the spring, went on a whirlwind tour of Spain for a number of weeks, then spent much of the summer in a cottony cloud of sweetness that rivaled Tucker's Candy Cane Cappuccino. By early fall, however, the sugar had started to melt. Sharp bouts of bickering continually punctured their meringue of constant cooing.

I didn't see this as any great sign of marital doom. Sooner or later every honeymooning couple had to deal with the struggles and drudgery of workaday life. Whether they touched down or crash-landed, newlyweds have been traveling the same trajectory for centuries.

"Maybe you should call her?" I suggested.

"Forget it," he said, then changed the subject. "You know, Clare, our Holiday Blend's a winner this year because of *you*. You created the blend; you perfected the roast."

"But you found the beans, Matt. *Your* beans are incredible." I didn't mind giving away the credit for this year's exotically spiced blend. Usually, Matt was so cocky it wasn't necessary. But because he'd gone humble on me, I stated the obvious: "That microlot of Sumatra you snagged on the last trip to Indonesia was superb. You made my job easy."

Matt's weary expression lightened at that, and I was glad to see him smile—until his gaze drifted over me. In anticipation of the evening's festivities, I'd fastened a prim choker of green velvet ribbon around my neck. In hopes of seeing Quinn, however, I'd squeezed into a new pair of *not*-so-prim, form-fitting low-riders. The holly-berry-colored cashmere-blend sweater wasn't exactly loose, either. It also flaunted a borderline audacious neckline. (What could I say? I liked Quinn's eyes on me.) Unfortunately, at the moment, it wasn't Mike Quinn doing the looking.

"Nice sweater," Matt said with an arched eyebrow, and before I could stop him he reached out to brush the melting snow crystals from my hair. "Have I seen it before?"

"The sweater's new," I informed him while carefully stepping beyond his reach.

Married or not, Matteo Allegro liked women. And because I was one, there was no getting around his occasional flirtations. I *could* get around his touches, however, and I'd found that a subtle dodge worked a whole lot better than a snippy lecture—it proved a lot less embarrassing in public, too.

Obviously, Matt and I had a history: the kind where

you live together for ten years as man and wife. For various reasons—most of them having to do with his addictions to cocaine and women, not necessarily in that order—a single decade legally wedded to the man had been more than enough for me. We did, however, still share a grown daughter as well as another kind of commitment: Matt's elderly mother owned this century-old coffeehouse and she'd bequeathed its future to the both of us. So once again Matt was my partner in *business*. I tried to keep that in mind whenever Matt's penchant for crossing lines sprang up.

Matt glanced around. "So where's your guard dog?"

"If you mean *Mike*, he's got police business in the outer boroughs. He might not make it."

Matt's dark eyebrows rose. "Too bad," he said, but his tone didn't sound disappointed. "Come on, I could use some warming up. The place looks great."

His arm began snaking around my hip-hugging jeans. I slipped clear.

"Thanks," I said. "You go ahead and hang up your wet coat in the back. I have to lock up again."

"I'll save you a seat," he said with a wink, then moved toward the back of the shop. As I turned to secure the door, however, it flew open on me.

A runway-model-tall woman jarred me and our store's new jingle bells without so much as a *pardon me*.

"I'm sorry," I told her. "We're closed."

Even with half of her face mummified by a scarf the color of latte froth, I could tell the redhead was a knockout. In her midthirties, she had a stunning, statuesque figure. Peeking above the costly pashmina, her nose and cheekbones appeared daintily carved; her eyes adorably big and brilliantly blue. When I spoke to her, however, the woman's wide, doll-like eyes collapsed into slits, squinting down at me as if she'd just noticed a bug under her boot.

"Like *hell* you're closed!"

Okay, the woman's tone was a tad nastier than the angelic face she showed to the world, but I forced a smile. For one thing, she was a new regular. I'd seen her in here several times over Thanksgiving weekend—wearing the same white fur-trimmed car coat and large sheepskin boots, both of which screamed designer label. Her hair was memorable, as well. From beneath her soft knit cap, her sleek curls tumbled down her shoulders in a silk stream of eye-catching scarlet, a striking contrast with the ivory car coat.

"Again, I'm sorry, ma'am," I said with polite firmness, "but we *are* clo—"

"You are *not*," she said, stamping her giant Ugg boot on my internationally festive welcome mat. "You have, like, *a dozen* people here!"

Anyone who'd spent five minutes in Manhattan realized that a percentage of its well-heeled population sashayed around the island with so much attitude that branding *entitlement* on their foreheads would have been redundant. In the presence of perceived "peers," these people could be downright charming. When dealing with no one of "significance"—say, a lowly coffeehouse manager—their behavior turned less than affable. As New York retail went, however, appallingly bad customer behavior wasn't anything out of the ordinary, so I simply stiffened my spine.

"I realize the snow's really coming down. But I'm not lying to you. This is a private party, and we *are* closed as you can see from the sign on the door—"

"Excuse me? *Who*, in their right mind, would notice some stupid little *sign* on a night like *this*?!"

By now, the buzz of discussions near the fireplace had come to a dead stop. All eyes had turned to us, which wasn't surprising. Everyone in the Big Apple loved a scene. Not that minding your own business wasn't still a primary objective in this town, but there was an important distinction: Just because New Yorkers didn't want to get *involved* in an unfolding drama didn't mean they weren't interested in gawking at it.

"I'll tell you what," I offered. "If you don't mind meeting and mingling with some new people, you can join our—"

"Whatever!" she interrupted. "You're closed!" Pirou-etting like a girl who'd never missed a ballet recital, Red yanked open the door and stomped her big Ugg-booted feet out into the snowy night.

I locked up and turned to find everyone still watching me. "Sorry about that."

"What do *you* have to be sorry about?!" Esther cried. "That woman was a total *be-yotch*!"

Although I agreed with Esther, I wasn't happy about ejecting anyone back out into a snowstorm. "I was trying to invite her to the party."

"Maybe if she hadn't cut you off and pitched a fit," Tucker said, "she would have *heard* the invitation! Talk about rude."

"The woman's agitation level was off the charts," Gardner said. "Looked to me like she needed her meds adjusted."

"O Valium, O Valium," Tucker sang, "how lovely are your trances—"

"That little display was nothing," Dante said, waving a tattooed arm. "Three out of the last five nights I closed, I had to physically eject some total A-holes. It's like the holi-day season's pissing everyone off."

"Yeah, me included," Gardner confessed.

"You?" I couldn't believe my most reliably mellow barista had lost his holiday spirit. "Why?"

"It's these nonstop loops of mediocre Christmas tunes," he said, gesturing to our shop's speaker system. "At least three radio stations have been repeating these same lousy playlists twenty-four-seven for weeks now, and practically every store I walk into has one of them on speaker—"

"It's like bad sonic wallpaper," Esther said.

"Whatever you want to call it, it's driving me sugarplum crazy." Gardner shook his head. "Three weeks to December twenty-fifth and I'm already fed up with the sounds of the season."

"Me, too," Dante said. "The CIA should abandon gangsta rap as a torture technique and try playing 'Jingle Bell Rock' a few hundred times in a row."

"Oh, man. *One* time's enough for me," said Theo, one of Gardner's musician friends.

"Wait!" Dante froze and pointed to the speaker system. "There it is again."

Jingle bell, jingle bell, jingle bell rock . . .

"Can we *please* cut the power on this stuff?" Theo begged.

Gardner nodded and moved to turn off the 24/7 Christmas carol station.

"But it's a party," I protested. "We should have *music*." (And I actually liked "Jingle Bell Rock"—and "Winter Wonderland" and "I'll Be Home for Christmas"—even if they were played twelve times in twenty-four hours.)

"Put on my ambient mix," Dante called to Gardner, then turned back to me.

"That's nice, mellow, latte-tasting music, don't you think?"

"But it's not *Christmasy*," I pointed out.

"That's okay by me," said Banhi, Dante's raven-haired roommate.

"Yeah. Me, too," added Kiki, the pierced platinum pixie.

I couldn't believe it. "Where's your holiday spirit?"

Everyone exchanged glances.

Finally Dante said, "Face it, boss. There's no holiday cheer out there because the holidays have become a grind. Everyone's fed up with tinseled-up stores pushing commercial kitsch."

"Yeah, what's *good* about gridlock season?" Kiki said. "Out-of-town tourists and bridge-and-tunnel bargain hunters swinging shopping bags like medieval maces? A herd of them nearly ran me over today rushing across Thirty-fourth!"

"And don't forget those corporate Scrooges all over the city," Banhi added. "I temp at an office where all they do is gripe about having to use half of their bonuses to buy gifts for their families."

"Well, don't talk to *me* about 'holiday cheer'—" said Esther, putting air quotes around the offending phrase. "I'm still gagging over my perfect, older, married sister's annual year-end newsletter about her perfect suburban life."

"I *should* have the Christmas spirit," Tucker admitted. "Given my latest gig."

"What's that?" asked one of the guys in Gardner's group.

"Dickie Celebratorio absolutely *adored* that limited-run cabaret I put together last summer, so he hired me to cast, direct, and choreograph his big holiday bash at the New York Public Library. We've been in rehearsal for two weeks now."

"Celebratorio's that big party planner, isn't he?" I asked.

Tucker's boyfriend, Punch, nodded. "It's being sold to the press as a fund-raiser for New York's public libraries, but it's really a PR event for that big-selling children's book they just turned into a movie."

"*Ticket to the North Pole?*" Esther said. "Isn't that whole thing set in Santa's workshop or something?"

Tucker nodded.

"So you've basically hired a bunch of actors to play Santa's elves?" Esther pressed.

Tucker sighed. "The money's excellent, but when you get right down to it, my job's essentially—"

"Head Elf," Esther finished with a smirk.

Tucker shrugged. "Like I said, I *should* be in the holiday spirit, but the material's just so *cheesy.*"

That's it, I thought. *I can't take any more.* "Santa Claus is *not* cheesy!" I cried.

Dead silence ensued.

"You're all forgetting what this season is really about!"

Everyone stared. I'd just become Linus in *A Charlie Brown Christmas.*

"Well?" Esther finally said. "What's it about, boss?"

I threw up my hands. "Giving! Selfless giving! That's what we're celebrating! The Christ child's birth is a *gift* of *love* to a weary world! All these symbols—the tree, the lights, the carols—it all comes down to *love!*"

No one moved as my words reverberated off the restored tin ceiling and echoed through the newly decorated shop. For a full minute, we actually had a *silent night.*

I shouldn't have been surprised at the flabbergasted expressions around the room. After all, this was the age of irony, when cynicism was the conventional norm, which was why a blasphemous string of curses would have gone over without a batted eyelash. The *truly* radical act these days was *sincerity.* Consequently, our silent night continued—until a single voice boomed—

". . . all right, Breanne! I *heard* you! *Don't* come, then!"

Matt had been striding into the main room from the back pantry area. Suddenly he stopped.

Yes, Matt, the entire tasting party just overheard the unhappy end to your personal call.

His cheeks, no longer ruddy from the frosty outdoors, began reddening again for an entirely different reason. Then his pleading eyes found mine—a search for rescue—and I immediately clapped my hands.

"Hey, everyone!" I shouted with forced cheer. "You know what this Taste of Christmas party needs?"

All eyes now abandoned Matt and turned to me.

"What, Clare?" Tucker asked. "What does it need?"

"Santa Claus!"

THREE

~~~~~~~~~~~~~~~~~~~~~~~~~~~~~~~~

UNFORTUNATELY, Santa was late.

Earlier in the day, I'd invited St. Nick to drop by our Fa-la-la-la Latte tasting, but he hadn't shown.

"I can't believe Santa would stiff you," Esther said. "Not with his daughter coming."

Santa's daughter happened to be my ex-barista, Vicki Glockner. And Santa Claus was really Alfred Glockner, our local sidewalk Santa, also known as—

"Alf?" Matt said. "Are you talking about Alf?"

I nodded.

Everyone in the neighborhood knew—and loved—Alfred Glockner. Even *without* his long white beard and Traveling Santa suit, Alf was a huggable guy. On the slightly paunchy side, he wore his graying hair in a retro sixties ponytail and his salt-and-pepper mustache in a slightly walruslike David Crosby–esque style. His ruddy face was close to jack-o'-lantern round, his vivid hazel-green eyes completely lit it up, and for the past month he'd been using the Blend to take a bathroom break or warm his bones.

Because his daughter had once worked as a barista here, I

could see why he felt at home in my coffeehouse; and because he was collecting for groups that helped the city's homeless and hungry, I was more than happy to supply all the free lattes the man could drink.

It was a fair exchange, too. Every time Alf came into the Blend, he'd work our customer line, making even our most jaded regulars laugh, then dig into a pocket to give a little. (And, believe me, getting a coffee addict to laugh *before* he gets his caffeine fix is no mean feat.)

One of my favorites of his shticks was Santa as urban rapper. He'd ho-ho-ho to a prerecorded hip-hop beat, then start old-school break-dancing in his padded costume. His retro moves included the Robot topped by a Michael Jackson moonwalk. Out on Sixth and Seventh avenues, I'd seen him warm up the coldest crowds, getting them to laugh, applaud, and finally dig out that loose change in their pockets and handbags.

"Alf's a real trip," Dante said. "Did you hear his joke this morning?"

"Was it another homeless-dude joke?" Esther asked.

"Homeless dude camps out in front of a Manhattan day spa," Dante recited. "'Ma'am,' the guy says to the first woman who comes out, 'I haven't had a bite to eat in two days.' 'Wow,' says Spa Lady. 'I wish I had your willpower.'"

Everyone laughed—just like my customers did this morning. It was a dark joke, but it was funny. And according to Alf, whenever he told his homeless-dude jokes to the men in the city shelters, they laughed the hardest of all.

On one of the many days I sat down with Alf on a latte break, he told me the Traveling Santa thing was "a great gig" for him because he was also working the comedy club circuit. Not only did the Santa act pay him a regular salary, it helped him hone his stand-up routine.

Twice a week, he even made time to bring his Santa act to soup kitchens and homeless shelters. "Those places can give a person a bed or a hot meal," he'd told me, "but what they need even more is laughter—a leavening of the life force, you know?"

He truly did embody the spirit of Christmas.

Matt stepped up and pulled me aside. "I saw your Santa on my way here."

"Where?" I asked. "Close by?"

Matt nodded. "He was pushing his sleigh down Hudson."

Unlike the Salvation Army, whose bell ringers staked out permanent locations throughout the city, the Traveling Santas lived up to their name by roving the busy streets. They pushed small wheeled "sleighs" in front of them while cheerfully coaxing pedestrians to throw money into "Santa's bag." As Alf himself said, the gig was made for him.

"So he was heading for the Blend?" I assumed.

"He might have been. But it looked to me like he was making a stop at the White Horse."

"He must have forgotten about my invitation," I said. "I'm going to get him."

Matt held my arm. "Let me, Clare. The weather's bad out there—" Just then Matt's cell went off. He checked the Caller ID and scowled.

"Breanne?" I guessed.

He nodded. "I'll just be a minute."

I shrugged and headed for the back pantry to get my coat. *Take all the time you need*, I thought. The West Village was a small neighborhood. Alf and his cheery ho-ho-hos would be easy to find.

As Matt quickly strode to a corner to continue arguing with Breanne, I zipped up my parka. *Alf will lighten up my griping baristas*, I thought, *put things in perspective*.

As I headed for the door, I saw Tucker opening it, setting off our festive new jingle bells once again.

"You're not *closed*, are you, Tuck?" boomed an impressive male voice from beyond the threshold.

I stepped closer to see an attractive man standing there. I'd seen him in the Blend a few times before, often chatting with Tucker. His fair hair and complexion were a stark contrast to his pitch-black overcoat and scarf. His boyish "look" was the kind I used to see on my daughter Joy's teen magazine covers—cute dimples, a golden shag, trendy chin stubble—only this guy was way beyond his teen years. My guesstimate was thirty-five, maybe older.

"It's a private party," Tuck informed the man. "But you can join us."

"Great 'cause I'm freezing my butt off out here!"

"And a very nice butt it is." Tucker laughed.

"Who's this?" I asked, stepping closer.

Tucker introduced us. "Shane Holliway, Clare Cosi."

"Charmed." Shane threw me a wink.

"Shane was in my cabaret last summer," Tucker explained. "We met when I was on that daytime TV show—*before* the writers killed my character! Shane played the suave private investigator with an eye for the ladies."

Shane shook his head. "Those were the days, weren't they, Tuck? Easy lines. Big paydays. Gorgeous females using shared dressing rooms—of course, that was a perk for *me* more than you."

I raised an eyebrow. *So Shane's straight*, I thought, *and a soap actor. No wonder he's so good looking.*

Tucker snapped his fingers. "No doubt."

"Now what's this I hear about your putting a show together for Dickie?" Shane asked.

"You mean the Elf extravaganza?" Tucker smirked. "Come on in and we'll dish."

"As long as there's a part for me," Shane said.

Tucker laughed. "You want to play a dancing elf?"

Shane shrugged. "I could use the gig. Dickie mentioned you needed another dancer and—"

"Nice to meet you," I told Shane, moving out the open door as his big boots clomped in. Then I caught Tucker's eye. "I'll be back in a few minutes," I promised as I flipped up my hood, "*with* our Christmas spirit."

Outside the heavy snowfall was tapering off into light flurries. The occasional icy flake pelted the hood of my white parka, then fell to the ground to join its brethren, but for the most part the storm appeared to be over. The glistening blanket it left behind, however, now draped every inch of the historic district—the cobblestone streets and narrow sidewalks, the parked cars and town house roofs.

There was nothing like walking through the Village on a snowy winter night. The few vehicles on the slippery street crept along no faster than horse-drawn carriages. Every surface appeared flocked with white; the pungent smell of active old fireplaces floated through the air; and bundled couples hurried past dark storefronts, eager to get back to their warm apartments or inside a cozy pub for a glass of mulled wine or mug of Irish coffee.

As I passed by St. Luke's churchyard, the whole world seemed to go silent, save the icy flurries that still pecked at my parka and the *crunch, crunch, crunching* of my winter boots. At one intersection I stood alone, watching a traffic light provide a signal for crossroads that had no traffic. Hands in pockets, I waited half-amused as the bright red light flipped to green in an unintentional Christmas display just for me.

Suddenly I was a little girl again, back in Pennsylvania, slipping away from my grandmother's house and carrying my cheap little red plastic toboggan to the dead end of her street. The other kids were tucked in for the night, but the snowfall was fresh, not a mark on it, and the vast, empty hillside was all mine.

That kind of exhilarating privacy was rare in Manhattan. Snow almost always melted to rain upon entering the heat and intensity of this crowded island. But tonight—for a little while, anyway—the world was mine again, a blank canvas, fresh and clean for me to mark as I pleased. And block after block, I did make my mark, each footfall breaking through the frozen crust to leave its momentary print in the soft powder.

When I finally reached the corner of Bank and Hudson, I sighed, stamped the snow off my boots, and reluctantly rejoined civilization. The White Horse Tavern was crowded despite the weather, and I knew Alf often stopped here for a burger or Coke. (Being an ex-alcoholic, he told me he no longer drank alcohol, but he still loved the atmosphere of pubs.) Unfortunately, I didn't see him inside.

I chatted with the bartender, who told me he'd served Santa a cranberry juice. "He came in to get warm, wait for the snow to ease up, you know? And we were just hanging out, shooting the breeze when he jumped up all of a sudden and left in a big hurry."

"Which way did he go?" I asked.

"West," said the man, pointing. "Toward the river."

That sounded wrong on a night like this, but I didn't say so. I simply thanked the bartender, left the tavern, and returned to the chilly sidewalk. Moving off the bright main drag, I headed purposefully down the side street. Within two blocks, however, my firmness faltered.

The picturesque charm of the officially designated historic district was gone now. This close to the river, there were no more legally protected Italianate and Federal-style town houses. The buildings here were mostly remnants of the nineteenth-century industries that once supported the working waterfront.

Protected or not, however, the location of these former factories, garages, and warehouses put them right next door to a real estate bonanza. With the West Village commanding some of the highest rents in all of New York City, developers had taken advantage over the years, converting these old white elephants into residences for new money.

To make matters worse, the flurries started changing back into serious snowfall again. The clouds had thickened once more, and the icy flakes were getting heavier and more frequent. Even the halogen streetlamps were straining to cut through the returning blizzard.

With a shiver, I flipped up my parka's hood. But my mood didn't get any warmer. Traffic was nonexistent on this stretch, and the few commercial businesses I'd passed were shuttered. Uneasy on this desolate street, I was about to throw in the towel and abandon my search when I spied a familiar sight a little farther up the block: Alf's bright green Traveling Santa sleigh!

For a moment, I was elated. Then I saw that the green sleigh was parked alone on the sidewalk, its red wheels propped against the curb, white powder piling up on its surface.

Okay, this makes no sense.

Under the weak glow of a streetlamp, I could see that the cash box was still on Alf's little cart. The box was really a round plastic container about the size of a large soup pot. The top of the container was molded to look like a pile of presents, and it slid into a much larger plastic case on the sleigh that was shaped to look like Santa's big red bag. Pedestrians threw their cash donations through a small hole at the top of the cash "present" box. Because it was removable from the sleigh by a hidden handle, Alf always brought the plastic cash box into the Blend with him. He never let it out of his sight. So there was no way he'd leave it unguarded on the street like this.

Alarmed now, I approached Alf's sleigh along the slippery sidewalk. The structures on this street were mostly brick, their ground-floor windows either curtained or shuttered, emitting little light. The sleigh had been left at the mouth of a narrow alley between two seven-story apartment buildings—twin century-old warehouses that had been gutted and remodeled into high-priced lofts.

Reaching the sleigh, I finally saw that Alf's plastic cash box was broken open, only a few coins left inside. More coins were on the ground, making little round sinkholes in the snow. There were footprints in the powder—*two* sets of prints. Both led away from the sleigh, into the alley. Only one set of footprints came out again. They continued down the sidewalk in the direction of the river.

Those can't be Alf's footprints, I decided. *Why would he head toward the river and leave his sleigh behind?*

I decided to follow the other tracks of footprints in the

snow, the ones leading *into* the shadowy alley. I had to make sure Alf wasn't lying at the end of those prints, hurt, bleeding, even unconscious.

I couldn't see much as I moved toward the narrow passage between the buildings, just a gunmetal gray garbage Dumpster. But as I moved farther in, I realized the alley eventually opened up into a snow-covered courtyard.

"Alf?" I called. A wind gust suddenly howled, swallowing my voice. I called out again, stronger this time, but there was no reply, no movement.

I dug into my pocket and pulled out my keychain flashlight. The beam was weak, but it was better than the dingy dark. I stepped forward, paralleling the two sets of snow prints that led into the alley. Both sets of tracks were larger than my own small boots, and I took care not to disturb either one.

As my flashlight beam glanced along the white surface, a flash of cheery red color suddenly made me stop. I pulled the light back and saw the Santa hat.

"Hello!" I shouted, more urgently than before. "Alf! Are you here?"

Again no one answered.

I stooped to pick up the hat, and that's when I saw the shiny black boots. They were sticking out from behind the gray Dumpster.

For a moment, I stood still as a gravestone, staring at Alf's boots, vaguely aware of St. Luke's bells ringing the hour. The church wasn't far—not physically—but in that frozen flicker of time those clear, innocent, beautifully pure peals sounded as if they were coming from another world.

A second later I was down, kneeling over my red-suited friend sprawled in the snow. "Alf, can you hear me? Alf!"

He couldn't. Choking back a scream, I realized Alfred Glockner was dead.

Four

～～～～～～～～～～～～～～～～～～

In the frigid air, my breath was still forming little pearl-colored clouds. No steam was coming from Alf's lips or nose because there was no surviving the gaping hole in his chest or the amount of lost blood pooled around his body.

Despite the clear evidence, I went through the motions, checking for any way to help him. I played the flashlight across his wide, unfocused eyes, looking for a reaction. There was none. His wrist had no pulse; neither did his neck.

I pulled out my cell and dialed 911. The call was answered immediately by a female operator who took down all the information. She told me to remain at the scene in order to speak with the investigating officers. Finally, the woman asked if I wanted to stay on the phone with her until the officers arrived.

"No," I said. "I need the line."

I was still kneeling, the cold, wet snow soaking through the legs of my jeans. I didn't care. I hit speed dial. When I heard the reassuring timbre of Detective Mike Quinn's gravelly voice, I started ranting—only to realize I was talking to his prerecorded message telling me to leave my name and number. When the tone sounded, I took a breath.

"It's Clare. Call me back as soon as you have the chance . . ."

I was tempted to say more, but Mike was on the job now. If he wasn't picking up, there was a good reason. He could very well be at a crime scene of his own.

After getting the commendation last spring for taking down a major West Side dealer of prescription drugs—a case I helped him solve—his superiors asked him to continue heading up the "OD Squad," the nickname for a city-wide task force recently formed out of the Sixth Precinct to document criminality in cases of narcotic drug overdoses.

Tonight he was overseeing an operation in Queens, which meant, even if he *had* picked up, he would still be an hour's drive away.

I wasn't the one who'd been shot in this alley; I was perfectly okay, and the police were on their way. A hysterical message from me wouldn't do either of us any good. So I ended the call, closed my eyes to gain some objectivity, and shifted the beam to illuminate Alf's wound.

Judging from the scorch marks on the breast of the velvet Santa suit, Alf had been shot at point-blank range. The lapel pocket was turned inside out—no doubt when the mugger rifled Alf's pockets. The killer had ripped open Alf's costume, too, using so much force that one of the big white Traveling Santa suit's signature buttons was ripped off.

I passed my flashlight over the nearby snow, but I didn't see the button. I did, however, see Alf's blood. There was so much of it pooled around him, it was impossible to miss. Its warmth had even melted the snow around it, forming a gory pile of pinkish slush.

I stilled, realizing something for the first time: *Alf's blood hasn't frozen solid yet.* In weather like this, that could only mean one thing: *He was shot very recently.*

About then I noticed my hands were shaking. I was upset

about Alf, of course, and beginning to feel very cold, but I knew something else was making me shiver.

I reminded myself that the perpetrator of this horrible crime was gone. I'd called out to Alf enough times that anyone lurking in the shadows would have been scared away. And that single trail of footprints I'd noticed coming out of the alley was heading away from the scene and toward the river. *That had to be a trail of the killer's prints,* I thought.

But what if they aren't?

There was a slim possibility that Alf's murderer was demented enough to hang around the crime scene. The shooter could be lurking in the shadows, watching me right now. I swallowed hard and hit *another* button on my speed dial.

Matt answered on the first ring. "Clare! Where are you? You left without me—"

"It's Alf. I found him lying in the snow. Someone shot him. He's dead."

Matt's breath caught.

"I'm not hurt," I quickly added. "I'm just waiting for the police."

"*Where*, Clare? What street?"

I told him.

"I'm on my way!"

I closed the phone and glanced down at Alf's body. Still kneeling in the snow, I collapsed back on my calves. The tears came then. Hearing myself tell Matt what had happened made it all personal again. My new friend was dead.

Someone had mugged and murdered Santa Claus!

For a flashing moment something far less serious but just as ugly rose out of my memories . . .

After Matt and I had divorced, I'd raised my daughter in a modest home in the Jersey suburbs. Matt's mother always came to join us for the first and last nights of Chanukah as well as Christmas dinner, and Matt always made it, too. For most of the season, however, Joy and I were on our own doing the baking, decorating, and holiday card writing.

By the time Joy was twelve, we'd developed our own little girls' club traditions, like buying a tree the first week in December. We put up our front-yard lights and decorations together on the same day, too, and one of my favorite displays was a plastic Santa. He was four feet tall and had a big red light for a nose. Chipped and fading, he was nevertheless a beloved piece of sentimental kitsch from my childhood front yard—and not just the yard of my late grandmother. My four-foot Santa with the glowing nose had started out his life in my family's yard when it had still *been* a family, before my mother had left my dad and me to run away with some passing salesman to Florida (all the explanation I'd ever gotten).

Joy had grown fond of that funny little Santa, too. She loved the red glow of his nose, strong enough to cast a bit of festive color through her bedroom window during the dark December nights.

Unfortunately, on one of those nights—the longest of the year—a foursome of local punks got drunk enough and mean enough to want to kill Christmas. They set about smashing holiday decorations all over town. One of their victims was our much-beloved Santa. I can still recall the morning I had to comfort my tearful daughter, while trying to explain the unexplainable to a little girl.

A decade later, kneeling in the snow, I was the one who felt like a little girl, needing the unexplainable explained to *me*. I said a prayer for Alf, but it answered nothing. In fact, talking to God only turned my feelings of grief and shock into an onslaught of other emotions.

How could this happen to a good man like Alf?! Do you hear me, God?! What are you going to do about it?!

Tears welled and spilled. I swiped them away; when my vision cleared, I saw something I hadn't noticed before. Right in front of me were more footprints in the snow.

I noted the size and shape of the prints and played my flashlight on the sole of Alf's slightly pointy boots. The prints in the snow were identical. Standing up, I used my little flashlight to illuminate this new trail of Alf's pointy boot prints. Oddly, they were coming *out* of the courtyard.

What in the world?

The killer's rounder-toed prints stopped in the snow next to Alf's body, then backtracked out to the street again. That meant Alf was coming *out* of this building's courtyard and through its side alley when the killer mugged and shot him.

But that made no sense for a street robbery. A mugger would have confronted Alf on the sidewalk, taken his donation box, and (God help me) forced Santa *into* the alley at gunpoint to prevent him from identifying the criminal in a lineup. But the marks left behind in the snow didn't tell a story like that. According to the boot prints, Alf came into this alley alone, went back into the courtyard for some reason, and met his killer on his way out again.

Why would Alf go into this dark courtyard alone? Why was Alf even on this desolate street during a snowstorm?

I knew at once that the detectives assigned to this case needed to see these prints. But where were they?!

I glanced skyward. The fat white flakes were falling even harder now. If the police didn't arrive soon, this evidence would be completely covered. I listened for the sound of a siren but heard nothing. Worried the prints would be obliterated by the weather, I moved farther into the alley to track them myself.

Inside a minute, I'd followed Alf's footprints through the alley's shadows and all the way into the snow-covered courtyard. The prints appeared to pause in the middle of the small yard, and I got the impression Alf had stood here for a moment, shifting from left to right, as if studying something.

But what were you studying, Alf?

His prints moved from this spot to the back wall of the building, where another gray metal Dumpster stood with three blue plastic recycling bins lined up beside it. I noticed a steel door to the building near these bins, but Alf clearly wasn't interested in going through this service entrance because his prints deliberately bypassed the door, heading instead for the far end of the blue bins.

I moved my flashlight beam around the snow-covered ground and saw his prints ending near an empty wooden crate. The snow was pretty scraped up in the area, but it was clear to me, following the scrape marks, that the crate had been dragged from a pile a few yards away and placed next to these blue bins.

Why would Alf do that?

I stepped back a moment to consider the question and realized that the building's fire escape stairs—high off the ground—would be reachable if someone were able to boost himself up using these recycling bins.

Alf must have paused in the middle of this courtyard to consider how to get up on the fire escape. He pulled that crate over to use it as a step. Then he climbed onto the recycling bins and most likely onto the fire escape.

I stared up at the tangle of iron grilles looming over me and wondered why Alf Glockner would climb an icy set of outdoor stairs in the middle of a winter snowstorm. If you asked me, Alf was too chubby to be a part-time cat burglar, and far from the sort of person I'd peg for a peeping Tom.

Just then, I became aware of a high-pitched wail in the distance. *An emergency siren! Finally!* A police car was approaching from the street I'd left. I checked my watch and realized with a start that less than six minutes had passed since my 911 call. Given the state I was in, it only *seemed* like hours. Still, I was glad I'd had the time to investigate. Now I was more than ready to give my statement to the detectives, show them what I'd found.

That's when I heard the voices.

"Police!"

"Freeze!"

Men were shouting between buildings from the other side of the courtyard.

"NYPD!"

"Stop, police!"

Frost-crusted snow crunched behind me. As I turned to see who was coming, a hooded figure rocketed across the small, dark yard. I tried to make out the person's face, but I didn't have more than a nanosecond before the figure slammed into me.

The impact tore me off my feet. I flew through the air, and two seconds later I knew what a blitzed quarterback felt like when he hit Astroturf.

FIVE

∾∾∾∾∾∾∾∾∾∾∾∾∾∾∾∾∾∾∾∾∾∾∾

"Ms. Cosi? You okay? Ms. Cosi?"

The voice sounded earnest, youthful, and familiar. I blinked against the flashlight's glare. A silhouette formed in my blurred vision. Narrow shoulders blocked the falling snow. The young man bent down to the icy ground beside me, and that's when I noticed the nickel-plated badge pinned to the dark blue uniform.

"Officer Langley?" I whispered. He and his partner, Demetrios, were regular customers at the Blend. (Langley was a latte man; Demetrios, double espressos.)

"You really took a tumble," Langley said.

Still flat on my back in the snow, I felt an icy clamminess creeping over me. Slush was trickling down the back of my parka, and I tried to sit up. Officer Langley gently restrained me.

"Don't move, Ms. Cosi. An ambulance is on the way."

"You're kidding, right? 'Cause I'm freezing down here!" I sat up—then clutched my ribs. "Ouch." I moaned.

"You shouldn't move until the paramedics check you out," Langley said. But I refused to remain on the frigid ground any longer, and the young cop gave up trying to fight me.

With a sigh of defeat, Langley helped me up. Loose strands of my shoulder-length hair were hanging in my face. As I brushed them away, a wind blast knifed through the courtyard. I groaned from the cold and noticed Langley shiver as he spoke into his police radio. Under his uniform's hat, the man's fair complexion blanched pastier than an albino thrown into a meat locker. After this long in the cold, I figured my own olive skin tone had gone nearly as pale.

Teeth close to chattering, I flipped up my hood and asked, "What happened?"

"We were chasing a suspect, Ms. Cosi. You got in the way."

"Oh my God!" I cried, my chill suddenly forgotten. "You saw the killer? Did you catch him? Did he tell you why he shot poor Alf?"

Confused, the officer gave me a sidelong glance. "There's no *killer*, Ms. Cosi. Just a mugger. We were chasing a purse snatcher, that's all, and—"

"Langley!"

The deep, harsh call came from the side of the building where I'd found Alf's body.

"Where the hell is he? Langley!"

We moved across the courtyard and up to the mouth of the alley. My eyes widened at the small army of police and crime-scene officers now gathering around Alf's corpse. Two uniformed men began spooling out a roll of yellow police tape to cordon off the area around the metal Dumpster.

"Yo! Langley," the man called again.

"Over here, Detective!" Langley waved.

A male figure broke away from the pack and moved toward us up the alley. "Give me the rundown," he demanded from the shadows.

"Me and Demetrios heard a scream on Perry Street," Langley explained. "A woman was being robbed. We pursued the perpetrator through that alley over there." He gestured to the other side of the courtyard. "The perp fled through this yard, where he ran down Ms. Cosi here. I stopped to help her while Demetrios continued the chase with officers Wu and Gomez, also from the Sixth—"

"Those guys are after a *shooter*, Langley," the detective said, still veiled by the darkness. "We got a DOA by the Dumpster over there."

Langley tensed and exchanged a glance with me.

That's when the detective finally stepped out of the shadows. Most detectives I'd met wore suits, ties, and overcoats. This guy wore cowboy boots and a Yankees jacket, and his head was covered by a red, white, and blue bandanna—an urban fashion statement my shaved-headed barista, Dante, once informed me was a "do-rag."

"Some female called the dead guy in, then took a hike," the detective said.

"Excuse me," I interrupted, "but that *female* would be *me*."

The detective appraised me with eyes as cold and gray as the dimly lit snow. I returned the courtesy.

The man was average height—which is to say at least seven inches taller then my five two—early thirties, maybe a little older. His skin was dusky, his features betraying a mixed heritage of what might have been Hispanic, Italian, and possibly Russian; in other words, a typical New Yorker. With one gloveless hand, he scratched his chin's dark brown stubble.

"You know this woman, Langley?" he said, shoving a square of nicotine gum between his lips.

Langley nodded. "She manages the Village Blend on Hudson."

"So *you're* that coffee lady I've heard about," the detective said, working his jaw. "Never been in your place. My drink's Red Bull."

"My *name* is Clare Cosi," I replied.

"And *you* found jolly old St. Stiff over there?"

"His name's *Glockner*, Alfred Glockner."

The detective paused a moment and studied me again. "You knew the victim?"

I nodded.

"Sorry." He glanced away then back again. "I didn't realize you knew him. Sorry for your loss." His tone was sincere—or at least he'd blunted its street edge enough to make it sound that way. "Did you witness anything suspicious, Mrs. Cosi? Hear a shot? See the man who mugged your friend—"

"It's *Ms.* Cosi, Detective—what's your name?"

"Franco. Sergeant Emmanuel Franco."

"Well, I'm not so sure he was mugged, Sergeant Franco. Or if he was, I'm not so sure something else wasn't happening, too—"

"Excuse me?"

"I'd like you to look at these footprints I found in the snow—"

"Why didn't you stay close to the victim like the 911 operator asked?" Franco continued as if I hadn't spoken at all.

"I'm trying to tell you. After I found the body, I followed Alf Glockner's boot prints, and I'm thinking it doesn't add up to a mugging."

Sergeant Franco glanced around the snow. "*What* prints are you talking about?"

"Follow me. They're right over here—"

It was still snowing as I led Franco and Langley into the center of the courtyard, but the heavy downfall had once again tapered off into light flurries. I pushed back the hood of my white parka in order to see better. It didn't help.

"Where are they?" the detective asked.

"They *were* right here."

Officer Langley scanned the ground with his flashlight, but the clean trail of prints I'd followed had been obliterated by the mugger, the policemen chasing him, even Langley when he'd stopped to help me.

"Do you see any evidence of the victims' footprints here, Officer Langley?" Franco asked evenly.

"No, Sergeant," Langley replied. "Sorry, Ms. Cosi."

Franco shifted his attention to me. "What is it you think you saw, Coffee Lady?"

"I didn't *think* I saw anything. There *were* footprints here. Alf's prints. I saw them. It looked to me like he pulled that wooden crate over to those garbage bins—" I pointed. "Then I'm deducing he climbed them to get onto the fire escape for some reason."

Franco exchanged a glance with Langley. "So it's St. Nick the Cat Burglar, now?" he said. His expression remained neutral, but his tone was obviously flip.

"Just look for yourself," I said tightly.

Franco held my gaze a moment, saw that my glare was dead serious, and, with a sigh of obvious male annoyance, flipped on his flashlight. He walked over to the crate and examined the box and the ground. He took a long look at the bins and finally the fire escape above them. As he walked back to me and Langley, an electronically garbled voice interrupted us. Franco lifted his radio to his ear, listened for a moment, and cursed a blue streak. Finally, he turned to Langley.

"Four of you in pursuit and you *still* manage to lose that perp!"

Langley sheepishly shrugged.

"Fine. You *and* your partner can do some overtime." He shook his head. "Me and Charlie aren't going to be the only ones bracing local skells all night to find an 'armed and dangerous' stupid enough to actually pull the trigger—"

"Excuse me, Sergeant, but what makes you think the mugger these men were pursuing is the same person who killed Alf? I found Alf's body before the mugger ran through here."

Franco faced me, his denim-covered legs braced in the slippery snow. "Ms. Cosi, some scumbags work in teams. Some move from street to street in the same area, targeting victims. This perp hid Santa's body pretty well from anyone passing on the street—it's clear the shooter didn't expect his victim to be found anytime soon, which would mean he was free and clear to keep looking for victims nearby. As to your friend here, his pockets were turned out, his wallet is missing, and the money box on his little green wagon was looted. Two and two is four. The motive here was obviously robbery—"

"*Unless* the robbery was *staged* to make you *think* this was just a random mugging. What if it wasn't? What if there was some *other* reason—"

"Stop!" The harried detective spat his gum into a wrapper and stuck the wad into the pocket of his Yankees jacket. "Listen to me, Coffee Lady. You're cold, you're tired, and you're probably feeling some level of shock or you're not human. But I don't see anything out of the ordinary back here in this courtyard—other than the mass of footprints from the police chase. There's no sign of blood under the fire escape or anything else all that suspicious. The crime we're investigating obviously took place in the alley and on the sidewalk, where the victim's little cart was parked. So let *us* take it from here, okay?"

"I fully intend to, but I do have a theory of the case—"

"A *theory of the case*? Jesus—" Franco laughed, short and sharp, then glanced at Langley. "She's a cute one, isn't she?"

"Sergeant!" I cried. "I'm serious."

Franco faced me. "Honey, if you and me were in a nice warm bar, I'd let you talk to me *all* night about your theory. But I don't have time to play here. This was obviously a street crime. The mugger led the poor son of a bitch into the alley at gunpoint and"—he made a gun with his thumb and forefinger—"Bang! Bang! Santa's dead."

"Except your scenario's wrong, Sergeant. Alf wasn't forced into this building's alley. The footprints I saw clearly showed he was coming *out* of this courtyard when he was shot."

Franco shrugged his shoulders. "So?"

"So . . . find out why Alf was in this courtyard and you might find out why he was killed."

"Did it ever occur to you that maybe Santa Claus had to drain his pipe?"

"What?"

"This place is private," Franco said, gesturing. "An old

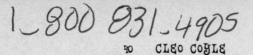

geezer like that likely had a prostate the size of a cantaloupe. Santa probably had to take a leak."

Officer Langley shifted on his feet as Franco exchanged a glance with him. "Maybe we ought to canvass the crime scene for yellow snow, eh, Langley?"

Langley lifted a hand to hide a smile, then moved it to pat my shoulder. "I'll find a paramedic to look you over, Ms. Cosi."

The second Langley left, I stepped up to Franco. "Listen, Sergeant, Alf was only fifty-two, hardly a 'geezer.' I'm reporting what I saw. I think it's germane to your case."

"Good," Franco replied. "The PD wants your *germane* statement. Okay? Feel better?"

"Stop patronizing me."

The man's jaw worked so hard I got the impression he was trying to pull his next few words out of the cavity in his left molar. "Let's just say I see the events coming down differently than you do: a simple robbery gone very freakin' bad, all right?"

I sighed.

Franco glanced toward the mouth of the alley as if to make sure Langley was out of earshot. "Look . . ." He took a step closer to me—a lot closer. "How about we make nice, you and I?"

"What do you mean?"

Franco's dark eyes studied me some more. "I mean you and I should get together. I just came on for a night tour, but I'll be off duty in the morning."

"I, uh—"

His voice went low and soft. "You serve jelly doughnuts at that coffee shop of yours?"

I folded my arms. "A jelly doughnut *latte*—we just added it to the menu for Chanukah."

"Coffee and no doughnuts?"

"It's not that kind of coffee shop."

"Jeez—"

"Clare! Clare Cosi! Are you in there? Clare!"

Matt's bellow cut through the buzz of voices around the crime scene and echoed all the way into the desolate courtyard. I moved across the snow and around the corner of the building to find my ex-husband at the other end of the alley, shouting like a crazy man from behind the yellow crime-scene tape.

Franco came up beside me. He tilted his head in Matt's direction. "You *know* that guy?"

"He's my . . . business partner—"

"Clare!" Matt shouted when he finally saw me. "Over here!"

"Well, go shut him up," Franco commanded, his sweet overtures immediately souring after one glance at Matt. "We don't want to disturb the citizens in these nice, expensive apartment buildings any more than we need to, right?"

I didn't reply, just continued through the alley, now painted ruby red by flickering emergency lights. As a uniformed officer lifted the yellow tape to let me pass, I glanced one last time at the still figure lying beside the Dumpster. Alf's corpse was surrounded by members of the crime-scene unit, examining him, taking notes, flashing photos.

Swiping new tears away, I ducked under the tape and groaned—the bending had aggravated my bruised torso. Just then, Officer Langley appeared at my shoulder. "The paramedics are here, Ms. Cosi." He pointed to an ambulance behind the half-dozen police vehicles. "They can check you out. If you'll just come with me—"

"Thanks, Officer Langley, but I don't need a para—"

"You got hurt?!" Matt interrupted, rushing to my side. "You said on the phone you were okay!"

I shrugged. "I got the wind knocked out of me after I talked to you, that's all." I explained about following Alf's boot prints and getting nailed in the process by a police chase across the courtyard. "My side's pretty sore at the moment, but I'm fine—"

"You don't know that!" Matt insisted. "You could have a cracked rib!"

Before I could prevent him, my ex pulled off his gloves, unzipped my parka, and began running his hands along my bruised body.

"What are you doing?!" I cried so loudly several cops glanced in our direction.

Matt ignored them. "Remember a few years ago, when I was in Rwanda and Timo flipped that Land Rover?" he asked, his fingers still busy probing my chest. "He cracked his rib and I had to wrap his torso with canvas to prevent his lungs from being punctured. We were stranded for a whole day and a night. Poor Timo could have died."

"So?"

"So I know what to look for," Matt said. He felt me up for another few seconds. "You're okay, Clare. Nothing's broken."

"Good." I said. The examination was clearly over, but Matt's hands remained planted on my hips.

"We're done, right?" I said.

His eyes held mine. "Are we?"

"Yes!" I assured him, nudging his hands away.

As I zipped my parka back up, Sergeant Franco approached me again, this time with another man in tow. The man looked younger than Franco by a few years and appeared to be of Chinese heritage. He was also more conventionally dressed, his athletic frame draped in a suit, tie, and camel hair coat.

"Give Chan here a statement, Coffee Lady," said Franco. "Tell my partner everything you remember. Then you and *your* partner here can both go home and get on with your fondling in *private*."

"Matt was *not* fondling me," I clarified. "It was purely medical. He was just making sure—"

But Franco was already striding away. His partner shook his head as he watched him go. Then he turned to me and flipped a page on his detective's notebook.

"Your name is *Coffee*?" he asked.

"Cosi," I corrected. "And you're Detective *Chan*?"

"My name is Charlie. Charlie *Hong*," he said.

"Not Chan?"

Hong smirked. "You'll have to excuse Sergeant Franco's sense of humor."

While I gave Detective Hong a statement, Matt hovered close by. The process took no more than ten minutes, and through it all my discomfort level grew. The flurries had stopped completely now, but the snow down my parka had turned to water, my side still throbbed, my nose was running, and my voice was raspy from the cold.

Finally, the detective thanked me and closed his notebook. He gave me his card and told me to call if I remembered anything else.

"And what about the footprints I told you about, Detective Hong? What do you think?"

Hong shrugged. "I'm inclined to agree with my partner. What the victim may or may not have been doing in the courtyard is irrelevant. He was confronted, robbed at gunpoint, and murdered in the building's alley, most likely by the man the police were chasing down Perry Street."

He offered me his hand, and I shook it. "Thanks for your help, Ms. Cosi."

As soon as Hong departed, Matt swooped in again. "You should really get your chest x-rayed," he said, reaching out for me again.

"Forget the hospital," I said, stepping back. "*And* my chest. I just want to go to bed."

"Good idea."

"*Alone.*"

Six

~~~~~~

Morning came, cold and bright, and I was outside again, but now the snow around me was much deeper than the low drifts of the city. The field I stood in was flat and continuous like an aerial view of unending clouds.

Jingle, jingle, jingle . . .

The bells surprised me. The cheerful sound swirled across the wind on a gentle gust. Then a voice called my name—an impossible voice—

"Clare!"

"Alf? Alfred?" Filled with hope, I turned. Sunlight struck my eyes. The glare off the snow was blinding. "Where are you, Alf? I can't see you!"

"Look *up*!"

I lifted my arm to shield my eyes and finally did see him. Alf was *alive*, waving at me from the top of an enormous white mountain. He looked small up there, like a tiny Christmas ornament, yet every detail of his being appeared strangely clear to me—the red velvet suit, the shiny black boots, the big white Traveling Santa buttons down the front of his costume—all but one. *One* button was missing.

"Alf!" I shouted. "I was looking for you!"

"Sorry, Clare! I have to go!"

"No, wait! I'm coming to bring you back!"

I took off across the snow, but when my boots hit the base of the incline, my progress slowed. With every step north, the snow became deeper, the climb more difficult.

Jingle, jingle, jingle . . .

Alf's bells kept ringing and *ringing*! The endless repetition soon made them seem tinny and hollow, until they sounded more like cash registers ringing up sales.

Cha-ching! Cha-ching! Cha-ching!

Slapping my hands over my ears, I kept moving, exhausting every muscle in a sweaty, angry slog. But with every foot closer, Alf seemed to move another yard higher. I felt so thwarted, I wanted to cry. Then I tripped, taking a hard, bruising fall before rolling down the slope in an unending tumble—

"Ahhhhhh!"

I opened my eyes.

My body felt sore; my heart was still pounding, but I was no longer outside. I was inside, lying under a warm comforter, on a soft bed, in a dark room. *My bedroom*—and I wasn't alone. Between the two mahogany pillars at the foot of my four-poster, I could see a shadowy figure moving suspiciously. The intruder was male, I realized. The man stood up and then crouched down.

What's he doing? Searching for something?

Still groggy and disoriented, I swallowed hard and reached a hand out from under the covers. Groping at the side table for any sort of weapon, my fingers closed on the base of a Tiffany lamp—one of Madame's heirlooms. I didn't want to break it, but I had no choice.

I slid the lamp base closer, trying to gain a better grip. The slight scraping sound gave me away. The intruder turned quickly, and I sat up, priceless weapon ready.

"Clare?"

I froze, watching a red orange glow suddenly rise up behind the man's silhouette. That's when I realized two things: This "intruder" was my boyfriend, Mike Quinn; and his "suspicious" movements were the result of his lighting a fire in my bedroom's hearth.

Quinn regarded me sitting up in bed, lamp base in hand, arm cocked to bash in his head. "You know," he said, appearing more amused than alarmed, "if you're having trouble turning that thing on, you might have better luck using the switch."

I blinked. "I thought you were a burglar." Quinn's dress shirt sleeves were rolled up, his tie pulled loose. I noticed his suit jacket draped over a chair.

He folded his arms. "Did you forget you gave me a key?"

"No, of course not."

How could I? It was the same key Matteo had handed me the day he'd married Breanne. It had been big of Matt to do that, considering his mother had given us both permission to live *rent free* in this duplex above the Blend (one of Madame's many failed attempts to get us back together). Eventually, however, Matt acknowledged my feelings (that I was *never* going to remarry him) as well as my dilemma (homelessness). With rents in the historic West Village among the highest in the city, I couldn't afford a place of my own close to the Blend, and a commute would be hard on me, given the hours I put in running the place. So after he'd married Breanne, he gave up his key.

"Sorry, Mike." I set down the lamp. "I had a bad dream."

Without a word, he moved to the bed, his solid frame depressing the edge of the mattress. I put my arms around him and he pulled me close.

Our embrace was far from glamorous. I wasn't expecting him, so my nightwear was nothing fancy, lacy, or overtly alluring—just my usual oversized Steelers jersey and a pair of cotton underpants. With his leather holster still strapped across his shoulders, the butt of his service weapon dug into me a little, aggravating the bruise along my rib cage. I didn't care. We hadn't slept together in a week, and I missed the feel of him: the affection in his touches; the strength in his muscles; even the smell of his skin, warm and male and slightly citrusy from his aftershave. In a phrase, Mike Quinn felt good—and I liked hanging on to that goodness.

After a minute, he leaned back and I studied him. His pale Irish complexion had gone to the ruddy side—no doubt from the business of starting the fire in my bedroom's hearth. His dark blond hair was cropped (the usual) no-nonsense short. His jawline looked as square as ever, his chin dependably strong. Like most men in their forties, he had crow's feet and frown lines etched into his face, badges of surviving life's tragedies, fighting its battles. His blue eyes were as sharp as ever, too, and clearer than a glacial lake.

On the street, Quinn's eyes were stone-cold cop, unwilling to give away an iota of intention. For a long time, his true feelings were my own personal guessing game—at times a frustrating enterprise. (*Is the man only mildly irritated?* I'd wonder. *Or pissed enough to start shooting up the room? Is he turned on by my risqué references to his handcuffs? Or am I just making an ass of myself?*)

That kind of bewilderment was rare now. When we were alone together, Mike's chilly cop curtain was swept aside. Whatever he was thinking or feeling, he usually showed me. (*Usually* being a necessary qualifier—Quinn was, after all, still a man.)

"You should have told me about Alf, Clare."

"You heard what happened?"

"Not until I was ending my tour." He gently brushed stray locks of hair from my cheek. "Sully and I picked up the radio chatter about Santa being shot near the Sixth, and I asked about the DOA. Langley told me it was you who found him."

I nodded. "He was shot point-blank. I found him in an alley."

Mike shook his head. "I got your voice mail. You didn't say a *word*, Clare. Not one word in your message was about *why* you were calling." His voice carried a bit of annoyance, but his eyes weren't flashing with anything close to rebuke. Instead, his brows were drawn together with concern.

"You were on duty. I didn't want to worry you—"

"Well, I sure as hell wish you had. I called you back the second I played your message. Why didn't you pick up?"

"I should have . . . I was just so drained by then. I couldn't handle telling the whole story one more time—not over the phone. By then I'd already given the account to so many people: Langley, the two detectives, Matt—"

"Matt?" Quinn stiffened. "*Allegro* was there?"

I nodded. "He showed up at the Blend for my tasting party. So I knew he was nearby, and when I called, he picked up right away."

Quinn's jaw worked. "I'm sorry I didn't."

"Stop apologizing. You were on duty. I knew if you weren't answering your cell, you were probably in the middle of a crime scene of your own—"

"I was."

I could tell from his tone it didn't go well. "What happened?"

"Our suspect was high when my guys got there with the warrant. He barricaded himself in his bedroom with his teenage girlfriend as a hostage, claimed he was holding her at gunpoint."

"Oh, no."

"Your call came about the same minute I realized I had a fubar on my hands."

"What happened?"

"We got a sniper in place on the roof across the street. Had a clean shot to take him out, too, right through the open window blinds, but I didn't think he'd really hurt the girl."

"Why not? He had a gun on her, right?"

"No. He had a gun in the room, but not pointed at her,

and he kept talking with me, so I kept working on him—
explained we wanted information, that we'd plea down the
charges if he gave up the associates in his ring."

"This was the hospital worker you told me about?"

Quinn nodded. "Been supplying OxyContin to dealers
around Queens College, Hunter, NYU."

"So you didn't have to shoot him?"

"We would have, if he'd forced our hand. But, like I said,
he wasn't pointing the weapon at the girl, and he continued
talking with me until I persuaded him to surrender. Then
we got all the evidence we needed out of the apartment, took
the girlfriend to her mother's unharmed."

I smiled for a second, proud as anything, then poked his
chest. "See, now I'm glad I didn't leave a hysterical message.
Although I almost did . . ."

"Almost?"

"I started ranting as soon as I heard your voice—then I
realized it was your prerecorded voice and I pulled myself
together."

"*You* were hysterical?" Quinn's grim expression lightened
a fraction.

"Listen, Lieutenant, I'm not a professional. I admit
it, okay? But I have seen a dead body or two, as you well
know."

Quinn's crow's feet crinkled in amusement, no doubt
with a memory of one of the criminal cases I'd helped the
NYPD clear. Not that anyone with a badge and a gun would
acknowledge me as anything more than a "helpful witness,"
excepting, of course, the cop sitting on my bed.

"So what did you tell the detectives?" he asked.

"It doesn't matter. They didn't deem it 'important' to the
case."

"Who didn't? Who's the lead detective?"

"A sergeant named Franco. Emmanuel Franco."

"The General."

"Excuse me?"

"Don't ask me how he got the nickname. He's new at the

Sixth, although not with the PD. He's had a lot of success running street crime task forces in the boroughs. In case you haven't heard, street crimes haven't exactly been on the decline since the economy tanked."

"*Yes, someone's* mentioned that to me once or twice already."

"So what do you think, Detective Cosi?" Quinn asked. "You think Alf's death was more than a mugging?"

"I think there are a lot of unanswered questions about why he was on that particular street during a snowstorm and what exactly he was doing in that building's courtyard."

Quinn studied me a moment—*read* me, actually. "So you and Franco locked horns."

"For about a minute, yes," I admitted. "He was condescending and I was angry. In the end, the man did show an interest in my theory, but only if I was willing to discuss it with him off duty, over coffee and doughnuts. I'm pretty sure he was hitting on me."

"Is that so?" Quinn's eyebrow arched. "And?"

"And what?"

"And did you tell him you're *my* girl?"

I laughed. "It wasn't that big a pass. He was just starting to suggest we 'make nice' when Matt showed. Ten seconds later Matt was touching my chest in front of everyone, so Franco jumped to the conclusion that Matt and I—"

"*Whoa*, back up! Allegro did *what* to your chest?"

Oh, God. "It's not what you think. See, I got caught in the middle of this police chase. The perp ran me down and Matt was worried I'd broken a rib—I hadn't, but he wanted to check me out. I mean check my chest out. I mean my *ribs*—and Franco saw the whole thing and got the wrong impression—"

"*I'm* getting the wrong impression. And I'm completely lost. Start at the beginning."

I did. I ran down the entire evening, the crime scene, the footprints in the snow. "Sergeant Franco said, 'Two and two is four.' But the man must be using new math because there's definitely more to the story. Alf went to that deserted street for a reason, and I believe he was climbing the fire escape in the courtyard for a reason, too."

"And you think those reasons will add up to why he was killed?"

"I realize there's plenty of circumstantial evidence to support Franco's version of the events, but I think there's more here to investigate."

Quinn went silent a moment. "Tell you what. I'll keep an eye on how the case progresses. Who's Franco's partner?"

I told him.

"Good. I know Charlie Hong. He's an easy guy to deal with, methodical, even-tempered—"

"You mean as opposed to this Franco character?"

Quinn avoided a direct reply. "I'll have a chat with Charlie," he simply said. "Find out when they pick up and charge that mugger who eluded capture."

"Thanks, Mike. Looks like I'm going to owe you one again."

His eyebrow arched suggestively. "Hold that thought."

I laughed. But he didn't. His gaze was too busy moving over me; his callused fingers too interested in sliding up my bare thigh.

I shivered—*happily*. For the first time tonight, my quaking had nothing to do with freezing cold weather, residual fear, or latent reaction to a bloody crime scene. Nevertheless, I stilled his hand.

"You want something to eat first?" I whispered, knowing he'd just come off duty after a very long day. "Some fresh coffee?"

I moved to get out of bed, but he stopped me.

"Stay put, Cosi. For once, I made a treat for you."

"You're kidding."

Quinn rose from the bed and crossed the room to an end table near the fireplace. As my gaze followed him, I found myself actually noticing the decorations I'd put up that morning: the evergreen wreath hanging over the hearth's ivory-marbled mantel, the tiny white lights framing the French doors, the gold tinsel draped along the top of the antique gilt-framed mirror.

The crackling fire had brought a glow to the room, and despite the chilling events of the evening, I felt my spirits rising again. Mike Quinn had built more than a fire in this room; he'd brought the warmth of the season back to me—along with a neatly folded brown bag.

"I was sorry about missing your tasting party," he explained, sitting back on the bed. "But I did take your challenge."

"What challenge?"

He held up the brown bag. "Didn't you ask your staff to figure out what Christmas tastes like?"

"I did but I didn't expect you to—"

"Close your eyes."

"You're kidding."

"Close 'em, Cosi."

I did. Next I heard the brown bag rustling, then a plastic container popping open. The earthy smell of cocoa immediately hit my nostrils. A moment later, I felt Mike's fingers slipping something cool and smooth between my lips. The morsel was round and fairly hard. I bit into it, hearing a gentle snap. The shell of rich chocolate burst open in my mouth, delivering a velvety taste of sugary fruit laced with the tart brightness of alcohol.

"A cherry cordial!"

"You like it?"

I opened my eyes. The plastic container in Quinn's hand was filled with a dozen chocolate-covered treats. The candy was far from perfect. Some of the pieces were lopsided, some dunked in too much chocolate, others too little. But the effort alone left me gobsmacked.

"You actually made these?" I couldn't believe it. The first time I'd baked corn bread in the man's new apartment, he reacted to the oven timer as if it were an air raid siren. Quinn had skills—plenty of them; cooking just wasn't one.

He smiled. "My mom made cherry cordials every Christmas. She gave me the recipe last week. I was going to pass it to you, but"—he shrugged—"the directions were so straightforward . . ." He popped a homemade treat into his own mouth and smiled again. "I thought I'd surprise you."

I sampled a second. *"Mmmm,"* I said, "tasty surprise."

Then Quinn leaned in and gave me another.

His lips were warm and loving as they brushed across mine. His mouth was sweet from the chocolate, his tongue tart from the alcohol, but after a few soft tastes of me, all gentleness fled. Quinn's kisses became deeper, his mouth downright hungry. Thrilled to keep pace with the man, I hooked my arms around his neck and worked myself into his lap. We were locked together like that in the firelight for an entire transcendent minute before his cell went off.

On a groan of frustration, he pulled away. As he checked the Caller ID, I tried to pretend I wasn't catching my breath.

"Police business?" I finally whispered, unable to read his squinting gaze.

"I'll just be a minute."

His blue eyes had already gone cold.

"What is it?" he asked the caller, his long legs crossing briskly to the window. The shortness in his voice was barely perceptible, but its meaning was clear enough to me. Quinn wasn't just irritated by this interruption; he didn't think it necessary.

A substantial pause followed. As Quinn listened to the caller, he absently pushed back the window curtains, checked the street. *Forever the cop*, I thought.

"Oh, really?" he said at last. "Well, not me."

His tone was openly sharp now.

"That's not a good idea," he added. And finally, just before ending the call—"*Stop*. This is *not* the time."

Something was wrong, *obviously*.

Quinn was almost always in control of his temper. But this unexpected call had really set him off. Even across the shadowy room, I could see the level of ire in his movements. He tugged off his shoulder holster and hooked it sharply over a chair. Then he smacked his badge, cuffs, and wallet onto the dresser. Finally, he came to me, roughly unbuttoning his dress shirt.

"Let me," I whispered, and he did.

As I gently removed the garment, my mind raced with the possibilities of who was calling and why. I asked him if he wanted to talk about it, but he waved me off.

"It's not important," he said, "and I'd prefer we get back to what *is*."

Impatiently he pulled off the rest of his clothes; then he turned his attention to undressing me, first tugging off my worn football jersey, then slipping his hands over my hips to remove my last scrap of modesty. The second I was naked, he hauled me close.

I didn't know why Quinn's need for me was suddenly so acute, but I wasn't about to slow the man down. More than ever, I wanted sweet oblivion, and that's exactly what he gave me.

The flickering shadows of his fire rendered my bruises invisible. The heat of his kisses melted my bitterest fears. And when his body covered mine, he made every last thought in my head disappear.

SEVEN

~~~~~~

MORNING dawned again, cold and bright—only this time I wasn't dreaming. The rhythmic scraping of a snow shovel woke me, and I knew it was Tucker downstairs, clearing the sidewalk before he opened.

With last night's fire thoroughly burned out, the room felt slightly acrid and plenty chilly. I turned under the comforter to find Mike still in a deep sleep. Like any sane woman would, I kissed his bare shoulder and snuggled up to his big, warm body. Unfortunately for me, dreamland was over with one sound—

Mrrrooow!

Feeling a light tread of paws up the bedcovers, I opened my eyes to white whiskers and a pink nose. A fur ball the color of a roasted arabica bean settled onto my chest and began loudly purring. I considered nudging away the little brown tabby, turning over to show her my back, but I didn't have the heart.

"Okay, Java, you win," I whispered on a yawn. "Let's get you some breakfast."

Rolling out of bed, I stifled a groan. The bruises along

my side had been easy enough to forget about while Mike was making love to me. In the light of day, the pain wasn't so easy to ignore. The hot shower helped; so did the Advil with espresso chaser. Within a half hour of waking, I was feeling much better—and much worse.

My contentedly full kitty was watching pigeons on a wire out the back window, my man was happily catching zzz's in the bedroom upstairs, but I was far from serene. In the quiet stillness of the duplex's kitchen, sipping my second espresso of the day, I couldn't stop my mind from returning to that dingy alley down the street.

How did it all go down? I wondered. *Did the creep demand money from Alf first or just start shooting? How long did it take my friend to die there in the snow? Was that ugly gray Dumpster the last thing he saw on earth?*

I felt myself beginning to shake again—but not from fear or cold or Mike's touches. This time what shook me was fury. I wanted to do something *for* Alf, not just sit here and think about what the killer did to him—

I suddenly stood up at the kitchen table.

I need to be busy.

Tucker was already downstairs in the shop. One of our new trainees was helping him open, and I was supposed to have the morning off. I considered getting dressed and going down to the coffeehouse anyway, but I didn't want to abandon my still-sleeping Mike.

I know. "I'll bake!"

Java's ears barely twitched at my announcement, which she deemed far less significant than her pigeon watching. Given my line of thinking a moment before, I figured the cat was right—

Baking was a pathetic alternative to pursuing an active criminal investigation that could nail Alf's killer, but it *would* keep me from climbing the walls this morning; and it was practical, too, because whatever new cookie, tart, or muffin I devised, I could ask my baker to re-create for the Blend's pastry case and sell it downstairs for a profit.

Cha-ching!

I cringed at the sudden memory of my dream—Alf's Santa's bells transforming into ringing cash registers. Then I remembered yesterday's holiday decorating blitz when we'd replaced the Blend's front door dinger with jingle bells.

Is that why I dreamed what I did? Every jingle of the door's bells signals a new Blend customer, doesn't it? And every customer is another chance for my cash register to ring . . .

I closed my eyes. *How can I use Alf's Fa-la-la-la Latte idea now that he's been murdered? I'll feel like a heartless mercenary.*

Stop it, Clare! Stop thinking. Just bake!

I started pulling out the flour, sugar, butter, and the old wooden bread board that Nonna had brought with her from Italy. An hour later I was carrying a breakfast tray upstairs. On it was a French-pressed pot of Matt's annual shipment of Jamaica Blue Mountain and my modern twist to my grandmother's biscotti.

I replaced her traditional anise with vanilla and used roasted pistachios to give the cookie a delicate nutty flavor as well as a hint of green for the season. Dried cranberries added a cheerful shade of Christmas red while a decadent drizzle of white chocolate evoked icy-fresh winter snow. My secret ingredient, however, was ground cinnamon. The bright, bittersweet spice—once used in love potions by wealthy Romans—may have been an unconventional addition for biscotti, but it struck a surprisingly harmonious chord with the cookie's other flavorings while lacing the air with an evocative aroma for the holidays.

As I reentered the still-chilly bedroom, my spirits rose like a yeast panettone. Mike's being here for me felt like an early Christmas gift. At the very least, it was a wish fulfilled. Not so very long ago I'd daydreamed a scenario exactly like this: me serving the sandy-haired detective his morning coffee in this beautiful mahogany four-poster.

There'd been times I never thought it would happen, not that Mike hadn't been thoroughly miserable in his marriage. Between his wife's lying, cheating, and mood swings, the man had been living in the equivalent of an emotional war zone. For the sake of his two kids, however, he'd made every attempt to keep his marriage together. His wife was the one who'd ended things.

I'd never met Leila Quinn, and I often wondered what she'd been like when he first married her. I'd heard about the end of their marriage, of course, but I was curious how they'd originally met, what made him fall in love with the woman and decide to marry her.

Mike never told me. He didn't like talking about his ex or his past with her. And whenever the subject came up, he changed it. For now, I let him. When I'd first met the man, he'd been reduced to a shell-shocked zombie where relationships were concerned. The last thing I wanted to do at this stage of our fledgling bonding process was open barely scabbed-over wounds.

"Rise and shine, big guy," I sang in his ear.

Without opening his eyes, Mike smiled.

I set the tray on the nightstand. "Your coffee is here, and you can try my newest recipe with it: Red and Green Holiday Biscotti."

Mike's eyes were still closed, but his nostrils moved. "*Mmmm*, the house smells good," he murmured, "like my mom used to make it smell at Christmastime when I was a kid. You weren't actually *cooking* this early, were you?"

"You don't know the third tenet of the homemaker's credo?"

"Never heard of it."

"I bake, therefore I am."

Mike laughed. "What are the first two?"

"I clean, therefore I am; I grocery shop, therefore I am; and there are at least seven more." (During my Jersey days, when I was freelance writing to make ends meet, I'd listed them all in one of my old In the Kitchen with Clare columns.) "But my favorite is still baking."

"Lucky for me," he said, closing his fingers around my wrist, "because, as it happens, I'm still starving." Then Mike pulled me back under the bedcovers; and that's when I knew two things—it was absolutely brilliant planning on my part to pour the Blue Mountain into a thermal carafe (because we wouldn't be getting to it for a good half hour), and those wealthy Romans were right about the cinnamon.

A short time later, Quinn was back on the job and so was I. After tying on my Village Blend apron, I helped Tucker recharge our lunchtime crush of caffeine-deficient regulars, then relieved him and our trainee.

Dante and Gardner were scheduled for the evening shifts, and we were short-staffed at the moment, which meant the Blend was all mine for the next three hours.

Only a few café tables were occupied, and after I whipped out another dozen sporadic take-out orders, there were no customers left in line. This was usually my favorite time of day—the quiet afternoon between lunch and dinner, the calm before the after-work crowd stormed our doors. But I didn't like the calm. Not today. Not one bit. My deserted coffeehouse suddenly felt like a widow's empty kitchen, once boisterous with family laughter, now as silent as the viewing room of a funeral home.

Around two o'clock, a number of chatty tourists and chilled holiday shoppers passed right by the shop without even glancing in. I frowned, considering writing up that sidewalk chalkboard featuring our new Fa-la-la-la Lattes, but I thought of Alf again—how the whole Taste of Christmas thing had been his idea—and my heart just wasn't in it. So I swept the floor and wiped down our unoccupied tables.

Just before three, I felt myself tensing. Alf almost always stopped in at this time to "warm his mittens," as he put it, and I'd take a break with him, grab a latte, and sit by the fire. At one minute after the hour, the jingle bells rang. I glanced up, half expecting to see my Santa, and instead found Matt standing there.

I smiled.

He returned my smile, clomped his snowy hiking boots across the wood plank floor, and took a load off at my espresso bar. I was a little surprised to see him dressed like the old days (before fashionista Breanne's influence) in paint-stained jeans and a battered old parka. As he pulled off his coat and settled onto the bar stool, I took a moment to thank him for his help the previous night—and not just for coming to the crime scene.

I'd been so distraught after finding Alf that I didn't think I could tell my staff about the murder without breaking down. Matt had understood. While I'd gone up the back stairs to collapse in bed, he agreed to return to the tasting party, break the news to my baristas, and handle locking up.

"Tucker didn't say much about Alf's death this morning," I told Matt. "Just that it was *too* depressing. How did everyone else take it?"

"They were upset, of course," he said. "But I didn't tell them right away. I let the tasting go on as planned—"

"You *what*?" That decision stunned me.

"I broke the news near the end of the party. You wanted the tasting info, didn't you? Oh, that reminds me—"

He shifted on the bar stool and pulled a folded sheet of paper out of his back pocket. "Here are last night's reactions to the latte flavors. It went pretty well overall. There were only a few duds and a couple of suggestions for tweaking the recipes."

I ignored the folded paper. "I can't believe you let that tasting party go on! What were you thinking?! What about Vicki—"

"Vicki Glockner never showed, Clare. If she had, I would have told her about her father right away. Give me a little credit."

"Oh." I frowned, processing that. "Why didn't Vicki show? Do you think the police got to her first? Called her to give her the news?"

"I don't know."

"Didn't Esther try to reach her? Call her cell?"

"Yeah, sure, but she just got Vicki's voice mail, and—" Matt shrugged. "Esther wasn't about to inform her friend that her father was murdered on a recorded message."

I closed my eyes. "Of course not." My heart really went out to Vicki—especially after I saw the morning papers. The death of her dad wasn't just news. It was a tabloid bonanza.

Ho-Ho-Homicide, screamed one front page in red and green letters. *Santa's Final Sleigh Ride*, declared its rival. Randy Knox's scandal sheet wasn't about to miss the fun. *The Grinch Who Plugged Santa Claus* was the lead story for the *New York Journal*, complete with the head of Dr. Seuss's Grinch Photoshopped over the body of a gun-waving street punk.

All over the Five Boroughs, beleaguered parents now had to explain the news to distraught youngsters who'd heard on television that jolly old St. Nick would no longer be riding his sleigh—or pushing it, in Alf's case.

"Clare?"

I opened my eyes.

"You okay?" Matt asked.

I nodded.

"Espresso then," he said, "if you don't mind."

"No problem."

I was relieved to turn my attention to something so familiar, not to mention fundamental—the espresso being the basis for most Italian coffee drinks. After burring the beans, dosing the proper amount of grounds into the portafilter, and tamping them in for perfect distribution, I locked the handle into place and sent a small amount of hot water under high pressure through the puck. In less than thirty seconds, the water extracted the flavor from the freshly roasted beans, producing that quintessential full-bodied, aromatic liquor topped with *crema*—the term for that dark golden foam that defines a correctly drawn espresso shot.

After finishing the pull, I set the white porcelain cup on its saucer and slid Matt's shot across the blueberry marble counter.

Customers sometimes ask me if I ever grow tired of smelling coffee. I never do. Unlike perfume or incense, the caramel-sweet aroma of a perfectly pulled espresso is neither overbearing nor monotonous. To me, it's a living scent, rising and falling with the life of the cup. Intoxicating yet invigorating, it's like a song I never tire of hearing; the sight of an old friend stepping again and again through my front door . . .

"Getting back to last night," Matt said as he brought the demitasse to his lips. "Did your guard dog ever call you back? Or are you frosted at him for ignoring you?"

"Mike dropped by after work. And I'm not *frosted* at him. There was a very good reason he didn't come to the crime scene."

"Another woman?"

Spare me. "No. As I recall, that was typically *your* reason for not returning my calls. But only when we were married."

Matt grunted. We'd run our wagon wheels over this road so often, the grooves reached the earth's mantle.

"And how's Breanne?" I asked after a long, awkward silence.

"Breanne is . . ." Matt looked into his cooling cup, where the exquisite *crema* was slowly beginning to dissipate. "The same as she ever was."

"What's that supposed to mean?"

Matt shrugged. "You know how she gets."

"What exactly are you two fighting about?"

"At the moment?" Matt shifted on his bar stool. "She's obsessed with micromanaging her magazine's holiday party: all the details, the food, the music, the guest list—"

"Guest list? I thought a company party was supposed to be for the employees? You know, to pat them on the back for a job well done over the past year."

"Well, that's your version. Breanne sees it as a networking opportunity for *Trend*. She's invited name designers, press people, celebrities—she's got her staff working after hours on an 'exclusive' holiday issue for the attendees. Photographers will be there to capture every Technicolor moment. She's determined to garner national buzz."

"I see. And how do you fit into all this?"

"I don't. And frankly, Clare, I'm sick of being ignored by my own bride. I mean, I come home after a two-week tour of Central American coffee farms and what do I get? The cold shoulder. She comes to bed after I'm asleep, gets up before I'm awake—"

No sex, in other words. I arched an eyebrow. For Matt, that was tantamount to no food or water.

"I'm just going to stay out of her way till this holiday crap blows over. But it really pisses me off. I cleared my travel schedule for December. I thought we were going to celebrate a nice, romantic Christmas together. Now I can't wait until January second."

Great, I thought, *another bah-humbug refrain.* "Well, you shouldn't be so eager to see the holidays come and go. Our daughter's flying all the way from Paris to spend time with us."

"Joy's coming?"

I nodded. "She called yesterday morning—morning my time, I should say, with Paris six hours ahead. She asked for two weeks off to celebrate the holidays with us. She says the restaurant's sure to be busy, but she's owed a lot of time off and her bosses are willing to give it to her."

Matt's expression lightened. "That's the best news I've heard all week. You know, you're right, Clare, I should focus on our daughter . . ." He reached out and took my hand. "You want some company tonight? I mean, you're probably still upset about Alf and everything."

"I'm fine. I don't need company," I gently reclaimed my appendage. "Listen, can I give you some advice?"

Matt exhaled. Loudly.

"Breanne's just stressed right now. A combative attitude from you is not going to help the situation. Try to be patient with her. And while you're waiting for her workload to lessen, don't go looking for love in all the wrong places."

Matt glanced away. "Whatever."

It was then I noticed his neglected espresso. Its thick, golden foam was shrinking and collapsing, breaking up into ugly patches that revealed the black pool beneath.

"Your drink's gone cold," I told him.

Matt should have known better. Espresso was a tricky commodity. Once the harmony of the *crema* was lost, the experience could turn bitter.

"I'll just have a new one then," he announced. "*Doppio*, please."

After that, he settled in near the fireplace with his double espresso, his cell phone, some industry trades, and his PDA. Every once in a while, he'd look up at me and wink. But that was Matt, ever constant in his inconstancy.

As the day wore on, business picked up, and I was glad to see Dante arriving on time. Tying on his apron, he joined me behind the counter to deal with the crescendo of the after-work crowd. By six thirty—far too early for my bottom line—the rush began to slow again. That's when Dante spotted my relief coming through the front door.

"Gardner's here!" he called at the register. "And look who else decided to show on her night off . . ."

I glanced up from my espresso machine to see who was walking in behind Gardner's easygoing strides. *Esther Best*. And she wasn't alone. Sweeping in after her on a blast of frigid air was the last person I expected to see tonight— Vicki Glockner, the daughter of my murdered Santa Claus.

EIGHT

∾∾∾∾∾∾∾∾∾∾∾∾∾∾∾∾∾∾

"VICKI, I'm so sorry about your father." I came around
the counter to embrace my former barista.

She nodded her head, setting off the tiny jingle bell earrings. "Thanks, Ms. Cosi. That means a lot."

Her pretty face was florid; her eyes, which were the same
bright hazel green as her father's, were now puffy from crying and shadowed from lack of sleep. Under her fuzzy yellow beret, her mass of salon-streaked, caramel-colored curls,
usually silky and soft, were frizzy and windblown. She tossed
back a handful and sniffled.

I pointed out an empty table. "Have a seat, girls; I'll get
us some drinks." A few minutes later, I brought three mo-
chaccinos over on a tray.

Vicki sniffled again as Esther and I helped her off with
her long, belted beige coat. She pulled off her yellow hat and
matching scarf, then wiped her eyes with a tissue. Esther
and I took seats flanking her.

As we drank in silence, I couldn't help recalling some
of the last words I'd said to Vicki almost eight months
earlier . . .

"No opening shifts. No closing shifts. I'm sorry, Vicki, but I can no longer trust you with the keys to this coffeehouse."

Within two weeks of hearing those words, Vicki had quit—via a cell message. She'd wanted more hours to earn more cash, and I wasn't willing to accommodate her.

Vicki's skills weren't the problem. She'd come to me from a recently closed restaurant on Staten Island, already trained on a professional espresso machine. She started out loving the coffeehouse experience—experimenting with the bar syrups, learning how to prep our menu of coffee drinks. She was great with the customers, too, (crucial for a true Italian barista), but food and beverage service wasn't only about skill and affability.

Vicki had started coming later and later for her shifts, forcing her coworkers to cover for her, and her behavior at work was becoming far from reliable. One evening, I found Gardner alone, dealing with a growing crowd. Vicki had gone downstairs to fetch supplies, and she hadn't come up for thirty minutes.

I found her down there, all right, making out behind the roasting machine with a cute customer. She didn't know the guy. He'd simply been flirting with her and she'd invited him down there for a necking session—and I'm being polite. When I'd interrupted them, their hot-and-heavy focus was moving a lot lower than the neck.

I liked Vicki; it was hard not to. A full-figured girl with an equally full personality (just like her late dad), she had a mile-wide smile with adorable dimples. She laughed easily and at only twenty-one years old joked around with the customers with a level of ease I typically saw in someone much older.

Because Esther and Vicki had gotten to be good friends during the time Vicki worked for me, I'd actually asked Esther to help straighten her out. She'd told me Vicki's parents had separated recently, and I assumed the girl's erratic behavior was akin to Joy's "acting out" after her father and I had split. The backlash was understandable. Alf and I even discussed it one afternoon over lattes . . .

"*Vicki was always a good kid,*" he told me. "*I know she made some bad choices when she was working for you. But I don't blame her. Childhood's an insecure enough ordeal without having your parents screw up your universe, you know?*"

I didn't disagree with Alf. Even though "childhood" was a debatable term for a twenty-one-year-old, I knew how much psychological stock young adults put in having their childhood world still available to them, whether they went back to it or not.

My heart went out to Vicki because I assumed she felt some of the same fears I'd felt around her age—which, frankly, was what tipped the scales for me toward marrying Matt. At nineteen, my fine arts studies were going well, but my grandmother had recently died and my father had just sold off our family grocery. Yes, Matt had gotten me pregnant and I wanted to legitimize Joy's birth, but a big part of me felt adrift at that time. My past was gone, my future uncertain. I'd wanted ties again, stability, someone to love and lean on, a family to belong to.

Unfortunately, my sympathies for Vicki did little to change her. Not even Esther could straighten her out.

"*That girl,*" Esther told me, "*has a mind of her own.*"

Vicki was always sincerely apologetic after she was caught messing up. Her behavior would improve for a week or so, but she'd always backslide again. Then she started picking up guys from dance clubs, bars, God knew where. One day there'd be a preppy white student from the Upper East Side waiting for her shift to end, the next a black kid from Greenpoint in basketball sweats, a week later an Italian street tough from Ozone Park.

Finally, one night, she'd been responsible for closing and "forgotten" to set the security alarm and bolt the back door. A lot of managers would have fired her for that alone, but I still didn't have the heart. I read her the riot act instead, limited her hours, and kept her off key shifts. She pulled the plug herself, leaving the Blend for a waitressing job at a bistro on the Upper West Side.

I hadn't seen her since—until tonight.

"I really liked your dad, Vicki," I assured her as she sipped her mochaccino. "If there's anything I can do to help—"

"There is!"

I blinked, a little surprised by the speed and force of her reply. "Okay. Tell me."

"It's that thing you do," she said.

"That thing I do?" I paused. "You want me to make espressos for the wake?"

"No, not that thing. The other thing."

I glanced at Esther, who looked suddenly uncomfortable. "Sorry?" I said.

Vicki leaned toward me and dropped her voice. "What you did for Joy. I need you to do that again."

"I'm not sure I know what you—"

"I know everything, Ms. Cosi. The real reason your daughter went to work in Paris; Esther spilled the whole story. She said you were the one who got Joy cleared of *double* murder charges. She said the police stacked the evidence against your daughter, but you still found the real killer."

As Vicki wiped her nose, I shifted uneasily. Although I was proud of bringing Tommy Keitel's killer to justice, my daughter's involvement in that sordid affair was something I didn't like spread around. I shot Esther enough of a frown to get that across. She replied with a typical Esther shrug—part sheepish, part defensive. I could almost hear her arguing: *Okay, boss, I feel bad about gossiping, but what did you expect? It was in the papers!*

"I know you liked my dad," Vicki went on. "And he really liked you. He told me how much he looked forward to his latte breaks with you at the Blend. You want to see his killer brought to justice, don't you?"

"Of course I do, but the police are working on it. I've spoken with them—"

"You mean that clown with the do-rag? Sergeant Franco?! He thinks Dad was shot by some anonymous street punk. I know better, but Franco and his partner don't believe me."

I frowned. "What don't they believe, exactly?"

Vicki's gaze locked with mine. "I know my father was *executed*."

Once again, I glanced at Esther. This time she looked a little freaked and shook her head—*Don't ask me!*

I turned to Vicki. "Who would want your father executed? I mean—"

"Omar Linford is his name," Vicki replied. The sniffles were all gone now, her jaw set, her hazel green eyes flashing. "The man lives right next door, too."

"Next door where? To your dad uptown?"

Vicki shook her head. "No, back home on Staten Island. He lives next to the house where I grew up and my mom and I still live."

"So Linford's *your* next-door neighbor?"

"He used to be close friends with my dad, but they had a falling out. Linford's a shady businessman, Ms. Cosi. He may not have pulled the trigger on my father, but I'm *sure* he's involved. I want you to find the proof—"

"Slow down, Vicki. How is this man Linford shady exactly? What's your evidence?"

"It's, like, obvious. He calls himself an importer, but no one seems to know *what* he imports. And he's got 'business interests' in the Cayman Islands." Vicki made air quotes around the words *business interests*.

"That still doesn't tell me why he'd want your father killed. What motive would he have?"

"Motive! My dad borrowed two hundred thousand dollars from Linford!" Vicki's reply was so loud a few heads turned our way. She lowered her voice again. "But he lost the restaurant anyway."

"Restaurant?" I said. "What restaurant?"

"Dad never told you?" Vicki studied my surprised face. "He owned a restaurant for years—a steakhouse with a wine cellar. It was in our Lighthouse Hill neighborhood, right near the Island's La Tourette golf course. It was *way* pricey, but he did pretty well, laughed it up with the Wall Street guys, you know?" Vicki paused to sip her mochaccino. "That's why it didn't surprise me when he started doing the stand-up thing in New York."

"I don't understand."

Vicki shrugged. "He was practically doing it every night in the restaurant. Telling jokes, making his customers laugh—he loved doing that. Then the economy tanked, and those financial district guys lost their jobs and half their life savings. In, like, six weeks, Dad's base just dried up."

"So he lost the restaurant?"

"Not right away, Ms. Cosi. He *loved* his business to death, like, *literally*. He refused to close, just kept borrowing money to keep it going, spent a ton on ads in the papers, discount coupons, online stuff, but it didn't work. Then his drinking got really bad and my parents' marriage went right down the tubes with his business. That's when I came to work for you. I was supposed to take over the restaurant one day, run it as *my* place. That's why I didn't even bother with college. I figured my future was all worked out, you know?"

I blinked, still absorbing this revelation. "I remember when you first applied to work here, Vicki. You told me you had hostess and barista experience, but you never said your dad owned the place."

She shrugged. "I thought it would look better if I didn't mention that Daddy gave me a job seating guests and making espressos. I mean, it worked, didn't it? You hired me."

And very nearly fired you, I thought but didn't say.

That's when I remembered checking Vicki's references—an older woman at a Staten Island number had sung her praises over the phone. Had that been her mother? Well, it didn't matter now. I remembered Alf telling me that he was a reformed alcoholic. He'd confessed he'd had to live in the New York shelter system for a few weeks earlier this year. But the only thing he'd told me about his old life was that his marriage failed after he lost his income and life savings.

"So you see now, Ms. Cosi? That's why Omar Linford had

my dad killed," Vicki declared, staring at me as if I were supposed to follow her logic.

I shook my head.

"Dad *never* paid Linford back. Not one red cent."

I took a breath. "Listen, I understand how upset you are, but it's common knowledge that restaurants are a risky business venture. More of them fail than succeed. Bankruptcy isn't uncommon. This next-door neighbor of yours—this Linford—he had to be aware of the risk going in."

"Linford isn't some bank. He operates outside the law."

"Is he a loan shark, Vicki? Is that what you're saying? Because if this man is involved with organized crime, we should contact the FBI."

"No. He's not a gangster, Ms. Cosi, at least not the kind the FBI bug and take photos of and stuff. The loan *looked* legit. It was drawn up by Linford's lawyer—but it was made through one of his business accounts in the Cayman Islands."

"So?"

"The Cayman Islands! Hello! Tax cheat heaven. Home of crooked investment bankers and laundered drug money. Linford even lives there for part of the year!"

"That still doesn't mean Mr. Linford is a killer. Your dad never mentioned any of these things to me. Did this man Linford ever actually threaten your father—with a phone call or note, anything like that?"

"Nothing I can prove. But I'm sure Linford is involved in my father's murder—" Tears sprang into her eyes and the pitch of her voice turned almost heartbreakingly desperate. "I'm afraid he's going to go to my mother next, force her to sell our house or something, you know? Pay up or the same thing will happen to her."

I exchanged worried glances with Esther. "Has this man contacted your mother? Threatened her?"

"No, but he might. He might even come after me, use me in some way to force her to pay the debt!"

"You told Detective Franco all this?"

"He said he'd 'follow up' on it," she said, again using air quotes. "But I could tell he thought I was just paranoid, that Dad's killer was just some random mugger, not part of a conspiracy or something. He kept looking over at that other guy—the Chinese cop, Detective Kong."

"Hong," I corrected.

"Whatever." She threw up her hands. "Look, they were both nice and polite and everything on the surface, but I could tell they thought what I was saying was dubious. That's why I need you, Ms. Cosi. You and Daddy were friends. I need someone to help who actually cares."

I checked my watch, remembering that Mike had mentioned he was going to speak with Franco's partner and give me an update on the case. But I hadn't heard from him since we'd parted this morning. Alf's case was an NYPD matter now; the next move on solving it was really Sergeant Franco's and Detective Hong's.

Sergeant Franco, I muttered to myself, recalling the man's insufferably condescending attitude. *Sergeant Franco . . .*

By rights, I should have been fine with letting the professionals handle this and persuading Vicki to do the same. If nothing else, the conventions of modern life—from push-button pod coffeemakers to the 24/7 media—wanted us all to act like nothing more than passive observers. After leaving my fine arts program to have a baby, however, I never considered myself a passive anything.

"These cops will never catch Daddy's killer," she said, taking hold of my arm. "I'm begging you, Ms. Cosi. Check out this Linford guy. *Please.* Do it for my dad—"

"Okay, Vicki," I said, quieting the nerve-racked girl. "I'll look into it. I will. I'll see if I can find something that will get the NYPD to take you seriously—"

Or else get you to calm down and see that you're wrong.

Vicki nodded enthusiastically. I didn't know yet what I was going to do, but seeing the relief on the girl's face made me believe I'd at least said the right thing.

As I gave her another hug, I glanced at the occupied tables

around us. Professional journalists regularly canoodled with
their laptops in coffeehouses all over this city, and mine was
no exception. The accusations Vicki made—naming Linford
so loudly as her dad's killer, pleading with me so emotionally to get involved—weren't exactly the kind of thing I'd
want to read about in tomorrow's tabloids.

But the few people with laptops were absorbed in their
work, and I knew them as regulars—two NYU undergrads,
a young lawyer from a nearby firm, and a doctor from St.
Vincent's Hospital up the street. There was only one person
looking our way: that gorgeous thirtysomething redhead
who'd nearly run me over the previous night at the Blend's
front door.

She was sitting alone, a few tables away, nursing a latte,
her scarlet curls framing high cheekbones draped in porcelain, her doll-like eyes staring openly at me. She was studying me with such intense interest that I wondered if she
wanted to talk.

Maybe she actually wants to apologize for her rude behavior?

I deliberately met the woman's eyes to see if she would
gesture me over—but she immediately looked away.

I let it go.

I doubted very much that she was any kind of writer or
reporter. The previous times I'd seen her in here it was never
with a laptop, PDA, or work of any kind. Travel brochures,
exclusive catalogs, and high-end fashion magazines were all
I'd ever seen her paging through as she nursed a drink.

Socialite. Trust fund baby. Trophy wife—any or all of these un-
generous labels were what I affixed to the woman in the banks
of my memory, and I dismissed her interest as either boredom
or some sort of imagined vendetta she now had against me for
our momentary confrontation the night before.

*Great, that's all I need in my life: an aging Paris Hilton with
a sociopathic grudge.*

Meanwhile, Vicki was explaining to me that she had to
leave. "I have to meet with Brother Dominick about Dad."

"Alf had a *brother* in the city?"

"Not that kind of brother. My dad didn't have any siblings. His parents are dead, too. Brother Dominick was Dad's boss at the Traveling Santa headquarters—"

"He's a Catholic monk?"

"He used to be. His first name's really Pete, but all the guys playing Santa call him 'Brother,' even though he left the order years ago. Anyway, Brother Dom is the one making arrangements for my dad's funeral."

"Why isn't your mom doing that?"

"Mom doesn't want any part of it," Vicki said, a little bitterly. "I doubt she'll even show."

"Oh," I said, pausing as that sank in. "Well, don't be too hard on her, Vicki. When a marriage breaks up, it can be painful. Your mom's probably still focused on her anger, and she may even be in denial. The grief for your dad will come in time."

Vicki's mouth tightened, and her hazel green eyes went cold. "You don't know my mother," she said, and then she rose and grabbed her coat. "Well, thanks for doing what you're going to do, Ms. Cosi. You have my home phone number, and Esther has the number for my cell. Call anytime."

We hugged again, and then Vicki headed for the door. When she was out of earshot, Esther turned to me. "I don't know if she's paranoid about this neighbor of theirs or not, boss, but I'm sure Vicki will appreciate anything you can do."

"What do you mean, anything *I* can do? *We're* going to be working together on this one."

Behind her black glasses, Esther's eyes went from their typical, world-weary squint to freak-out wide. "Excuse me?"

I bolted back the remains of my mochaccino and set down my cup. "I just decided. You and I are going to start investigating Alf's death right now."

"What?!"

"Listen up, Esther. If I'm going to do this, I'm going to need a partner—and tonight you're it."

NINE

~~~~~~

"WHAT are you wearing?" Esther whispered fifteen minutes later.

"For what we're about to do, I needed something black and grungy."

"Well, boss," she said, making a theatrical show of looking me up and down, "you scored."

In the apartment upstairs, I'd shed my pressed slacks and sweater, replacing them with scuffed black denims, a navy turtleneck, a faded *Best Mom in the World* sweatshirt, and worn hiking boots leftover from my snow-shoveling days in Jersey. I'd draped a dark hoodie over it all and weighed down its deep pockets with a few devices I thought I might find useful on the little outing on which I was about to embark.

"What about me?" Esther asked, gesturing to her ensemble. "Don't I need to change, too?"

From her rectangular glasses to her steel-toed shoes, Esther was usually dressed for skulking around in the dark. Tonight was no exception: shiny dark pants (leather, pleather, vinyl?) topped with knee-high boots. I paused for a moment, considering the Renaissance level of cleavage bulging out of her sweater's plunging neckline—a garment layered over what looked like a deep purple lace-up bustier. (Since she'd started dating BB Gunn, aka Russian rapper Boris Bokunin, elements of Esther's wardrobe had taken a decidedly racy turn.) Then again, her Doctor Who scarf was the length of a football field and her ankle-length black duster would certainly provide enough warmth.

"You're fine," I told her.

Unfortunately, our route to tonight's snoop wasn't.

Dante Silva had begun bussing empty tables near the front door. When he saw my street duds, he laughed—loudly—and moved to stand right in front of us.

"*Carumba*, boss! Heading out for a rumble?" With one hand he brushed his shaved head in what I took to be a gang sign. "Did you join the Crips or the Bloods?"

"The Latin Kings," Esther replied flatly. "Her café con leche won them over."

Dante folded his tattooed arms and regarded us. "No kidding, you two, where are you cruisin' together?"

"Out," I replied, grabbing Esther's arm and hustling her around the overly curious painter.

So far, so good, I thought, until someone else noticed me.

"Sister Clare! Is that you?!" The voice was male, the Jamaican lilt all too familiar.

I looked across the room, surprised to see Dexter Beatty sitting with Matt. *When did he get here?*

"Come *yuh*!" Dexter waved me over with a grin. "Come, come!"

Dex was in his early forties; his Rasta dreadlocks, which he always tied back on the job, were now loose, framing his light-skinned African features like a cocoa-brown mop. As Esther and I approached his café table, he pointed to us and said something to my ex-husband.

Matt turned in his chair, and his gaze immediately narrowed on my oversized black hoodie. "What are you dressed for?" he demanded.

"The latest trend," I said flatly. "*Gangsta chic.* I'm surprised Breanne didn't tell you about it."

"Clare, what are you up to?"

"Not a thing," I lied. "Java needs Cat Chow. Esther's coming with."

Matt scowled. "You mean you're not all dressed up to play detective again? Because I'll tell you right now, Clare, it's a bad idea. You shouldn't get involved in—"

"Don't be paranoid! I told you where I'm going." *Time to change the subject.* I turned to Matt's friend. "And how are you, Dexter?" I chirped with more perkiness than a caffeinated Brady sister.

"Good, good," Dex answered with a nodding grin. "You must come to Brooklyn, Clare, and see my shops all decorated for the holiday."

"Yes, of course. You know I love your shops!"

No forced perkiness there. I really did love them. Like my grandmother's grocery, which had kept the Italians in her zip code supplied in fresh mozzarella, prosciutto di Parma, salt-packed Sicilian anchovies, and chestnut flour; Dexter's three Taste of the Caribbean shops kept the pantries of West Indians stocked up with pigeon peas, chicken feet, freshly cut sugarcane, ginger beer, scary-hot Scotch bonnet peppers (for your jerk seasoning), and burnt sugar syrup (for your black cake).

Also like my Nonna, Dex was a stickler for authentic products, and that included coffee. Given the world market, the Caribbean was far from a major coffee-growing player, but Matt routinely sought out its coffees for Dex—from Haiti, the Dominican Republic, Puerto Rico, even St. Vincent, where a single coffee farmer was attempting to bring back the crop to his tiny island home.

Dex also depended on Matt to acquire one of the most expensive varieties of coffee on the planet: Jamaica Blue Mountain. Some roasters mixed JBM with less expensive beans to make a blend. But Jamaica Blue was such a smooth, mild brew that cutting it negated the entire reason for drinking it. My Village Blend JBM was pricey, but it was pure—which was one reason Dex dealt exclusively with us for that particular import.

Anyway, with the winter holidays Dex's busiest and most profitable selling season, I was surprised to see him here this evening.

"And speakin' of holidays," Dexter continued. "This Blend of yours, she looks magical. The lights, the tree, the little jingle bells—to the fullness, sister!"

"Thank you," I said.

"And this holiday latte—" Dexter raised his glass. "Sweet!"

"Sweet, huh?" Esther broke in. "Which one are you drinking? Because I still think Tucker's candy cane concoction is borderline insipid."

"Well, that one may be. But this one's a marvel!"

Okay, now I was downright curious. It must have shown, because Matt caught my eye and explained.

"I asked Gardner to mix up Dex his Caribbean Black Cake from last night's tasting."

Dex took another sip. "The flavor of rum comes through first. Then the nutty sweetness of the brown sugar. And cinnamon is ticklin' my tongue at the end, the way it tickled my nose at the beginnin'. I taste a note of heavy fruit flavor, too—"

"That's the black currant syrup," I said.

Dexter sipped again. "There's a hint of somethin' more. Somethin' dark, sweet, earthy—"

"Chocolate." I smiled. "Gard and I agreed that authentic black cake is so rich it tricks the taste buds into thinking chocolate is one of the ingredients; we compensated with a splash of my homemade chocolate syrup."

"Clever! And what other flavors are you offerin', Clare?" He glanced around the shop. "Where is your holiday menu?"

I shifted uneasily. "To tell you the truth: I had mixed feelings about putting it up. Something happened to a friend of mine last night and suddenly the whole Taste of Christmas thing feels . . . I don't know . . . *wrong*."

"Cha!" Dexter threw up his hands. "This Black Cake Latte brings me right back to the islands. I tell you that's a gift, Clare, a gift for your customers, bringin' them back to a time and a place with the simple magic of flavor. I sip this drink, and I'm with my *madda* and aunties again, weeks before holiday bakin' day, when they all got together and started soakin' their black cake fruits in wine."

Before I could reply, he turned to my ex. "What do you think of these drinks, Matteo?"

"Sorry." Matt shrugged. "Fa-la-la-la Lattes just aren't my thing."

Dexter frowned at his friend's reply. "Hmmm, well now . . ." Dex said, catching my eye. "We know what *is* Matteo's thing, don't we, Clare?" He pointed to a very familiar glossy-paged publication among the papers and trade magazines on the café table.

I smirked when I saw it. Talk about being brought back to a time and a place. For my ex-husband, the Christmas season didn't start until the Victoria's Secret holiday catalog arrived in the mail. Perusing its pages was an annual event.

"You never change, do you, Matt?"

Matt squinted. "A man has a right to shop for lingerie gifts, doesn't he?"

"Yes," I said, "but my problem was never with your giving the gift of lingerie, just the number of women you gave it to."

Dexter opened the racy catalog. Many of its pages were marked with Post-its—color-coded Post-its. What the coding system was, I could never bring myself to ask.

"That one's a stunner." Dex tapped one of the scantily clad models.

Matt frowned. "Are you blind? She's got beady eyes, her lips are too thin, and her legs are bowed."

Dex laughed. "Oh, *mon*! Haven't your heard that ol' island song? 'How me love swimmin' with bow-legged women.'"

Esther frowned. "Isn't that a line from the movie *Jaws*?"

Dexter nodded. "It's also a very old pirate ditty. Port Royal, you know, was once their biggest haven in the Caribbean." He winked. "Underneath, we're all buccaneers."

"If you mean all *men*," Esther said flatly. "I'm in complete agreement."

Dex flipped through more glossy pages. "So, Matteo, what lady in here is to your likin'?"

Matt pointed to a leggy blonde.

"Her? *Cha*!" Dex shook his head. "She looks *fenky-fenky* to me!"

"What's *fenky-fenky*?" Esther asked.

"It means she looks proud," Dex said. "Stuck on herself."

Esther snorted and leaned toward me. "Sounds like Matt's new wife."

I cleared my throat. "Well, we really should be going—"

"Don't you know that ol' Jamaican saying?" Dex interrupted as he thumbed through the Post-it-tagged models.

"Not another one." Matt muttered.

"Sweet nanny goat have a runnin' belly."

"Excuse me?" Esther said.

Dex turned to face her. "It means, what tastes good to a goat at noontime might ruin his belly by nightfall."

Esther adjusted her black glasses. "I need more."

Dex shrugged. "Some things that seem good to a man now, can hurt him later."

"Oh, I get it," Esther said. "The running belly is the goat eating too much bad grass and then getting diarrhea."

"Diarrhea!" Dex vigorously nodded, sending his dreadlocks bouncing again. "Now you're gettin' it, sister!"

"O-kay!" I interjected. "Now that she's *got* the diarrhea, we'll just let you two continue your, uh, browsing."

I grabbed Esther's arm.

"Clare, wait!" Matt called. "Where are you really going—"

I heard the worry in Matt's voice, but I didn't care. Ignoring his question, I left my ex-husband to his lingerie models and pushed Esther out into the chilly night, my only reply the echo of jingle bells above our shop's door.

W**HEN** I finally let go of Esther's arm, she skidded on a patch of sidewalk ice. I grabbed her in time to save her from a tumble.

"You okay?" I asked.

"For now," she said, shifting her big black leather shoulder bag from one arm to another. "But I'd really like to know why we're returning to the scene of Alf Glockner's murder in the dead of night?"

I had to strain to hear her words over the traffic on Hudson Street, not to mention the howl from a stiff wind coming off the nearby river. It didn't help that Esther's chin was tucked deep into the coil of her mile-long scarf.

"It's not the dead of night," I pointed out. "It's only a little past seven."

A steamy sigh escaped Esther's mouth. "Okay, maybe it's not the dead of night, but it feels like it. It's dark and cold and windy, which raises the question—no, two questions. Is this trip really necessary?"

"Yes." I flipped up the hood of my giant black sweatshirt. "We're returning to the scene because I have a new theory about what happened to Alf in that courtyard. What's your second question?"

"It's rhetorical, actually."

"What?"

"Why-oh-why didn't I go down to Florida with my parents this year?!"

I took her arm. "Come on . . ."

"So, Boss," Esther piped up again as we took off down the sidewalk. "What is this new theory of yours?"

"Sergeant Franco is searching for a random mugger, but I think he's wrong." I kept my voice low. There was no snowstorm tonight to scare pedestrians inside, which meant plenty of people were now strolling the Village sidewalks, including a middle-aged couple carrying bags of takeout right behind us.

"How is Franco wrong exactly?" Esther whispered, taking my let's-keep-this-private cue.

"I think the killer had more to lose from Alf identifying him. I think the killer was a serious criminal, either fleeing or just beginning a break-in. That would explain the footsteps to and from the fire escape."

"So you think Alf was trying to stop a burglary? And caught a bullet for his trouble?"

"Maybe."

"But . . . why was Alf in that courtyard in the first place? I mean, how could he know there was a burglary going on?"

I fell silent for a moment. "Franco claimed Alf went back there for an innocent reason. As he put it: 'to clean his pipe.'"

"You mean pee?" Esther said. "*Ew.* Out in the open? In the middle of a blizzard?"

"I don't believe it, either. Alf had just left the White Horse Tavern on the corner, where he could have used a nice, warm men's room. And he wasn't that old—even though the Santa disguise makes him look that way—so I doubt very much that Alf had a prostate the size of a cantaloupe."

"A what?"

"That was how Franco put it."

Esther rolled her eyes. "This dude sounds like a real class act."

"Well, he's the lead detective."

"But you think he's wrong, which means you still have to answer my question. What made Alf go into that courtyard?"

Under my voluminous black hoodie, I shrugged. "Maybe he spied suspicious activity from the sidewalk and went in to check it out."

"But wouldn't a burglary have been reported to the police by now?"

"Maybe it already has. But that's police business, so it won't be easy to find out."

"Can't your cop boyfriend help with that?"

"Mike will help if he can. Of course, there are reasons burglaries go unreported, too. The victim could be out of town and not even know his or her place was ripped off—"

"*If* it was ripped off. Of course, it *is* the holiday season. Lots of expensive gifts in shopping bags sitting around these posh apartments."

"True," I said, "probably a lot of extra cash, too."

"And the people who got robbed might be criminals themselves, right?"

"That's possible, too," I said. "Police involvement would be the last thing someone like that would want."

Esther snorted. "I guess a drug dealer isn't going to tell the NYPD his stash was stolen—but I still don't get what we're doing out here in the *dead of night*. What are we looking for, exactly?"

"Physical evidence of a burglary. Broken glass. A jimmied apartment window. Obvious signs of illegal entry. And it's not the dead of night. Stop saying that."

"But haven't the police been all over that place?"

"All over the alley, yes, certainly the courtyard, too, because the policemen chased the mugger through there, but Franco shrugged off my concerns about the fire escape."

"The fire escape." Esther stared at me a second. "You're not going to *climb* it, are you?"

I nodded.

"What if you're caught? That's trespassing, isn't it?"

"I won't be caught. Not with you watching my back."

"'Esther Best, accessory to felony trespass.'" She framed her words like a headline. "Boris would love that. I mean, talk about gangsta chic—"

"Look, if you want to back out—"

"No way, boss. You know I like to live on the edge."

"Uh-huh."

Five minutes later, we were standing on the sidewalk just outside the alley where Alf died. "Are you sure this is the right place?" Esther asked. "I don't see any police tape."

I suppressed a shiver. "This is the place."

"Then let's go—"

I stopped Esther and gestured toward an elderly couple heading right for us along the narrow sidewalk. "We can't go into the alley yet," I whispered. "We have to let these people pass so they don't notice us and get suspicious."

"We can't just loiter here," Esther whispered back. "That's suspicious, too. Maybe we should walk on, then double back. There's no one coming from that direction."

Just then, two young men entered the block from the opposite direction and across the street.

"Crap," I muttered.

"Quick, pretend to tie your boot," Esther suggested.

I glanced over my shoulder. The older people were still moving toward us, but at a glacial pace. "I could tie my laces three times and those folks still wouldn't be here."

Esther nervously shifted from foot to foot. "What do we do then? Maybe we should just leave—"

"Spill your bag," I said.

"What?"

"Spill your bag. I don't have one. You do."

"No way, I—"

I pulled the purse from Esther's shoulder and dumped it onto the frozen concrete. Esther tried to catch it, and slipped on a patch of ice for her trouble. She grabbed my arm to steady herself, and we both went down.

Now I felt like an idiot. "I'm sorry, Esther," I said, taking my time scooping up change, makeup, and a pen off the ground. Across the street, I heard the two men snicker.

Esther smirked. "They think we had a girl fight."

The elderly couple finally reached us. The woman inquired about our safety.

"Just slipped in the snow!" I chirped. "Have a nice day!"

Esther watched the couple pass. "Good thing nobody noticed us, right, boss?"

"I think I've had enough irony for one night."

I opened Esther's bag to dump her stuff back inside and was surprised at how heavy it was. So I took a closer look.

"My God, Esther! You have half a brick at the bottom of your purse."

"It's protection," she said.

"Protection? From what?"

"Those fashion mags with their anorexic models are a crock, you know? It's Rubenesque girls like me who bring out the worst in the guys with *real* testosterone. The home-boys in Air Jordans I can handle; even construction workers aren't so bad. But when some of these Middle Eastern dudes and south-of-the-border guys spot curves like mine, they go bonkers. Their tongues loll and their eyes bulge like the wolf in that old Tex Avery cartoon." Esther sighed and shook her head. "Sometimes, to dissuade them, I have to resort to the brick. That's how I roll."

"Okay," I replied, refilling the purse.

Esther scanned the street. "The coast looks clear, boss."

"Good," I said, rising. "Then let's get rolling."

Ten

~~~~~~

$\mathbf{A}$s we slipped into the private alley, I stared at the in-famous gray Dumpster. It stood in the shadows, lid open, contents emptied.

"This is where I found Alf," I said softly.

"Oh." Esther blinked at the trash container. "Weird."

"What?"

"I guess I expected something more ominous. It looks so . . . normal."

Esther was right. The police tape was gone by now, and so was most of the snow. There were no traces of blood on the concrete, no chalk outline, no sign that a violent crime had taken place here.

From my talks with Quinn, I knew this was the work of the crime-scene unit. In their search for a murder weapon or forensic evidence, crime technicians would have metic-ulously combed through every garbage and recycling bin, then had the trash carted away and stored in case they'd missed anything during the initial search.

I understood the procedures on an intellectual level, but the emotional effect was unsettling. It felt as if Alf never existed. Like this wonderful man had been wiped away by bureaucrats of a heartless metropolis that had no time to mourn the death of its citizen.

In twenty-four hours, Alf went from human being to crime victim; tabloid folly to complete eradication. The speed of erasing a person in this town was too unsettling to contemplate—*and anyway*, I promised myself, *I'm not going to forget him.*

"What did you say, boss?"

"Nothing. Come on."

We moved through the dim alley and into the darkened courtyard, where the second metal Dumpster stood beside the line of blue plastic recycling bins.

From one of my hoodie's deep pockets, I fished out a small flashlight, one more powerful than the keychain light I'd had the night before. I flipped it on and scanned the fire escape above the trash bins. Then I moved to those crates I'd seen, stacked against a far wall. I hauled one off the top of the pile and dragged it over to the blue recycling bin to act as a step—exactly the way I was sure Alf had.

"You're really going up there?" Esther whispered.

"Yes."

"You sure?"

"Just watch my back and warn me if someone comes." I turned to start climbing.

"Wait!" she rasped. "How can I warn you if you're all the way up there and I'm down here? I'll have to shout."

"You're right." I thought it over. "We'll use our cell phones like walkie-talkies."

We made the connection a moment later. "Keep the line open the whole time I'm up there," I whispered. Then I pocketed the open phone and boosted myself to the top of one of the blue bins, bruising an elbow in the process.

"Ouch."

"You okay?"

"I'll live."

I climbed to my feet, boots thumping dully on the frigid

plastic lid, and made sure my footing was secure before I reached into my pocket to check the connection.

"Still there, Esther?"

"Affirmative. What next?"

"I'm going to climb the fire escape ladder up to the second-floor landing."

"But those ladders are always locked in place for security," she warned.

"Yeah, I know," I said, eyeballing my Everest.

The wrought-iron framework appeared pretty typical for an apartment building of this age and type: metal staircases connecting narrow grilled balconies that sat parallel to each story. In an emergency, a simple sliding ladder allowed tenants to move from the second-floor balcony to the ground. When not in use, the ladder was locked high off the ground—to keep people like me from trespassing.

"I'm going to pull myself up," I told Esther, my focus on the ladder's bottom rung, just above my head. "Stand by; I may need help."

Okay, I thought, *so I haven't done a pull-up since high school gym class, but my job has its daily physical demands and I swim laps semiregularly in the local Y's pool. I'm in passable shape. How hard can one stupid pull-up be?*

Taking a deep breath, I jumped up to grip the wrought-iron rung and heaved with all my might. But my body didn't lift up. Instead, the freezing black bar shot out of my hands as the heavy metal structure rolled down its runner with a wince-inducing grinding. Then the bottom of the ladder slammed the ground with an explosive *clang!*

I froze.

"Crap," Esther said over the phone. "That was loud!"

"The ladder wasn't locked!" I rasped into the cell. "If anyone comes out, just tell them you're a new tenant and you were emptying your trash!"

We waited nearly five minutes, just to be safe, but no one came to investigate. Then on a deep breath of bracing winter air, I gripped a cold metal rung and began to climb.

At the top of the ladder, I stepped onto the second-floor balcony. That's when I noticed that the security release hook had rusted through—

It wasn't unlocked, I realized. *It was broken.*

There was still snow and ice on the grillwork. My gloved fingers grabbed the guardrail, and I knocked free an entire row of tiny icicles. With a crystalline tinkling, they rained down on Esther.

"Watch the shrapnel, boss!" she complained over the cell. "And keep the noise down, too."

"Sorry."

Using the tiny beam from my pocket flashlight, I searched for anything out of the ordinary. Two windows faced the second-floor balcony—presumably different apartments. Both were curtained and dark, and the glass on each window appeared intact and undisturbed.

On my way to the third floor, a blast of arctic wind swept through the courtyard. The fire escape bucked under my feet like trick stairs in an amusement park fun house. Freaked a little, I clung to the rocking metal until the wind subsided.

That's when I heard a loud *bang* from the courtyard below. I put the phone to my ear and heard Esther's frantic whisper. "Boss? Are you there?"

"I'm here."

"Someone came out of that steel back door."

She said nothing more for several long, tense moments. Finally, she spoke again, but not to me.

"Hi, I guess you're emptying your garbage, too."

A woman's voice replied, but I couldn't make out the words.

"No. I just moved in." Esther again.

More conversation.

"Thanks," Esther told the stranger, "but I'm not going back inside. I was on my way out anyway, so I'll just hit the street through the alley."

A moment later, I heard the steel door clang. I kept the phone to my ear and waited.

"Boss?"

"I heard what happened, Esther. Where are you?"

"Back on the sidewalk out front," she replied. "That woman was *way* suspicious. She waited till I left the court-yard before she went back inside. Now I'm stuck on the street. And there are like a million dog walkers out here. I can't get back to the courtyard without being seen."

"Don't worry, Esther. I'm okay up here—" And now, given that tenant's reaction, I figured she was more likely to draw attention to what I was doing than prevent anyone from noticing. "Just wait for me on the corner, in front of the White Horse Tavern."

"Fine," Esther said. "But if it's all the same to you, I'd rather wait *inside*. It's freezing out here, in case you haven't noticed."

I'd noticed. "Just keep the line open, okay?"

"Roger."

I pressed on. When I got to the escape's third-floor land-ing, I heard laughter and conversation muffled by drawn blinds and a closed window. I flipped off my flashlight. Examining the landing and the windows on this floor, I couldn't see anything out of the ordinary, so I moved on.

It was the fourth floor that gave me what I'd come here looking for: Light from a bare window spilled onto the metal grillwork. The illumination wasn't just bright enough to make the icicles glisten, it cast a spotlight on something peculiar just below the window ledge. A small, round hole had been punched into a mound of snow. The tiny crater re-minded me of those chilling little sinkholes I'd spotted the night before on the layered sidewalk—random white resting places for the change that scattered when Alf's "Santa Bag" had been broken open and robbed.

Careful to stay hidden beneath the brightly lit window, I dropped to my hands and knees and crawled up to the pitted snow. Something shiny and smooth sat in the center of that little indentation. As I snatched it up, a shadow suddenly crossed the light.

Someone's moving inside that apartment!

I reared back—only to be stopped short when my hoodie snagged on a sharp object hanging just below the window ledge above me. It took me a moment to detach myself from what looked like a loose cable television hook.

Finally free, I sat back on my haunches and studied the object in my hand. It appeared to be a white button. A little larger than one of those old Susan B. Anthony silver dollars, it had four holes in its center and a bold *TS* design embossed on both sides.

TS—Traveling Santa . . . Oh my God.

This was the missing button from Alf Glockner's Santa suit!

I'd assumed Alf's attacker had ripped the button off while trying to get to the dead man's wallet. But Alf obviously lost the button in front of this window, probably on the same hook that just snagged my hoodie!

"Okay, Alf," I whispered, half believing his spirit was still swirling around me on the winter gusts, "what the heck were you doing all the way up here?"

"What did you say, boss?"

I swallowed hard and put the cell to my mouth. "Stand by, Esther."

Think, Clare, think . . .

When Mike talked to me about his cases, he talked *method*, too; most of that method involved reconstructing possible scenarios of past actions based on discovered evidence.

"*It's really not that complicated,*" he'd once told me, "*not if you have an imagination.*"

Right, I thought. *Ask questions. Imagine the possible answers . . .*

First question: Why was Alf in this courtyard? The evidence of his button, right under this intact window, pretty well answers that one. Alf was spying on someone in this apartment.

"*And?*" I could practically hear Quinn challenging me. "*Next question? Isn't it obvious?*"

"Who?" I murmured into the night air. "Who lives in this apartment?"

I tucked the button into the pocket of my jeans and went back to my hands and knees. The metal was freezing. Suppressing a shiver, I crawled forward.

I could see that the window blinds were half open—enough to get a good look inside. Carefully, I peeked over the ledge and saw the corner of a cherry wood end table. On its glossy surface sat an expensive-looking man's watch, a black leather wallet, a thick ring of keys, some loose change, and what looked like a photo ID badge on a cord. Beyond that, I saw a hardwood floor and designer showroom–esque leather furniture. A halogen floor lamp, mimicking fusion as bright as the sun, reflected off the polished coffee table, where several glossy little shopping bags were lined up in a row.

Hardly daring to breathe, I pulled out the tiny pair of opera binoculars I'd brought along. A few years back, Madame had given me and Joy the pair as a memento of the night she took us to see *Cosi fan tutte* (one of Mozart's lesser-known works). I peered through them now to make out the writing on the glossy bags: Tiffany, Tourneau, Saks—all elite uptown stores. More shopping bags were labeled with the names of high-end boutiques located here in the West Village.

Looks like someone's already doing the holiday shopping, I noted, *very pricey holiday shopping*.

Adjusting the magnification on the opera glasses, I moved my focus to the end table. Next to the black leather wallet sat a Rolex watch as well as a security ID badge for a place called Studio 19. Under the studio's logo, I saw the photo of a handsome black man in his midthirties. The name on the badge was *James Young*. There was smaller writing on the card, but I couldn't read it.

When I tried readjusting the magnification level again, the light streaming through the window flickered—as if

someone were passing in front of the floor lamp. I looked up
to see a man's figure moving swiftly out of the room.

Had I been spotted? Probably.

"Uh-oh . . ."

I crawled away from the window and descended the fire
escape stairs as quickly as I dared, which wasn't all that fast
because the structure was still icy. Then between the second-
and third-floor balconies I heard a loud *clang!*

I stilled, realizing the building's steel back door had
opened and closed again. It was too dark to see what was
going on below me, and with Esther now sitting in the
White Horse Tavern, all I could do was cling to the handrail
and wait.

A moment later, I heard the grinding squeak of that big,
metal Dumpster lid, the one next to the blue recycling bins.
With an exhale, I relaxed. *Someone's just emptying their trash
again*, I decided.

I let another few minutes tick by. Except for the winter
wind, the courtyard fell silent. I waited for the sound of a
steel door opening and closing again, but it never came, so
I decided the person emptying the garbage must have departed by way of the alley, just like Esther, and I continued
my descent.

A sharp gust of wind blew off my hood, but I didn't pause
to flip it up again. As soon as I reached the second-floor
landing, I scrambled onto the ladder. *Almost there.* Rung by
rung, I moved south. Just a few feet from those blue plastic
recycling bins, I thought I was home free.

"Got ya, *bitch*!"

Two bruising hands closed on my upper arms.

"Ahhhhhh!" I shouted. "Let me go!"

The jerk who grabbed me didn't. He ripped me from the
ladder, literally tossing me into the air. I felt myself falling,
yelling all the way, until I hit a low pile of plastic garbage
bags at the bottom of the metal Dumpster. The lid had been
left open, and the bin swallowed me up like a fetid, black

monster. I'd barely hit the garbage bags before I heard a clang above my head.

That jerk closed the lid on me!

I scrambled up so fast I banged my head against the freezing metal.

"Crap!"

Crouching down again, I glanced around the smelly box, but the darkness was absolute. I reached for my flashlight and couldn't find it. The thing was gone, most likely lost among the garbage bags under my feet, so my hands became my eyes. I reached up to feel the lid above me. The metal was colder than the shelves of a deep freezer, but the temperature did little to diminish the stench of rotting food and God knew what else. Nearly retching, I placed the palms of my hands against the heavy lid and pushed with all my strength. The lid rose about an inch—and clicked against the latch.

Locked! I'm locked in!

"Help!" I shouted, banging against the Dumpster's side with a *clang, clang, clang!* "Let me out of here!"

"Shut up, bitch!"

I didn't recognize the jerk's voice. And I wasn't about to listen to it!

"Let me out!" I shouted even louder, banging again and again. "Help! Someone help me!"

Then I remembered Esther and my mobile phone!

I'd shoved the cell into my pocket on the climb down. Now I reached into my clothes for it. In the pitch-darkness, the little screen glowed like a lighthouse beacon on a storm-tossed sea. I sighed with relief until I saw my iceberg—a *single* tiny bar in the screen's upper left corner!

"Esther? Hello? Esther!"

Nothing. No partner. No connection. No cellular signal.

I went back to pounding (and gagging).

A minute later, I heard male voices shouting at each other. I stopped to listen.

"Let her out. Now!"

Matt? Is that Matt's voice?!

"Mind your own business and get the hell out of here!" The jerk's gruff bark.

More yelling.

Then Matt and the jerk started to threaten each other. Something was slammed against the Dumpster with enough force to rock the heavy container. I yelped and fell backward, my spine hitting the wall with a hollow thud. More pounds came from outside, and over the echoing din I heard angry voices, too.

"Matt!" I shouted. "HELP!"

A meaty *thwack*! More scuffling. Finally, all motion ceased. I listened hard, peering into the dark. There were more male voices—none that I recognized—and I couldn't make out the words.

"Bastards!"

That word I'd heard. It was Matt's, his curse followed by a scuffle.

Finally, the lid was thrown open. Beams from a half-dozen flashlights blinded me.

"NYPD!" bellowed a male voice. "Show me your hands now!"

Blinking against the glare, I raised my arms above my head. Someone reached out and snatched the cell phone from my fingers.

"Grab her," another man commanded. "Get her out of there!"

Still blinded, I felt rough hands seize my arms. Two uniformed officers half lifted, half dragged me out of the bin and set me on the ground.

Relieved, I exhaled. "Thanks, I really appreciate—Hey!"

A large African-American officer was pulling my arms behind my back.

"What are you doing?!" I yelled.

"You're under arrest!" he yelled right back.

"For what?!"

"Trespassing, for starters!"

The cold click of cuffs snapped around my wrists.

"What do you mean, for *starters*?!" I demanded—no longer yelling because my voice was getting hoarse.

The cop turned me by the shoulders and pointed at a paramedic a few yards away, taking care of a six-two, two-hundred-eighty-pound (at least) guy wearing a torn doorman's uniform. The man was sitting on the ground, his head tilted back, blood seeping out from under a pressure pad the medic was holding against the man's nostrils.

"A *doorman*?" I said. "Is that the doorman for this building?"

"He's the one who reported a burglar on the fire escape," the cop informed me.

"So he's the jerk who locked me in that Dumpster! You should arrest *him*!"

"Let's go," the cop said, tugging me—none too gently—along the alley. "Your partner in crime's being charged with assault."

"My partner in what—?!"

"And before the night's over, I'm guessing breaking and entering's going to be on both of your sheets. For now, let's just get you to the precinct."

Two more uniformed officers flanked me. On my way to the curb, someone read me my Miranda rights, which I already knew—including and especially my right to remain silent.

A crowd had gathered on the sidewalk, and no fewer than three police cruisers and an FDNY ambulance were parked on the street. Among the bystanders, I spotted Esther, her eyes bugging.

"You okay?!" she mouthed.

Fearful the cops would see my original partner for the evening, I used shifting eyes and jerking head to signal her to take off. One of the cops opened the back door of the police car and pressed down on my head so I wouldn't bump it.

Climbing inside, I finally confirmed what I already suspected. Right next to me on the cold vinyl car seat was a bruised, cuffed, but unbowed Matteo Allegro.

New York's finest had been wrong. They hadn't arrested my partner. They'd arrested my *ex*-partner (not counting our business arrangement, but I'd never considered that a crime).

"Are you all right?" I whispered.

"Yeah," he said, short and sharp. "You?"

"I'm fine."

"Good."

"Well . . . thanks, Matt," I finally added after a long, chilly silence. "I mean for trying to help."

On the short drive to the precinct house, I considered babbling an explanation, but after all we'd been through together, I knew Matt didn't really need one.

"I just knew you were up to something," he muttered.

Eleven

~~~~~~~~~~~~~~~~~~~~~~~~~~~~~

SERGEANT Emmanuel Franco swaggered into the holding room, an unopened can of Red Bull in one fist, a bag of Nacho Cheese Doritos in the other. When he spied me and Matt, his smug grin vanished and he kicked the cement-block wall with his size-twelve motorcycle boot.

"I thought you had two righteous suspects here!" he bellowed at the arresting officers.

"We caught them both in the building courtyard," the big black cop replied defensively. "The scene of last night's murder. Man-and-woman team is what it looks like to me. Neither was armed, but we found devices on the woman that could be used in a burglary."

I cleared my throat. "Excuse me, but I'd really like those opera glasses back, if you don't mind . . ."

The three men stared at me.

I shrugged. "Sentimental value."

"They also resisted arrest," added the big cop's partner.

"Excuse me again," I called. "Point of clarification? *I* didn't resist."

Franco spat a curse. "*Great* job," he told the officers. "You didn't nail me two suspects. All you brought in was the local coffee lady and her grab-ass boyfriend!"

"Ex-husband," I corrected.

"Just get the hell out of here!" Franco barked at the uniforms. "And close the door behind you!"

Muttering between them, the two officers departed.

Beside me, Matt was bristling. I knew this situation needed to be defused fast. Not only did Franco look pissed, my ex appeared ready to blow deadlier than Vesuvius.

To his credit, Matt had kept his lips zipped while the cops marched us through the precinct and into this holding room. He'd kept his mouth shut as they forced us to sit down on this long, scuffed wooden bench. He even held his tongue while they chained his handcuffs to a metal bar running behind it.

When they did the same to me, however, Matt cursed out both men in uniform—which was okay by me, because being trussed up like a Sunday roast chicken gave me all the comfort level of a peasant woman being accused of witchery during the Spanish Inquisition.

Around then is when Franco strutted in, his boot hitting the wall. Now the sergeant was glaring at me full out, his face flushing as red as the stripes in the American-flag do-rag covering his shaved head. (How many of those did he have, anyway?)

"I understand you waived your right to an attorney," he said, dropping his Doritos and Red Bull on a chair in the corner. "You want to talk to me, Coffee Lady? Are you waiving your right to remain smart, too?"

"I have nothing to hide," I stated, "and neither does Matt."

Franco stepped closer. "Okay then. Talk."

"Sure, Sergeant. How are you?" I saw no reason not to be civil. "You wouldn't want to reconsider that coffee and jelly doughnut offer you made me last evening, would you? Explaining everything would be a lot more comfortable in my coffeehouse, don't you think?" I rattled my cuffed wrists to make my point.

"You think this is funny?"

"I assure you, Sergeant, there's nothing about my friend's murder that I find the least bit amusing. But this arrest? That's downright hilarious. So would you mind unmanacling me now?" Once again, I *cha-chinged* my S&M wristbands. "This is positively medieval. Plus I'm really hot under all these layers."

"So . . ." Franco folded his arms and leered. "You want to *strip* for me now, honey? Is that it? Tops or bottoms first? I vote tops."

"You son of a—"

That did it. Matt blew. Straining against his cuffs, he angled his body on the bench enough to violently kick out at the detective's private parts. Franco jumped back—in plenty of time—as if he were expecting it.

"Calm down, Pit Bull," he warned, "or I'll have you *put* down."

The threat was harsh, but Franco's expression appeared borderline amused by the little dance. Matt replied by cursing him out—in several languages.

Franco moved down the bench and kicked the wood, hard. I felt the jolt all the way up my already aching spine.

"I said calm down! Unless you actually *want* leg shackles and additional charges."

Matt's jaw worked, but he settled back and zipped it.

Then Franco stepped closer—a fairly plucky move, considering his privates were once again within my ex's target range. "Look, Rover, I know you're tough, okay?" he said, his voice actually carrying a modicum of respect. "That doorman used to be a bar bouncer and he's no pushover. But understand this. I'm armed."

"Yeah, Matt," I whispered. "Stand down already."

Matt shot me the kind of look you reserve for a kitten who claws you up right after you save her from a nasty mutt. I didn't blame him. Being hassled by corrupt uniforms in banana republics left Matt lacking respect for pretty much anyone flashing a badge and a gun. Given Franco's unprofessional manner (and leering comment about my giving him a strip show), Matt's reaction was downright valiant. But if he didn't chill, he wouldn't be sleeping beside Breanne tonight. He'd be sharing a cell on Rikers with a much less attractive anorexic, pierced person.

So I leaned closer to his ear and whispered, "You don't need to keep defending me. I can handle him."

Franco smirked, obviously overhearing. "Is that right, honey? Go ahead, then. Handle me."

"Listen to me, Sergeant, I found something important in that courtyard. Something germane to Alf's case—"

"Christ," he laughed, rubbing his eyes. "Nancy Drew's got another germane clue."

"I found it on the fire escape—"

Franco met my gaze. "So you admit you trespassed?"

I blinked. "Of course."

Franco went quiet. My direct admission obviously surprised him. He moseyed back to the chair in the corner, opened his Doritos, munched a few, then popped his Red Bull and took a swig—a cover, it seemed to me, for figuring out how to handle *me*. Finally, he shook his head.

"Twenty-four hours after a murder takes place next to that building, you have the nerve to climb that fire escape? Are you certifiable? Or just one of those bubbleheaded broads who've sniffed too much nail polish remover?"

"Don't you *get* it?" Matt snorted with disdain. "She was looking for something you idiots probably missed. Then that scumbag doorman locked her in a Dumpster. In a Dumpster! He should be the one chained up here like a dog! Not me!"

"Listen, dude . . ." Franco cast me a sidelong glance, then locked eyes with Matt. "Your little ex-wifey here is dressed like a gangbanger, and I'm the one to know, believe me. For all that doorman knew, Coffee Lady could've had a Glock tucked between those tasty butt cheeks of hers."

"Shut your damn mouth about my wife—"

"Ex-wife," I corrected.

"—or I swear to God I'll shut it for you."

Franco put the Red Bull to his lips again—less to take a swig, it seemed to me, than to hide a chuckle.

I groaned, half convinced Franco's antisocial behavior was part of some good-cop/bad-cop ploy. But only half. For one thing, where the heck was the good cop?

"Sergeant, will you please stop trying to provoke my ex-husband and listen to me. I have something for you. Just uncuff me and I'll show you."

Franco eyed me for a long, silent moment. "Where is it? This thing you want to show me"

"It's right here in my pocket." I gestured with my chin.

"I don't know about uncuffing you, Coffee Lady. You look pretty unpredictable to me. You might even go for my gun." He took another swig of Red Bull. "Plus you look kinda hot, all chained up like that."

"Fine. Have it your way. Don't uncuff me. Just put your hand in my pocket and get it yourself."

Franco smiled. It wasn't a cheerful, have-a-nice-day sort of smile. It was the sort of smile bad boys give you before they start easing down your zipper.

Matt gritted his teeth. "Don't go *near* her."

Franco's eyebrow rose. "You heard her. She wants me to."

"Don't *touch* her."

Oh, good God. "Matt, will you stop letting this guy push your buttons?" I shifted my body so Franco could easily reach into my front jeans pocket. "Just reach in and get it!"

The cocky sergeant stretched out a hand, glanced furtively at Matt's cocking leg, and stepped around me—positioning his privates far, far away from Matt's itchy foot. Finally, he dipped his fingers into my pocket.

For all his roguish taunting, Franco didn't play around. His hand came right out again, clutching the white button.

"Recognize it?" I asked.

"It's the missing button from Santa's costume," Franco said without meeting my gaze. For the first time tonight, he dropped the swaggering supercop act. "How did Crime Scene miss this and you didn't?"

"Because it wasn't on the ground. I found it all the way up on the fourth floor of the fire escape—"

"At the window you were looking through when you got spotted?"

"Yes."

Franco nodded while he turned the button in his hand. "Okay. So your Santa friend may have been a peeping Tom. Or maybe even a burglar."

"No. I think Alf was murdered because of something he *saw*—"

"On the fire escape?" he said doubtfully. "When he looked through that apartment window?"

"Yes!"

"Sorry, Coffee Lady. Finding this on the fire escape isn't evidence of anything like that—only that he may have been some kind of pervert."

"Alf was *not* a pervert!"

"How do you know?"

I met Franco's stare. "The same way you know I'm not a murderer."

The detective frowned, then looked away.

"I found the body, didn't I?" I quietly challenged. "I knew the victim. Yet you never once considered me a suspect. Why?"

"Because . . ." Franco's dark eyes returned to mine. "I didn't see evil inside you."

"Excuse me?"

"You heard me."

It's true. I'd heard him. I just couldn't believe what he'd said. "So . . ." I continued carefully, "you can see evil in a person? Just like that?"

"Yes."

I paused to study the detective in front of me. The man's tone was no longer taunting. He sounded deadly serious, and his unrelenting stare felt borderline chilling. I knew most cops had hunches, trusted their instincts on reading people. But this was something else—something kind of bizarre, if not downright disturbing.

"Don't you think a little thing like a trail of evidence would be helpful?" I asked the man. "I mean, if the DA's office wanted to pursue charges based on something other than your insightful, apparently infallible intuition. What do you do after your nightly tours, turn in a list of who's naughty and who's nice?"

Franco's eyes flashed. "A little advice, Coffee Lady. Sarcasm's not the way to 'handle' me."

"What about Vicki Glockner's allegations?"

Franco's irritation changed quickly to surprise—unhappy surprise. "What do you know about Glockner's daughter?"

"She came to me earlier this evening. The girl's convinced Omar Linford had her father executed, or even did the job himself. Don't you think you should—"

"I spoke with the victim's daughter already. I'm well aware of her accusations. And let me tell you something, Coffee Lady, everybody's got a conspiracy theory in this case. I'm waiting for the Zapruder film to pop up next."

"But aren't you going to look into this Omar Linford person Vicki was talking about?"

Franco appeared to tense. "I already have—not that it's your business."

"Alf Glockner was my friend. His daughter came to me. So, yes, it's my busi—"

"Okay, all right, I'll tell you—" He might as well have added *just to shut you up.* "Omar Linford has made no threats or shown himself to be guilty of anything. He has no state or local criminal record, and there are no charges pending. There's no DEA file on him, and a personal contact I have at the FBI claims they have nothing on the man and no interest in him."

"But Linford's loaded. If he wanted to, he could have hired a hit man."

"So could Donald Trump. But why would he?"

"Donald Trump didn't lend Alf Glockner two hundred thou. Money he never got back."

Franco narrowed his eyes. "How could offing St. Nick score Linford his Benjis? Answer me that."

"Vicki thinks it might have been a warning, that this Linford character is going to use Alf's murder as a scare tactic, pressure her mother into selling their home or the same might happen to her—or even Vicki."

"Look, honey, if Omar Linford really is guilty of hiring the gunman or if he proceeds to make threats, we'll build a case against him. But first things first. We have to arrest the perp who pulled the trigger. Locating the murder weapon would help, too."

"Or you could talk to the person who lives in that fourth-floor apartment," I said. "Find out if he knows anything. Heard or saw anything. Is *guilty* of anything—"

"We canvassed the building," said Franco, cutting me off. "I questioned the occupant of that apartment—"

"You mean James Young," I stated as if it were fact, even though I wasn't at all certain. Sure, I'd spotted a Studio 19 identification badge issued to a James Young; but for all I knew, that badge belonged to a friend or relative of the person who lived in that apartment. Crossing my slowly numbing fingers—still locked behind me—I prayed Franco wouldn't notice the ploy. He didn't. A second later, he confirmed what I'd dug up.

"Mr. Young had nothing significant to say regarding our investigation."

"Mr. *James* Young?" I pressed.

"Are you deaf? *Yes.* James Young!"

"And you're certain he's the only tenant in that apartment?"

"As far as I know."

I heard male voices in the hallway. The door opened and a man leaned in—Franco's partner, Detective Charles Hong.

"Yo, General," he called, gesturing.

"General?" Matt whispered.

Franco drained the last of his Red Bull, crumpled the can with ease, and smirked at Matt. "Stick around, Fido. I hear there's an in-flight movie."

Matt shifted on the bench.

"Temper," I whispered.

"*General* Franco," Matt muttered, shooting me an unreadable look. "Now I've got this guy's number."

Twelve

~~~~~~

STILL chained to the rail behind me, I maneuvered my body as much as I could to get a view of the hallway outside the holding room. Through the half-open door, I saw Franco and Hong conferring with a fortyish Hispanic man in an unbuttoned trench coat—an assistant district attorney I'd seen once or twice before. There was a fourth man, too, a preppy type in his early thirties.

By now it was close to ten at night, but the preppy newcomer looked fresher than just-squeezed breakfast juice. Blond hair impeccably coiffed, designer suit cleanly pressed, he carried a slim attaché case in his right hand and sported a Harvard ring on his left. His chiseled features displayed one of those slick smiles that almost always carried some kind of noxious threat behind it.

I knew we were in trouble when the ADA departed and Franco ushered the preppy into the room with an almost merry disposition. Detective Hong followed, closing the door behind him.

"Bad news, people," Franco began. "But first—the introductions." He jerked his thumb in the direction of the Ivy

Leaguer. "Meet Chip Castle, a lawyer for the management company that owns the property you two were trespassing on. It's the same company that employs the doorman Rover here assaulted."

"I hardly tapped him," Matt muttered.

Castle eyed Matt, then me—pretty much like we were bugs. (Of course, the stench of garbage still lingering on my *Boyz N the Hood* ensemble wasn't exactly a public relations booster.)

"We're pressing charges against you both," Castle announced with a kind of gleeful spite. "Criminal trespass. Felony assault."

I blinked, Matt cursed, and Castle grinned through a fortune of pearly orthodontia.

"Nothing personal," he added. "My clients have no choice but to pursue the matter through the legal system. It's in the insurance agreement for the property, you understand? We're required to do this."

Franco stepped forward. "Matteo Allegro, you're charged with felony—"

"Screw you, *Generalissimo*!" Matt barked straight into Franco's face. "You're letting this A-hole lawyer railroad us because *she's* doing your job for you!"

"Matt, don't make it worse—"

"She's trying to solve a case you *can't*, or *won't*, solve yourself."

Franco lunged for Matt, fist cocked. He'd finally gotten a taste of having his own buttons pushed. Unfortunately, Matt's strategy—to nail Franco with police brutality charges—also meant he'd have to endure a beat down.

"Stop it, Franco! *Chill*, man!" Hong threw himself between Franco and Matt. "The guy's in cuffs! You can't touch him!"

"Touch me, Generalissimo!" Matt yelled. "Come on! Smack me around! You're just a tin-pot dictator like your Spanish namesake! You want to, Generalissimo! Do it!"

That's when I noticed the lawyer. The smarmy grin never left Castle's face, but now he was backing toward the door.

Okay, boys, playtime's over!

"EXCUSE ME!" I shouted at a level of female shrill that was disturbing enough to cut through the testosterone-fueled bellows. "I have something *germane* to say to Mr. Castle!"

Fists clenched, Franco broke free of his partner's grip, but he stepped away from Matt instead of toward him. (Thank goodness.) Hong froze. And Castle stopped inching toward the door. He regarded me for a silent moment.

"I'm listening," he finally said, his tone still insufferably superior. He even made a show of glancing at his watch. "You have a germane comment, do you?"

"I'm a businesswoman, counselor," I replied, "so I know the score."

Actually, I'd learned the score from Matt's mother. Before teaching me how to run a shop in the heart of Manhattan, Madame Dreyfus Allegro Dubois had run it herself for half a century—that meant decades of dealing with corrupt inspectors and mobbed-up garbage handlers; unethical real estate developers and slip-and-fall lawyers. Channeling Madame was getting to be a habit, and taking this guy down was going to be a pleasure.

"Your clients are forcing you to press charges because they're afraid of rate increases from the insurance company," I said. "But what if this insurance company found out how easily I was able to breach your clients' building security? Wouldn't that raise rates, too?"

"I don't know what you mean."

"For starters, you have no security gate blocking access to the courtyard from the street—"

"We had some construction going on a short time ago. That's why there's a Dumpster on the side of the building, as well as the—"

"You have bins positioned against the back of the building and crates piled up nearby. That's hardly secure. Your own building management has made reaching the fire escape child's play."

The lawyer tossed his perfectly styled mane. "Such a situation is easily rectifiable—"

"But most egregiously, Mr. Castle, the security hook on the fire escape was rusted completely through. All I had to do was pull down the ladder. Why, under those conditions, building management might as well hang out a sign that says *Please Burglarize Our Tenants*. I'm sure those very tenants would be interested to know how little management cares for their safety and security. And if we go to trial . . ." I paused to shoot Mr. Billable Hours a sharklike smile of my own. "I guarantee they'll all find out."

Castle's superior smirk started to waver.

"Of course, to prepare for trial, I'd insist on official reports from the FDNY and Department of Buildings. I'd definitely want them to check out that fire escape. The way it was rocking in the wind, I have doubts about its structural integrity."

Poof! Just like that, Castle's smirk disappeared. He loosened his tie.

"Now listen to me, counselor, because here's the *real* story: I was on that fire escape for an innocent reason—to search for evidence the police might have missed in my friend's murder the night before. Your doorman didn't ask what I was doing there. He simply assaulted me and threw me into that Dumpster. The only reason my ex-husband here took a few swipes at the man was because he heard me screaming. He was trying to get me out of that Dumpster—to make sure I wasn't hurt or bleeding or raped or dying. Your employee locked me in there, by the way—with the garbage—but I'm sure your nose already told you that. So if you press charges against me and my ex-husband, I'm not only going to sue your doorman in civil court, I'm going to sue your client for five million dollars."

Everyone was looking fairly sheepish now. Everyone but Charlie Hong, who appeared to be suppressing a smile.

"Take a good look at me, Mr. Castle. I'm five two in stocking feet, a single mother of a grown daughter, and a well-known shop manager in the community with no criminal history. Your doorman is a six-two, two-hundred-eighty-pound former bar bouncer. Which version of this story do you think a jury will side with?"

Castle stood in silence for a moment. Then he motioned to Franco and Hong to follow him out the door. Lucky thing, too, because I'd just run out of options—and threats.

After conferring with the detectives, mostly Hong, and making a cell call (presumably to that departing ADA), the Franco bomb detonated again: "What do you mean you're not pressing charges?!"

Mr. Castle muttered something I couldn't hear. Then he turned his back on the sergeant and strode away. After that, Hong and Franco started talking. I overheard one telling phrase on Hong's end: "Lieutenant Mike Quinn." Inside a minute, Franco was striding away with obvious frustration, and Detective Hong returned to the holding room. He unlocked Matt's cuffs first.

"You're free to go, Mr. Allegro, and I suggest you leave right now."

Rubbing his wrists, Matt stood. "Not without Clare."

"Fine," Hong said. "Wait outside, then. I want a private word with Ms. Cosi."

Matt didn't budge, just looked at me.

"It's okay," I said.

Matt crossed the room and closed the door behind him. Hong released my cuffs, and I shook my arms to restore the feeling in my fingers.

"I checked you out," Hong began, sitting down next to me. "And I know you know something about police business. Lieutenant Quinn contacted me today, as well. He's a good man. I think a lot of him."

"So do I."

"Look, Ms. Cosi, I don't want you to think that Franco and I aren't working hard to find the man who murdered your friend. That's pretty much all we're thinking about right now. I wanted you to know that—and that I fully understand your interest in this case."

"I'm glad *one* of you does."

Hong sighed. "I know Franco seems like a hard case." The detective's stony face cracked. "Hell, he's got a chip the size of Battery Park on his shoulder. But he's a good cop and a good detective."

"I find little evidence of that."

"Believe me, it's true. If anything, my partner can be extreme in the pursuit of justice."

"What do you mean by *extreme?*"

"Let's say he has a rep for getting the job done and leave it at that."

I didn't want to, but I could see Hong did.

"Just curious," I asked as he stood up. "Why did that 'Generalissimo' thing set him off so badly?"

Hong paused a moment, as if he were deciding how to answer me. Finally, he sighed. When he spoke again, his voice was much quieter. "Franco likes to let people assume his nickname comes from the street—you know, 'General' as slang for 'leader.'"

"Where did it come from, then?"

Hong shook his head. "Franco and I got hammered one night and he admitted what your ex-husband just guessed."

"What's that?"

"I'm really not old enough to remember, but apparently back in the seventies, the network news anchors kept announcing Spain's dictator was near death. When he finally kicked, *Saturday Night Live* put a joke in their weekly fake news routine: 'This breaking news just in . . . Generalissimo Francisco Franco is *still* dead.'"

"Okay. Not actually funny. And what does it have to do with your partner?"

"On his first day at the police academy, Franco had an instructor who was into that vintage *SNL* stuff. He's the one who gave him the nickname *Generalissimo*. Franco hated it. Took him years and a few transfers before he finally got *General* to stick. That's it."

I shook my head. "What is it with you men? Why do you let your egos dictate—"

"If it's all the same to you, Ms. Cosi, I'd rather you not lump us all in the same category."

I was about to reply when the door flew open, banging explosively against the back wall. With that preamble, I expected to see Sergeant Franco standing there again, but it was Matt—with Mike Quinn in tow, an unreadable expression on his still-as-stone face.

"There she is," Matt declared, pointing his finger at me. "You try talking some sense into her."

.

THIRTEEN

~~~~~~~~~~~~~~~~~~~~~~~~~~~~~~

"**Sweetheart**, it's almost midnight."

"I don't care what time it is. I missed dinner."

My hair was still damp from the long, hot shower. My Dumpster clothes, down to the socks and underwear, were currently spinning in a double-strength detergent wash. With a sigh, I knotted the belt of my short terrycloth robe.

"You could eat, too, right?" I asked.

Quinn didn't reply. One sandy eyebrow simply arched in a way that said he had the enjoyment of something else in mind.

I turned and headed for the bedroom door. "I need to cook. I'll be downstairs."

I really couldn't blame the man for his spicy train of thought. After all, he'd just finished showering, too—with me. I'd been under the pulse setting of the Water Pik so long he'd stripped down and joined me. Under the warm spray, the man's shoulder massage felt wonderful, but I was too wired about the events of the evening to just let go and "get with him," as my current crop of collegiate customers liked to put it.

Quinn saw I needed time and let me pull away. Now he was pulling a white T-shirt over his torso and a pair of gray sweats over his long legs. Barefoot, he padded after me down to my duplex's kitchen. His dark blond hair looked even darker in its dampness; his rugged expression was turning a lot less readable than I'd been used to lately.

I uncorked a chilled bottle of Riesling and poured us half glasses. He sat back in silence at the kitchen table, sipping the crisp, sweet nectar, his glacial blue eyes on me as I began following my grandmother's recipe by heart—putting the water on to boil, mincing the scallions and garlic, chopping the parsley.

It was so quiet in the little room. Every so often I'd glance over, just to make sure the man was still there. He was—his eyes remaining fixed on my movements, his mouth taking slow sips of wine.

Unhappy with his silence, I flipped on the radio.

Christmas 24/7 was still going strong—and, presumably, still driving Gardner Evans sugarplum crazy.

Not me.

Frankly, I'd endured enough upheavals in my life to consider the seasonal loop of old chestnuts reassuring instead of boring, like an old family recipe you've made a thousand times and will happily make a thousand more, just because it reminds you of a time or a place or a person that you loved with all your heart.

So "The Little Drummer Boy" accompanied my sautéing of onions and garlic. "O Holy Night" orchestrated the addition of flour and milk, and "Winter Wonderland" provided the beat to whisk my white sauce lump free. Next came the clams, reserved juice, and "Merry Christmas, Darling."

On a refill of Riesling and the umpteenth replaying of "Jingle Bell Rock," I tossed in salt, pepper, and parsley, then stirred and sipped; sipped and stirred . . . and when the white clam sauce finally thickened enough, I turned off the burner, covered the pan, and allowed the flavors to blend while I boiled the linguine—just the way my Nonna had taught me (in a big ol' pasta pot with a splash of olive oil to keep the noodles from sticking and enough sea salt to mimic the Mediterranean).

At last, with my wineglass nearly empty and my patience with Quinn's *Quiet Man* act worn through, I turned off the Christmas music and turned on the cop.

"Aren't you ever going to say anything about my arrest?! You haven't asked me one question all night!"

Quinn slowly stood up. Without a word, he casually poured more wine into my glass then his own.

"Well?"

"I told you already," he softly replied. "Allegro filled me in plenty."

"He also ordered you to talk some 'sense' into me!"

Quinn cracked a smile at that.

"What?" I prodded. "You find that funny?"

"Yeah . . ." Quinn's fingers brushed some damp hair off my cheek, curled it around an ear. "As a matter of fact, I do."

"And what exactly is so funny?"

"*Allegro.* The guy was married to you for a decade and he still doesn't realize that no one can talk sense into you. That's what's so funny. It's a complete waste of vocal cords."

"Ha. Ha."

"Listen, Cosi . . ." Quinn reached around me and began using the tips of his fingers to work the stiff tendons in my neck. "The day I met you—" He stopped, smiled. "The *minute* I met you I knew you had a mind of your own. I accept it. I like it. I'm not about to lecture you on the fact that you put yourself in a precarious, even unduly dangerous position tonight. You know that already, right? No one needs to tell you that."

"But you know why I did it."

"Yes . . . I just wish you had waited for daylight, asked permission of the doorman. You know, done it legally."

I might have been annoyed at the subversive way Quinn was putting across his censure, but his magic fingers felt too good.

"The trouble with doing it safely is hearing the word *no*,"

I pointed out. "Then what? Another freak evening storm, this time with rain instead of snow, and that button I found would have been washed away."

Quinn's eyebrow arched. "True."

"And don't forget, Lieutenant, it was you who taught me to bend the rules. Remember how you lied to that super up in Washington Heights so he'd let us illegally search an apartment?"

"I can see I've been a bad influence."

Before I could argue, Quinn's fingers encircled my wrist and he tugged me toward the kitchen table. Sitting back down, he coaxed me onto his lap.

"Now what? Am I supposed to tell you what I want for Christmas?"

Quinn grinned. "That'd be a good start."

"I want to discuss Alf's case with you."

"That's what you want for Christmas?"

"Now that you mention it, yes—Alf's killer brought to justice with a jingle bell bow on top."

"I see . . . and do you have a theory?"

"Not yet. But I'll tell you one thing: I do not trust Sergeant Emmanuel 'Do-Rag' Franco. Do you know Detective Hong practically implied the man was a vigilante? What do you think of that?"

"I've heard rumors."

"Do you think it's possible . . ." I hesitated, then felt Quinn's fingertips return to working my neck muscles. I sighed. That spine slam I'd endured against that Dumpster wall was finally melting away.

"I know this may seem out there," I continued, "believe me, I do. But do you think that Franco might have been involved somehow in killing Alf?"

Quinn went quiet for a long moment. "Why? Why would Franco want to kill Santa Claus?"

"What if Franco caught Alf doing something bad or illegal—or thought he caught him doing something like that. Maybe Franco decided to exact street justice."

"You want me to ask around about him? I know some guys in the borough precincts where he worked street crime task forces."

"Could you?"

Quinn nodded. "I can make a few calls."

"There's also another man, James Young. He lives in the apartment that Alf was spying on the night he was murdered. Franco says Young had nothing significant to add to the investigation, but maybe the man didn't want to talk to the cops. Maybe, if he has something to say, he'll talk to me."

"Good lead, Cosi. But guess what . . ." By now, Mike's deep voice had thickened as beautifully as my white sauce. His lips were so close to my ear, his low, gravelly buzz felt downright ticklish. "I don't want to talk about this anymore—"

"You don't?"

"No," he whispered. "But I'll make you a deal."

"What kind of deal?"

"We can talk all you want tomorrow."

Quinn's nearness, his fingers, his lips were all getting to me, but I was reluctant to drop the subject. "What are we supposed to talk about tonight, then?"

"Anything else."

"I don't understand."

"I just want you to let go for a little while, Cosi. Give your head a rest."

"You think I can't handle the stress of an investigation?"

"It's not you. It's the job. Everyone has to learn to let go. Some guys lift weights. Some guys lift a bottle." He tilted his head toward the Riesling.

"You think I have a problem?"

"No. I think you're still new at this and you should take my advice. Let go. Give it a rest."

"Let go?"

"Yeah, and guess what?" he whispered into my ear. "I'm going to help you right now. Close your eyes . . ."

"Mike—"

"*Close* 'em."

I did.

"Now forget about anything related to evidence or procedure or even criminal mischief—"

Quinn's little teasing kisses were moving as he talked: from my earlobe to the back of my neck to the hollow of my throat. Finally, he reached for the belt of my short terrycloth robe, and his mouth continued its downward path.

Oh, God, Mike . . .

A few minutes later, I realized why Mike Quinn didn't need free weights, a Nautilus machine, or a bottle to forget his stresses and give his brain a rest.

His chosen method of distraction wasn't exactly something one could do in public, but it wasn't exactly torture, either, so I went with it; and for the next few hours, anyway, the Lieutenant and I had a deal.

Fourteen

~~~~~~~~~~~~~~~~~~~~~~~~~~~~~~~~~~~~~

"Good morning," I whispered on a yawn.

Quinn kissed my head. "Get enough sleep?"

"I got what I needed."

The night had been a blur of sweet vino, creamy clam-sauced linguine, 24/7 Christmas tuneage, and Quinn's intense lovemaking. A dead-to-the-world sleep followed, and when I awoke the next morning, I was sure the light of leprechaun gold had found a shining path through the cracks in my curtains.

Quinn's mood, however, wasn't even close to that good. He was still next to me on the mattress, wide awake, cradling me in the crook of his arm, but his gaze was far away—and not on the other side of the proverbial rainbow.

"What's wrong?" I asked when his good-morning smile faded too quickly. "You having second thoughts about being annoyed with my arrest?"

"No. Nothing like it."

"What then?"

"I didn't want to bring it up last night. I needed to let things go for a little while, too, you know?"

"Let go of what? What's the matter?"

"I've got a cold case heating up . . ."

Rubbing the sleep out of my eyes, I sat up. "I'll make coffee."

✦TEN minutes later, we were back at the kitchen table, but on opposite sides of it this time.

With a freshly pressed mug of my Breakfast Blend in hand, Quinn started talking about his job—something he'd been doing with me for years now, first as a barista, then as a friend, finally as a lover.

"You remember Thanksgiving night, when I was called in?" he began.

"Sure," I said. "I finally got some bonding time with your kids."

Molly Quinn was nine; Jeremy had just turned eleven. Typically, Mike would spend time alone with his daughter and son. He explained why, of course. After Mike's wife left him for a slightly younger, much wealthier Wall Street whiz, she moved their children from their Brooklyn home to her fiancé's Long Island estate. With new schools, a new home, and the new man in their mom's life, Mike wanted his kids to get comfortable with visiting his new apartment in the city before introducing another new person into their already drastically changed world.

I respected that. I also suspected, given Mike's years of marital problems, that he wanted to make sure he and I were on solid ground before he started complicating our relationship.

Well, the day before Thanksgiving, Mike's ex-wife did that for us. Leila decided to accompany her super-rich fiancé to Connecticut for a Thanksgiving Day social gathering with some even wealthier people who suggested their guests leave the kiddies with the nannies. Leila had a housekeeper who also looked after the kids, but the woman had the week off, so Leila ended up dumping the pair with Mike.

As for my Thanksgiving Day plans, I'd already accepted Madame's invitation to attend a party at Tavern on the Green. Mike was supposed to be my dinner date—until his ex changed plans on him. So I changed my plans, too.

I bowed out of Madame's dinner, went to Mike's place instead, and cooked a turkey with all the trimmings. Mike offered to treat us to a restaurant, but I knew a homemade Thanksgiving dinner would help make his new apartment feel more like a home to him, Molly, and Jeremy. The kids couldn't have been sweeter. We even bundled them up that morning to see the Macy's parade.

The dinner turned out to be a huge success. Like their dad, the kids practically swooned over my cooking. And when Mike was called out on a case that night, I sat with the pair. We stayed up till the wee hours, watching a Disney movie, playing cards and Scene It?, and eating slices of my pumpkin praline tart until Daddy came home again.

"The kids are still talking about your food, you know."

"Good thing." I laughed. "Because I'm lousy at cards. They beat the pants off me at Crazy Eights."

Quinn nodded, but his smile was fading fast.

"So, anyway," I said, trying to help him along. "You said something about a cold case heating up?"

He nodded again. "It's connected to the one I was called to consult on Thanksgiving night—"

"You mean the Pilgrim's Daughter case?"

I listened as he recited the facts. A wealthy young blueblood was found dead, alone in her apartment, the previous Thursday night. The woman, Waverly "Billie" Billington, was a Mayflower descendant and an heiress of the founder of Pilgrim Investments—a firm with the less-than-original catchphrase "Solid as Plymouth Rock."

Just like they did after Santa's slaying, the tabloids had a field day with their Black Friday headlines: *Pilgrim's Daughter OD's on Pills Instead of Turkey*, *Plymouth Rock Heiress Found Stone-Cold*, that sort of thing.

Up to now, Quinn hadn't said much about the girl's tragic

death, and I assumed it was because the case was open and shut. Taking too many drugs or mixing the wrong ones was not a homicide—although it could very well be a suicide.

I said as much.

"There are complications with that conclusion," Quinn replied.

"Such as?"

"Such as . . . the young woman's family is friends with the mayor, the police commissioner, two state senators, and an influential city council member. The Billington girl attended schools with some of their children and occasionally socialized with them in Manhattan clubs. So they want it all to go away as fast as possible. My captain's down our necks with this one. He's made it known the case should be cleared as an accidental death."

"Even though it could have been suicide?"

"They want it closed."

I studied Quinn's set jaw. "I get a feeling there's a *but* coming . . ."

"The details on this one started me thinking about a cold case from last Thanksgiving. Another attractive young woman, about the same age, living alone, died the same way. Cora Arnold had far less money and fewer connections than the Billington girl, so she didn't make front-page news."

"She overdosed?"

Quinn nodded. "Died Thanksgiving evening last year. Except the Arnold girl didn't have a domestic, so the body wasn't found until that Sunday night when she failed to show up for her sister's birthday party."

"You think there are similarities in the cases?"

"Not just the timing—both dying on Thanksgiving night. But both died from ingesting the same prescription drug, an opioid narcotic, one that neither of them had been prescribed."

"No other pills in the apartment?"

"No. The girls were drinkers and known to be promiscuous. They both had a male guest sometime that day."

"Sex?"

"They had sex. They drank. And he ate junk food."

"Junk food?"

"Both girls were very slender and had hardly any food in their apartments. No junk food in the cupboards or fridge. Yet there were empty bags of potato chips, pretzels, Doritos—but none of that food was found in either of the girls' stomachs."

"You have semen, I take it?" I paused. "That came out wrong. What I meant was—"

Quinn smiled. "I know what you meant. DNA isn't the problem. Finding the match is. These young women had a lot of people in and out of their lives—friends, relatives, strangers. Fingerprints were taken, but nothing matched perps with previous records. No matches on known boyfriends."

"Given her level of society and the social-circle issue with the bigwig offspring, I take it interviews are a touchy potato. How aggressively can you question friends and family?"

"What do you think?"

"Your bosses want the case closed. That's what I think."

Quinn took a long, sullen sip of coffee. "I think this girl was a victim, Clare, not a suicide, and not an accidental death. I think there's a guy out there who's partying with dangerous drugs. He may not have meant to kill these girls, but he did, and he's at least guilty of manslaughter. He must know about this latest death, given the headlines, but he hasn't stepped forward. And I don't think he will. He drugged both girls—even if they took the stuff willingly, he left them unconscious without a second thought. And I think he'll do the same thing again."

"Then you have to find him, Mike. No matter what your bosses say."

"I know."

"What did your superiors say when you told them all this?"

Quinn's frown deepened. "Circumstantial similarities. It doesn't help my theory that both girls had a history of using drugs recreationally—although rarely."

"Didn't the domestic worker see anyone come into the apartment?"

"The domestic's a young, single woman—a live-in. She was given the day off, which she spent with her sister's family in Queens. She returned around eight that night. That's when she found her employer."

I sipped my own coffee, considering the facts. "What did the victim do that day?"

"We know that Billie went to a party that morning on the Upper West Side—a large apartment that had a view of the Thanksgiving Day parade."

"That kind of parade-watching party is pretty common in the city," I said. "What did the people at the party tell you?"

"Billie talked to almost everyone there. She watched the parade and left the party alone. She entered her building alone. The doorman never announced anyone for her, and the lobby security camera confirms the doorman's story. There's a service entrance to the building, no camera on it, but it's securely locked from the inside and there's no sign of a break-in."

"The man must have lived in Billie's building, then, right?"

"That's what we think; even though Billie had no history of sleeping with anyone in her building, it could have been a solitary sexual fling. We're still working on getting DNA samples from the male residents—including the married men. It's a touchy legal issue. Most have lawyers who are fighting it. This is a tough one, Cosi."

I sipped more coffee, then drummed my fingers on the tabletop. "Wouldn't the DNA help your theory? If the Billington and Arnold girls had sex with the same man—even if you can't ID the guy yet—wouldn't that prove the pattern you're arguing?"

"Yes, it would, and I'm trying to get that test done."

"Maybe there are more victims, too. Did you think of that? Cases with those same things in common? And if you find those, you might find other things in common—like the killer."

Quinn gave me a half smile. "Logical next step, Detective. And, yes, Sully and I thought of that." Sully was short for Sergeant Finbar Sullivan, Quinn's right-hand man on the OD Squad.

"He and I are going to work that angle this week, *quietly*, along with our regular caseload. We're going to review the cold-case interviews with Cora Arnold's friends and family; look for anything in Cora's life that might intersect with the facts we've gathered about the male residents of Billie's building. I wanted you to know because it's going to mean some late nights and early mornings. It's important you understand . . ."

"I get it, Mike. You're warning me that you won't be around much."

"I want to help with Alf, Clare—"

"I know you do, but I can handle it. I can. How hard can it be to ask James Young a few questions, judge his reactions?"

Quinn studied me. "You need to have a partner watching your back."

"I know. That's why I took Esther with me last night to the courtyard."

"But she left you."

"That was my call."

"Well, do me a favor, sweetheart; bring backup and keep it there, okay?"

"Okay. I will. Don't worry."

"Can't promise that." He smiled. "In the meantime, I'll see what I can dig up for you on Franco."

"Thanks. I mean it."

He shrugged. "'Tis the season for favors. And you did tell me what you wanted for Christmas." We both smiled at that.

"Speaking of Christmas," I said, "we haven't discussed plans for the holiday. Do you have time scheduled with your kids? I was thinking we could take them ice skating in Bryant Park, see the tree at Rock Center. There's always frozen hot chocolate at Serendipity, and Macy's windows are really nice this year. Is Molly too old for Santaland? Joy loved doing that until she was almost eleven."

"Whoa—slow down." Quinn shifted in his chair. "The kids won't be around, Clare. My wife's taking them to Florida. Her boyfriend's family's down there and she wants them to meet the kids—

"Ex-wife," I said.

"Excuse me?"

"You called her your wife."

"I did?" Quinn frowned. "Habit, I guess. Anyway, since they'll be gone for two weeks, I also agreed to be available for coverage over Christmas and New Year's—favors owed, you know? The guys who have families know I'm divorced now, so I agreed."

"Oh. You really are going to be off the map."

"It's no big deal, is it? I mean, you've been pretty excited about Joy coming back from Paris for the holidays. You warned me you were going to spend some serious girl time together, right?"

I nodded, smiling at the thought of seeing my daughter again, catching up with all the exciting things she was learning and tasting and cooking in France. "You're right. I've really missed her."

"I know you have, sweetheart. So look at the bright side: You'll be so busy visiting with her, I doubt you'll miss me much."

My heart sank a little at that. Of course I would miss him, especially at this time of year. But I didn't say so. I mean, I didn't want to lay on the guilt. I understood about the demands of his job (it was one of the things that broke up his marriage), and it seemed to me what he needed most now was reassurance that overtime wasn't going to hurt our relationship.

"You're right," I joked, forcing a smile. "I'll be way too busy to miss you."

Quinn's reaction wasn't what I expected. His smile faltered, and he actually looked a little hurt. I was about to clarify that I was joking when his cell went off.

"Excuse me," he said, checking the Caller ID.

"Police business?"

He didn't indicate yes or no, just said, "I have to take this."

"I understand."

What I didn't understand was why he didn't just take the call at the kitchen table instead of leaving the room. I moved to the doorway and cocked a curious ear.

"No. I'm having coffee." Pause. "Yes, I plan to." Longer pause. "Yes, I do. I *do*. I just can't talk right now." Pause. "Because I *can't*."

I frowned. The conversation certainly didn't sound like police business.

Just then, my own phone rang—but not my cell, which was still recharging in the bedroom. This was the landline to the apartment. I picked up the kitchen extension.

"Hello?"

"Hi, Mom!"

"Joy!"

Her call couldn't have come at a better time. Just hearing her voice made me feel grounded again. We talked a little about what she was doing and what I was doing, and then she said she had something to tell me. Her voice suddenly sounded strained.

"I'm really sorry, Mom. Really sorry, but . . ."

"What is it, honey?"

"As it turns out, I can't come home for the holidays. I have to work at the restaurant after all. Forgive me?"

My heart went through the floor. For a few seconds, I had trouble finding my tongue. "Sure, honey," I finally managed to get out. "I'm so busy this year . . . don't worry about it."

A few minutes later, she ended the call, and I went to find Mike. All of a sudden, I felt a little numb. I couldn't believe it, but this would be the first Christmas, the very first, that my little girl and I would be spending apart.

I needed to tell Mike about it. Not that I expected him to change his plans—but I suddenly needed an empathetic ear, a sympathetic hug. I also needed to reassure myself that he and I were on solid ground. I was afraid he'd gotten the wrong impression from my reaction to his overtime speech.

But Quinn was no longer on his cell in the living room. I found him in the bedroom, fully dressed, shrugging into his shoulder holster.

"You're not leaving already? I was about to whip up some of my Golden Gingerbread-Maple Muffins—I was thinking of adding a warm glaze with some holiday spice notes. I thought you'd like to sample a couple."

"Sorry, sweetheart. Save me a few, okay?" His expression was unreadable as he grabbed his badge and wallet off the dresser. "There's an issue. I have to take care of something."

"What?"

"Nothing important. I'll give you a ring later."

"But I wanted to tell you—"

"Later, Clare. I promise," he said. And with a too-quick kiss on my cheek, he was gone.

Fifteen

~~~~~~

LIKE most New Yorkers, James Young was not an easy man to contact. For one thing, his phone was unlisted. On the Internet, I found plenty of info about Studio 19, including its address. But the only number I could find was for the general public. A message service answered when I called but refused to put me through directly to Mr. Young—although they did confirm he worked there.

The most maddening part was that I knew the man's home address, down to his apartment number, but I dared not approach the place. If the Matt-battered doorman saw me again, I was pretty sure he'd find a way to have me arrested, most likely for "harassing" his tenant.

I didn't have time for some half-assed stakeout of his place (to collar him before he went into or came out of his building), so I decided to contact a partner, just as Quinn advised.

Madame Dreyfus Allegro Dubois was more than my boss, my landlord, my former mother-in-law, and my daughter's biggest champion. Madame was my very best friend. She also happened to be the most beloved (and elegantly dressed) snoop in the vicinity of Washington Square Park.

After Quinn left, I dumped the dregs of his java, which had grown unpalatably cold during our long talk, and pulled out my Moka Express pot. In more ways than one, I needed to get some hot jolts into my system. Using Alfonso Bialetti's stovetop invention, I quickly produced the rustic version of coffeehouse espresso that Italians have been enjoying for nearly a century.

On my third energizing shot of the day, I phoned Matt's mother and told her everything that had happened—from Alf's murder to my arrest for trespassing the night before. She started out sounding a little sleepy, but with each new revelation, she became more animated.

"You actually climbed a fire escape in the dead of night and peered through a stranger's window?" Madame said. "I certainly hope you saw something juicy."

"Sorry to disappoint. I only saw a photo ID for a man who works at a place called Studio 19. It's an independent television facility located on Nineteenth Street, near Eleventh Avenue—"

Madame laughed.

"What's so funny?"

"I know all about Studio 19, dear."

I nearly dropped my demitasse. "What are you? Psychic?"

"Even better. I'm nosy. And a good neighbor."

"Excuse me?"

Madame laughed again, but she wouldn't tell me anything more—except to say that she'd "make a few calls" and get back to me.

Thirty-six freshly baked Golden Gingerbread-Maple Muffins and one four-hour barista half shift later, I was sitting beside the silver-haired matriarch, inside the cavernous Studio 19. We'd come to see the taping of one of the most popular television shows in the country, *The Chatsworth Way*.

According to Madame, an illegal Pekingese is what gained us admission. "There's a two-pet minimum in my building, you see," she explained, which still left me confused.

"And how exactly do the rules of your apartment building translate into instant tickets to a TV show with a three-month-long studio audience waiting list?"

"Well, when someone snitched to the building manager," Madame's voice dropped conspiratorially, "and I have no doubt that someone was that music producer's paramour on the second floor, the one who sleeps until noon and parties until four AM. *Pooh*, what a terror. Bohemians I can tolerate, but *her*—"

"You were telling me about a Pekingese."

"Oh, yes. Someone snitched to the building manager that Mr. Dewberry and his wife Enid had a third dog, so I pretended the dog was mine. I walked Ming two or three times a day until the whole thing blew over."

"So it was Mr. Dewberry who got you these tickets to the taping?"

Madame nodded. "Mr. Dewberry is the major stockholder in the company that syndicates this program. He was very appreciative of my efforts on Ming's behalf. So here we are."

I was appreciative, too.

Now we watched from our front-row seats as technicians crisscrossed a darkened soundstage. Several large monitors dropped from the ceiling to flank the shadowy stage, each with a *Chatsworth Way* logo on a field of pastel pink or powder blue.

"I have to say it. You're amazing. Tickets and backstage passes in less than twenty-four hours."

"You really ought to include me in your sleuthing from the start, Clare," Madame said flatly. "It's lucky you caught me today at all, because tomorrow morning Otto and I are off to a charming little bed-and-breakfast in Vermont."

Otto Visser was Madame's latest flame. A younger man (at nearly seventy), Otto was an urbane art dealer and appraiser who'd been smitten with Matt's mother from the moment he "eye-flirted" with her across a French restaurant's semi-crowded dining room.

"Have you found that 'perfect' gift for Otto yet?" I asked.

"What do you buy a man who collects medieval illuminated manuscripts?" she asked with a wave of her beringed hand. "But I thought about it long and hard, and finally settled on a fraud."

"Excuse me?"

"I acquired an image of the Madonna and Child that appears to come out of a medieval manuscript, but it's really a forgery perpetrated by the Spanish Forger, a legendary counterfeiter who created hundreds of medieval fakes in nineteenth-century France." Madame smiled, her gentle laugh lines impishly crinkling around her brilliant blue eyes. "Otto will absolutely adore it, I'm sure. A real conversation piece among his colleagues."

"It's certainly unique," I replied.

"So when is Joy scheduled to arrive?"

I'd dreaded this moment. I hadn't yet broken the bad news to either Madame or Matt.

"I'm sorry. I need to tell you. Joy phoned me earlier this morning. She's not coming home after all," I said. "She couldn't get the time off."

Instead of registering disappointment, Madame nodded with a knowing smile. "That's why I made sure her plane tickets were open-ended."

Now I nodded knowingly. "You assumed she'd get stuck working."

"Working?" Madame shook her head. "Joy's not working, Clare. It's a boy. She's suddenly madly in love and can't bear to be apart from him."

"She told you that?"

"No! I just know my grandchild. I'm quite sure you'll discover that she's fallen for some adorable, flirtatious, irresistibly cocky French cook in her brigade. I can only hope the feeling is mutual, for her heart's sake . . . What's wrong?"

"I just . . . never considered that."

"She's left the nest, dear. She wants her own life." She

leaned closer. "Don't you fret now. It was hard for me when Matteo did the same, went off to Europe for an entire summer, but then he came back with you, didn't he?"

That was the abbreviated version of a much longer summer-of-love story that ended with me pregnant. Without that sweet *bambina* bun in my oven, however, I doubted very much the freewheeling, extreme-sports-loving, twenty-two-year-old Matteo Allegro would have taken me home to Mama.

My frown deepened. The momentary glimpse down memory lane left me anxious—now I couldn't stop wondering whether Joy had been listening during our talks about birth control.

Madame squeezed my hand. "Just remember this, Clare. When Joy gets married and has a child of her own, she'll need you more than ever."

An usher interrupted us. He was moving through the audience, handing out a brochure about the show. As Madame leafed through it, I scanned the studio for any man who resembled that ID badge photo of James Young.

"Today we're going to see a very special seasonal episode about holiday stress," Madame informed me, a pair of reading glasses perched on her nose.

"Timely," I said.

"It also says here that Dr. Chaz is a trained psychologist born and raised in Southern California. His wife, Phyllis, is a marriage therapist originally from the Twin Cities. They met during college, and *The Chatsworth Way* began as a local program in Minneapolis. The nationally syndicated version of the show is devoted entirely to the subject of mending splitting marriages and healing damaged relationships."

"*Hmmm . . .*" I glanced at the eager congregation around us. "That might explain why four fifths of this audience is female."

"Last year *The Chatsworth Way* went into syndication, and it is now the fourth most popular daytime show behind *Oprah*, *Dr. Phil*, and *Rachael Ray*." Madame arched a silver eyebrow. "And apparently this James Young you're looking for is the show's executive producer."

Before I could express surprise, a spotlight appeared in the center of the main stage. The beam illuminated a man and woman perched side by side on tall stools. Both were surrounded by a bevy of assistants, several cameras, and a pair of teleprompters. I didn't recognize the renowned man-and-wife counselors until excited chatter, then a smattering of applause, broke out around me.

"I love you, Dr. Chaz!" a lone woman's voice cried out from the middle of the studio audience.

"I love you, too!" he replied.

Laughter—mostly female—followed.

While a technician slipped a tiny microphone under his tie, Dr. Chaz continued grinning and returning waves from various women. Tall and fit, he exuded an easy, boyish charm. Adding an air of sagelike distinction to his appearance, the handsome face was crowned with thick waves of prematurely white hair.

In contrast, Therapist Phyllis was a short, slender brunette with a cropped, no-nonsense 'do. Unlike her effusive husband, she completely ignored the audience during the last-minute stage prep. Oblivious to the female adoration her husband was garnering, she remained deep in conversation with a leanly built man visible only in silhouette.

Finally, from a glassed-in control booth, the director ordered the stage cleared. That shadowy figure Phyllis Chatsworth had been speaking with gave her arm an affectionate squeeze. Then the man stepped into the glare of the spotlight.

It was James Young, looking very much like his ID photograph.

A minute later, the show's upbeat theme song began to play. The digital prompters ordered *APPLAUSE!* and the audience complied.

Then came the announcer's voice: "Husband-and-wife relationship therapists for two decades, Dr. Chaz Chatsworth and Therapist Phyllis will guide you through the pitfalls and pleasures of love, romance, and marriage. And now, the most *understanding*, *compassionate*, and *insightful* couple on television . . ."

The spotlight reappeared in time to catch the couple casually smooching. Then Dr. Chaz and Phyllis pretended to look guilty at being caught in a kiss. They clasped their hands above their heads, jumped off their stools, and faced the audience.

"Bills! Gift lists! Company parties! Prickly family members! Pricklier in-laws! Are you feeling the pressure to create the 'perfect' Christmas, Chanukah, or Kwanzaa?" Dr. Chaz asked.

Phyllis stepped forward. "If all this holiday tension is ruining *your* marriage or romantic relationship, stick around. Today we'll deal with holiday stress, and ask the question, can love survive it?"

"Our 'Chatsworth Survival Guide' may just keep this holiday season from ending in divorce," Dr. Chaz added, "or worse . . ."

"Worse?" I muttered. "What's worse? *Homicide?*"

Madame chuckled. "It's *The Chatsworth Way*, dear, not *Nancy Grace*."

The monitor blinked: *APPLAUSE!*

Almost immediately, the show segued into its slick B-roll, showing couples arguing at holiday parties or on shopping trips. Quoting a list of statistics, Dr. Chaz and Phyllis discussed the dangers of high "perfect holiday" expectations versus disillusioning realities. They cited the troubles that come from reuniting dysfunctional families or attempting to work out fair visitation in divorced ones. They spoke about dealing with disapproving in-laws and demanding grandparents, while keeping your sex life from slipping into a coma. By the time the opening segment ended, the audience could come to only one conclusion—

The holidays are hazardous to your mental health!

"Time for a break," Dr. Chaz finally said. "When we come

back, we're going to meet two couples. One husband and wife who learned how to cope with the season's stress—"

"And another couple that *didn't*," Phyllis said, exaggerating a frown.

Then the pair turned their backs on the audience, lovingly clasped hands, and strolled back to their seats while the stage faded to black. After the cameras cut away, the stage crew appeared to carry in stools for the day's guests.

Dr. Chaz and Phyllis remained in their chairs, and I noticed that the kissy-kissy couple was far less cordial when the cameras weren't rolling. At one point, Phyllis, script in hand, swept aside her husband's assistant to point out what she obviously felt was a glaring error in the next segment. I regretted that their microphones were off, because the animated argument went on for nearly thirty seconds.

James Young's arrival put an end to it. The lanky African-American executive producer seemed to be a calming presence on the set. After a few minutes in a heads-together conference, Young made changes that both of his media darlings could live with. Then the exec producer was off again when a technician alerted him to a problem backstage.

The taping resumed and the audience was introduced to an onstage couple whose last holiday season could best be described as a model train wreck.

Sobbing, a thirtysomething blonde identified only as "Tracy from Memphis" described her "worst Christmas ever," which took place last year.

"It was a week before Christmas when I found out the truth, Dr. Chaz. I arrived late to my husband's office party to find Todd and a coworker doing the *nasty* under the Rudolph the Reindeer display in the company break room!"

Members of the audience gasped.

Dr. Chaz nodded knowingly. "And how did that make you feel, Tracy?"

"Angry!"

The audience began to mumble unhappily. Sitting beside

his estranged wife, Todd shifted in his seat and worriedly eyeballed the disapproving (mostly female) audience.

"So, Todd, tell me. What the heck were you thinking?"

Todd's shrug was sheepish. Then he glanced at the sea of frowning females and cleared his throat. "I guess I was hurt, Dr. Chaz. Really, really hurt."

The crowd around us began to mumble again. They seemed less angry now and leaned forward with interest.

"Hurt, Todd? Why?" said Dr. Chaz, feigning extreme curiosity. "Who hurt you?"

"My wife."

Now the women in the audience began whispering. Todd began to act reluctant to speak, as if this were very hard for him to do. At the doctor's slightest urging, however, he cut loose.

"I was hurt by my wife when she ran up our credit cards buying gifts we couldn't afford for a ridiculously long list of family members and friends." He shook his head. "I felt our kids' futures were at stake, you know? That's how I felt about it. Can you blame me?"

"I see. Anything else?" Dr. Chaz prompted.

"Yes! I was hurt that my wife couldn't find the time between decorating the tree and stuffing the stockings to pay attention to *my* needs!"

"Sounds like you both made some mistakes," Dr. Chaz said, nodding sagely.

In the second half of the program, Therapist Phyllis took over the questioning. Ironically the story of "Mona and Bill from Columbus," aka the happy, *functional* couple, was far less interesting to the audience.

"Sad but true," Madame remarked to me. "Train wrecks make front page news, not on-time arrivals."

The final segment was a regular feature called "People Are Still Having Sex," where both Dr. Chaz and Phyllis advised couples to keep romance alive during stressful times. "It's important you find those little pockets of intimacy with your lover, especially during this crazy, hectic season."

Film footage rolled, showing couples kissing beside a Christmas tree, embracing on a winter sleigh ride, exchanging perfectly wrapped gifts in bed.

"Mistletoe and music," Therapist Phyllis suggested.

"Candy canes by candlelight," added Dr. Chaz.

By the time the springy closing theme filled the studio and the hosts waved us all good-bye, the audience had swallowed enough soma to jump to their feet in teleprompted *APPLAUSE!*

As the music died, the exit doors opened and the crowd filed out. Madame and I gathered our things and approached an usher.

"Excuse me," Madame said. "My daughter-in-law and I have a backstage pass. I wonder if—"

"Oh, you need to see Heidi," he said, gesturing to a slender, ice blonde in a tightly fitting gray business suit. "Heidi Gilcrest."

The woman took tiny steps, her high heels clicking like castanets as she hurried from the opposite end of the studio to greet us. "Well, hello!" Heidi's eyes went nearly as wide as her pearly grin. "Mr. Dewberry told us to expect you, Ms. Dubois. Isn't he a wonderful man? And those dogs of his are just scrumptious. Follow me and I'll show you the place."

The long-limbed dynamo led us through a maze of cables, curtains, and equipment. She paused patiently at a metal fire door, waiting for us to catch up.

"Here we go," she finally said, pushing through to a long, carpeted hallway. "Back here we have our dressing rooms and offices." She pointed to a line of mostly closed doors along the hallway. "If you'll wait right here, I'll see if—"

Right beside me, a door with a silver star on it suddenly jerked open and Phyllis Chatsworth charged out.

"Watch out," she said, nearly knocking me over.

"Oh, Mrs. Chatsworth!" Heidi exclaimed. "I'd like you to meet two dear friends of Mr. Dewberry's. This is Ms. Dubois and—"

Ignoring us completely, Phyllis Chatsworth addressed

Heidi. "Did Simon get my e-mail about the bottled water?"

Heidi's head bobbed. "I'm sure he did, Mrs. Chatsworth. I printed it out as a reminder and put it on his desk myself."

"Well, there isn't any water in my dressing room! The refrigerator's empty, Heidi. Empty! And it's been that way since before the taping started."

"I'll find out what happened—"

"I love the way you make sure my husband's snacks are delivered like clockwork, but I have to wait for a few lousy bottles of water."

"I assure you, Mrs. Chatsworth, I want to make you happy—"

"Then you tell Simon to straighten it out. *Now.* And while you're at it, tell maintenance the overhead light in my bathroom has died. I don't care if one of these guild bums has to work overtime for once. I want the light fixed today!"

Before the statuesque assistant could play doormat again, her "understanding, compassionate, and insightful" therapist boss slammed the door in our faces.

Sixteen

~∿∿∿∿∿∿∿∿∿∿∿∿∿∿∿∿∿∿~

MADAME and I squirmed during Phyllis Chatsworth's cranky fit, but the nasty tone of the confrontation didn't appear to dampen Heidi Gilcrest's enthusiasm one iota.

"You can see how busy things get around here!" she chirped, lifting the receiver on a wall phone. "Let me buzz Simon, then we'll continue our tour."

A moment later another door with a star on it opened.

"What's Phyl griping about now?" the male half of the Chatsworth duo garbled around a mouth stuffed with food. Then he noticed us and froze.

I have to admit, Dr. Chaz was even more striking up close. Still armed with easy charm and a ready smile, he also possessed a kind of natural elegance that even a pair of snack-stuffed chipmunk cheeks failed to diminish.

Stuck on the phone, Heidi mimed an apology to the doctor for not introducing us. Finding the situation amusing, Dr. Chaz crunched and crunched and finally swallowed his potato chips.

"Sorry about the food," he said with a sheepish laugh. "I'm always ravenous after a taping. It's the intensity of the show, I guess. Would you like one?"

Dr. Chaz offered the bag to Madame first.

"No thank you, Doctor. I prefer *pommes frites*!"

The doctor chuckled warmly at that. After I also declined the snack, he tossed the half-empty bag back into his dressing room and wiped his hands with a handkerchief, winking at us to dispel any awkwardness.

Madame introduced herself, then me, adding, "I enjoyed your show today, Doctor. I'm not able to watch every day, you understand, but I did especially like your episode on men who remarry but still love their first wives," she said, shooting me a meaningful glance.

Oh, brother.

"That was one of our most popular episodes," Dr. Chaz replied. "Especially among first wives!"

Madame laughed. I didn't. (Matt's wedding was supposed to put an end to that particular argument. From the look on Madame's face, however, I could see old habits were going to die hard.)

Then Dr. Chaz fixed his eyes on me. "Did you enjoy today's taping, Miss Cosi?"

"It was, uh, memorable," I said diplomatically.

He gestured to Heidi, still on the phone, clearly having an intense argument. "It seems you lost your tour guide."

"She's got an issue with Simon," I explained.

"Simon's a good guy; he's just busy and can't do everything for everyone every day," Dr. Chaz said, rather loudly—loud enough, no doubt, for his wife to hear behind her own star-marked door. Then he changed his tone to a much warmer one. "Is there something I can show you?"

Madame glanced at me. "Well—"

"Actually," I said, taking the cue. "I've come backstage to meet your executive producer, James Young. He and I are . . . *neighbors*, as it turns out. Though we've never actually met, I've, uh, *seen* him around."

Dr. Chaz studied me for a rather long moment and then raised an eyebrow. "Lucky for James, *he* isn't married."

"Excuse me?"

He leaned closer and lowered his voice. "You are interested in James, aren't you? I mean, that's why you asked, right?"

"Sure," I said, forcing a smile.

"*Phew!* I'm glad about that." He laughed. "Can't have a 'relationship specialist' getting something like that wrong, can we? And I do like a woman who knows what she wants and goes for it." He winked again. "We're doing an episode on that next month—maybe you'd like to be a guest?"

"Uh—I don't think—"

"I'll be sure to mention it to James." Then he took my arm and gallantly wrapped it around his. "Let me introduce you two right now. Will you join us, Ms. Dubois?"

"Oh, no," Madame replied. "I'll give those two their privacy. I'm content to wait here with young Heidi."

Dr. Chaz led me down the hall to a faux-mahogany door, on which he knocked once, then walked in. We caught James Young in the middle of removing his tailored sports jacket.

"Someone I'd like you to meet, James," Dr. Chaz announced. "It seems you and the lovely Ms. Cosi here are neighbors. She's an acquaintance of Mr. Dewberry, as well."

"Mr. Dewberry. I see," James Young said with an understanding nod and extended his hand. "Good to meet you, Ms. Cosi."

"Call me Clare."

Dr. Chaz glanced at his watch. "Got to run. Squash at the club. Good luck, Ms. Cosi." Yet another wink.

Then the door closed, and I glanced around Young's office. The room was spacious—but it felt small and cramped. The clutter was the reason. Digital recordings, scripts, and mounds of paper packed the room. I wondered how the man navigated through it all.

"Won't you sit down, Clare."

He offered me a chair, then sat down behind his desk and coolly steepled his long fingers. "So how long have you lived in the West Village?"

"A few years now—but I'm a returning resident. I managed the Village Blend coffeehouse, on Hudson Street, right out of college. Then I went to New Jersey to raise my daughter. Now I'm back in the city again."

He brightened at the mention of the Blend. "I know the place. A number of friends in the neighborhood are hooked on your lattes. I'm into tea myself—white tea lately—so I don't frequent your establishment. Nothing personal."

"No worries," I said, realizing this guy's Rolex wasn't the only indication he had plenty of disposable income. White tea was among the rarest and most expensive varieties on the planet.

Young looked at me askance, as if he were trying to place me. "You do live in my building, right? Chaz said you were a neighbor."

"Actually, I live several blocks away. But I'm familiar with your building, and the property around it. It's usually a fairly safe part of the city, but the other night, there was a murder on your street. You know about that, right?"

Young nodded. "I read about the shooting. Apparently it happened in the alley right outside my residence."

"I knew the victim, Mr. Young. He was a friend of mine."

"Oh?" he said. "I'm very sorry."

"Thank you."

At the mention of knowing the victim, I noticed a subtle change in the man. His coolness began slowly evaporating and he began to fidget.

"The victim's name was Alfred Glockner," I explained. "He was an aspiring stand-up comedian, and he worked as a Traveling Santa. Does his name mean anything to you?"

Young pursed his lips and then frowned. "I never heard of a Mr. Glockner. Should I know him?"

"That's a question I want answered. You see, I'm privately investigating Mr. Glockner's murder, and just last evening the police received evidence that proves Alf was on the fire escape, right outside your apartment window, just minutes before he was gunned down."

Young's fidgeting form froze. He was silent for a few moments, and then he said, "I'm stunned to hear that. I really am. I mean, I didn't see or hear anything out of the ordinary that night. Not even sirens."

"Well, I was wondering—why do you think Alf was on your balcony?"

Young's eyebrow arched, a little cruelly. "I guess he wasn't delivering presents, was he, Ms. Cosi? I mean, I would have expected Santa to use the chimney for that, wouldn't you?"

"I'm serious, Mr. Young."

"I know you are, and I'm surprised you're even asking that question. Burglaries increase during the holidays. That's one of the things I learned researching today's show . . ."

As he spoke, Young glanced several times at his Rolex. His gaze then began darting back and forth between me and his closed office door. *Is he hoping for an interruption? Or is he worried who might suddenly walk in and become a party to this conversation?*

"I was out much of that day, holiday shopping," Young continued. "Perhaps this Glockner fellow saw me with shopping bags around the neighborhood and followed me back to my building with the intent to rob my apartment."

I recalled what the bartender at the White Horse had told me. Alf was there that night. He'd ordered a cranberry juice and then left in a hurry without finishing it. I also recalled the small shopping bags I'd seen on James Young's coffee table—the ones labeled Tiffany, Tourneau, Saks.

Did Alf notice James Young walking home that night? Was Vicki Glockner right? Was Omar Linford pressuring or threatening Alf over the money he'd lent him? Was Alf so desperate to pay back Linford that he'd turned to burglary? If he had, was James Young Alf's first try—or had Alf done it before?

The phone on Young's desk buzzed.

"If you'll excuse me, Ms. Cosi," he said, reaching for the receiver. "I have work to do."

RELUCTANTLY I left James Young's office to search out Madame again. After thanking Heidi for her help, we flagged a cab on Eleventh.

"What did you find out?" Madame asked as we settled into the backseat.

"James Young is an attractive, confident, financially comfortable man. That's what I found out."

"Don't those sorts of men commit murder, dear?"

"Not my point. If James Young caught Alf Glockner in the act of burglary, would a man like him have gone all the way down to the alley, shot him, and then robbed the Traveling Santa cart to make it look like a random mugging?"

"Patently ridiculous."

"Agreed. Just last night, Young saw a dark figure on his fire escape—*me*—and all he did was call his doorman."

"Who *did* attack you."

"Yes, the Neanderthal also locked me in a Dumpster. But he didn't shoot me. He called the NYPD. I'm sure he would have done that for Alf, too . . . Still, there's something about James Young that doesn't feel right . . ."

"What's that?"

"Young became very tense when I brought up Alf, as if he were hiding something. Or at least knew more than he was telling me."

"Perhaps he was just uneasy with your grilling him about a terrible crime that occurred right outside his home."

I drummed my fingers on the cab's vinyl seat and watched restaurants, storefronts, and apartment houses roll by. "Young is certainly perceptive enough to know that I was suspicious of him—or at least of Alf's being on his balcony."

"Wouldn't it make you nervous to have someone suggest you may have something to do with a murder?"

"I guess so."

"So where are we now?" Madame turned in the car seat to face me. "The trail hasn't gone cold, has it? Perhaps Mr. Young left you with another lead? Do you have a new theory?"

I raised an eyebrow. "You've certainly picked up on the gumshoe slang, haven't you?"

"No mystery there, dear." Madame waved her hand.

"You're not the first coffeehouse manager who's regularly provided hot stimulants for men in law enforcement."

Having heard more than a few racy stories of Madame's bohemian years, I wasn't at all sure how to interpret that remark. Before I could clarify what exactly she meant, however, our taxi pulled up to the curb. We paid the driver, climbed out, and gasped. The line to get into the Village Blend was literally around the block.

"My goodness!" Madame gawked. "I thought you told me afternoon business has slowed considerably since the economic downturn."

"It has."

"Well, my dear, I haven't seen this kind of enthusiasm for a retail refreshment since *Seinfeld* aired an episode on the Soup Nazi! Did some television show film an episode about our Village Blend?"

"Not that I know of . . . Come on."

Rather than fight our way through the crowd, I led Madame around to the back alley, pulled out my keys, and unlocked the back door. We entered through the pantry area, passing the service stairwell that led down to the basement and up to my private apartment.

"Would you rather we go upstairs to talk?" I asked.

"And miss finding out what all the fuss is about? Not on your life!"

Seventeen

❧❧❧❧❧❧❧❧❧❧❧❧❧❧❧❧

"PEOPLE, people!" Tucker yelled, clapping his hands. "Will you puh-*leeze* give your order a *thought* on your way up to my counter! And have your money or credit card out *before* you get to me!"

The espresso bar looked like a caffeinated zoo—but a well-run caffeinated zoo. I still couldn't believe the shop was so busy. When I'd left earlier to go to Studio 19, the place had already slipped into its typical weekday-afternoon coma. Now the main floor was raucously packed. Tucker's shift had started, but Esther was still here, mixing drinks with Dante behind the espresso machine—she'd obviously agreed to stay past her scheduled departure time to help handle the thirsty tsunami.

I turned to Madame. "I want to pitch in here, but I need to ask you something important first."

"Of course." Madame nodded. "I'll find a table."

I could see from my quick scan of the first floor that she wouldn't have a problem. Despite the line out the door, quite a few tables were still empty. The drinks my baristas were mixing were mostly "with wings"—aka to go. A lot of the patrons were new, but just as many faces belonged to former regulars—customers I hadn't seen in here for some time.

I noticed Tucker's friend, the ex–soap actor Shane Holliway, as boyishly appealing as ever with the golden shag and trendy chin stubble. He was sipping a drink near the fireplace, a scarf rakishly thrown over his shoulder. When he saw me checking him out, he gave me a big smile and a wink.

Another winker, I thought. What was it with these guys on TV? Did those klieg lights affect their vision or something?

I waved politely—and that's when I noticed the thirty-something redhead, the one I'd clashed with the night of Alf's murder. She was back, sitting in a far corner of the shop, still gorgeous, still angry, her eyes focused on me as if I'd thrown a *macchiato* in her face.

I wasn't intimidated. Not even a little bit. I met her gaze with a direct stare. She looked away.

Mentally dismissing the grudge-carrying socialite, I tapped my assistant manager's shoulder. "What's going on, Tuck?"

"Ohmigawd, Clare!" he said, finally noticing me. "It's our Fa-la-la-la Lattes!"

"What? How can that be? I only just put out the sidewalk chalkboard this morning!"

As reluctant as I'd been to cash in on Alf's Taste of Christmas latte idea, I'd changed my mind for two reasons. The shop badly needed an economic shot in the arm, and as a business manager responsible for the sustainability of this shop and its employees, I had to be willing to try anything. The second reason was Dexter Beatty's nostalgic reaction to Gardner's Black Cake Latte the previous evening. If Alf's idea could bring back even one happy holiday memory for a customer, I figured it had to be a worthy addition to our menu. But I never expected a reaction like this. It didn't even make sense!

"Tucker, all these people can't be random foot traffic!"

"We're all over the Net, Clare. Two major foodie bloggers frequent the Blend. They wrote about our lattes first thing this morning—loved the Fa-la-la-la holiday theme. Actually, one of them loved it, the other one kind of derided it as 'twee.' But both thought the variety and flavors were outstanding. Then two more foodie writers came in, much bigger ones: Grub Street Digest and the-feedbag.com! They took digital pics. Someone else took a YouTube video! We're the talk of the foodie Web world! A *Post* reporter was just here, and a *Times* photographer called to confirm our address!"

"Excuse me! Hello!" A young woman in heels and hose plopped her designer handbag on top of the cash register. "I'm on a work break. Are you people going to take my order, or what?!"

Tucker whipped his head around. "Chill-ax, honey! I'll get to you." He snapped his fingers. "And get your Kate Spade *off* my register!"

"Give me ten minutes and I'll relieve Esther," I told Tuck. "Madame's waiting for me at a table."

"It's okay, Clare. We're going just about as fast as we can anyway. Another pair of hands won't help Dante pull those espressos any faster."

"And we don't want him to, either."

"I know—quality is why we're in business after one hundred years. But I warn you, I have a choreography rehearsal at seven sharp for my *Ticket to the North Pole* production number. The benefit party's next Tuesday evening, so there's no time to spare. All of the dancing elves and singing Santa's helpers are on my call sheet."

"Is that why Shane's here?" I gestured to him in the corner, noticed he was still watching me, and quickly dropped my pointing finger.

"Oh, is Shane here already?" Tuck glanced across the room and waved. "Well, the rehearsal space is just down the block. And, yes, Clare, he is one of my dancing elves. Apparently Dickie Celebratorio—"

"The party planner?"

"The same. He's throwing this bash and he owes Shane some big favor, so I had to hire the man, but that's fine with me. I figure the ladies at the benefit party will be more than happy to see him in tights. Anyway, I've paid for the rehearsal space already, so I can *not* give you any overtime."

"No problem, Tuck. I'll cover." I ducked over to Esther, thanking her for staying past the end of her shift.

"What's to thank, boss? You are paying me, right?"

I squeezed her shoulder, pushed up my sweater sleeves, and a few minutes later approached Madame with two freshly made Fa-la-la-la Lattes and a quick update on why our store was suddenly swamped.

"Well," she said, after sampling my own late addition to the latte line-up, "if all your new flavors are as delightful as this Chocolate Cherry Cordial, I'd say we've struck gelt."

I laughed. "Speaking of gelt—you should try our Apricot-Cinnamon Rugelach and Raspberry Jelly Dough-nut lattes."

"For Chanukah!" She hooted. "Wonderful!"

"Esther's idea." I smiled, but then glanced at the line again, a little worriedly.

"Come now, Clare, you don't have to entertain me when the shop's this busy. Ask me your question and get on with your day."

I leaned closer. "I need to know if you know a man named Omar Linford."

Madame paused a moment, thinking it over, and frowned. "Now that's a name that does *not* ring a bell for me."

"Too bad. I'm out of leads and Alf's daughter's theory is actually starting to make sense."

"How so?"

"Alf Glockner was a warm, generous, thoughtful human-itarian. The only way I could see him turning to burglary was if he was pressured or threatened into it. He owed this man Linford a great deal of money. Alf may have turned to crime to get it, but if he had, he obviously wasn't paying

Linford fast enough and the man decided to make an example of him instead."

"Have police questioned this man?"

"Yes, but they say he has no criminal record and they don't see him as a viable suspect for what appears to be a random street crime, especially now, when street crime is on the rise."

"Could the police be right, Clare? Perhaps Alf was going to burglarize this nice man James Young, but he had second thoughts and then he himself was mugged and killed—a terrible irony."

"Yes, it could be that simple. But Vicki Glockner herself claims it isn't—"

And although I didn't mention it to Madame, I still had my suspicions about the lead detective in the case. "Generalissimo" Franco's own partner practically called him a vigilante, and his hostile treatment of me, for butting into the investigation, not to mention his oddly intense statement about not "seeing evil" in me left me wondering. The night of Alf's murder, Franco had told me he'd just come on duty. Could he have shot Alf himself in some twisted form of street justice? Or was Franco somehow involved in covering up the real truth about Alf's murder? He wouldn't be the first corrupt cop to take a bribe for looking the other way, especially when it involved the shooting of a man he judged to be a criminal himself.

"I have to talk to Linford," I finally told Madame, "see what I can find out. Even a denial can be telling if the man's not a good liar."

"You'll need a partner for that, too, dear."

"I have to get a handle on this guy first. I know where he lives—next door to Vicki Glockner—but Vicki wasn't very helpful about his background. I need to know more about him, his business, his associates. I need to know how to question him."

Just then, a wiry young man with spiked blond hair and a pale complexion approached our table. He wore baggy jeans, motorcycle boots, and a shiny, outer-boroughs black leather blazer. The young man nodded politely, then struck a slouching hip-hop pose.

"Clare Cosi, Clare Cosi; you're a fresh Village posy; now release my czarina; so with me she can mosey!"

Madame's eyes widened. She glanced at me and addressed the rapper: "And who is your czarina, young man?"

"The Best girl, in the West, girl! *That* sweet-booty babe-with-the-chest girl!" The young man lifted his closed fist, shook his pinkie and index finger free, and pointed both toward the espresso bar.

"Esther?" Madame glanced at me, just to make sure.

"This is Boris Bokunin," I said. "He's a Russian émigré, slam poet, and urban rapper." He was also a hardworking assistant baker in Brighton Beach, but I knew he preferred the other identifiers. "Did I get it right, Boris?"

Boris gave a little bow. "BB Gunn. That's my hip-hop handle! Just ask me ladies and—" He clapped his hands and pointed at us. "I'll light your candles!"

Madame glanced at me, her laugh lines crinkling. "He reminds me of the beats!"

Boris's eyes widened. "You need someone beat down?"

"She means *beat poetry*, Boris," I said. "But that's a whole other century." I rose from my chair. "Tell Esther I'll relieve her in a minute."

BB grinned at that, saluted me, bowed to Madame, then spun on his motorcycle boots and headed for the counter.

Madame touched my arm. "Do keep me informed of the developments on catching Alf's killer. I'd like to help if I can."

I patted her hand. "Have a good trip to Vermont with Otto. The bed-and-breakfast sounds amazing. Your beau certainly knows how to keep the romance in the holiday season."

"Mistletoe and music, my dear." She winked. "Candy canes by candlelight."

I nodded, ignoring a surge of mixed feelings. With Joy

away and Mike trying to crack a cold case, this Christmas wasn't going to be a very merry one for me. On a quiet sigh, I bent down and gave Madame a good-bye hug.

I could only hope my daughter was finding the same sort of happiness in Paris that her grandmother was enjoying in New York. Despite the theme of today's *Chatsworth Way*, it appeared the holiday season really could be the most romantic time of the year for some women. I simply wasn't one of them.

Eighteen

~~~~~~~~~~~~~~~~~~~~~~~~~~~~~~~~~~~~

A few days after wishing Madame a good trip, I was on my way to Staten Island to have lunch with Omar Linford. I even brought backup. With Madame still away on her long romantic weekend, I tapped my old partner in anticrime, Esther Best.

We finished our morning shifts together and she agreed to do the driving—mainly because I didn't want to burden her with balancing my *struffoli* on her lap all the way to Lighthouse Hill.

According to Dexter Beatty, bringing a home-baked gift was a sign of affection. A black cake would have been a better choice, given Linford's Jamaican roots, but I didn't have three weeks to macerate fruit in Manischewitz or travel to Brooklyn and back for a jar of authentic West Indian burnt sugar.

Instead, I made the famous little "Italian Christmas tree" pastry that I'd loved as a child, hoping it would start us out on the right foot (as long as I could prevent the whole thing from ending up on the dashboard, that is).

Esther had been doing fine in the bumper-to-bumper

traffic across the Brooklyn Bridge, but now that we'd hit 278, she was tearing down the highway like a Goth out of hell.

"Esther, slow down! We've only gone from Lower Manhattan to Brooklyn Heights. Not to Monaco's Grand Prix!"

"Sorry," she replied, easing up on the pedal. "It's just that this part of the drive is seriously tedious . . ."

As its name suggested, Staten Island was in fact an island, connected to the borough of Brooklyn via the Verrazano-Narrows Bridge. Commuters without cars took the famous Staten Island Ferry.

"It would have been much easier to take the ferry from Battery Park," Esther pointed out.

It would have, except she knew as well as I did that cars had been banned from the ferry since the 9/11 attack.

"We have no choice. We have to go through Brooklyn."

Esther sighed and hit the gas again. "So, boss. You never told me how you managed to wrangle this invitation."

"It was Dexter's doing," I explained as we zipped along the highway. "I did a little snooping and found out he knew Linford."

"Oh, I see. No big deal, then."

Actually it was a big deal.

I'd started my research on Saturday morning. After typing Linford's name into a couple of Internet search engines, I learned he'd founded and managed a hedge fund called Linvantage. The fund was based in Antigua and had its prospectus posted online. It appeared to be very profitable, and I noticed the minimum investment was high enough to keep the client list exclusive.

Further research uncovered Linford's name on the roster of half a dozen import/export companies, all of them based in the Caribbean.

Of course, when I thought of the Caribbean, I always thought of Matt's friend Dexter—an absolute pillar of the Brooklyn Caribbean community. Any bigwigs from the Islands in the New York area probably made themselves known to Dex at one time or another to purchase authentic West Indian products for a party, family gathering, or traditional celebration.

So I called Dexter that afternoon to ask if the name Omar Linford rang any bells. Strangely, Dex claimed he'd never heard of the man, politely excused himself, and got off the phone. At first I believed him, but that night my research revealed that Linford owned a tiny Jamaica-based specialty food importer called Blue Sunshine.

Back in 2000, shortly after the U.S. Food and Drug Administration lifted its ban on a potentially toxic Jamaican fruit called *ackee*, I remembered Dexter boasting that he had "a *big-up* import guy" who sold canned ackee for seventy-five dollars a case.

At such a low wholesale price, Dex was able to peddle the Jamaican staple in his Brooklyn stores for six or seven dollars a can—about half the going rate everywhere else in the United States. Price points like that made Dexter's Taste of the Caribbean stores very popular, especially around Christmas when the price of ackee almost always rose because of increased demand.

"I'm not sellin' that hinky stuff, no neither," Dex had insisted. "Gettin' me the top brands for my customers. Nineteen-ounce tins of Island Sun."

On its Web site, the Blue Sunshine company boasted that it had the lowest wholesale price for Island Sun brand Jamaican ackee on the East Coast. I put two and two together (old-school math this time) and made a pest of myself by phoning Dexter a second time.

"I really put the pressure on during the second call," I continued explaining to Esther. "And Dex finally admitted that he has a 'confidential business relationship' with Omar Linford. Not just the man's Blue Sunshine company, but Omar himself."

"That sounds kind of fishy," she said, arching an eyebrow. "What kind of relationship?"

"Not the kind Vicki Glockner was thinking about. I'm

pretty sure Linford isn't supplying marijuana for Dex to sell out of his stores."

"*Pretty* sure?"

Esther was right. I wasn't all that sure about anything when it came to Linford's business interests. Even after I'd confronted Dex with circumstantial evidence that he'd been doing business with Linford's company for years, he still refused to come completely clean about the extent of his relationship with the importer.

And while all of Linford's business activities seemed legitimate, so what? If anybody knew how legitimate businesses could operate in a way to mask illegal activity, it was the daughter of the local sports bookie.

In the middle of my second call to Dexter, I remembered how he'd shown up at the Blend—abruptly and unexpectedly—the very same night that Vickie Glockner came to ask for my help in solving her father's murder. Again, my mind started working and I asked Dexter point-blank if he'd been *spying* for Omar Linford, too.

Dex wouldn't confirm or deny anything regarding the man, but he did get nervous enough to finally agree to arrange a "sit-down" lunch meeting at one o'clock sharp on Monday so I could ask Linford any questions "straight up" to his face. He wasn't interested, he said, in being "caught between the diver and the pearl."

On Sunday I phoned Matt for some kind of explanation on Dexter's bizarre denials regarding Omar Linford, but Matt couldn't talk more than a few minutes. Breanne had roped him into a last-minute trip to Connecticut for a "weekend in the country"—not for mistletoe and moonlight but for networking with her magazine's publisher and his board of trustees.

"I'll stop by the Blend after we get back on Tuesday," Matt insisted. "I didn't know that Dex knew this man Linford or did business with him, but I have a feeling I know what this is about. I just can't talk about it now."

"Why not? My meeting with the man is Monday, Matt. Why can't you just explain it to me?!"

"Because it's not fit conversation for a cellular line, that's why!"

Now Esther was guiding my battered, decade-old Honda over the Verrazano-Narrows Bridge. Soon we were passing La Tourette Park, part of the Staten Island Greenbelt that included the woods around Richmond Creek and the manicured lawns of the La Tourette Golf Course. It was frozen and snow-crusted now, but I could still remember how lush and leafy this exclusive landscape looked a few summers ago.

I'd driven out to the Lighthouse Hill area only once before, to get a glimpse of the landmark Crimson Beech house, the only home in New York City designed by Frank Lloyd Wright, one of the many architects I'd admired during my fine arts studies. The original owners had it manufactured fifty years ago in kit form, and fewer than a dozen of these prefabricated houses were ever built.

Linford's house was not prefabricated. From what I could see of it on my Google map, it had a much bigger footprint than the Frank Lloyd Wright house; the location was a more elite part of the neighborhood as well, one that included a view of the water.

"There's the turn," I cried. "You're supposed to go left!"

Esther swerved so suddenly we nearly tipped onto two wheels. I managed to keep the *struffoli* upright, but barely.

"Sorry," Esther said, glancing at my pastry. "What is that mound of doughnut holes, anyway?"

Esther was being flip, of course; the little fried dough balls of the *struffoli* were more petite than doughnut holes. After drenching them with a honey glaze, I'd molded them into their traditional Christmas tree shape (kind of a rounded pyramid), then fairy-dusted the entire sculpture with rainbow sprinkles, let the whole thing dry, and carefully tented it with plastic wrap.

"*Struffoli* is actually a very old tradition," I informed

her. "The honey glaze is supposed to 'sweeten' family relationships—"

Esther snorted. "Maybe I should bring some to my sister's this year!"

"Italian nuns also used to make these in their convents and distribute them to noble families at Christmastime—a kind of thank-you for acts of charity."

"Sort of appropriate for Linford, then," Esther replied.

"What do you mean?"

"If Linford didn't actually have Alf whacked, then lending him all that money was kind of an act of charity." Esther shrugged. "Of course, the dude probably doesn't see it that way if he expected to be paid back."

"I didn't actually think a glazed pile of fried dough balls would end up compensating the man for two hundred thou," I flatly replied.

Esther turned onto Oceanview Court and we rolled up to the impressive address. We both raised our eyebrows at the man's front lawn.

Esther glanced at me. "Is this guy into Christmas, or what?"

Every bush and tree had been strung with lights. There were two full-sized sleighs, three animated elves, a big lighted Santa and Mrs. Claus, and eight tiny reindeer trotting across the house's sloped roof, a scarlet-nosed Rudolph in the lead.

"Add one ginormous electric menorah and this could be my sister's place in Westchester," Esther declared. "She married a Catholic guy, so they're doing the whole 'multiple traditions' thing: Chanukah bush, dreidels, Nativity scene. Last year she added some kind of African harvest symbol for Kwanzaa. I'm betting this year I'll find Tibetan prayer wheels spinning in the front yard, too."

I released my shoulder strap and popped the door. The frigid December air hit me immediately. I thought the day was cold back in the Village, but up here on the cliffs of Lighthouse Hill, the wind was almost cruel, lashing in off the Atlantic with cutting force.

I'd dressed professionally for today's lunch in a charcoal gray pinstriped pantsuit over a cream-colored camisole. My stacked high heels and belted slate coat looked polished enough, too, but they weren't very warm. As the arctic air knifed through me, I shivered, from the tips of my pointy toes to the hint of cleavage cresting the V of my buttoned-up blazer.

Esther came around and held the *struffoli* dish while I climbed out.

"This won't take more than an hour—right, boss? That's what you promised."

"Don't worry, Esther, I'll have you back in the city by three for your four o'clock exam. We'll have plenty of time."

It was then I noticed the tricked-out SUV in the driveway. With all the Christmas kitsch in the front yard, its garishness wasn't immediately apparent, but now that I saw it, my jaw dropped.

"What the heck is that?"

As we moved up the driveway, Esther looked over the vehicle with interest. "Tinted windows, electric blue racing stripes, chrome spoilers, and illuminated hubcaps."

"Are those bullet holes?!" I bent a little to examine what looked like punctures along the side of the vehicle.

"They're fake," Esther informed me.

"Fake?!"

"Yeah, it's a pimped-up ride effect—like that oh-so-tasteful masterpiece along the back." Esther pointed to the airbrushed scene of Viking warriors sacking a village with half-naked babes thrown over their arms.

I shook my head. "Fake bullet holes. What'll they sell next? Chalk outlines and toe tags?"

"Probably."

I shook my head. "Dexter described Omar Linford as a conservative businessman in his fifties. Could this be his car?"

"No," she whispered. "I'm sure it's *his*."

Esther gestured to a young man in his late teens swaggering out the front door. Tall and plenty big through the shoulders, he wore a studded leather jacket, stressed black denims, and a battered DJ fedora over his thick, wavy ponytail. His complexion was light brown, his eyes darker than French roast, and his chrome-tipped boots clicked as he walked down the cobblestone drive. Finally, the young man noticed us examining his car. He paused and stared, saying nothing.

I waved, but I needn't have bothered. He just kept staring suspiciously—first at me, then at Esther, whom he looked up and down with a kind of openly wicked leer that made her shift the huge bag on her shoulder.

"I've still got my brick," she whispered to me.

A moment later, the kid turned his back on us and opened the SUV's door. Before climbing behind the wheel, he brushed his arm across the leather seat, sweeping a tumble of junk food wrappers onto the driveway. Then he slammed the door and gunned his high-performance engine. A moment later, the placidness of the upscale neighborhood was shattered as the aspiring hoodlum roared off.

"What a charming encounter," Esther said as she kicked an empty bag of jalapeño-flavored corn chips off her boot.

"*Who* the heck was that?"

"I'm sure it was Linford's son, Dwayne. Vicki described him to me once. She dated him in high school."

"Interesting," I said, then started up the drive again. "Come on, Esther. Let's see how far that wannabe gangsta's fallen from the family tree . . ."

Nineteen

∞∞∞∞∞∞∞∞∞∞∞∞∞∞∞∞∞

THE double front doors of Linford's home were made of heavy polished oak and decorated with the largest holiday wreath I'd seen outside of Macy's sales floor. While Esther rang the regal-sounding doorbell, I stood by her, still holding my hand-painted dish of Italian *struffoli*.

A narrow-shouldered man of average height greeted us.

"Ms. Cosi, I presume? I'm Omar Linford."

Linford's light brown skin was the same shade as that of the young man who'd just peeled out of the driveway. But there the resemblance ended. Omar was in his fifties, not his twenties, and he wore his salt-and-pepper hair in a short-cropped style. A small, neatly trimmed brown mustache, threaded with silver, graced his upper lip. A bright red bow tie cheered up an otherwise dowdy three-piece suit—only a tad plump in the vest—and small, round, retro 1930s glasses made our host look more like a museum curator than a shady businessman.

"Please, Mr. Linford, call me Clare. This is my associate, Esther Best."

"Come in, ladies . . ."

As we stepped inside, Mr. Linford pointed to my *struffoli* and his smile widened. "I see you've brought a gift! Let me help you with that."

But Linford didn't lift a hand. Instead, a mocha-skinned woman in a maid's uniform appeared at my side, relieved me of the dish, then withdrew as quietly as she'd arrived.

"Delightful to meet you both," Linford said. "Follow me to the dining room. Everything's ready for our luncheon."

The interior of Linford's sprawling, glass and stone house was as hyperdecorated for the holidays as the exterior. The living room's gigantic Christmas tree filled the whole floor with the scent of pine. A fortune in antique Victorian ornaments appeared throughout the house, and a much smaller illuminated tree sat in the large dining area.

We paused before a polished mahogany table, dripping with a delicate lace tablecloth and set for three. Beside it, a line of silver service buffet trays rested on a large serving cart. A roaring fire in a brick-lined hearth provided warmth, and a glass wall offered us a spectacular view of the Staten Island Greenbelt and the blue green waters of New York Bay beyond.

"Please make yourselves comfortable," Linford said, holding my chair.

The maid returned with my dish of *struffoli*, now neatly placed atop a sterling silver serving tray. The honey glaze I'd drizzled over the tiny balls of fried dough gleamed in the sunlight. *Struffoli* was traditionally served as a communal after-dinner sweet, with guests tearing off pieces of the confection between sips of hot, strong espresso.

As soon as the maid placed my little Christmas tree in the middle of our table, however, Linford tore off the top and took a bite. "Forgive me for digging in," he said with a smile. "I forgot how much I loved this!"

After chewing and swallowing, he dabbed the glaze from his fingers and mouth with a white napkin. "Delicious! I can taste a hint of citrus. Did you use lemon halves to position the hot dough when you formed the tree?"

I blinked. "How did you know?"

Linford laughed. "I'll tell you, Clare, when I was seventeen I went to sea. I was young, so of course I had plenty of romantic delusions."

"Didn't we all," I muttered.

"Well, things didn't work out as planned. I caught pneumonia in Sicily, and the ship on which I was billeted sailed without me. It would have been a lonely Christmas in a strange land if a fisherman and his family hadn't taken pity on me."

Linford patted the modest bulge in his vest. "I must confess that I never ate better in my life."

"Wow, Sicily," Esther said, shooting me a pointed glance. "Did you happen to meet any *Mafia* bosses when you were there?"

It was an awkward, obvious question, but now that it was out, I watched Linford carefully for a reaction. He seemed amused more than anything, shaking his head *no* and laughing. Then he turned to his maid.

"Cecily, you may serve now."

Into our crystal goblets, Cecily poured a blend of guava and mango nectars. She then removed the lid from a silver tray and a salty, briny, peppery scent filled the dining room.

"Funky smell," Esther blurted out. "What is it?"

"Ackee and saltfish," Linford replied.

Cecily spooned some of the fish and fruit stew onto Esther's bone china plate.

"Ackee?" Esther whispered to me. "Isn't this stuff toxic?"

I turned my head, raised the napkin to my lips, and whispered, "Only if it's not ripe."

"Excuse me," Esther said loudly, "is this ackee *ripe*?"

Linford nodded. "Of course. It's canned in Jamaica and approved for import by the FDA. It has to be processed correctly. Ackee can be poisonous, otherwise."

Esther swallowed hard and stared at her food.

"I actually prefer *fresh* ackee with this particular dish," Linford told me. "But the fruit is only harvested in the warmer months."

The ackee fruit had the consistency of scrambled eggs; the fish was firm and resembled the Italian variety of dried codfish called *baccala*—something I ate as a child, but frankly didn't miss (an inevitable truth of life: Not every foodie memory is a good foodie memory). Apparently, Esther agreed.

"This reminds me of *dag maluah*," she said. "That's Jewish saltfish." Then she gave me a private look that said, *This sort of stuff is vile in* any *language.*

Luckily, Linford served the saltfish dish with freshly baked hard dough bread and boiled bananas on the side. (I thought at first they were plantains, but Linford informed me that boiled green bananas were also a traditional pairing. The fruit was boiled in its own skin with the tips and sides sliced to make peeling easier after cooking.) Then Linford dug in and so did I. Esther pushed the fish to the side of her plate and ate the bananas and bread—both of which were quite good.

As the conversation lulled, I cleared my throat. "Speaking of ackee, Mr. Linford—"

"Call me Omar, Clare. We have a mutual friend, which makes us friends, too, doesn't it?"

"Yes, of course. And I understand our friend, Dexter Beatty, purchases import items from you?"

Linford sat back in his chair. "From my company, yes. You are here seeking a purveyor of Caribbean foods for your store, aren't you? Dexter told me you had questions for me about my Blue Sunshine company. It's a very reliable source, as Dexter can attest."

"Actually, I had the impression that you and Dexter were involved in a number of business deals."

"Dexter and I do have a private arrangement, Clare."

"Importing and exporting?"

"Surely you're not here to invade our friend's privacy. If Dexter wanted you to know what he and I were doing together, he would have told you himself."

"I'm here, Mr. Linford, to talk about another one of your business ventures. One that wasn't so profitable."

Linford's smile began to slip away. "You're referring to?"

"Alfred Glockner."

Linford exhaled. An expression of relief appeared to cross his face, like he'd just dodged a bullet—which made me suspicious of Vickie's "shady" sobriquet all over again.

He cleared his throat. "I don't mean to be rude, but how in the world would my private dealings with the late Mr. Glockner concern you?"

"I was Mr. Glockner's friend. After his murder, someone close to Alf asked me to . . . step in and investigate."

"You must be referring to the money I loaned to Mr. Glockner."

I nodded. "Money he never paid back."

Linford met my eyes. "Let me begin, Clare, by assuring you that Alfred was my friend, too, and that not all of my investments are profitable. Quite frankly, in Alf's case, I suspected I would never see a return on my outlay."

That surprised me. "If you wanted to help Alf, why make it a loan? Why didn't you simply give him the money?"

"I don't operate that way, Ms. Cosi. My charitable donations are always made with tax deductions in mind, and Alf's business wasn't a charity. At the time, you must understand, the loan to Alf made sound business sense."

"How sound was it, if you lost the money?"

Linford smiled—a bit tightly this time. "You're very direct. Dex warned me that you would be. Let's say I had my reasons for lending Alf a hand."

"Such as?"

"The same reason I'm in a business relationship with our friend Dexter: to keep my profile high in a community of people from whom I draw hedge fund investors. *This* community on Staten Island, Alf's community, has changed over the years. But it wasn't always so inviting to someone of mixed race."

"What do you mean exactly?"

"Alf's steakhouse catered to a wealthy, mostly white clientele, and I used it for networking, a place to connect with my well-heeled neighbors. Everyone in the community loved and respected a born-and-raised Staten Islander like Alf, and I hoped he could open a few doors for me. I also hoped Alf could keep his business going, but in these hard times, that proved impossible. And the shambles the poor man made of his personal life didn't help."

"Alf told me about his separation and pending divorce."

"Did you know about his drinking?" Linford shook his head. "One morning, near the end of his marriage, I found Alf passed out in my driveway. Alf was so drunk Shelly—his wife—locked him out. He tried to come over here for a place to sleep, which I would have happily provided, but he never made it to the front door. My son, Dwayne, nearly ran him over coming home from one of those disc jockey club jobs of his."

From the stories Linford told, I learned that Alf Glockner wasn't just a failed restaurateur. He'd always been a borderline alcoholic who'd spiraled into dysfunction after his restaurant went belly-up. As the drinking intensified, Alf's marriage disintegrated. The man finally hit bottom, ending up in a hospital with acute alcohol poisoning.

"I visited Alf there and met another man," Linford said. "A high school chum, Karl Kovic is his name. Alf moved in with Karl, and shortly after, Karl got him involved with that Santa Claus thing in Manhattan—"

"The Traveling Santas." I made a mental note to question Karl, see what he could tell me.

"I thought Alf was well on the road to recovery," Linford continued, "until I received a rather disturbing letter from him a couple of weeks ago."

"Alf wrote you a letter?"

"He didn't sign it, but I know it came from him," Linford said, his face taut.

"What did the letter say?"

"Say?" Linford shook his head, his expression looking almost pained. "It was a threat, Clare—Alf's clumsy attempt at blackmail."

"You're joking."

"I never joke about blackmail. The note demanded I forgive the debt completely—as an early 'holiday' gift. I was also to come up with fifty thousand more dollars by Christmas in exchange for his silence about alleged unlawful activities—"

"About your investments?"

"The allegations were not about me," Linford said, mouth tight. "The letter suggested my son was involved in criminal activities."

"What activities?"

Linford shook his head. "It doesn't matter. The claims were all lies."

Hard to believe after my encounter with the kid driving the tricked-out gangsta ride. But then Omar Linford wouldn't be the first parent who'd blinded himself to his offspring's malfeasance.

"Do the police have the letter now?" I asked.

Linford shook his head. "I didn't want to get Alf into trouble, so I never alerted the authorities."

"I see," I said, but the claim only made me more suspicious.

"Alf was a good man at heart." Linford held my eyes. "And the letter made no sense. I mean, Alf was the one who insisted on paying me back in the first place."

"He *was* paying you back, then?"

"Not much—a thousand or so one week, a few hundred another. Out of respect for his pride, I took the money. I decided he must have written that letter on a bad night—probably he'd slipped and started drinking again, or he was feeling embittered and helpless. I'd planned to talk with Alf about it. My goal was to resolve the matter without bringing in the police. Then, when I read the terrible news about his death, I filed away the whole affair."

I didn't know whether or not to believe Omar Linford, but here was the acid test—

"You still have Alf's letter, right?"

Linford nodded.

"I'd like to take it with me, then," I said firmly. "You see, I've been advising the NYPD on this case, and the letter might help them solve Alf's murder."

"If it will help you catch Alf's killer, Clare, then have it by all means."

Linford gestured to his maid. "Has Mac come back yet?"

Her reply was a silent shake of her head.

"We have one problem with your request, Clare. Mrs. MacKenzie, my secretary, filed the letter God knows where. My wife might be a help, but she's left on another holiday shopping spree, so I doubt very much we'll see her before dark!" He smiled at the thought of his wife, then checked his watch. "Mac should be back here soon, certainly within the hour. When she arrives, I'll ask her to locate the letter and hand it over to you immediately."

Esther had remained silent through most of the questioning. But now she loudly cleared her throat. "What do we do until then?" she asked. "It's freezing outside, you know?"

"By all means, continue to make yourselves comfortable in my home as long as you like . . ." Linford rose from the table. "Now, if you'll excuse me, ladies, I have work waiting in my study."

Twenty

~~~~~~

ESTHER glanced at her watch for the third time in five minutes. Her black knee-high boot began *tap-tap-tapping* down each second as it passed. I understood her impatience—not that the waiting was unpleasant.

Linford's maid had escorted us to this glassed-in solarium well over an hour ago. From the sunporch, the view of the surrounding neighborhood was sedately suburban. Cecily provided us with a stack of current magazines, as well as a crackling fire in the charming potbellied stove, a fresh pot of Jamaica Blue Mountain, and slices of a freshly baked flourless chocolate Jamaican rum cake, which, she confided, came from a recipe used by Dexter's Taste of the Caribbean shops. The dessert was sinfully rich and fudgy, served on a warm little pool of coffee-rum sauce.

Everything was cozy, delicious, and copacetic—except for the fact that we'd seen no sign of Linford's personal secretary, "Mac" MacKenzie, or the blackmail letter he'd promised to hand over to me.

"Sorry, boss, but we've got to roll," Esther said, rising.

"My final exam is in one hour. I own this test, but I've got to *show up* to pass it!"

This was the moment I'd dreaded. I knew Esther had to get back to Manhattan, and I even began to wonder if this whole "misplaced letter" wasn't a ploy to discourage us, force us to leave without the note—something I was not about to do.

On the other hand, my best barista didn't deserve to fail an academic test over this.

"Take my car and go," I told Esther. "I'm going to stay and wait for Linford's secretary to show."

"How will you get back?"

"Easy. I'll call a car service to take me down to the ferry."

"Are you sure?"

"I'm not leaving here without that letter, if there even *is* a letter."

Esther nodded and I called the maid to bring her coat, explaining she had to go but I was staying. As we waited, Esther noticed something going on at the house next door.

"I think that's Vicki's mother," she said, pointing.

A tall, slightly heavy woman with short blond hair, wearing workout gear, running shoes, and a pink headband, was moving down the tiled walkway that bisected the expansive yard. She stooped down, picked up a *Wall Street Journal* that had been badly tossed onto the snow-covered lawn, and shook it free of snow. With her newspaper retrieved, she rose and stepped back into the house.

"That's definitely Shelly Glockner," Esther said. "I met her last year at Vicki's birthday party."

I nodded with interest. This was too good an opportunity to pass up. I mean, I'd come all the way from the West Village to Lighthouse Hill; I might as well shake another well-trimmed tree for information.

"Come on," I whispered after the maid retrieved Esther's coat. "I want to talk to that woman."

The sunporch had a door that led to a wraparound cedar

deck. A few steps down and I was on the lawn at the side of the sprawling house and already shivering. Away from the crackling fire, sans coat, I really felt the December chill!

"My car's close to an antique," I warned Esther. "Make sure you warm up the engine for at least five minutes before you drive away, or you might stall out."

"I got it, boss. But I still feel rotten leaving you like this—"

"Go!" I gently pushed her. "Take your test. I'll be back at the Blend in a few hours."

With a reluctant nod, Esther headed toward the curb where she'd parked my Honda. I cut across the snow-covered yard, leaving little pointy-toed prints on the field of pristine white. Then I carefully stepped over a low row of leafless bushes that separated Linford's elegant residence from the Glockners' more modest home.

Of course, the word *modest* could only be used in comparison. The Glockner house—a split-level brick ranch with a double garage and what appeared to be a built-in pool, freestanding sauna, and glass-enclosed hot tub in back—was quite grand by New York City standards. In this neighborhood, the place could easily command a cool million or more, even in these overleveraged times.

A few moments later, I arrived at Mrs. Glockner's front door (a single door this time), with a small wreath hanging there the only concession to the season.

I rang the doorbell, waited a polite ten count, then rang again. The curtain on the bay window stirred.

"I'll be there in a minute," a woman's voice called.

I guessed that Mrs. Glockner was making herself presentable. But much more than a minute passed before the door opened. Freezing on her stoop, I counted the seconds.

When Mrs. Glockner finally answered, she was oddly still wearing the same sweats, and her short-cropped yellow hair was still banded by the pink elastic. *So what had she been doing all that time?*

"Hi," she said.

"Mrs. Glockner? My name is Clare Cosi. And—"

"Come on in," she interrupted, giving my hand a strong, no-nonsense shake. "Call me Shelly."

Good, I thought with relief, *at least she's not going to give me indigestion.*

She was a foot taller than me and a bit heavier, but Shelly Glockner's size didn't affect her carriage. As she led me inside, she walked with the proud, confident grace of a principal dancer.

Alf had mentioned that his wife was around his age (mid-fifties), but she looked much younger with high, sculpted cheekbones, and—like her pretty daughter—a generous mouth and dimples in both cheeks. Sans makeup, her face showed only the subtlest signs of a skilled plastic surgeon's work around the eyes, chin, and neck.

We walked through a foyer into a spacious living room with a small, retro 1950s aluminum Christmas tree in the corner. The hardwood floor of almost black mahogany set off stark white walls covered with framed black-and-white prints. The furniture was mostly white, the tables and lamps all chrome and glass. A large fireplace of white brick dominated one wall of the large room, but there was no fire—and no sign there ever was one. The hearth looked as clean as a convent's kitchen floor.

Along the mantel, I noticed an array of photographs, all framed in heavy silver. There were a number of pictures of Vicki at various ages; other pictures appeared to be of friends and relatives. Not one photo of Alf.

Mrs. Glockner neatly set aside a few black throw pillows, then sat down on her sleek sofa of white leather—not a scuff or smudge on it. With a gesture she invited me to take a seat in a matching chair.

"I expected you later this afternoon, but since you're here now, it's good that we can just get this over and done with." She smiled widely. "I hope you brought the check for me!"

I blinked. "Excuse me. What check?"

"You're kidding, right? You do have papers for me to sign?"

"I have a few questions for you, Mrs. Glockner. That's all."

The woman's sunny disposition clouded and a thunderous flash of pique bolted across her pretty features. It suddenly reminded me of her daughter's mercurial moods—I'd seen plenty of them when the girl had worked for me.

"I thought I answered all of your questions," she said, almost petulantly.

"I've never spoken with you before, Mrs. Glockner."

"I can't believe you people don't talk to each other down at that office!" She threw up her hands. "How can you make a profit when you don't manage redundancies like this!"

"What?"

She stared at me and I stared back. "You're from the insurance company, right? You're here to close out my late husband's policy."

"I'm sorry you misunderstood, Mrs. Glockner. I'm not from any insurance company. I was simply a friend of your late husband's."

She sat back, smirking, and crossed her long legs. "A friend of Alfred's, huh? What kind of friend?"

"Alf was a customer at my coffeehouse. I also employed your daughter, Vicki, at one time; and to tell you the truth, Mrs. Glockner, Vicki was the one who asked me to step in and look into her father's murder. She has concerns that the detectives on the case are on the wrong track—"

"Well, she's right about that!" The woman cried. "Two of them showed up at my real estate office to question me—and on one of my busiest days, too! The jerk with the red, white, and blue babushka almost scared one of my clients off for good!"

"You're talking about Detective Franco?"

"Yes, that was his name."

I raised an eyebrow at that. *Why would Detective Franco bother to interview Shelly Glockner? Oddly thorough for a cop who claims he's only looking for an ordinary street thug in a random mugging.*

Mrs. Glockner shook her head. "That's always been one of my Vicki's *many* problems."

"What has?"

"She's just like her father. Can't let anything go!"

I gestured to the Alf-free pictures on the mantel. "I can see you don't have that problem, do you?"

"Why?" Mrs. Glockner narrowed her eyes. "Because I don't keep my husband's picture around for sentimental reasons?"

"I understand. I know he was about to become your *ex*-husband."

"New York State law requires that a couple live apart for a year before a divorce can be finalized. We'd just reached that merry milestone when Alf began dodging my lawyers. Not that it matters now." She sighed. "You see, Ms. Cosi, I met Alf in high school. We married a year after graduation. Vicki was born later—a pleasant surprise after years of thinking we couldn't even *get* pregnant." With a deep breath she rose, crossed to the mantel, and reached for a framed photo tucked behind the others. "We spent more than thirty years together, but this is what Alf truly loved."

She shoved the framed photo into my hands. It was an old one, showing a younger, slimmer Alf standing under the green awning of his restaurant: *Alfred's*. Beneath the name, in much smaller print were the words *Steaks, Chops, Fine Wine*.

"It was a traditional New York–style steakhouse bordering the La Tourette Golf Course. He borrowed and borrowed and mortgaged this house to open that restaurant. For a lot of years, it was a success. People came because they loved Alf. It was like a party every night—folks around here still tell me they miss it. Not that they did much to help keep him in business . . ." She fell silent.

"What happened?" I asked. "To Alf's restaurant, I mean."

Shelly Glockner took back the picture and stared at it. "The recession. The entire New York financial sector taking it in the neck. That and Alf's drinking, which got worse and worse as his business declined. Of course, it didn't help that he hadn't changed the menu or that dark, imposing decor in fifteen years. Tastes change, and that dump was so old-school! I told him so. Many times. Then Alf finally decided I might be right. He remodeled twice, changed the menu, offered deals, advertised. Nothing helped."

She set the picture behind the others and faced me. "Stupidly, I let him continue the farce. Really stupid because we hadn't saved much over the years."

"Why not?"

She waved her hand. "Vacations, spas, a pleasure boat, remodeling the house, the hot tub and sauna in the back—"

Plastic surgery for you, I silently added.

"We never expected the Manhattan financial sector to collapse, for heaven's sake! That it would take down dozens of restaurants all over the city! Anyway, Alf refused to close, tried to keep his place afloat by burning through the small nest egg we did have—which was *my* hard-earned money as well as his. But then his whole identity was wrapped up in that business."

"What do you mean his whole identity? He was a husband, a father—"

"Oh, please. That was never enough. Alf couldn't imagine doing anything but being a restaurateur. When he lost his place, he just"—she shrugged—"lost himself."

Just then, the phone rang. "Excuse me." She took the call, standing and staring into space. Then she barked into the receiver. "No! I told both parties that already. If Mr. Mahoud wants to back out, that's fine. But *we* keep the deposit. I haven't had a commission in six months, so I'm not playing here. You just warn him that I'll see him in court!"

She hung up and faced me again. "Are we done? I have a session with my personal trainer in twenty."

"Just a few more questions. What happened after Alf spent your nest egg on the restaurant?"

Mrs. Glockner exhaled with obvious impatience. "Alf wanted to take a second mortgage on our home, that's what happened. We'd just paid off this house after twenty-five years. I wasn't going to sit still for that, so I put my foot down and refused to allow it. Banks wouldn't help him, so Alf took out that ridiculous loan from our neighbor."

"Ridiculous? Why?"

"Because I knew the restaurant was dead by then, that's why! I knew we could never pay Omar Linford back—not without selling this house! Alf was deluding himself, Ms. Cosi. He was a failure and a drunk, and only digging himself in deeper with that loan. That's when I knew it was time to move on. So I had my lawyers draw up papers and I asked a judge for a separation."

I frowned, wondering how I might have fared with a marital partner like Shelly Glockner. Maybe it wasn't very nice of me to judge the woman, since I hadn't walked a mile in her cross-trainers. But I was a first wife, too. A bad marriage with an addict could hard-boil any woman's heart, but it appeared to me, after all those years together—not to mention Alf being a father to their daughter—that Mrs. Glockner was suspiciously unaffected by her husband's murder.

Once again, I began to wonder about that blackmail letter . . .

"I just had lunch with Omar Linford, Mrs. Glockner. Are you aware Mr. Linford is alleging that Alf tried to blackmail him?"

"That's preposterous."

"I heard the whole story from Mr. Linford himself."

"And you believe that pirate?"

"Mr. Linford claims he has proof. In fact—" I checked my watch. "I'm headed over there right now to pick up the note and turn it over to the NYPD, where it will be analyzed. With forensic science today, they can determine if the letter was really sent by Alf—fingerprints, fibers, DNA. It's amazing what they can do."

Frankly, I didn't know what the police could accomplish, but I wanted to shake Mrs. Glockner's brittle little tree, see what might come loose.

It worked. The second I mentioned the NYPD, her face flashed redder than Rudolph's nose.

"Why are you doing this?!" she demanded.

"I told you, your daughter asked me to find out——"

"It's Christmas, for heaven's sake!" She stomped her running shoe. "Why don't you just mind your own damn business and let Alf rest in peace!"

I locked eyes with the irate woman. "Don't you have something you want to tell me, Mrs. Glockner? Something that might help the police solve Alf's murder?"

That did it. Her face went from berry red to almost snow-white. She went quiet and her voice turned low and calm: "You have to leave *now*."

"Mrs. Glockner—"

"I have a busy day ahead of me."

Yeah, with your personal trainer. Then there's that highly lucrative moment when you sign off on the insurance policy and cash in on your husband's murder.

I rose. "If you change your mind about talking to me, you can reach me in the city at the Village Blend. Thank you for your time, Mrs.—"

The door slammed behind me, sending the tiny holiday wreath tumbling to the ground.

With a deep breath of wintry air, I retraced my pointy footprints across the snow-covered yard, back to Linford's sunporch. I was hoping that I hadn't been missed, but it didn't work out that way. Approaching the solarium, I paused when I heard angry voices. Peeking around a manicured bush, I spied Omar Linford and young Dwayne arguing in the room that Esther and I had vacated.

". . . and I'm not going to stop! I told you already!" Dwayne shouted.

"You have to listen to me, son," the older Linford calmly replied. "This is your life I'm talking about. Your whole life. You're gambling with your own future—"

"I told you, Dad. I told you all weekend. I'm going to do this *my* way!" Dwayne shouted, and then he bolted from the room.

"Don't be a fool!" Linford shouted after his son, then shook his head and sat down heavily in the solarium.

Better not go in that way, I decided, *or he'll know I was eavesdropping.*

I turned, moved around the house, and headed for the front entrance instead. Barely a moment after I pressed the bell, the double doors jerked open. Frowning down at me was a big-boned, Caucasian woman with strawberry-blond hair and a line of freckles across her patrician nose.

What's with all these amazons on Staten Island? Must be something in the water!

"Ms. Cosi?" the woman asked with a slight British accent.

"Yes."

"We wondered where you'd gone off to!"

"I'm sorry. My assistant had to leave," I explained quickly. "There were things I needed to discuss with her in private before she left."

"I see. Well, I'm Mrs. MacKenzie, Mr. Linford's executive assistant. Here's the letter you requested." She thrust a small manila envelope into my hand.

"Thank you." I stuffed the envelope into my bag. "May I wait inside to call a car service? I need to get to the ferry terminal."

The woman shook her head. "No need for a taxi. I was about to take Mr. Linford's car out to run some errands. I'll be happy to give you a ride. You'd better come in and get your coat."

As I did, I noticed the Linford boy standing a few feet away in the foyer, big arms folded. He said nothing, just glared. Then his pumped-up body brushed roughly past me and out the front door.

A minute later, I heard an engine gunning and tires squealing. Glancing out the window, I watched Dwayne's tricked-out SUV, with its fake bullet holes and airbrushed Viking raiders, disappearing down the tree-lined street.

Twenty-one

~~~~~~

"**Thank** you for the ride," I said, popping the car door.

"No bother, Ms. Cosi," the unsmiling Mrs. MacKenzie replied. "I have many errands today. You were just one of them."

As I stepped onto the walkway that led to the St. George Terminal, Mac pulled away from the curb. I noticed, however, that she didn't leave the area. Instead, she swerved the BMW toward the terminal's parking lot.

Odd, I thought.

Either Mrs. MacKenzie was taking the ferry herself today and didn't care for my company, or she was picking someone up on an arriving boat.

As my gaze followed her car into the lot, it snagged once again on that garishly tricked-out SUV that could only belong to Linford's son. Clearly, he'd caught a ferry to Manhattan already—or else he was waiting inside now and I'd be sharing my ferry ride with him, too.

The crowd was light inside the terminal's neo-deco waiting area. The vast space with the soaring ceiling reminded me of one of those big-box Costco-type warehouses, except this structure was trimmed in *Jetsons*-like polished steel and illuminated by flood lamps.

A ferry was docked and waiting, and I quickly boarded, although I needn't have hurried because it wouldn't actually take off for another ten minutes. In the interim, I traversed the flat decks of floating metal and found the little refreshment stand onboard. I stood in line to buy a cup of hot cocoa and was just taking my first sips as the ferry finally chugged out of its slip.

There weren't many passengers for this twenty-minute journey—not surprising at this time of day. Most riders were work commuters who packed the boat before nine and after five. As the engines throbbed, I moved quickly through the cavernous interior, skipping rows of sparsely populated benches for a choice position near the stern.

Despite the near-freezing temperature, I took a spot outside, close to the rail, just above the lapping waves. With the Blend now packed from morning till night and my mind working overtime to decipher the truth about Alf Glockner's tangled life, a few moments of peace was exactly what I needed.

I closed my eyes, and as the crisp salt-tinged wind whipped through my hair, I imagined it was clearing my mind, too. Then I leaned against the metal railing and relished the contrast of cold bracing sea against my cheeks and steaming hot chocolate against my lips.

If I commuted every day on this route, I might have become jaded about the ferry-crossing experience, but I wasn't. Not even close. As the boat swiftly cut a wake through Upper New York Bay, I opened my eyes again, drinking my fill of the cobalt blue chop, glistening in the afternoon sun.

In the distance, a black ocean liner smudged the pale horizon, its most likely destination the renovated docks of the Upper West Side. A sleek white pleasure craft zoomed by at twice our speed, slicing the water with a groove of froth as it veered toward the East River. Behind us, a little orange tug chugged along buoyantly; an FDNY fire boat motored steadily behind it.

Soon we were coming up on Liberty Island and its adjacent partner, the old immigration station of Ellis Island, now a historic landmark run by the National Park Service. Finally, there she was, Lady Liberty, soaring right above me, continuing her watch for the world's wretched refuse.

I gawked at the steel-framed sculpture, her copper sheeting oxidized green after more than a century at her post. She looked so strong and sturdy in the middle of the bay, lifting her lamp to light the path to our harbor. Emma Lazarus had called her the "Mother of Exiles," and I thought how right she was as I imagined how millions of immigrants to this country (my grandmother included) must have felt when they first saw her rising from the water, her gold-leaf torch held high.

When the Lady's noble features finally receded, I turned my attention back to a business that wasn't so noble. Reaching into my shoulder bag, my gloved fingers carefully fished out the manila envelope Mac had handed me.

Inside I found a smaller envelope, this one plain white. Linford's name and address were printed by what appeared to be a standard computer printer. A Santa Claus stamp carried a postmark from Manhattan's busy main branch on Eighth Avenue.

I'd hoped the letter would be handwritten, but no such luck. The writer typed the note and appeared to have printed it with the same computer printer used to address the postmarked envelope:

Dear Omar: I have a new proposition for you. If you care about your son's future, you will read every word of this note and do what it says. I know all about Junior Linford's little hobbies. Do you know what he is up to in those clubs? I do. If you don't want the NYPD and DEA to know too, then forgive my debt.

Just call it an early holiday gift! While you're at it, wire 50K more into my account by Christmas and I will stay quiet for good. My bank account number is below. That will finish our business forever. Bother me or fail to pay and I will tell what I know to the right people. Your son's future is now at stake. Do not try to contact me. Just do what I say in this letter and you will never hear from me again.

I read the letter twice. It didn't sound like the Alf I knew. Not at all. There was no signature, either. But the bank account number, typed at the bottom of the letter, was a clear lead. The NYPD could definitely check that out—make sure it really was an account controlled by Alfred Glockner. I suspected it wasn't. And if it wasn't, then another name would need to be added to my list of murder suspects.

My trip to Staten Island had yielded good information. I knew then that I'd made a smart decision waiting around for this letter. With the sense of a job well done, I carefully refolded the note and slipped it back into its envelope. Then I placed it into my shoulder bag and firmly zipped it closed.

I'd show the letter to Mike Quinn first. Then we could go to Detective Hong. (I still didn't trust Franco.) I only hoped Omar was right about his son's innocence, because I knew I couldn't stop Hong from tipping off the narcotics division and DEA, just in case.

I took another sip from my cooling cup and turned my thoughts to Shelly Glockner. Frankly, she struck me as likely a suspect for murdering Alf as Omar Linford. Her husband's life insurance policy was an obvious motive—though I couldn't imagine she would have pulled the trigger on Alf herself. No, for that, someone like Shelly would have used an accomplice—

My mind was so preoccupied with puzzling out the possibilities that I barely registered the clanging steps crossing the deck behind me. Before I could fully turn around, I felt a jolt at my shoulder. Someone had snatched my shoulder bag!

As if in slow motion, I saw my cup of cocoa tumbling from my gloved hands into the churning waters below. Then I followed it—but not of my own accord.

Strong hands lifted me like a sack of green coffee and tossed me right over the rail! The sunny harbor blurred for a moment; then I struck the churning waves. Frozen concrete would have been softer.

The ferry's roiling wake began spinning me literally heels over head. My nose, ears, and mouth filled with freezing water. The cold was mind numbing, but I was so *angry* I used my rage to fight against the shock of it.

Don't panic, Clare! You're a good swimmer! Don't panic!

But I couldn't even tell which way was up. The water was dark and murky, and I was still *spinning*! I was running out of air, too. I had to do something—

My coat!

The long, thick material was heavy with salt water and already half off. I ripped it free, letting it go. Feeling more than seeing, I noted which way the garment began to sink.

If that way is down, then this way must be up!

I kicked out immediately, shedding my blazer and slacks as I swam, giving my limbs the least possible drag as I propelled myself upward.

Light! I can see light!

I needed air. My lungs were burning so badly that I was ready to give in to the impulse and breathe in water. But I knew it would be the end of me, as good as giving up. So I fixed my gaze on that flickering sunlight above me, pictured the Mother of Exiles holding her golden torch, and stepped up my struggles.

Breaking the surface, I gasped and sputtered, then stared in horror at the vast field of choppy blue waves. The ferry was gone! With hardly any commuters on board, no one had noticed I'd been tossed over the side!

Desperately treading water, I cast about, wondering

which way to swim. The cold was excruciating—like a thousand icicles stabbing every pore in my body. Already the bone-deep chill was stiffening my muscles, making it hard to breathe, harder to stay afloat.

No, dammit! I'm not going to die like this!

I thought of my daughter and fought harder to stay conscious, tread water, stay alive. That's when I saw the orange tug and the fireboat! The two vessels had been sailing just behind the ferry!

"Help!" I shouted, the weak sound seemed lost in the splash of waves, the cries of circling gulls.

I yelled again and choked on a wash of briny liquid. I knew I was mere minutes—if not seconds—from freezing to death or drowning. That's when I heard the tug's loud horn, male voices shouting—

"To the starboard, Sean!"

"Donnie, toss me that hook!"

"Get a safety line around her!"

"No time, Connor. She's about done. I'm going in!"

I felt the rumble of an engine in the water, smelled diesel fumes. Something big, heavy, and canary yellow hit the water beside me. The splash itself almost sent me under again. Then strong arms closed around my numbed, nearly naked body.

"I got you, honey," a deep voice promised in my ear.

I lifted my face to find a strapping man holding me, his big, reassuring grin wide under a prominent nose and bushy dark eyebrows. "Don't pass out on me now! Hang on!"

I tried to speak, but shivers overwhelmed me and my teeth were chattering like a dentist's wind-up toy.

"Haul her up! Come on, quick! Her lips are turnin' blue!"

I think I blacked out at that point because the next thing I felt was a cold steel deck behind my back and bare legs. My camisole was soaked and half torn off, my lace bra leaving very little to the men's imaginations. I tried to speak, but strong, warm hands were pushing down on my diaphragm— hard enough to force salty water up my throat and out.

Gagging and sputtering, I finally realized that half a dozen burly firemen were standing around me, all in bright yellow FDNY life jackets.

"You're okay, ma'am. Let's get you warm."

As I sat up, a number of large hands wrapped thick blankets around me.

"Is there anyone we can contact for you?" asked one of the firemen.

"M-m-m-mike," I stammered. "Mike Quinn. He works at the—"

"I know Big Mike!" The dark-haired man who'd jumped into the water to save me patted my shoulder. "I'll put in a call. What's your name?"

I told him, my voice weak as I pulled the blankets closer around me. The deck was so cold! I tried to rise but stumbled. Several firemen instantly came to my aid. One simply hoisted me up and carried me inside the fireboat. The cabin was warm, and the man placed me on an aluminum-framed canvas stretcher and piled on another blanket, which I appreciated, even if I couldn't thank him.

I was shivering so hard now I couldn't speak. I couldn't see straight, either, but I think that was because my eyes were still stinging from the salt water. A new blanket was tossed over me, this one electric. The warmth felt delicious, like a fortifying drink I could gulp and swallow.

A few minutes later, I was starting to feel better and began to sit up. The dark-haired fireman who'd pulled me out of the water had been watching over me close by. He quickly returned to my side in sweats and a T-shirt, a towel around his neck, and handed me a cup of strong tea.

"No need to worry, pretty lady. You'll be okay. You said your name's Clare Cosi?"

"Clare," I repeated.

"I'm Sean. I just talked to Big Mike, *personally*. He'll be at the FDNY dock when we pull in."

"Thank you," I said.

"You were lucky we saw you. You wouldn't have lasted five minutes out there."

I sipped the tea but then felt woozy again. "I think I have to—"

Sean took my cup as I fell back on the stretcher. While I closed my eyes again, I could feel him tucking the blankets closer around me.

"You're in shock, pretty lady, just rest . . ."

The next thing I remember was the fireboat bumping up against a dock, men shouting to each other as the fire crew secured the vessel. A few minutes later, I heard whispers, felt a hovering presence.

I opened my eyes and stared up at an absolutely immense man, probably in his late forties, with bright scarlet hair, a cleft chin, and an absurdly large handlebar mustache (circa 1890). He stared at me, too, the skin around his blue gray eyes crinkling with amusement. Behind him, the rest of the fireboat's crew gathered, obviously curious.

"I've had many a damsel call out my name in her darkest hour—or in the dark of night," the big man loudly announced to his audience. "But I think I would have remembered *this* one."

"Excuse me?" I propped myself on my elbows. "Who are you?"

"Captain Michael Quinn of the FDNY, darlin'. Big Mike to my friends and a holy Irish terror to all others."

He smiled, a single gold tooth flashing, as he stroked his crimson mustache. "They told me your name's Clare Cosi and said you asked for me. How did you end up in the drink?"

"I was pushed off the ferry. My handbag was stolen."

Big Mike gestured to a member of the crew. "Radio the terminal. It's probably too late to stop the assailant from getting away, but maybe we can recover this poor woman's purse."

The imposing fireman faced me again. "I thought these

boys probably got it wrong, Clare, so I put in a call of my own before I came down here. You were looking for Little Mikey, right? Sixth Precinct. My cousin, Mike Quinn, the cop?"

"Detective," I clarified.

"Black sheep," he replied.

"Black sheep?" I repeated. "Mike's not a black sheep. He's not *little*, either. He's one of New York's finest."

The firemen watching us exchanged amused glances. Big Mike raised a bushy red eyebrow. "He's little compared to me, darlin'. And the Quinns are firefighters. New York's *bravest*. Little Mikey's the only *cop* in our clan." He cast a glance at his brothers in boots. "Black sheep."

The men laughed, and then a voice called from the deck. "Here come the boys in blue!"

A minute later, Detective Mike Quinn entered the fireboat's cabin, pushing through a wall of doting firemen to get to me. Dropping down beside the stretcher, he hugged me tightly.

"Clare, sweetheart, are you okay? What happened?"

"I'm fine," I said, soaking up his steady warmth. "I was on the ferry. My bag was snatched, then I got picked up and tossed over the side."

"Who did it, Clare? Did you see the person?"

"No," I said, then lowered my voice to a whisper. "But I'm almost positive I can hand you his head on a platter."

"Good, I'm glad, and we'll get to that. But first you're going to an ER—"

Before I could reply, Sean stepped up. "She's a tough one, Detective. Managed to make it to the surface after that arctic plunge in the ferry's chop. Saved her own life doing that."

"No," I clarified. "*You* did that, Sean. All of you did. Thank you."

Mike joined me in thanking the men—and that's when he noticed the big redheaded captain standing among the others.

"That's what firemen do, Mikey boy," the man declared with a smirk. "You hand out parking tickets. We save lives."

Mike released me and rose stiffly, facing the other Mike Quinn.

"Michael," he said flatly.

"Little Mikey," Captain Quinn replied, folding his arms. "Are the traffic violations keeping you busy?"

The men around us glanced uneasily at each other, clearly picking up on the bad blood between the two cousins. I frowned at the tense exchange and almost blurted out: *What's the beef between you two? You're family!*

But I held my tongue instead. This obviously wasn't the time or place for an in-depth history lesson on the mighty Quinn clan.

Fortunately, a pair of female paramedics interrupted us. "Okay, let's get you to the hospital," said one of the women.

"What?" I replied, shaking my head. "I'm fine. I don't need a—"

"Zip it, Cosi," Mike warned and leveled a gaze at the medics. "Do not listen to her. Listen to *me*. Get her on a stretcher and get her into your ambulance. *Now*."

THE ER doc assigned me to a hospital bed for "overnight observation." Once more, I tried to argue. Once again, Quinn wouldn't let me.

He never left the hospital, either. While I was being examined, I could hear him on his police radio, then on his cell phone to his partner, Sully. By the time the hospital staff moved me from the ER stretcher to a proper hospital bed, he'd even retrieved my stolen handbag.

"The ship was already emptied out by the time our uniforms got there," he explained, taking a seat on the edge of my hospital bed. "Your attacker was long gone, but they searched the ferry and recovered your purse. It was shoved under a bench on deck."

I took my bag and examined it. The strap was ripped. My wallet, cash, and credit cards were gone. My brush, makeup, and other incidental items were still there; even my keys to the Blend and my duplex apartment were still zipped inside their little pocket.

With a jolt I realized something else was missing. "The letter!"

Mike frowned. "What letter?"

"I had a letter in this bag. It was evidence of someone trying to blackmail Omar Linford." I was still pretty much convinced the note had not come from Alf. "It's been stolen, too! And that proves my case!"

"What case, Cosi? You better start from the beginning."

I brought Mike up to speed on everything I'd uncovered. ". . . and I'm sure it was Dwayne Linford who tossed me over the rail. I saw his tricked-out SUV in the parking area—I know it was his. Before he tore off, he was even fighting with his father about taking care of something *his* way. And that letter he tried to kill me to get was all about incriminating him."

"So the punk tossed you overboard to shut you up, too."

"He knew I was there with his father. He knew I was looking into Alf's murder. His father handed me a letter that practically declared the kid a drug dealer!"

Mike nodded. "Motive and opportunity." He reached for his police radio. "I'm calling Hong and Franco on this. It's their case."

"You think Dwayne Linford shot Alf, too, don't you?"

"Or had him shot. Yes. And made it appear to be a mugging—exactly your theory, Detective."

I shook my head. "Franco's going to be pissed."

"Why? He's right, too, isn't he? Think about it. If Dwayne Linford is a drug dealer, then he probably has known associates who are gangbangers. He could have hired one of them to do the hit on Alf and make it look like a street crime. We'll get a warrant to search Dwayne's property. Question him. If we're lucky, we'll get a confession, maybe the murder weapon, maybe the name of the person who did the hit."

"Just get him off the street, Mike."

"I will, sweetheart." He smiled, then took my hand and squeezed it. "Looks like you'll be getting what you want for Christmas, after all."

As I leaned closer for something a little more intimate than a hand squeeze, a light knock came on the half-open door. The heavenly smells of fresh-baked crust, tangy tomato sauce, and floral oregano preceded a familiar voice—

"Someone here order two pies?"

I glanced up to find a pair of giant pizza boxes coming toward me. Above them floated the carrot-topped face of Detective Sergeant Finbar Sullivan.

"Loaded?" Mike asked his partner.

"*Fully* loaded," Sully assured him with a grin.

Mike motioned him closer and turned to me. "Hungry?" he asked, lifting one of the box lids.

Closing my eyes, I inhaled the scent of pepperoni and sausage, roasted peppers and mushrooms. "Oh, Mike . . . ," I gushed as my empty stomach gurgled.

As usual, the man knew just how to make me swoon.

Twenty-two

~~~~~~

"**AND** then you *what*?!"

"I went into the water."

My ex-husband gritted his teeth. "Clare, why the hell didn't you leave with Esther?!"

"Because if I'd left with Esther, I never would have gotten the information to nail Alf's killer! And I'm perfectly fine, as you can see."

"Dumb luck, Clare. Emphasis on the *dumb*."

The next day was Tuesday and the Blend was as busy as ever. Matt stopped by during a late-morning lull, and I took a short break, grabbing a stool next to him at our espresso bar's marble counter. Sipping reviving jolts, I brought him up to speed on my adventures on Staten Island and literally *in* New York Harbor.

"So Dwayne Linford is in custody now?"

Matt pulled off his fisherman's sweater, too thick for the warmth of the cozy coffeehouse, draped it over his broad shoulders, and began rolling up the shirtsleeves on his well-developed forearms, the ones that came in so handy for me when I was locked in that Dumpster last week.

Unlike Matt, the heat of the roaring fire and steaming hot java didn't bother me. Not in the least. Frankly, after my freezing dip, I couldn't get warm enough.

"The police arrested Dwayne late last night at a Manhattan club," I explained. "He's got a high-powered lawyer—no surprise. But detectives are reviewing digital images from every Staten Island Ferry security camera they can get their hands on. They have warrants to search his home and SUV, and they already have him booked on a drug charge."

"What's the drug?"

"Marijuana. Mike said they found a 'nickel bag' on him when they picked him up. What's that mean, exactly?"

Among other things, my ex was a veteran lounge lizard. Name a remote outpost on the world's vast coffee belt and he'd give you detailed directions to the nearest place to party. If anyone knew what drug slang meant, it was Matt.

"A nickel bag is fifty dollars' worth of pot. It's like four or five joints max. They won't be able to hold him long for that, Clare. It's just possession, not sale."

I frowned. "I'm sure they'll find more evidence."

"Are you sure you didn't *see* him throw you over that rail. Just a glimpse?" Matt's brown gaze speared me. "Wouldn't that solve your flatfoot boyfriend's problem with the charge?"

"I'm not going to lie. Not to Mike. Not to his fellow cops on the force, and certainly not under oath in court."

"Dumb." Matt muttered again. "You said you know he did it, Clare. Isn't that enough to warrant a little lie?"

"No! Not when that lie is tantamount to perjury. And Mike would agree with me."

"Dudley Do-Right." Matt bolted the remains of his espresso, then shook his head. "If you only knew . . ."

I frowned, not liking the sound of that. "Knew what? Something about Mike?"

"Forget it." Matt looked away. "I shouldn't have said anything."

I stared at my ex. "Okay, *spill*. What do you know about—"

"Wait," Matt cut me off. "Didn't you ask me here to talk about Dexter?"

"You're changing the subject, but, yes, I did."

"Please, Clare, let's talk about that. What did you want to know?"

I stewed for a second, unhappy that Matt was keeping something from me about Quinn, but I didn't have time to argue. I was only on a short break, and when my relief came, I had to change fast and get up to Union Square for Alf's memorial service. I'd already sent up the boxes of goodies. The thermoses of coffee would come with me via taxi.

"Okay, Matt." I met his eyes. "I want to know why Dex was so cagey about his 'confidential' relationship with Omar Linford. Because if Dex is selling drugs, you better warn him he's about to get caught."

"He's not selling drugs, Clare. I spoke with him already, and he admitted what I suspected. Linford is Dex's silent partner in all of his Taste of the Caribbean shops."

"What's so secret about that?"

Matt leaned closer. He lowered his voice. "Dex took capital-improvement money from the city. If the bureaucrats knew Linford was Dex's partner, they never would have granted him the money to remodel his stores and purchase new freezers."

"Why didn't Dex just get the remodeling money from Linford straight up?"

"Because that's how Omar Linford ended up owning the Blue Sunshine company, that's why. Dex doesn't want Linford putting any more money into the business than he has already."

"But if Dexter and Omar took that money from the city, they're committing a crime."

"Which is why he was paranoid about admitting his business relationship, get it?"

"Hey there, Cosi Lady!"

I glanced up at a familiar voice and did a double take. A five-foot-eleven Santa's elf, complete with green leggings, velvet tunic, and a felt hat with a feather was grinning down at me.

"Shane? Shane Holliway?"

"In the flesh," he said. "Or in the tights, whichever you prefer, Clare."

The ex—soap actor took the bar stool beside me. Matt shot him a wary glance. Shane had shaved off his trendy stubble. He looked better with the clean chin, and his golden shag, lean cheek dimples, and twinkling blue eyes made him perfect elf material, too.

"I take it you're in a dress rehearsal with Tucker down the street," I said.

"Perceptive." Shane winked. "But then Tucker did tell me you're an amazing sleuth."

I laughed. "Well, your tights are a dead giveaway."

"The benefit party's tonight at the Public Library's Main Branch on Forty-second. Are you coming?"

"Oh, no," I said. "That thing's exclusive. Invitation only."

"Tuck can get you in! Come on, Clare. You don't want to miss my tight green buns leaping over sugarplum props, do you?"

I laughed again. "You make it sound tempting. I'll think about it, okay? Can I get you something in the meantime?" I asked, standing up.

"Are you kidding? *Method's* my middle name: Candy Cane Latte—easy on the whipped cream. This outfit's pretty unforgiving."

"You don't have to worry," I said, heading behind the coffee bar again. "You look great."

"Thanks."

As I whipped up the latte, Shane called over to Dante. "Hey, Silva, I saw you on YouTube! You're an official World Wide Web star!"

"I know!" he replied from behind the espresso machine. "My roommates told me I have almost as many hits as Keith Judd holiday shopping on the Upper West Side!"

"My girlfriend saw that one, too," Gardner mentioned as he worked the register. "She's been into Judd since that fighter pilot movie he did ten years ago. Now she wants to check out every boutique he went into."

"You're kidding?" I said. "People care about that stuff?"

"Oh, yeah," said Dante.

"You bet." Gardner nodded.

"I don't believe it."

"It's no joke, boss," Dante said, quickly tamping fine grinds into the espresso machine's portafilter. "Do you know every single store Judd was shown going into has a line out the door today?"

I blinked at that. New York 1 news had just done a story on how slow the shopping season was this year. Many shops were in real danger of going under.

Gardner handed change to a customer. "If you ask me, whoever took that Keith Judd footage should have gone to those stores and asked for a cut."

"I guess I can't object," I murmured. "I mean, the Web is why we're doing so well this year."

I finished mixing Mr. Elf's Candy Cane Latte: fresh espresso, crème de menthe syrup—with a pump each of cherry and vanilla—perfectly microfoamed milk, a kiss of whipped cream, and sprinkles of crushed candy cane and shaved chocolate. I slid it across the bar.

"On the house, Shane," I said. "It's the least I can do for a Santa's helper."

"Oh, you're a babe." He took a few sips and made orgasmic noises. "Sweet . . ."

I smiled. "Good?"

"Good? Listen, Cosi Lady. After the benefit, I'm coming back here for another. Then how about you and me do a little work in my *tool* shop tonight?"

Matt rolled his eyes.

"I think you mean *toy* shop, don't you, Shane?" I replied.

"No. I meant what I said."

Oh, brother. "That's very flattering, I'm sure. But I'm in a relationship with someone special."

Matt grunted at that. I shot him a look.

"Come on," Shane pressed. "You don't have to get *serious* with me. We can just, you know . . ." He winked at me again. "Play."

"Really, I mean it," I said firmly. "No thanks."

Shane just smiled wider. "I'll see you again, Cosi Lady. 'Cause *challenge* is my middle name." After yet another wink, he was gone.

Matt smirked. "I thought *method* was his middle name."

I shrugged.

"I don't know," said Matt. "Maybe you should consider it."

"Consider *what*?"

"The elf."

"Not funny."

"I'm half serious, actually."

"Now why would you even half-seriously suggest a thing like that?"

"Because I don't want to see you hurt."

"Excuse me?"

"Clare . . ." Matt looked down at his empty demitasse. When he glanced back up again, he met my eyes. "I don't think you and your guard dog are on the same page."

"What page is that exactly?"

"The exclusivity page."

"Come again."

"Look, I'm going to be straight with you here. I've seen Quinn around with another woman."

"What do you mean, 'another woman'?"

"I mean you mentioned to me that the man was doing all this overtime and was so busy. But last week I stopped in at Enoteca's bar and saw him having dinner with a really beautiful redhead."

"A redhead?" I stilled, remembering that stunning woman I'd seen in here a number of times. The one with the obvious grudge against me. *It can't possibly be the same woman, can it?*

"And then I saw the two of them again, having breakfast early one morning in the East Village—very early. Early enough that I can imagine what they were doing the night before. Doesn't the man bunk over there?"

"Yeah, his apartment's in Alphabet City. But there must be some explanation. Maybe she's part of a case."

"Quinn was in an intense conversation with this lady both times. It didn't look professional. It looked personal. And this redhead—she looked familiar to me, too. Then I finally remembered where I'd seen her before. So I looked her up."

"What to you mean, you looked her up?"

"She was a Victoria's Secret model about fifteen years ago. Really hot. Cover model material. I keep all the holiday issues. They put her on the cover with a Santa hat, little black boots, and a naughty Mrs. Claus baby-doll nightie."

"You're making me want to throw up."

"Sorry," Matt said. He blew out air and ran a hand through his short, dark Caesar. "I wasn't going to tell you, Clare, but the elf actually looks like a good time, and"—he shrugged—"I thought maybe you deserved that. I mean, why save yourself for a guy who obviously wants an open relationship?"

I blinked, dumbfounded for a moment. "You can't be right," I finally said. "I don't believe you."

"Suit yourself," Matt said with another shrug. "But don't say I didn't warn you."

"Hey, boss!" Dante suddenly called. "We can use a hand again! Things are backing up."

"Okay!" I rose on legs that were suddenly a little shaky. Then I mentally shoved Matt's claims aside, deciding there had to be an explanation, and went back to work.

Matt departed with a sad little wave. An hour later his mother came in waving, too. But her gestures weren't sad or little—they were big and frantic.

"Clare, dear!" she called, motioning me to step away from the espresso machine.

"Take over, guys," I told my two-man crew. "I'll be right back."

Madame looked stunning this morning in a jacket of whipped-cream soft suede and matching slacks. A hat and gloves the color of cappuccino foam, both trimmed in fine-spun faux fur, completed the ensemble.

"You look gorgeous," I said, pecking her cheek.

"Thank you, dear! It's sleigh-ride couture." She laughed. "I bought it especially for my little Vermont getaway with Otto." We sat down at a café table near the fireplace. "We just got back this morning."

I smiled. "Candy canes by candlelight?"

"Yes, yes—it was all quite romantic, but that's not what I've come to tell you. Something alarming has occurred."

"Are you talking about the ferry incident? Did Matt tell you?"

"Ferry incident? No, there's nothing here about a ferry . . ." She reached into her blond leather tote bag and pulled out a tabloid newspaper. A yellow Post-it marked the Gotham Gossip column. "This is what I'm talking about!"

"Oh my God."

Splashed across the tabloid's fold was a series of color photographs, set up frame by frame, showing an intimate moment between Phyllis Chatsworth and her executive producer, James Young. The two were standing in the foyer of a storefront, looking at jewelry. James put his arm around Phyllis and squeezed. She put her head on his shoulder. And in both of their hands were shopping bags—Tourneau, Saks, and Tiffany. The exact same bags I'd seen in Young's apartment the day after Alf was killed!

"Didn't Mr. Young tell you he was out shopping the day Alf was murdered?" Madame whispered. "Didn't he tell you he thought Alf saw him with bags from high-end shops and decided to burglarize him?"

"Yes."

"Well, what Young obviously didn't tell you was that a photographer was following him, too."

I quickly looked at the photo credit. "Ben Tower!"

Madame nodded. "Mr. Dewberry is very upset, Clare. *The Chatsworth Way* is an important asset for him, and these photos threaten that asset."

She was right. I skimmed the column, written by a man both Madame and I had tangled with before—scandal hound Randall Knox. Knox speculated whether the married relationship counselors who hosted one of the hottest TV shows on the air didn't need counseling themselves.

I added it up. "Madame, did Mr. Dewberry approach you with this? I mean, does the man expect you to do something about it?"

"Yes, but I should explain. You see, Otto and I have had a number of very nice dinners with Mr. Dewberry and his wife. They're very generous people. And Mr. Dewberry has a very good memory. He recalled my mentioning our previous dealings with Randall Knox *and* Ben Tower, the photographer of record here."

"You're dining out on tales of our sleuthing, aren't you?"

Madame looked sheepish. "Well, they are good stories, dear. Quite entertaining!"

"Okay . . ." I sat back in the café chair. "What's your plan?"

"I have a few angles to play with our Mr. Tower—and I wanted to know if you'd like to accompany me. I thought you might be curious, given the timing of his pictures, so close to Alf's murder."

"I *am* curious. Tower may have seen something incriminating. He may even have a proof sheet that shows more . . ." I quickly brought Madame up to date with Dwayne Linford's arrest. "But the police still haven't found a murder weapon or gotten a confession from the kid. So every little bit of evidence is going to help the authorities pin him to Alf's murder."

I checked my watch. "I'm going to Alf's memorial service right after my shift. You go to see Ben Tower and do your thing. Let's talk afterward, okay? You can tell me what you dig up."

Madame nodded, her blue eyes brightening. "What fun!"

Twenty-three

"**CLARE**, I'd like you to meet someone . . ."

Vicki Glockner approached me with a shaky smile; her hazel green eyes, so much like her dad's, were still red and puffy from the moving memorial service we'd attended in the storefront church above. We were now mingling in the church basement—a brightly lit space with colorfully painted walls and a big Christmas tree in the corner.

At least two hundred Traveling Santas packed the place. Homeless men and soup kitchen workers had come, too, people who remembered Alf from his entertaining "stand-up Santa" visits in the shelter system. Even some of Alf's old Staten Island friends were here. Omar Linford was not among them, and I wasn't surprised. Shelly Glockner wasn't here, either. But Vicki had warned me a week ago that her mother probably wouldn't come to today's service.

Like me, Vicki had worn a simple black pantsuit for the event. Her mass of caramel-colored curls was tied back in a tame ponytail. Walking close beside her now was a big, bald man. Tall and only slightly paunchy, he was dressed simply in black slacks and an open-neck black shirt. The man's cheeks were cheerfully ruddy, his brown eyes lively under bushy brows, and the soft brown beard, trimmed close to his face, was shot with only a bit of sliver.

"Clare," she said. "This is Peter Dominick."

"Just call me Brother Dom," the man insisted. He smiled down at me from his substantial height. His voice was very deep but soft and kind. "I understand you're the lady to thank for the delicious boxes of cookies and muffins and all those hot thermoses of coffee."

"She's the one!" Vicki nodded, her jingle bell earrings ringing.

Vicki had been wearing those same earrings a week ago, the day after Alf had died. I suspected they'd been a gift from her dad, which probably meant they wouldn't be coming off her ears anytime soon.

"Clare's been great," Vicki said. "She's doing *a lot* for Dad right now."

"How's that?"

Vicki lowered her voice. "She found Dad's killer."

Brother Dom's bushy brown eyebrows rose. "So you're a policewoman, too?"

"No, no! I'm a coffeehouse manager. I just asked a few questions and helped the police out."

"Vicki!" One of the Traveling Santas was waving for her to come to the goody table. "There's a girl here asking for you!"

"I'll be right there!" she called. "Excuse me."

Brother Dom and I talked for a few minutes about Alf— and I was glad to have this chance to question the man. Dom had founded the Traveling Santas a few years before. A former Franciscan monk, he now worked with the city and several of the city's churches to bring aid to the homeless and hungry.

"It's funny," I told Brother Dom. "The more I pieced together about Alf's life, the more I wondered about the gaps in it. There are so many things that make no sense about the man."

"Like?"

"Like I know he was a failed restaurateur. I know he had an alcohol problem and his marriage fell apart—"

"Yes, Alf was an alcoholic, struggling to work through the twelve-step program. When I first met him, he had a lot of problems."

"But when I met him, he wasn't struggling at all. He seemed so certain about life, so happy, so together. He was full of optimism and purpose. His primary concern whenever I spoke with him was helping others. I just can't reconcile the stories I'm hearing about his past—and his past actions—with the living man I knew. Or thought I knew."

"You have questions, Clare. Ask and you shall receive answers—" He laughed. "If I can provide them . . ."

"Okay—what do you think turned Alf around? I mean, what made him suddenly want to do charitable work?"

"*A Christmas Carol.*"

"A song?"

"The book." Brother Dom's attention wavered when someone came up to speak with him.

Just then, my cell phone went off, vibrating in my pocket because I'd silenced the ringer for the service. I saw from the Caller ID that it was Quinn.

"Mike?"

"I have bad news."

I braced myself—suddenly remembering Matt's ugly story about some redhead. But Quinn's news wasn't personal.

"Dwayne Linford's going to walk, Clare."

Crap. "What happened?"

"There's nothing we can hold the kid on. The cameras in the St. George Terminal parking area confirm his story. Dwayne picked up a man on the incoming ferry—a college counselor from NYU that his father set him up to meet. His dad wants him to get a degree in music instead of trying to make a living as a club DJ. That's what Dwayne claims you overheard them fighting about. His father wanted him to keep the appointment with the counselor."

"Did you confirm his alibi?"

"Of course. The guy checks out—Grant Bass works at NYU. We spoke with him. As a favor to Omar, he took the ferry over to meet with Dwayne. The kid was angry, but he didn't disobey his dad's wishes. He picked up the man at the ferry for their meeting. There's no way Dwayne was on that ferry so there's no way he could have stolen the blackmail note and thrown you overboard."

I closed my eyes, tried to think. "Linford had a secretary. A woman named Mrs. MacKenzie. She didn't pull out after she dropped me off. She parked her BMW in the lot."

"I don't know, Clare." Quinn exhaled. "A woman wouldn't have had the strength to toss you the way you described."

"This woman was *big*, Mike. I think she could have."

"Come to the Sixth as soon as you can and take a look at these digital recordings. If you know what she looks like, you'll have a better shot at spotting her movements."

"Okay, I'll come to see you within the hour."

"I won't be here. Sully and I have a meeting uptown. Ask for Hong or Franco. They'll help."

I shuddered at the thought of seeing Emmanuel "Do-Rag" Franco again. "I'll ask for Hong," I replied.

"Fine—just be careful, Clare. *Do not* go anywhere alone today. Okay? Are you hearing me? Whoever threw you off that boat is *not* in custody. Do you understand?"

"I understand, Mike. I do. I won't take any chances."

After saying good-bye to Quinn, I noticed that Brother Dom was still hovering close by. He turned away from another conversation to get back to ours.

"Have you ever read it, Clare?" he asked me, motioning me toward the goody table.

Read it? "I'm sorry?" I said. My mind was still spinning from Mike's news. "Read what?"

"Have you read *A Christmas Carol*?"

"Oh, right. You were saying that book was important to Alf . . . No, I've never actually read the Dickens story. But everyone knows about Scrooge, right? The terrible misanthrope who hated Christmas?"

Dom filled two paper cups with hot coffee and handed me one. "What else do you remember, Clare? About Scrooge?"

"Well, let's see . . . he was a rich man but he was also very unhappy—and greedy and selfish and cynical. He loved money and had no use for humanity or humanitarians. *Bah humbug.*"

Dom smiled and sipped his coffee. "Go on."

I paused, trying to remember the story, and took a long caffeinated sip from my own cup—as mystified as ever how the simple sharing of a warm cup o' joe could be both comforting and fortifying at the same time.

"I think Scrooge had a business partner, didn't he?"

Dom nodded. "His name was Marley."

"Yes, I remember now . . . the story opened with Marley already dead. It was Christmas Eve and Scrooge went home alone. That's when Marley's ghost comes to his home to haunt him. And then what happens?"

"Marley warns Scrooge that he's going to be visited by other specters—"

"Oh, right! The spirits of Christmas Past, Present, and Future."

Brother Dom nodded. "And through those visits, Scrooge is made to remember the man he once was, examine the man he truly is, and consider the man he might still be. Most important of all, Clare, Scrooge makes a decision about the man he no longer wants to be."

"And you're telling me that single book changed Alf's perspective?"

"A single chapter, actually. You see, Alf lost everything—his worldly clothes were stripped away. And when that happens to a man or woman, he or she has nowhere to hide any longer. That human being must face the ultimate question of identity: Who am I? Without my clothes and job and worldly goods? Without even my friends and family? What is it that makes me who I am? And more important, who do I want to be in this life and in this world?"

Brother Dom's voice was deep and strong and full of earnest passion. I could see the fire in his eyes, the certainness of his purpose and place in the world. He was a natural minister, and hearing him speak helped me understand something more about my late friend. Alfred Glockner hadn't gotten out of the dark woods all by himself. He'd followed in the footsteps of a man who knew the way.

"When we crossed paths," Brother Dom continued, "Alf was simply looking for work. The Traveling Santas do make money for their time. They work hard and they take a percentage of what they collect. But before one of my Santas puts on that beard and red coat, I have a long talk with him over coffee—"

He lifted his paper cup and winked at me.

"I then ask our aspiring Santa to read *A Christmas Carol*. Alf took the book the day we talked and came back to me. He stopped reading after one chapter."

"Why?"

"Because that's all he needed to read."

"I don't understand."

Brother Dom motioned for me to follow him. I did. We moved out a door, away from the loud hum of the talking crowd and into a long, quiet hallway that had been white-washed clean—but then covered anew with colorful posters and photos. There were families and children beaming at me, smiling elderly people, waving groups of men. I got the impression they were people that Dom's organization had helped. He confirmed it. Finally, the man opened another door, ducked inside, and came out again.

"Read the book, Clare," he said, handing me a worn copy of Charles Dickens's beloved tale. "I think you'll see what Alf saw. There's a passage at the end of the first chapter that moved the man to tears, made him understand that it wasn't too late for him to change his perspective. I'm glad he had that reconciliation before he died."

"Thank you for this," I said, holding up the book. "My life's been crazy busy lately, but I'll read it soon."

"That's the trouble with the holidays," Dom said with a smile. "People forget the reason—"

"—for the season, I know!"

As we walked back to the wake, I glanced again at the array of faces on Dom's hallway walls and asked about this year's donations. Given the economy, I expected the news wouldn't be great, and it wasn't.

"Donations are low this year, I'm afraid. I doubt very much we'll meet our goal."

"I'm sorry to hear it."

"A sad irony—with the top rungs feeling the pinch, hands remain clenched. But the people on the bottom rung need help more than ever. Losing Alf is tough for that reason, too. His collections were among the highest in the city, right behind his roommate, Karl Kovic."

Karl—that's right. "I've wanted to talk to Karl, Brother Dom. But I don't know what he looks like. Can you introduce me?"

"I wish I could, but Karl didn't come to the service today."

I stopped walking. That sounded wrong. "He didn't come to the memorial service of his own roommate?"

"That's right." Dom turned to face me.

"Why not? Do you know if they were estranged?"

Brother Dom sighed and folded his arms. "The two were longtime friends—since high school. It was Karl who introduced Alf to me and got him the job as a Traveling Santa."

"Then why isn't he here?"

"I'm afraid it's my fault."

"Your fault?"

Dom nodded. "Word came to me a few days ago that Karl has been rather, well—*naughty.*"

"Naughty?"

"It's not a sin what he did, you understand, just not something I approved of. He was shooting YouTube celebrity sightings while on duty as a Traveling Santa."

"Celebrity sightings?"

Dom shook his head, obviously embarrassed. "The Traveling Santa suit let him blend into the background on the

Upper West Side—the area Karl's been covering for several years now. Because he was roaming the city streets all day, he decided to keep his eyes peeled for celebrities, actors, TV stars entering boutiques and shops or eating at restaurants. He filmed them with a small camera, and then he'd approach those establishments and ask if they wanted to buy the footage. Many of them did, and then they'd release it—usually to the Internet for viral publicity."

"Karl took kickbacks for celebrity photography?" I remembered that footage the guys at the Blend were discussing of actor Keith Judd shopping at some Upper West Side boutiques.

"It's legal," Dom pointed out. "He was filming in public places. And whether the store owners paid or didn't pay was entirely up to them. It was simply a form of advertising. But I didn't consider it a good reflection on our charity. So I decided to clip his wings. I told him I was taking him off the street and putting him to work in our offices. He didn't like that. We argued and he quit. Karl's not the most patient man. I've tried ministering to him, but he's remained hard—a much harder case than Alf ever was."

As we returned to the party, more people came up to speak with Brother Dom. I thanked him for his time and the book, and stepped away, considering his words.

If Karl Kovic was filming video on the Upper West Side for money, was Alf doing the same thing in the Village? The two men were old friends. They shared the same apartment. They were both Traveling Santas . . .

The economic downturn meant retail businesses needed every advantage to pack shoppers into their stores. Most would pay for that advantage. Alf probably saw that kind of thing as helping the stores anyway—it certainly helped mine.

It was all legal, too, just like Dom said, but what if Karl and Alf wanted a bigger payday? Ben Tower was a professional photographer who was able to get big payoffs for celebrity photos like the ones Madame had just shown me in Gotham Gossip of James Young and Phyllis Chatsworth.

Could Karl and Alf have gotten involved in that kind of photography, too?

That's when it hit me. The pictures of Young and Phyllis, the timing of that day—it all added up! Suddenly, I knew why Alf was on James Young's balcony—it wasn't to burglarize his place! Pulling out my cell phone, I strode swiftly back to that quiet hallway and speed-dialed Madame's cell.

She answered immediately. "Yes?"

"It's Clare. Are you with Ben Tower, by any chance?"

"Why, yes. We're having drinks right now at a bar on—"

"Tell Tower you're hearing from a source *right now* who's confirming that he's been buying photos from Alfred Glockner and Karl Kovic."

"Yes. Hold please."

I heard some low voices in the background. Then Madame's voice more clearly. "I cannot reveal my source, Ben."

Madame came back on the line. "Yes, Ben is confirming what you've discovered."

Oh, my God. "Put me on with him."

"Are you sure, dear? I thought you were trying to remain anonymous?"

"It doesn't matter now."

"Hello? Who is this?" Ben's voice was familiar—a little tentative and also a little slurry. Madame wasn't stupid. Treating a man like Ben to a liquid lunch would loosen his tongue in record time!

"This is Clare Cosi, Mr. Tower."

"Oh, God," he muttered. "The coffee-slinging *snoop*."

"Charmed, I'm sure."

Our exchange wasn't pleasant or long, but it did yield what I'd suspected. Alf Glockner had been sending digital images to Ben Tower the day he was killed.

"Alf sent me photos of James Young and Phyllis Chatsworth in the afternoon. He lost the pair for many hours, then caught up with them again going into a bistro across from the White Horse Tavern. That's the last photo I got from Alfred."

And that explained why Alf had been sitting in that tavern and abruptly rose and ran. He hadn't been following James Young to rob him. He'd been following James Young and Phyllis Chatsworth back to Young's apartment building to get more photos of them.

I remembered the night I found Alf's body. His boot prints in the snow had led into the courtyard, where he appeared to pause and loiter. *He probably stood out there in the dark, watching for a light to go on among the building's windows. Then he climbed the fire escape hoping to get some pictures of the couple together in Young's living room.*

It all made sense now—Omar Linford had told me Alf was paying him back a little at a time: one thousand here, a few hundred there. Alf was also doing the twelve-step program; and one of those steps was to make *amends*. He was obviously trying to pay back his neighbor, pay off a loan that Omar had made him in good faith.

Although I couldn't condone what Alf had done, I could understand why he'd done it. Making money on those photos wouldn't just help him make amends to Omar. As long as he was continuing to pay back the man, Alf could feel that he was protecting his wife and daughter from being pressured in any way to sell their house and repay that loan.

The only question now was, who shot Alf? Did James Young do the deed after all? Phyllis Chatsworth? How the heck was I going to prove *that*? And *who* the heck threw me off that ferry? Linford's amazon of a secretary still seemed the most likely suspect for that.

"There you are!"

As I reentered Brother Dom's crowded basement, I looked up to find Vicki coming toward me with Esther Best in tow.

"Hey, boss!" Esther greeted me with surprising energy. "I've had exams all morning—and, man, am I glad my finals are finally over!"

"Is that why you missed the service upstairs?"

"Yes, but I made it for the wake—" She put an arm

around Vicki's shoulder and gave her a squeeze. "Anyway, I should have called you last night, but I was cramming."

"Called me about what?" I asked. Esther still didn't know about the ferry incident, but this wasn't the time and place for that particular update.

"I have something weird to show you."

"Show her! Show her!" Vicki pointed to Esther's cell phone.

I studied the images on the little screen. "What is this?"

"It's some guy coming out of the side door of Vicki's mother's house. When you went in the front door yesterday, I was still warming up your old car, but I noticed this guy coming out. See . . ."

Esther reached over and toggled the photos forward. Frame by frame they showed a man who looked a lot like Alf. He was about Alf's height and weight with longish gray brown hair and a mustache. He wore a long, white terry-cloth robe and slippers, and the digital photos showed him moving out the side door of Shelly Glockner's ranch, then toward the back of the house—where there was a glass-enclosed hot tub and sauna.

"Who is this guy?" I whispered.

"Karl!" Vicki blurted out so loudly that a number of heads turned our way. "That's my father's roommate, Karl Kovic!"

Alarms were going off in my head. "Your mother is involved with Karl?"

"If she is, it's news to me," Vicki said looking fairly freaked. "And I can tell you I'm not happy about it. That guy is so *mean*. I can't stand him!"

I stepped closer. "Mean how? Could he have hurt your dad?"

"Oh, no. I don't think so. They were good friends. Karl never said much to me when I visited my dad at their place. He mainly kept to himself. It's the kitten. That's why he's mean."

"What kitten?" Esther asked.

"My dad found a little white kitten a few weeks ago, in an alley—"

"Oh, the kitten!" Alf had told me about the little thing. He'd been forced to sneak it into Karl's apartment because the building didn't allow pets.

"I asked Karl to keep the kitten for a short while," Vicki explained. "My mom won't let me have a pet at home, but I'm planning on moving into the city in a month or so. Then I'd be able to take care of it. Karl's refusing to keep it for me until then! He says he's just going to dump it in the city shelter."

I scowled. "That *is* mean."

Vicki's hazel green eyes, still red from crying upstairs, began welling once more. "Can you help me again, Clare?"

I nodded. "Of course, I'll stop by this evening and pay a visit to Karl. I have a cat already—I can certainly take care of another for as long as you like. And anyway, it seems to me Karl Kovic and I have quite a few things to talk about."

Twenty-Four

∼∾∾∾∾∾∾∾∾∾∾∾∾∾∾∾∾∾∾∾∾

"**THERE** he is. Thanks!"

The second I saw Matt, I paid the cabbie and climbed out of the idling taxi. It was past six o'clock, already dark, and for a few minutes I was actually worried I'd phoned my ex-husband with the wrong location.

Vicki supplied the address, but it wasn't an address that made sense to me. I mean, in the past Alf had mentioned he lived uptown, but I assumed it was *way* up, some tiny apartment on the fringes of Harlem where rents were in the realm of being reasonable.

This part of the Upper West Side, just north of midtown and west of Central Park, was dominated by stately historic buildings sandwiched between gleaming new co-op towers and high-rise offices. The whole neighborhood seemed way too pricey for a lowly Traveling Santa to afford.

All around me, young professionals were hurrying home from office jobs. Backslapping businessmen were ducking into bars, socialites were strutting their stuff in designer ensembles, and couples in evening wear were discreetly debating places to have a light bite before attending Handel's *Messiah* at nearby Lincoln Center.

In my worn jeans, scruffy sneakers, and old parka, I suddenly felt underdressed. My ex-husband, by contrast, fit right in. Six feet tall with broad shoulders, Matteo Allegro cut a dashing figure in his black-tie formalwear and tailored topcoat. More than one strutting socialite turned her salon-perfected head as she passed him on the sidewalk. I flagged him down with a waving arm, my bag (a new one after the ferry incident) slipping off my shoulder.

"Where were you when I called?" I asked, setting Java's cat carrier down on the sidewalk to haul my shoulder bag back up my arm. "On your cell it sounded like a party?"

"It was."

"Well . . ." I gave his designer tux the once-over. "Thanks for coming, Double-Oh-Seven."

"Very funny."

"No kidding, Matt. I'm glad you can help me out here."

He waved a gloved hand. "I wasn't even at the main event—that's at eight at the public library. Bree and I were at this pre-party happy hour thing that Dickie Celebratorio is throwing."

"Celebratorio?" I raised an eyebrow. "I didn't know you were going to the big Dickie party."

"Neither did I. Bree gets the invitations. I escort her—and since this 'benefit' thing is really just a PR stunt for some kiddie holiday movie, Bree's a VIP guest."

"Because she's press?"

"Yep. She assigned a writer and photographer—I think she wants as many shots of the celeb attendees as the event itself."

"Well, Tucker deserves the coverage. He spent hours rehearsing some kind of Santa's workshop production number for the thing. Make sure you give him a big hand when the show's over."

Matt blew a hot breath into the frosty air. "I doubt we'll

stay long enough to see the show. Bree's kind of like a shark. She has to keep moving."

"Moving where?"

He shrugged. "She typically gets to a party, orders one drink, circles the room, and by the time I've settled in, she's snapping her fingers telling me it's time to move on to the next event. I'm beginning to feel like a freaking nomad."

"That's rich, given your globe-trotting gene."

"New York used to be my chance to *stop* moving for a little while."

"Well, I appreciate your coming. You know I wouldn't have called if I didn't really need your help, and I promise I won't get you arrested this time."

"Actually, Clare, compared to the dulling sameness of Manhattan social gatherings, Dumpster diving with you was kind of fun." He smiled. "So, what's up?"

"No Dumpster diving. All we're going to do is have a little talk with Alf's former roommate, Karl Kovic. I'm going to *persuade* him that it's in his best interest to hand Alf's orphaned kitten over to me, rather than ship it off to the city pound."

"We're here to steal a *kitten*?"

"Yes."

Matt groaned. "And you need me because . . ."

"You're the persuasion. I also plan to quiz Kovic about a few things."

"Like?"

"Like the particulars of his naughty extracurricular activities." I updated Matt on Brother Dom's revelations. "And as far as I'm concerned, this posh address is just another nail in Karl Kovic's coffin. Ben Tower confirmed to me that Kovic was selling him celebrity photos."

"Alf's friend Karl is beginning to sound like the grifters I see in every major city on this planet."

"Yeah, I know the type: Man of a Thousand Schemes."

Matt's smile was suddenly gone. "Guys like that can be pretty nasty, Clare." He flexed his gloved fingers. "It's a good thing you asked me to come along."

"Well, Mike read me the riot act on watching my back. I'm trying to listen."

"The flatfoot's right. Anything else I should know about this guy?"

"He's in some kind of relationship, probably sexual, with Alf's wife, Shelly. If he denies it, I have proof."

"Photos?"

I nodded. "Esther provided me with cell phone shots that would make a low-rent PI proud."

Matt was smiling again. "I can see being your muscle is going to be a lot more fun than being Breanne's arm candy." Arching a dark eyebrow, he slipped into a Sean Connery brogue. "Though perhaps I should have brought my Beretta, Miss Moneypenny."

"I'm sure the threat of your left hook will be enough." I picked up Java's carrier. "Come on . . ."

I led Matt up the avenue, then down a side street. A few minutes later I found the address. "This is it. The Wiseman Apartments."

Matt tilted back his head to take in the six-story brick building. It appeared newly renovated with big windows, restored pediments, and freshly painted wrought-iron grilles.

He glanced back down at me. "Pretty nice digs for a Traveling Santa."

"My thought exactly."

The lobby of Wiseman Apartments had eggshell walls and inset tile floors in a black-and-white checkerboard pattern. Lucky for us, there was no doorman. A young woman leaving the place in an open coat and a holiday party dress sweetly held the door for us (really for *Matt*), and we slipped inside. There were rows of polished brass mailboxes with buttons under each to ring the tenant.

"K. Kovic, Five C," Matt read. "Shall we buzz him?"

"He might not let us in if we ask, so let's not give him the option."

The solitary elevator seemed stuck on three, so we took the stairs and reached the fifth floor a few minutes later. The climb was a chore for me——but it seemed to invigorate Matt. (No doubt a conditioned effect from trekking all those steep trails on high-altitude coffee farms.)

"Let's steal this cat!" he said, cracking his leather-gloved knuckles.

"Not stealing," I reminded him as we stepped out of the stairwell. "Persuading."

He moved up to the apartment door and knocked once. Instantly, the wood swung inward, giving way under his sharply rapping knuckles. He shot me a confused look.

"Hello! Mr. Kovic?" I called into the quiet, dimly lit apartment. "Karl Kovic?"

I thought I heard some scuffling in another room as I stepped over the threshold, found a light switch, and flipped it. Recessed bulbs illuminated the foyer and hallway. Matt followed me inside and closed the door.

"Hello?" I said again, louder this time.

I took a step forward——then yelped as a little white fur ball rocketed between my sneakers.

"Here, kitty, kitty," Matt cooed.

The kitten scurried behind an umbrella stand, where it sat on its haunches and studied us, pink nose sniffing the air.

"I think she's afraid of me," Matt said after he tried to approach the skittish animal.

"You'd be scared, too, if a mountain draped in Armani came at you."

I saw Matt tense and realized that he was now sniffing the air. "Smell that?"

"What?"

"Cordite."

My brows knitted. "Cor——?"

"Gunpowder."

"You mean——"

Matt shushed me. "Stay here. And don't touch a thing."

Matt crept down the short hall. I moved to catch up with him, entering the apartment's living room.

Nothing appeared out of the ordinary. A dirty coffee cup

sat beside an easy chair, old newspapers and magazines were piled on the floor, and a Santa costume in a dry-cleaning bag was draped over the end of the couch, next to a man's overcoat.

Matt noticed me following him and scowled. Then he stepped around the littered coffee table and moved deeper into the apartment. I noticed that the white kitten had reappeared, following my ex's polished black shoes like a tiny white shadow.

Must be female.

I paused at the coffee table, where I spied a slim canvas wallet, keys, and a pile of change. I slipped on my gloves and gingerly opened the wallet with one finger. Karl Kovic's New York State driver's license photo stared back at me through a cellophane window.

He and Alf could have been brothers. Karl's eyes were muddier, more brown than green, but his face had the same round shape. Like Alf, Karl had a mustache, although his wasn't a bushy walrus; it was trimmed in a horseshoe shape more closely to his face. He also wore his hair long, but not long enough to do Alf's retro-sixties ponytail thing.

I heard Matt curse. "Son of a—"

"What's the matter?"

He reappeared, his face a shade paler. "It's Kovic. At least I *think* it's Kovic. He's in the bedroom, Clare. He's dead."

Twenty-Five

Matt grabbed me before I got past him. "You don't want to see that."

"I have to!"

I pulled away and moved into the bedroom. The smell was more pronounced here. Like sulfur or burned hair combined with the slightly metallic stench of fresh blood. Kovic lay on the floor beside the bed, facedown, head turned, eyes open. For a moment, my feet felt frozen to the floor.

"There was no sign of blood or a struggle in the foyer or living room," I murmured. "The killer must have met Kovic at the front door, and then led him at gunpoint to this bedroom . . ."

The room was a shambles. Every drawer was pulled out, its contents spilled onto the floor. Even the mattress had been molested, the pillowcases stripped away, sheets and blankets tossed around.

"Obviously the shooter was looking for something. I wonder if he found it."

Matt stepped up behind me. "Doesn't matter. Not for this poor bastard." He leaned over the body. "Looks like he was shot twice in the back. Those bullet holes are too small to be exit wounds."

I remembered Quinn's stories about working crime scenes and stopped Matt from touching the body to confirm what the exit wounds looked like in the corpse's front. Instead, I bent low, trying to figure out something else. Staring at the dead man's face, I noticed that Kovic's wide-open eyes were moist. There was saliva on his chin. It hadn't dried yet. The spittle was still wet.

"Kovic wasn't shot very long ago," I whispered. "I think we just missed the killer."

Matt tensed. "Now I wish I had that Beretta."

Stepping out of the room, Matt moved back into the apartment's hallway. I joined him, noticing that the bathroom door was open, but a second door beside it was closed.

"Feel that?" I whispered.

He nodded. "There's a draft."

I pushed the closed door open. Immediately a gust of frigid air filled the hall. Inside we found a second bedroom, half the size of the one with Kovic's corpse. This room had been ransacked, too, and the window facing the fire escape was wide open, curtains blowing wildly on the freezing night wind.

"Oh, God," I said. "When we were coming in, I heard shuffling in another room—I thought it was Kovic, but it was obviously the killer. He must have heard us and fled through the window!"

Matt looked outside and down the dark fire escape. "I don't see anyone."

With my gloved hands, I picked up a silver-framed picture that had been knocked to the floor. It was a photograph of a beaming Vicki Glockner at her high school graduation. Her dad was standing at her side, his arm around her shoulders, his face so happy, so filled with pride.

"This was Alf's room," I whispered, my voice suddenly gone.

Matt frowned, watching me. "I'm sorry."

I shook my head, swiping wet eyes, and put the photo back on the dresser. "Whatever the killer wanted, I don't think he got. He obviously tossed Karl's bedroom, then Alf's room, and then he must have heard us coming in and run . . ."

Matt took my arm. "Let's grab that cat and get the hell out of here."

"No." I pulled away. "We have to call the police."

"Why? So they can pin this murder on us? Think, Clare. We're trespassing. Again."

We argued back and forth for a minute until we finally reached an agreement. Matt would take Alf's kitten back to my apartment above the Blend (and risk the high holy wrath of Breanne finally noticing that her escort had temporarily abandoned her). And I would call 911 and stick around for the police to show up.

But first we had to find the kitten, which seemed to have vanished.

"Here kitty," I cooed. "Kitty-kitty . . ."

As I began making kissy-kissy sounds, I heard something familiar—

Jingle-jingle-jingle . . .

The sound came from the kitchen, where I found the little fur ball batting around a single silver sleigh bell. The ornament had come loose from a red-and-green pet pillow with an image of Santa Claus in his sleigh embroidered across the front and jingle bells sewn into its fringes.

An open—and empty—can of BumbleBee tuna served as the kitten's dish. A smelly shoebox sat in an opposite corner, beside a trash can filled with illegally mixed garbage—more tuna cans and a lot of other detritus that should have been separated for recycling. The shoebox was lined with soiled newspapers and cat poo. I didn't see a water bowl.

The kitty's antics had intensified since I entered the room. With my gloved hand I took the empty can and trickled a little faucet water into it. The kitten was lapping it up when Matt entered, Java's carrier in hand.

"The NYPD forensics team will find kitten hair," I told Matt as he set the carrier down. "But they have to assume Karl got rid of it, so we have to make it look like that . . ."

"Meaning what?"

"Meaning you have to take that shoebox with you."

Matt took a look and shuddered. "No way."

I glared. "Way."

"Look, we found the door unlocked," Matt said. "Just tell the cops it was ajar and they'll think the pet got out."

"Got out where? We're on the fifth floor of an apartment building. Kittens can't reach elevator buttons!"

Matt folded his arms. "But taking that disgusting thing is interfering with a crime scene. People go to prison for that."

I faced him, hands on hips. "Stealing the kitten is interfering, too. And it's not like we're tampering with evidence. I'm sure the killer didn't go anywhere near that cat poop."

"Of course not," Matt said flatly. "We're the only ones stupid enough to do that."

"Mr. Outback is squeamish?"

"Yes. When Mr. Outback is dressed in pricey Armani and has to return to a cocktail party smelling of feline feces, he's as squeamish as Shirley Temple."

I scooped up the adorable kitten and cuddled it. The cute little thing immediately began to purr. "Awww . . ." Its soft fur was as white and silky as latte microfoam. "I think I'll call her Frothy."

She didn't mind being tucked into Java's carrier, as if she knew I was here to take care of her. But the box was so large and Frothy so small that I slipped the loose jingle bell and Santa Claus pillow inside, too. At least the tiny thing would have something familiar to cling to on her scary trip downtown.

Matt lifted the carrier. "I'm out of here."

"Wait!"

"What?"

"The key!"

Matt put the carrier down. I handed him the key to my duplex. He met my eyes. "You're sure?"

"Of course! How else are you going to get in?"

"Right."

"Listen," I said, touching the exquisite Armani fabric covering the man's forearm. "I've got a spare at Mike's. So please don't stress about getting the key back to me right away. You can hold on to it."

"Oh?" My ex-husband paused and studied my face with an odd intensity. "You're sure about this . . ."

"Yes, of course." I knew Matt would be party-hopping all night with his new wife, and I'd taken him away from her long enough. But he was looking at me so strangely. "Did I miss something?"

He didn't reply, simply arched his eyebrow with a kind of satisfaction. Then he took out his keychain, slid the key on, and picked up the carrier again.

"Wait!"

"Not again!"

"The *shoebox*!"

The box o' kitten poo was nested in its own lid. I picked up the stinky square of cardboard, peeled the lid off its bottom and capped the box shut.

Matt held the thing at arm's length. (I didn't blame him.)

"Give me a five-minute head start before you call in the law," he said, then slipped out of the apartment, the *jingle-jingle-jingles* of Frothy's Santa cat pillow diminishing as he disappeared down the building's hallway.

I hoped no one would notice Matt leaving the place, but I did realize that a hunky guy in a tux, carrying a tinkling cat carrier in one hand and a stinky box of cat crap in the other might be too much for even jaded New Yorkers to ignore.

With five minutes to wait, I decided to keep my gloves on and poke around the dead man's apartment. The bedrooms had been tossed already. But the killer hadn't had time to ransack the living room.

Could there be some kind of lead here?

I checked the answering machine. All the messages had been deleted. I looked for a computer, but all I found was a printer and an adapter cord. I suspected there had been a laptop here, but the killer had taken it.

After five minutes, I came up with zip, so I dug out my mobile phone to call the police. When I saw the mailbox icon on my cell's screen, I realized I'd missed a call. I'd forgotten to take the cell off its vibrator setting. Worried it might be Matt needing more time, I quickly played it. The message wasn't from my ex-husband but my ex-mother-in-law.

"Hello, dear, I didn't want to tell *(static)* while Ben Tower *(static)*, so I waited until . . ."

Reception was lousy, so I moved closer to the window to improve the signal. As I did, I brushed against the plastic dry-cleaning bag holding the Santa costume. The slippery plastic slithered onto the floor, taking the adjacent overcoat with it. That's when I noticed a white envelope peeking out of the coat's pocket. There was something familiar about the Santa Claus postage stamp in the corner.

Forgetting Madame's message, I stooped down and carefully slipped the envelope free. As the typed name *Omar Linford* revealed itself, the hairs on my skin began to prickle. I opened the envelope and pulled out the letter.

Dear Omar: I have a new proposition for you. If you care about your son's future, you will read every word of this note and do what it says. I know all about Junior Linford's little hobbies . . .

Oh my God. I'd found the note blackmailing Omar Linford—the one someone had tossed me off the ferry to get. Now I knew who that someone was.

"Karl Kovic, you son of a—"

I shook my head, at last putting it all together . . . After I'd left Shelly Glockner's house, she must have rushed to the back yard, where Esther noticed Kovic going out to the Jacuzzi. Then Kovic watched and waited until I left Linford's place. He followed me onto the ferry, grabbed my bag, and threw me into water with a temperature a *tad* chillier than Shelly's hot tub.

Gritting my teeth with fury, I grabbed a pen and piece of scrap paper from my bag and scribbled down the series of bank account numbers at the end of the note. I was willing to bet the account was a joint one controlled by Alf and Shelly Glockner—giving her access to the money as soon as Omar deposited it.

I'm sure she and Karl went behind Alf's back. But . . . did they kill Alf, too?

That part didn't make a lot of sense. *Killing Alf would screw up their plan, wouldn't it? Alf was their fall guy in case Omar went to the FBI. Why kill him?*

I remembered the life insurance money, but that didn't seem to fit, either. They could have waited until they got the payoff from Omar—unless he already told Alf he wasn't going to pay and they became desperate . . .

The permutations were making my head hurt, and it didn't address the question of who killed Karl, either. Would *Shelly* have done something like that? If she had, why would she have to ransack the apartment? Wouldn't she have sweet-talked Karl out of whatever she wanted, and then killed him?

I tried making Omar Linford the villain here—but that didn't seem to fit, either. If the point was to kill Karl because of his threat to go to the police about Junior Linford, then the deed was done. Why ransack the apartment? For the note, maybe? It *would* be incriminating, showing a motive for Linford to have murdered Karl and Alf. But then why would Omar have admitted to me that he was being blackmailed in the first place?

I shook my head, still unable to put it all together. The bank account numbers were a good lead, though, and I took care in refolding the note and returning it to Karl's coat.

With a deep breath, I finally placed the call to 911 and

reported the murder. I told the dispatcher I'd wait for the police and ended the call. While I listened for the sirens, however, I suddenly remembered Madame's recorded message and replayed the thing—

"Hello, dear. I didn't want to tell you this while Ben Tower was listening, so I waited until I poured him into a cab. My goodness, when someone else is footing the bar bill, that man can drink like Moby Dick!"

No surprise there.

"Anyway! Tower told me one more thing about the man you mentioned—Karl—sorry, dear, I can't remember the last name. I don't know if this will help at all, but near the end of our time together, Tower kept saying Karl's got something *big* coming. The payoff was going to put him in another tax bracket; that's how Tower put it, anyway. He said Dickie Celebratorio was involved, although I didn't get the impression Dickie was the center of this scandal, just a part of it."

Dickie?

"You recognize Dickie's name, don't you, dear? He's that big party planner, a real PR king. Mr. Dewberry says Dickie knows all the celebrities and politicians. He helps them out, does favors for them, and they attend his promo galas, benefits, and openings in return. Very high-profile man. Tower wouldn't tell me what kind of scandal Karl had discovered or who it actually involved. Frankly, I don't think he even knew the details, but he said Karl was sure one of Tower's tabloid clients would pay big for the story and photos . . ."

I frowned, hearing that new lead, suddenly wishing I'd waited to call 911. With sirens already wailing in the distance, I had little time to search anew based on Madame's call. What could I possibly find that could help me in just a few minutes? I glanced around, considered the Santa costume and then realized—

The coat. Of course!

I'd found the blackmail letter in Karl's left coat pocket. Why stop there? Frantically, I went through the rest of

Karl's pockets. I dug out change, a Metro card, some throat lozenges, and . . . a folded scrap of paper.

The sirens were much louder now, only a few blocks away. I quickly unfolded the paper scrap. Read the barely legible scrawl—

6 PM $$$ Dickie. Watch for CC.

The note had a date on it, too. Today's date! I checked my wristwatch. It was almost six thirty. I smiled with triumph, despite the tragic circumstances. If anyone else read this note, I doubted they'd have a clue what it meant. But I'd been on this case for days now and *I* knew—

Karl was blackmailing someone and Dickie Celebratorio was either involved in the scandal or acting as some kind of go-between. At six today, presumably at his own apartment, Karl was supposed to meet someone to hand over something (probably digital photo or video files) in exchange for money. But there was no exchange. Something went wrong and Karl was murdered. Or—

Karl was simply set up for a cold-blooded execution. And, according to the note in his pocket, the person who set him up was "Dickie."

Outside, the sirens finally stopped wailing. Loud voices were shouting on the street below.

I'm out of time.

I put everything back in Karl's coat pockets and then read the note one last time, trying to think everything through. That's when it hit me. Those words: *Watch for CC.*

"CC," I whispered, my flesh turning cold. "Clare Cosi."

Twenty-six

~~~~~~

THIRTY minutes later, I hit the sidewalk running outside the Wiseman Apartments, pushing through a curious crowd eager to learn why three police cars and a crime-scene van were camped in front of Karl Kovic's building. Curious eyes followed me as I dashed down the block and hurried to reach Broadway—the quickest bet for flagging a cab downtown.

When detectives from the Twentieth Precinct arrived on scene, I didn't have time to explain the saga of Alf Glockner, Karl Kovic, Ben Tower, and the Dickie Celebratorio connection. So I sold them a digest version of what had happened.

"I came here looking for Mr. Kovic. He hadn't shown for his roommate's memorial service, and I wanted to see how he was doing . . ." Which was true. "That's when I found Karl's corpse."

Fortunately, the responding detectives accepted my statement and released me. At this point, I knew the only cops who could truly understand the whole story were Mike Quinn, Charlie Hong, and (heaven help me) Emmanuel Franco.

Right now, *tonight*, I had a window of opportunity to

confront the jet-setting Dickie Celebratorio over his role
in this sordid mess—before he dashed off to Rio, Dubai,
Cap d'Antibes, or God knew where for the holidays—and I
wasn't going to pass that up.

Propelling myself forward, I dug into my shoulder bag,
pulled out my cell, and hit a speed-dial button. "Pick up,
pick up, pick up," I chanted like a mantra.

"He-LO-ooo," Tucker answered in a three-note vocal ex-
ercise. I could hear other actors warming up in the background, too.

"Tucker! Thank God."

"Clare!" he said, alarmed. "Please don't tell me there's an
emergency at the Blend. I'm getting ready to put on a show
here!"

"Everything's fine at the Blend. I need you to get me into
Dickie Celebratorio's big holiday bash, ASAP!" (*Because once
my friends with the gold shields arrive, we're all going to have a
little powwow with the dubious party planner.*)

"I can swing getting you in here," Tucker replied. "But
you *have* to do me a *huge* favor in return."

"How can I help?"

"There are massive delays on the Long Island Rail Road.
My two Candy Cane Girls aren't going to make it in time,
but I'm sure I can squeeze you into one of their costumes."

"Did you say *squeeze*?"

"Yes. Face it, sweetie, you're *chesty*, and I've hired professional young actresses for tonight's gig. You know the type,
vegan anorexics who purge after one lemon chai."

"I don't know, Tuck—"

"Please! I'm begging."

Glancing down at my old jeans, scuffed sneakers, and
worn parka, I realized I wasn't exactly dressed to blend in
with the invited glitterati. I exhaled hard, hating to admit
it, but disguising myself as part of the production number
was probably the smartest thing I could do to keep a low
profile inside that bash.

"Fine. I'll do it."

"You're a godsend, Clare! Don't worry, okay? No singing or dancing is required. All you have to do is wear this adorable Santa's Little Helper getup and pass out candy canes to the kiddies."

Once again, I cringed—not at the activity. I loved children. It was the adjective *little* applied to *getup* that made me wary.

"Where do I meet you?"

"Go to the first door on the Public Library's Forty-second Street side entrance. There'll be two staff members at a desk just inside. I'll call right now and have them add your name to my cast list. Someone there will direct you down to the basement room we're using as a dressing area."

I signed off and flagged a cab. On my way downtown, I placed more calls—the first one to Mike Quinn. Unfortunately, I got the man's voice mail. I asked Quinn to call either me or Detective Hong and dialed Hong's number.

Detective Charlie Hong was strike two. This time, I left a long, detailed message on his voice mail informing him that I'd found Alf Glockner's roommate dead in his apartment and discovered that the murdered man was selling celebrity photos and videos . . .

"I think the murders of Alf and Karl are linked. According to a source I have, Karl Kovic was blackmailing someone, and I found a note in Karl's coat pocket that I'm sure means Dickie Celebratorio helped set up Karl for execution . . ."

That's when I realized something else. Matt had mentioned that he'd left Breanne at Dickie's pre-event cocktail party to meet me on the Upper West Side.

"Dickie couldn't have done the deed himself," I added to Hong's voice mail, "because he gave himself the perfect alibi. Hundreds of people were seeing him at a pre-benefit cocktail party when Karl was shot! By whom, I still don't know. But Dickie almost certainly does . . ."

I gave Hong details on where to scoop up Dickie for questioning. "Come to the Public Library's main branch as soon as you can, Detective. I'll be at the party inside, keeping an

eye on Dickie's movements until you arrive. I'm getting in
as part of the show. Look for me in a Santa's Little Helper
costume."

I ended the call to Hong and stared at Emmanuel Franco's
cell number, written on the card that Hong had given me. I
punched in the man's first three digits and stopped—

No. I squeezed my eyes shut. *I just can't.*

Frankly, I figured I was better off alone than with Dudley
Do-Rag as backup.

Tucking the phone into my bag, I realized the cab was
pulling over between Forty-first and Forty-second streets.
I glanced across Fifth Avenue. The sprawling main branch
of the New York Public Library was bathed in soft golden
light. Chandeliers sparkled through massive windows and a
deep burgundy *Ticket to the North Pole* banner fluttered from
one end of the sculpted beaux arts facade to the other.

Limousines were lined up all the way around the corner of
Forty-second. In a kaleidoscopic parade, women in lollipop-
colored couture, men in black dinner jackets, their children
equally well dressed, passed between the famous stone lions
that guarded the library's entrance, then ascended the red
carpet, which flowed like a cherry stream down the wide
stone steps. At street level, uniformed police manned barri-
cades, where a mob of young women held signs and shouted
out to famous actors and recording artists.

I darted across the avenue, jaywalking through traffic,
and headed for the side entrance, just as Tucker had advised.
The party staff already had my name and directed me to the
basement maintenance area that was doubling as tonight's
dressing room. Tucker raced up to me as soon as I stepped
through the door.

"Slip into this fast!" He thrust a garment into my hand—
a scrap of red velvet trimmed in white fur. "The rest of my
elves and Santa's Little Helpers are already upstairs on the
floor!"

I dangled the scrap of material between my finger and
thumb. "Where are the *bottoms*?"

"Over there—" He pointed to a pair of frilly white pant-ies clipped to a hanger, then touched a finger to his chin and appraised me. "Don't bother with the push-up bra. You'll have cleavage to spare already and we don't want to risk spillage—"

"Spillage?! Tuck!"

"Sorry." He shrugged. "Just being practical. You'll also find nude tights and black go-go boots in the dressing room."

"That's *it*? That's all I'm supposed to wear? Are you kidding?!"

Tucker threw up his hands. "Just pretend you're a Rockette!"

I held the microdress up to my body. "More like a Bada-Bing pole dancer."

That was my last official protest. Tucker push/guided me into a communal dressing area created out of portable resin room dividers. Inside, folding chairs were scattered around a long table with makeup kits and lighted mirrors.

"Use the lockers over there for your clothes and bag," Tuck said. "And don't forget to pin on your Santa hat." He pointed to the hairpins on the table. "It might come off when you're bending down to hand out the promo candy."

"Bending down? In this thing?" I shuddered at the thought.

Five minutes later, I emerged from the dressing room, my face redder than the form-fitting outfit I had indeed squeezed into.

"You look fabulous, Clare," Tucker proclaimed. Then he placed his hands on his hips. "But you can't go through the entire event clutching your hem with one hand and covering your cleavage with the other."

"Why not?"

"Well, for one thing you need a free hand to pass out the promo candy!"

I gazed at my reflection in the mirror. The dress (for lack of a better term) had long sleeves trimmed with fake white fur around the wrists, so my arms were covered. But those were the only body parts on me that were modestly draped. My legs were sheathed in tights, but the nude shade made it look as if I were exposed all the way up to my—you know. And the plunging neckline, also fur trimmed, left little to the imagination. Plus the fur was ticklish.

"Don't worry about a thing. You look absolutely scrumptious," Tuck gushed, pulling me to the makeup table. "Now stand still."

In three minutes flat, he'd sponged pancake makeup on my face and chest areas; did up my eyes with (way too much) mascara, liner, and snow-white shadow; added gloss to my lips and rouge to my cheeks; and dusted every inch of bared flesh with some kind of sheer glitter powder.

"Tuck, that's too much makeup!"

"It's Santa's Helper stage makeup, honey."

"Santa's Helper? I look like Santa's Hooker!"

"Here's your bag, Candy Cane Girl!" He passed me a bulging red velvet sack with a long shoulder strap. It was packed with gourmet chocolate-dipped red and white candy canes and green peppermint sticks, *Ticket to the North Pole* printed on each cellophane wrapper.

"Whoa, this is heavy."

"Sorry—but you're now doing the work of *two* promo candy girls."

"Ouch. Don't elves have a union or something?"

"Okay, sweetie, get upstairs, *smile*, and show those folks the true meaning of a Hollywood Christmas!"

I climbed the wide marble staircase to the enormous Rose Reading Room. On a normal day, this stately space with its massive windows and majestic chandeliers was library-quiet, with brass lamps glowing on heavy tables of darkly stained wood. Tonight, raucous laughter and children's holiday ditties ("Frosty," "Rudolph," "Jingle Bells") were echoing loudly off the high ceiling.

The room's chandeliers were still burning brightly, but the reading tables had been replaced with twelve-foot-tall candy canes, toy soldiers, rag dolls, and a Santa sleigh as big as my Honda. On one end of the room an open bar had been set up in front of a wall-sized enlargement of a children's picture book cover—the one this Hollywood movie was based on. At the other end of the long space, a temporary stage was flanked by two foam "snow" mountains.

"Hey, there, little elf. Got something sweet for me?" called a male voice.

I turned to find an extremely tanned guy in a tux shooting me with a trigger finger.

Gritting my teeth, I reminded myself that this flashy PR event was also a fund-raiser for charity. But after fifteen minutes of passing out confections to little ones, I realized I'd attracted an embarrassing amount of Big Boy attention, and I looked for a place to hide.

That's when I spied Breanne. She was stunning, as usual, in a pine-colored taffeta dress with a kicky flared skirt and a bolero jacket dripping with hand-sewn gemstones. Her long blond hair was piled high to show off her annoyingly swanlike neck, and her slender back was turned to me (a lucky break).

As I moved to hide from her—behind a giant toy soldier—I realized a dashing, dark-haired guy in Armani was ogling my cleavage. A few seconds later, he finally noticed the face above it.

"Clare?!"

"Matt!"

"What are you doing here?" he whispered. "And why are you dressed like that?"

"I'm here to have a talk with Dickie," I replied.

"Dickie? Why? Wait! Don't tell me—" Matt took a long belt from the tumbler in his hand. "I don't want to know."

"You better get back to your wife."

"I know," Matt griped. "She's royally pissed at me for taking off to grab your new kitten—who's safe and snug in the duplex, by the way. I refilled Java's food bowl and bought some kitten chow at a convenience store. The box is in the cupboard."

"Thanks. I mean it."

"It's okay," he sighed. "Anyway, you're right. I better get back to Bree. If she saw me talking to you right now, with you dressed like that—" He took his good old time looking me up and down, then blew out air. "I'm pretty sure she'd be wearing my private parts for earrings come Christmas morning."

"Hello! Good evening!"

A diminutive man in a spotless white tux had stepped up to a microphone on the temporary stage.

"My name's Dickie. Welcome to my pah-ty," he said with what sounded like a slight Bronx accent.

Loud applause greeted the man. As it intensified, I made a study of the famed party planner. With dark hair slicked back, a spray-tanned complexion that bordered on burnt orange latte syrup, and a Botox-numbed face, the Napoleon-sized Celebratorio (whose younger photographs cast him as a Dean Martin lookalike), now struck me as a cross between George Hamilton, Austin Powers's Mini-Me, and a Madame Tussaud's wax figure.

I moved to get closer to the stage. If Dickie decided to dash away without notice, I wanted to be in a position to follow him. But my movements were halted when strong fingers wrapped tightly around my upper arm and a man's hot breath tickled my ear—

"Come with me, honey."

For heaven's sake! What is it about a skimpy Santa's Helper costume that puts male libidos into overdrive?

I turned, ready to push away whoever had taken hold of me—and found a five-eleven, golden-haired elf gawking down my neckline.

Oh, no! Not Shane Holliway. Not now!

Twenty-seven

~~~~~~

"We need to talk," Shane whispered in my ear.

"Let me go."

"Come on, honey." He pulled my arm again.

A few people looked our way. *Darn it!* In an effort to avoid a scene, I let Shane take my hand and lead me to a corner. With a jerk, he tugged me behind an enormous glass-bulb Christmas tree ornament and quickly bent over me. I slapped his face.

He yelped. "What's that for?!"

"I am *not* interested in you, Shane! Got that?"

"Wait, Clare! You've got the wrong idea—"

I turned to dash. He jumped in front of me. "Listen to me. Please, it's important."

"Ten seconds."

"Your life is in danger."

My tapping go-go boot stilled. "Okay. You've got my attention."

Shane moved closer again and whispered in my ear. "Listen, I'm in deep here, and this is my only chance to talk to you."

"Talk, then."

"You have to believe me, Clare, I never meant anyone to get hurt, and I certainly didn't know what I was getting myself into—"

"Just *tell* me."

"Right after Thanksgiving, Dickie Celebratorio called me up and asked me to help out a celebrity friend of his—"

"What friend?"

"Dickie wouldn't say. He wouldn't even let slip whether it was a man or woman. I only know this famous person was getting bothered and wanted the harassment to end. Dickie agreed to help this person, and I agreed to help Dickie . . ."

"Agreed to do *what* exactly?"

"To follow the dude who was hassling his famous friend. Find out the dude's movements."

"What do you mean his movements?"

"It was like an acting job. I mean, I'd already done the method research when I played a private eye on TV. It wasn't that hard. Dickie knew stuff about this dude already—had the whole 411 on his name and address. But this famous friend of Dickie's wanted the guy's routine, too. So for two days in a row, I waited outside this dude's apartment building. When he came out, all dressed for work, I followed him and made notes on where he went and when. But I thought it was all innocent—that *we* were the good guys."

"What do you mean?"

"Clare, the dude I followed ended up *murdered*."

"Oh, no." I felt sick, closed my eyes. "You were following Alfred Glockner."

"Yes. I followed a Traveling Santa out of his Upper West Side apartment building, down to Union Square, and then on to the Village. That's the pattern I handed over to Dickie. I didn't know there were *two* Traveling Santas, with two different work routines, both living at the same address! What did they want from me? I'm not a real detective! I just played one on TV!"

Oh, for pity's sake. "You're an accomplice, Shane, don't you see that? What did you do after Alf was murdered? Did you confront Dickie? Ask him if he had anything to do with Santa's getting shot?"

"God, no. Are you kidding? I played the dumb soap actor. By then he'd already paid me for the surveillance job and even sent me to the Blend to see Tucker. He said Tuck could give me a high-paying acting gig, and he was right. I needed the money, and I didn't want to upset the man, so I put on the elf suit—"

"He was paying you off, Shane, to stay quiet—"

"Well, of course! I know that *now*. But then Tucker happened to mention that Glockner's daughter asked you to look into her father's murder—" He shook his elf-capped head. "I got scared, Clare. I wanted to know what you knew. That's why I made the pass at you today. I was going to try again tonight, too, but all that's changed now—"

"What do you mean?"

"Half an hour ago, Dickie pulled me aside and asked me to do it again."

"Do what again?"

"Keep an eye on someone. Report on their movements."

"Was it Kovic?" I asked. "Karl Kovic?"

Shane blinked. "Who?"

"Alf's roommate. I found Karl Kovic's body in his apartment this evening. He was shot in the back."

Shane's glitter-dusted flesh went all the way white. "That's it. I'm not waiting until tomorrow. After this show, I'm on the very next red-eye to L.A.!"

"Wait! You can't leave!" Now I was the one dragging Shane back behind the giant tree ornament. "You have to talk to the police first. They'll be here any minute." *I hope.*

"And tell them what? That I followed Santa Claus around and made notes? That's not a crime. They can't arrest me *or* Dickie for that—"

"No, but—"

"Listen to me, Clare, okay? If you find a way to nail Dickie and this mysterious celebrity friend he's covering up for, I'll back your testimony. But until then, Hollywood here I come."

"Shane, don't go!"

"Sugarplum, do you know what that man's real name is?" He pointed toward the stage where Dickie was wrapping up his remarks. "Richard Torio. He's not some puff from Fire Island. He grew up in the Bronx—a borough so dangerous they had to film the remake of *Pelham One Two Three* in Woodside, Queens! This guy has the kind of associates the *Sopranos'* producers used to hire for authentic-looking thug extras."

"I get it! Just tell me one thing. Who is this new person that Dickie asked you to follow?"

He put a hand on my shoulder. "It's *you*, Clare. I swear I didn't tell him that you knew anything, but somehow he found out you were digging into Alf's murder, egging on the cops. They know what you look like. They know where you work and live."

Shane met my eyes. "I'd get the hell out of here before Dickie or anyone else he's hired spots you. Take care, Cosi Lady."

With a kiss to my stunned cheek, the golden-haired elf was gone. *Now what?* From my hiding place, I tried to spot Detective Hong, but there were so many people here, who could tell? He was probably trying to call me right now, but my cell was downstairs in the dressing room locker.

I have to get out of here . . .

Fortunately, the lights in the reading room dimmed. Tucker's show was about to begin. I zigzagged through the crowd and bolted for the exit, eyes peeled for Matt the whole way. But he and Breanne, the party shark, were nowhere in sight. They'd probably moved on to the next event.

I hit another knot of people and stepped around them. My timing couldn't have been worse. I passed right by Dickie himself. He was conferring with a man whose designer suit couldn't hide a cauliflower ear and a pockmarked face—the kind that would have been captioned "Known Associate" in a true-crime book.

Both pairs of male eyes followed me through the crowd—
damn this Santa Hooker outfit!

Another mob of partygoers slowed me down, trying to
maneuver their kids closer to Tucker's show. I dodged right,
then left. Finally free, I hit the deserted marble stairway. My
black go-go boot heels clicked quickly on the stone. I didn't
get far before I heard heavy feet following. I glanced over my
shoulder and saw what I'd dreaded—

Known Associate was on my heels. "Wait, miss!" he
called. "Mr. Celebratorio would like a word with you . . ."

I reached the basement dressing room but didn't go inside. I hadn't seen another exit in there, and I didn't want
to get trapped. Instead I kept on going down a long, empty
corridor. I could hear the man's footsteps stalking me.

When I turned the first corner, I found myself trapped in
a dead-end hallway with locked doors. I spun around, ready
to rush back to the main corridor. But Known Associate was
already on me.

"Will you *stop* running—" His big hands reaching, he
lunged for me.

The only weapon I had was this huge bag of promo candy.
Remembering Esther's brick, I swung the sack with all my
might and smacked him right in the face! The bag burst
open and the cellophane-wrapped goodies went flying everywhere. Some even pelted me. *Peppermint blowback!*

The man stumbled and I raced past him. He yowled,
turned to chase me, and slipped on the layer of cellophane
that covered the polished floor. As gravity took him down, I
turned the corner again, continuing down the long hallway
until I saw a *Fire Exit* sign above a pair of wooden doors.

By now, Known Associate was on his feet again and running toward me. I pushed through the double doors and
spun around. Using my empty velvet sack, I quickly tied
the door handles together. Then I bolted the few yards to
the steel fire door. Behind me, I could hear Known Associate
violently rattling the tied double doors.

He can't get through!

An alarm sounded as I depressed the fire door bar and stumbled into the frigid December night. When the heavy door slammed behind me, I knew I was locked outside—and that was fine with me, because the only way I was going back into that crazy holiday bash was with an armed SWAT team!

Twenty-Eight

∞∞∞∞∞∞∞∞∞∞∞∞∞∞∞∞∞∞∞

"Hey, little elf! I like your outfit!"

"Are you coming from a Christmas party?"

"Maybe she's from the North Pole."

"You want a ride, sweet thing?"

"I'll give her a ride. A real *nice* ride!"

The four men laughed. They were sitting in an SUV, keeping pace beside me on a dim, deserted stretch of Fortieth Street. At least three of them were sloppy drunk from some office party. Shivering in my flimsy red costume, I tightly folded my red velvet arms and quickened the pace of my black go-go boots.

With Bryant Park Grill dark, and no other open restaurants or stores on this block, I'd struck out for the police station in Times Square. If I was lucky, I figured I'd encounter a cop or squad car on my way.

So far, I wasn't lucky.

My cell phone, wallet, and even my spare change were presently locked inside the public library's basement. There were no pedestrians on this sleepy street paralleling the snow-covered rectangle of Bryant Park, and the only car coming down Fortieth in the last three minutes was this big, black sport-utility vehicle filled with four office workers in their late twenties, most of whom were hammered, all of whom were making assumptions about my line of work— *wrong* assumptions.

"Ask her how much," one of them complained to the other.

"What's the matter, little elf? Don't you like us?"

Eyes forward, I shook my head. "Not interested!"

"Come on!"

They began talking lower, among themselves. "You have cash on you, right?"

"What's she going to charge?"

I quickened my steps on the sidewalk, hurrying to reach the much brighter lights of Sixth Avenue, but the SUV continued keeping pace with me.

"We'll treat you right," one of them shouted. "Just get in!"

When I finally hit the corner, I figured I'd lose them. But the SUV turned sharply, cutting me off at the curb. The inebriated guy in the front passenger seat swung open his door and leaped at me—

"Hands off, asshole!" I shouted, rearing back.

WHOOP!

The earsplitting burst of a police siren cut the night. A dark blue sedan peeled through the traffic light and spun with NASCAR-level rotational drift. In seconds, the sedan's driver screeched his vehicle to a halt, expertly boxing in the front of the SUV.

I noticed the revolving red bubble light on the sedan's dashboard and sagged with relief. Sergeant Emmanuel Franco climbed out of his unmarked car, swaggered over to the men in the SUV, and flashed his gold shield. I was never so happy to see a red, white, and blue do-rag in all my life.

"Now I ask you, gentlemen: Is that any way to treat Santa's Little Helper?" His dark eyes speared the four. "You should be ashamed of yourselves. I ought to throw the book at you. Or maybe give your so-called designated driver a Breathalyzer."

The wolves turned suddenly sheepish.

"We didn't mean anything, officer."

"You're misunderstanding."

"We all just thought she might want a lift."

"Yeah, that's all—"

"Listen, Jersey Boys," Franco replied. "Put it back in your pants and go home—unless you'd rather spend the night in a holding cell instead of Lincoln Tunnel traffic."

While Franco stood and watched, the SUV backed up, laboriously maneuvered around his unmarked car, and sped away. Then the police sergeant turned to face me, gave my outfit a long, slow, frustratingly expressionless once-over, folded his arms, and said, "So, Coffee Lady, you want a ride or what?"

"Yes!"

Freezing, I ducked into the passenger side of his sedan. He got behind the wheel, shut the door, and glanced at me. Without a word, he turned up the heat.

"Thanks."

"You're welcome."

"Listen, Sergeant, inside the library, there was a man after me—"

Franco put a palm in the air. "Give me a second." He grabbed his police radio handset. "Dispatch, I have a possible DWI currently traveling north on Sixth Avenue. Issue a BOLO for a late-model black Ford Explorer, four occupants, with the following New Jersey license plate . . ."

Franco finished his radio call and turned to me. "You were saying?"

"Where's Hong? I called Detective Hong."

"I know you did. He played me your phone message— *several* times." Franco smirked. "When I heard the part about you dressing as Santa's Little Helper, I said to Hong, 'Charlie, this is one call I've gotta respond to.'"

"Dressing like this was the only way I could get inside the *Ticket to the North Pole* party—"

"I know, Coffee Lady. So . . ." Giving me another once-over, he arched an eyebrow. "You want to go to my place?"

"No."

"I'm kidding. Where to?"

"Take me to the East Village. I'll fill you in as we go . . ."

To Franco's credit, he let me get out the whole story—from finding Karl Kovic's corpse, to hearing an elf confess to possible accessory to murder, to braining one of Dickie Celebratorio's Known Associates with a bag of gourmet chocolate-dipped candy canes. Dudley Do-Rag actually listened to the whole thing without once cracking wise. A Christmas miracle in itself.

When we reached Mike Quinn's apartment building, I still hadn't finished the tale, so he pulled to the curb and kept the engine running to keep the car warm.

". . . and that's when you found me," I concluded.

"I see," Franco said. "And that's it?"

"Isn't that enough?"

He smiled. Not a smirk this time, but a real smile. "You've got a lot of guts, Coffee Lady, I'll say that for you."

"I'm just trying to find out who really killed my friend."

"I know. And I have some good news. We recovered the murder weapon."

I sat up straighter. "The gun that shot Alf?"

Franco nodded. "It was found in a Goodwill bin. Someone tossed it in there—by our calculation, the same night as the murder. We ran the serial numbers. The weapon was bought in North Carolina by a man who died two years ago." At my look, Franco added, "That's an MO for a weapon bought and sold illegally up here on the street."

"Fingerprints?"

Franco shook his head. "Wiped clean."

I slumped in the car seat. "I guess you're happy about that."

"Why?"

"Because after all I've turned up, you can still pin this on some random street criminal, that's why."

"Except I don't believe that anymore."

"You don't?"

Franco turned to fully face me. "No street mugger would throw away something as valuable as a handgun. He might resell it in the 'hood or stash it in his crib until the heat from his crime cooled off, but toss something like that in a Goodwill bin? That's as good as throwing away hundreds of dollars—the kind of a thing an amateur would do, thinking he or she was making a premeditated murder look like a random street crime."

I sat up straighter. "You're on my side now?"

Franco nodded. "I interviewed Shelly Glockner."

"I know. She's a piece of work, isn't she?"

Franco laughed. "I'd peg her as coldhearted enough to do the deed *or* hire someone to do it, but then . . . it seems to me there are others who had a motive. You've stirred up a pretty gnarly nest of suspects."

Franco was right about that. Dickie was after me. But I knew he couldn't have shot Karl—because Dickie had a solid alibi at the time Karl was killed (that VIP cocktail party he threw before the big Public Library event). I doubted Dickie pulled the trigger on Alf, either. Given what Franco had just told me about the murder weapon, I even doubted Alf's killer was a professional Known Associate of Dickie's. A professional assassin wouldn't have made the mistake of getting rid of the gun in a manner the police would find suspicious. No, according to Shane Holliway, Dickie was just the go-between, someone who was helping some famous person, whom Karl was almost certainly blackmailing (according to Ben Tower). Which meant there was someone else out there, someone who wasn't a pro, who was willing to pull the trigger—twice—for whatever it was Karl had stashed in his apartment.

"I think the person who killed Alf was the same one who killed Karl," I said. "Do you agree?"

"Based on your investigation—yeah, I'd say it's the same person. Keep in mind, though, whoever it was didn't use the same gun."

"If only there were some way to get fingerprints after they were wiped!"

"Actually, there is."

"What?"

"Ever hear of John Bond?"

"Don't you mean James?"

Franco shook his head. "John Bond is a scientific support manager at Northamptonshire Police and an honorary research fellow at the University of Leicester."

"Leicester, *England*?"

"That's right. He's been working with American law enforcement to solve cold cases."

"How exactly?"

"Bond's developed a new procedure for detecting fingerprints. He coats a fine conducting powder, something like what you'd see in a photocopier, onto a metal surface and applies an electric charge. Then guess what? If the fingerprint has been wiped off or even washed off, it leaves a slight corrosion on the metal—which attracts the powder when the charge is applied and shows us a residual fingerprint."

"Are you telling me this Bond guy can find a fingerprint that's been wiped off? That he can find out who handled Alf's weapon?"

Franco nodded. "The technique works on everything from bullet casings to machine guns. Even better if our killer likes junk food."

"Excuse me? Are you joking?"

He smiled but assured me, "It's no joke. Processed and pre-packaged foods put more salt into human sweat. Salty sweat helps the microscopic corrosion process."

I frowned at that, remembering Omar's favorite lunch of Jamaican ackee and saltfish—his son's messy SUV, all those empty bags of chips and snacks that Dwayne had swept into his father's driveway . . .

"Anyway, even if heat vaporizes normal clues, Bond can read the fingerprints of who handled the metal. I hear they're going to try applying the technique to roadside bomb fragments in Afghanistan."

"I see. That's really . . . amazing."

Franco smiled. "And you thought I was just another pretty face."

"No, Sergeant. What I thought was—I'm sorry, but I thought you might be the shooter, some kind of vigilante doling out street justice."

"I'm not all that surprised." He shrugged. "I know you had your boyfriend ask around about me. Whether I was a good cop."

"And?"

"And Mike Quinn got his answers. Ask him."

"I don't need to, Sergeant. Not anymore."

Franco nodded, looking pleased. "So . . ." He glanced at Mike's building. "Is your man up there?"

"I don't think so. Can I use your cell phone to call him?"

Digging into his pocket, he smirked. "As long as it's local . . ."

Quinn was extremely relieved to hear from me. "I left *five* messages on your voice mail, sweetheart."

"I'm sorry, Mike, I didn't have my cell phone with me—"

"When I couldn't reach you, I finally contacted Detective Hong. He filled me in. You should be pleased, Cosi." I could hear the pride in Quinn's tone. "Based on what you've uncovered, Hong is looking for evidence to link Alf's killing with Karl's. They might have come to that conclusion eventually, but you speeded up the process. And crimes have a much better chance of being solved when they're—"

"—hot, I know. What about Dickie?" I asked after recounting my adventures in the New York Public Library, including my candy cane tangle with the man's Known Associate.

"Hong's already reached out to the Two-Oh on that—"

"You mean the Twentieth Precinct, right?"

"Right, sorry. That's who caught the Kovic murder. They're picking up Dickie right now for questioning. I'll call Hong and let him know about the man who tried to assault you in the Public Library's basement. If Dickie doesn't give up a name, we'll have you go through mug shots. The Twentieth Precinct house is on Eighty-second. I'll take you myself tomorrow, okay?"

"Okay . . ." I sighed with relief and explained my current dilemma. "I'm sorry, Mike, but I don't have a key with me to get into my place or yours."

He told me what to do and asked me to put Franco on the line.

I did, thanking the sergeant again for his help, and then I climbed out of his unmarked car, punched in the front door code on Quinn's building, and took the elevator up to Dr. Mel Billings's apartment (a neighbor and coworker of Quinn's who kept a spare key to his place).

Mel let me into Quinn's one-bedroom, and I locked the door behind me. Then I rang Tucker, left a message on his cell to take my handbag and clothes with him when he left the library, and headed straight into a hot shower.

Toweling off, I heard the front door unlock and open. I smiled with relief, already feeling better because Mike was finally home. Using a small hand dryer, I took a few minutes to fluff up my chestnut hair. Then I sprayed on a bit of perfume, glossed my lips, wrapped a terrycloth robe around me, and began swinging the bathroom door out toward the bedroom.

"Hey, big boy! Guess who?"

I froze at the sound of a strange woman's singsong voice— and pushed the door the rest of the way open.

Sitting on Mike's king-size bed was a tall, slender, thirty-something woman. Her most striking feature—a silky curtain of red curls—framed a delicately sculpted face with a complexion of flawless porcelain. A Mrs. Claus baby-doll nightie barely covered the woman's long, slender torso. Her

Rockette-length legs were crossed; her pretty feet manicured with holiday red polish; and the expression in her big, blue, doll-like eyes was one of pure shock.

Okay, that made *two* of us in shock.

"Who are you?" I demanded—and that's when I remembered. This was the same Blend customer who'd been giving me nasty looks for the past week. I'd assumed she'd been holding a grudge because of our argument on the night of Alf's murder. Obviously, I'd been wrong.

"I'm Leila!" she now informed me. "Leila Quinn!"

"Mike's ex-wife!"

I closed my eyes. Mike never wanted to talk about Leila. He displayed no photos of her, and I'd never pressed him for details. I thought I was letting the man heal, allowing him space from bad memories. Now I could see what that naive trust had wrought.

Opening my eyes, I glared. "Why are you here?"

"Excuse me," she snapped, "why are *you* here?"

"Mike invited me!"

"Well, he invited me, too," Leila said with a pout. "And you know what? Three's a crowd!" She pointed to one of her wrists and, right in front of me, *handcuffed* herself to Mike's bedpost!

My God. Matt was right. He'd warned me that Quinn was seeing some redhead . . .

"You know what, Leila?" I said. "Three *is* a crowd."

Hurt, humiliated, and so angry I couldn't see straight, I moved to the drawer Quinn had set aside for me, yanked out jeans, a sweater, socks. I didn't have shoes here, but the black go-go boots would do. I went back into the bathroom, dressed, and began to storm out.

As I reached the front door, the man walked in.

"Get out of my way, you son of a—"

"Clare!" Quinn took hold of my shoulders, stopping me. "What's wrong?"

"What's wrong?" Through a filmy blur of exasperated tears, I glared at the lying, cheating, jerk of a—"I just witnessed your ex-wife *handcuffing* herself to your bed, wearing a Mrs. Claus nightie, and you ask me *what's wrong*?!"

For three mind-numbing seconds, Quinn's confused expression dropped into horrified shock. Then his face flushed with pure fury.

"Wait right here," he bit out.

"No! I'm leaving—"

"*Please*, Clare, *wait*. You need to see this!"

Swiping away my angry tears, I stiffly stood by the apartment's open door, vowing to give the man no more than thirty seconds for whatever stunt he was about to pull.

Twenty-nine

~~~~~~

Quinn kicked open the bedroom door.

"Get out."

"Oh, calm down," Leila replied with a little-girl voice. "You *want* me here, Mike. Admit it . . ."

"You have no right. *No* right to invade my privacy."

"You gave me a key!"

"I gave you a key because you can't seem to drop off our kids anywhere close to a time we've agreed on. I gave you a key for Molly and Jeremy, not to handcuff yourself to my damn bedpost!"

Quinn cursed a blue streak. I could hear him manipulating the cuffs, unlocking them. "Get dressed—"

"You'll change your mind. You will—"

"Listen to me, Leila. I told you *a dozen* times over the last week. I don't want you in my bed *ever* again. Have you got that?"

"You're just acting like this because *she's* in the next room listening."

"Get out. *Now.* Or I swear to God I will have you arrested for trespassing."

Leila laughed. "Go ahead. Why do you think I brought the toy handcuffs? Remember when we first got married? They used to be your favorite—"

Quinn cursed again. "Get out!"

I gritted my teeth as I listened to the scene, remembering too well how ugly things had gotten between me and Matt at the end of our marriage. As I heard Leila stomping toward the bedroom door, my whole body went rigid. A second later, her statuesque figure sashayed across Quinn's living room. She was fully dressed now—a cashmere sweater and little skirt, a dainty box handbag dangling on her slender arm.

"Here!" Mike grabbed her overcoat off his couch and flung it at her.

I'd never seen him so angry. This was no act. He was absolutely furious.

Leila picked the coat up off the floor and took her time putting it on. Her big blue eyes connected with mine, then collapsed into slits. "He'll change his mind about you." Her voice was no longer girlishly saccharine. The tone was bitter, guttural, threatening. "And when he does, I'll be there."

I said nothing to the woman. This wasn't my fight.

"Get moving, Leila. Get out."

"I'm going," she told Quinn sweetly, and with one last withering glance my way, she added, "For now," then shut the door.

The room fell silent. I felt numb. Mike was still furious; his harsh breathing was audible. Finally, I got up the courage to meet his eyes.

"I'm sorry, Clare," he said. "She just found out about you."

"*What?* After all this time, you never mentioned me?!"

"Sit down, sweetheart. Let me explain."

Frankly, I was tempted not to. This night had put me through the grinder, and all I wanted right now was a warm gingerbread steamer and a soft mattress. I'd wanted Mike's arms around me, too, but that wasn't going to happen. Not tonight. Maybe not ever again.

"Please hear me out." Mike's face was no longer filled with rage. As he studied me, his expression crumbled into an almost painful helplessness. "Sweetheart, *please . . .*"

I finally did as he asked, moving to the sofa and sitting stiffly on its edge. "Talk."

Mike took a deep breath, ran a hand through his hair. "Remember when Leila changed plans on me two weeks ago, dropped off the kids for Thanksgiving? You changed your own plans so that you could help me take the kids to the Macy's parade, make us that incredible turkey dinner, play with the kids when I was called away to consult on the Pilgrim's Daughter OD case . . ."

"Of course I remember."

He began to pace. "Well, Molly and Jeremy *loved* you, Clare. When Leila saw them again the following night, they couldn't stop talking about the food you made them and the games you played with them. It finally hit Leila that I had a woman in my life—" He stopped pacing and met my eyes. "An unbelievably good, incredibly beautiful woman . . ."

"Mike—"

"Leila lost it, sweetheart. She had to know everything about you—"

I closed my eyes, remembering all the times I'd seen the woman visiting my coffeehouse since Thanksgiving weekend. Had she simply been spying on me? Or had she been waiting for Mike to walk in so she could make some kind of scene? *Probably both*, I realized.

"She started showing up at my apartment," Mike continued, "calling me at all hours, literally throwing herself at me."

"Why?"

"Because my ex-wife is a spoiled brat, that's why!"

"That tells me nothing."

Mike shook his head and went back to pacing. "Clare, when Leila and I first met, it was professionally. She came to the city on her father's money. She was a party girl, a model, and she had plenty of men drooling after her—"

"That's not hard to believe. Matt said he saw you twice in restaurants with a gorgeous redhead—he didn't know Leila's name, but he remembered her from a Victoria's Secret cover fifteen years ago."

"Well, all that physical beauty attracted the wrong kind of male attention, too. She'd gotten herself a genuine stalker. A real creep. I was still in uniform back then, assigned to her case on a stakeout shift. I caught the guy, put him in jail, and then she called *me* for a date."

"Okay, I get it. Police badge as knight's shield—"

"It was role-playing for both of us. I liked the role of hero, protector. And she'd become skittish of male attention after the creep almost raped her. She clung to me, we dated for a while, got married. Everything was hunky-dory for a few years. Then I got promoted, earned my gold shield, we bought a brownstone in Brooklyn, and she woke up one day, realizing she was changing diapers in a borough that wasn't Manhattan, married to a civil servant who had a demanding job. She wasn't strong, Clare, and she was used to another kind of life—parties, travel, shopping excursions, male attention. What she got were crying babies and a stressed-out husband who lived for his job. So she began to cheat. It went on for years. I put up with it, told myself she deserved better. I expected her to leave me at some point, and finally she did."

"But now she wants you back?"

"Not to marry."

"I don't understand. I thought she was happy, got what she wanted. Isn't she engaged to some Wall Street whiz, a richer, younger guy—"

"Yeah and he's lousy in bed because he's selfish, just like her. Guys with no-limit credit cards expect the women they're wining and dining and footing the bills for to *deliver*. Leila's getting bored with getting him off and getting little in return of any consequence—a closetful of shoes and handbags, a trip to a spa, or an overpriced restaurant meal. She's finally getting old enough to understand what's truly valuable in this life. She's comprehending what she lost when she dumped me. She wants my *love* back, Clare."

"Oh, God."

"You have to understand, she got used to the pattern. She'd cheat with some rich guy—use him to party in Manhattan, get back to that carefree life she'd had at nineteen—and then she'd come back to my bed. Cheat and come back. I'd always be there for her, always forgive her. This week was the first time she ever heard me tell her to take a hike. She can't have me and she can't believe it. But I don't want her anymore. I want *you*, Clare. See, I finally realized that maybe *I* deserve better."

I shook my head. "All those mysterious phone calls that made you turn into a zombie—"

"They were from her."

"Why didn't you just tell me what was happening?"

"Leila's poison, Clare. I didn't want her to poison us—"

"Aw, Mike. That's just a cop-out."

"No! I have to deal with her if I want to see my children. But her calls and demands and complaints are my problem, not yours. You and I weren't getting enough time together as it was—I didn't want the time we had poisoned by discussions of Leila and her drama-queen act."

"But if she's your problem, she's mine, too. I thought we were in this together. Until tonight, I thought you trusted me . . ."

Quinn studied me for a long, silent moment. Seeing the pain on my face, he finally seemed to get it. "I'm sorry, Clare. The last thing I ever wanted to do was hurt you. I thought what I was doing was shielding you."

"No, Mike, what you were doing was shutting me out. It's your knee-jerk solution to crisis. You shut down emotionally, throw up a firewall—"

"I'm a cop," he said quietly. "That's what we do. We don't . . ." He shook his head.

"You don't let it all hang out. Yeah, I get that. It's your conditioning, what's required to survive the job. But if you want our relationship to survive—"

"I do. Please don't doubt it."

"Then you have to let me be a part of your life, share what comes at you—the good parts and the embarrassing parts and the toxic parts, too. It's all or nothing."

"*All*, Clare," he said without taking a breath. "I want you in my life. Don't you understand? Without you, I don't have one."

"That's very sweet, but you do, Mike. You have your work—you're absolutely devoted to it—and you have your kids. Molly loves you; Jeremy looks up to you so much. You have your mother who gave you that cherry cordial recipe—"

"You need to meet her."

"I'd like to. I mean, the cat's out of the bag now, right? I just met your cousin the fire captain, the other Mike Quinn."

Mike scowled at that. "Let's discuss him another time."

"Okay, as long as you understand what I'm asking."

"I do, Clare. Please, can we get beyond this now?" He paused, exhaled, ran a hand through his hair. "Have you eaten?"

"No. I'm starving, but I don't want to stay here tonight."

Mike's face fell. "Clare, please . . ."

"Just drive me home, okay? I need to process all this." I headed for the front door. "I need some time, Mike. Give it to me. Please."

Quinn didn't say a word, just worked his jaw, rubbed the back of his neck, and nodded. Then together we walked out the door.

THIRTY

~~~~~~

As we climbed into Quinn's car, I noticed him give a quick wave to someone across the street. A short, loud *whoop* replied, and I realized Sergeant Franco had stuck around, waiting for a signal from Mike to depart. Now his blue sedan sped away, heading uptown.

"He's going to the Dickie interrogation, isn't he?" I said.

Quinn nodded. "They probably have him in custody by now."

"I wish I could be there, too."

Quinn started the car. "I doubt very much a man like that's going to confess to anything, Clare. He's got a lot of money. He'll lawyer up."

I slumped back in the seat, and we both fell into an unhappy silence for the rest of the ten-minute drive. When we pulled up to the Blend, the lights were still burning. Esther and Vicki—a barista team once more—were just getting ready to close up shop. (As it turned out, Vicki Glockner wanted to make some extra cash over the holidays, and I badly needed another trained barista. So we'd agreed to give our working relationship one more try.)

Boris Bokunin was inside, too, waiting for his Best girl to finish her shift.

As Mike pulled to a stop by the curb, I automatically reached for a handbag that wasn't there. That's when I remembered—

"My keys!"

"You don't have them?" Quinn said. "Oh, that's right. Your bag's in that locker. Should we drive to the Public Library?"

"No . . ." My bag wouldn't help me. I'd given *Matt* my key to the duplex. "I was going to pick up the spare at your place, but then I found Leila, and . . ."

Quinn reached out and put his hand on my leg. "Come back to my place, sweetheart. Just come back."

"You have a key to my duplex, don't you? I gave you one."

Quinn stiffened. "Yes."

"Can I have it back, please?"

Quinn didn't answer right away. For a long, silent moment, he just held my eyes. Then he rigidly reached into his pocket and brought out his ring of keys. With a heavy silence, he worked my key off his circle and held it out.

"Thanks."

As I took it, he leaned toward me. "Clare—"

"Good night!" I climbed out, shut the door, didn't look back. I could hear his car continuing to idle as I walked quickly through the Blend's front entrance.

Jingle-jingle . . .

"Hey, boss!"

"Clare Cosi, Clare Cosi, the West Village posy . . ."

I said a fast hello to Boris, then Esther and Vicki, and headed right for the back service stairs. Emotionally drained, I was about ready to burst into tears and I didn't want them to see.

None of this was easy. I was tired and hungry, badly disappointed in Mike for not trusting me, freaked out by his conceited ex-wife's crazy behavior, and still unbelievably frustrated that after all of my efforts I wasn't able to bring Alf's killer to justice.

As I hauled my tired body up the stairs, a strong sensation came over me that something familiar was cooking—heavy and savory with hints of garlic and herbs. It reminded me of the holiday aromas in my Nonna's house, and for a minute, I thought maybe her ghost was in my kitchen now, fixing me a much-needed snack.

"Don't be silly, Clare . . ."

It's a hunger delusion, I decided. My stomach was so empty that some kind of foodie flashback was hijacking my senses. I slipped Mike's key into the lock, turned it, and even imagined hearing sounds coming at me from another room of my duplex: pots and pans, laughter and voices—

"You have too many in the pan!"

"I do not."

"You have to be *patient*, Daddy! Fry *small* batches. If the oil cools off, the shrimp will soak it up and be greasy . . ."

"I *know* how to fry shrimp, little girl."

"I'm the pro here. You should let *me* cook for *you*—"

"Oh, I will, muffin. I expect a *full*-course French meal this Sunday!"

I rushed toward the lighted kitchen. It was true! This was *real*. My daughter was back from Paris!

"Joy!"

"Mom!"

She looked so beautiful, so grown up, standing there cuddling Alf's little white kitten. Her chestnut hair was much longer now, spilling loosely over her shoulders. Her green eyes were bright, her wide mouth smiling in her fresh, heart-shaped face.

Her father was a few steps away, working at the stove, frying something with lots of garlic and oil.

"Am I dreaming?!" I murmured.

Matt grinned. "Glad you finally made it!" He was still in his tuxedo pants, his Armani jacket draped over a chair, his black tie undone and hanging around his partially unbuttoned white shirt.

I opened my arms. "My Joy to the World!"

Stepping up, she hugged me tight. "I wanted to surprise you, Mom. I tried your cell but I couldn't reach you, so I called Daddy."

"I had your key," Matt said, "so I came back to let her in."

"And he brought two pounds of this amazingly fresh shrimp!"

"I've been so sick and tired of sushi and raw bars and vegan fare—when I got Joy's call, I decided what I really wanted was to cook my little girl up a nice big batch of Italian fried shrimp."

I shook my head, still amazed Joy was home. "Where'd you get the fresh shrimp at this hour?"

"Easy, I was already at a private party in a restaurant. I just ducked into the kitchen and slipped a staff worker fifty bucks to grab me two pounds from their walk-in."

Joy and I laughed as we sat down. Matt fried up those jumbo, bread-crumb-encrusted babies and we popped the hot, deliciously crunchy results into our mouths. Then I brewed up a big pot of our Holiday Blend, opened up my cookie jar of home-baked biscotti, and for the next two hours we were a family again. Matt and I caught up with our daughter about so many things!

Finally, Matt began to yawn.

"I better get back uptown. I told Bree I'd meet her at the apartment." He checked his watch. "I'll see you girls tomorrow, okay?"

Joy kissed her father's cheek. I gave him a hug.

Then, arm in arm, she and I climbed the stairs together. As I made up the bed in the second room, I sensed there was something on her mind—and I remembered what Madame had assumed about Joy's initial change of plan. Had the grande dame been wrong? (She hardly ever was.)

"So," I pried, "your bosses *really* decided they could let you off, after all?"

"Why do you ask that way?"

"Oh, because the way you changed plans last week, your grandmother seemed to think a boy was involved."

Joy's expression faltered. "I didn't want to say anything."

Aha! "What happened?"

"I met a guy. He's French."

Big surprise.

"We work together on the brigade, so we've spent a lot of time together—"

Score two for Grandma. Man, she can really call it . . .

"He's so cool, Mom. He and I really hit it off . . ."

"But then?"

"But then he bailed on me. He was supposed to come home on this trip so you and everyone could meet him. But at the last minute, he said he didn't want to come. He said if I had any delusions about his moving to America, we needed to stop seeing each other." Joy's eyes were filling with tears. "I think he just got scared . . . and then I didn't want to come home, either. It felt like he totally ruined the holidays for me."

"Sit down," I said. She did and I put my arm around her. "I'm glad you told me. And I'm glad you decided to come home anyway."

"Why are men such jerks?"

"Women are jerks, too. We're all jerks when it comes to relationships. At one time or another we all let each other down. The miracle is when we figure out how to love each other anyway."

Joy rested her head on my shoulder. "I'm glad I came home, Mom."

"Me, too, honey."

EARLY the next morning, Joy found me at the bathroom sink. She was already dressed in stressed denims and a sweater straight out of her suitcase, wrinkles and all.

"Mom? You're up already?"

"I didn't want to wake you, honey. It's not even six. Go back to sleep, you must be exhausted."

Joy shook out her newly grown long hair and reached

into her pocket for an elastic band, automatically securing it into a tight, kitchen-ready ponytail.

"I'm still on French time," she said, "so my internal clock's gone completely to *merde*. Since I'm up, I thought I'd help around the coffeehouse today. That okay?"

I was still flying from last night's reunion, and Joy's words sent me soaring even higher. I was so happy she was home for the holidays, and here she was asking to spend the whole day with me? It was the best Christmas gift I could ever get.

She pointed to the sink. "What are you doing with Frothy's jingle bell pillow?"

"Oh, Java got territorial. She sprayed the thing. It's too bad. The two girls were getting along otherwise . . ."

Last night, a purring Frothy even curled up next to my bigger, older Java at the foot of my bed. But this morning, I found Java tinkling all over Santa's embroidered sleigh.

"I don't think Java liked the smell of this thing," I said, "but then it did come from a strange apartment . . ." (With a dead guy in it, but I left that part out.) "I'll give it a good soaking in strong soap, wash it out—that should do the trick."

"What can I do? Make coffee?"

"Not here. You can start opening downstairs, though. Our bakery delivery guy should be here in the next half hour."

"No problem, Mom. I'll take care of it." Smiling, Joy grabbed the coffeehouse keys off the table in the hall. "See you downstairs!"

I searched Frothy's pillow for a zipper, planning to soak the inside and covering separately. But there was no zipper, just a tear in the fabric that had been closed with a safety pin. I unclipped it, and a flat, green, oval-shaped capsule clattered onto the tile floor—

What the heck is this?

I picked up the little green capsule and realized it was a flash drive, a portable computer storage device. It looked just like the flash drives I used to back up my laptop data.

I put the device on the sink and searched the kitty pillow until I was satisfied it would yield no more secrets. Then I washed my hands and hurried down to the computer inside my small office on the second floor of the Blend.

I plugged the flash drive into my computer. It contained a single folder labeled CC.

"CC again?" I whispered. "Me? Clare Cosi?"

Uneasily, I opened the folder and a series of thumbnail images appeared, dated and arranged in progression.

"Macy's Thanksgiving's Day Parade?" I murmured, confused.

I clicked through pictures of the parade marching by an Upper West Side apartment building. Then I stopped and stared at a close-up of a man. The man's face was familiar to me—and millions of other American women.

Oh my God. The "CC" in the note I'd found—the one in Karl Kovic's coat pocket—it didn't stand for Clare Cosi! It stood for this handsome TV celebrity who was laughing with an attractive young woman, one who was clearly *not* his wife.

The next image was a close-up of the young woman. I recognized her as Waverly "Billie" Billington, the famous "Pilgrim's Daughter" heiress who died of a prescription drug overdose on Thanksgiving night. She was the victim in the case Mike was working on.

Just then I heard someone knock on the locked door downstairs. *The bakery delivery must be arriving . . .*

"I'll take care of this, Mom!" Joy called.

"Okay, thanks," I yelled back. As the *jingle-jingle* of the front door sounded, I placed a call to Mike Quinn's cell.

"Clare?" Quinn said, his voice sleep-groggy. "Are you okay?"

"Mike, I *just* solved your Pilgrim's Daughter case. And Alf's and Kovic's murders, too. And maybe even your cold case from *last* Thanksgiving—"

"Clare, sweetheart, have you been *drinking*?"

"No! Listen! I found Karl Kovic's computer *flash drive*! He was hiding it inside a Santa Claus jingle bell pillow! It has digital photos on it. The link you needed is here, Mike."

"What link? I don't understand—"

"I'm looking at a series of images on my computer screen. They show a big TV celebrity laughing with Billie Billington on Thanksgiving Day. The two must have met at that parade-watching party Billie attended hours before she overdosed. And I'm willing to bet that party was thrown by Dickie Celebratorio. He probably even provided the drugs for the two to party with—"

"Whoa, Clare, slow down. Where did this all take place?"

"Karl Kovic shot this footage on the Upper West Side with what looks like a powerful zoom lens. He was using the pictures for blackmail. That's why he was murdered. These images show the movements of the TV star he was blackmailing."

"Who is this guy? What's his name?"

I told Quinn but he didn't watch much TV. "Believe me," I assured him, "the guy's famous! Anyway, the images show him talking to Billie Billington on the street, but then he walks off alone in another direction. More photos show the man buying junk food at a deli and ducking into an alley. He makes a cell call and then, lo and behold, Billie Billington appears in the alley, holding open the building's side service door. The famous man slips inside, bypassing the lobby!"

"Billie slipped him into her building?"

"Yes! That's why the woman's doorman didn't see anyone go into her apartment! She sneaked this famous guy inside by way of the building's side service entrance! This is it! You can use this evidence to demand DNA and fingerprints from this man. No lawyer can protect him now! And then you can prove his guilt when you match his DNA to the crime scenes and maybe even his fingerprints to the gun that Franco recovered in Alf's murder!"

Quinn finally caught up. "I'm coming, Clare. I'll call

Hong and Franco, too. Tell them to meet me at the Blend. Stay where you are."

I figured it would take Mike at least ten minutes to get from his apartment in the East Village to my West Village coffeehouse. Feeling a combination of triumph and relief, I decided I'd finally earned my first cup of morning joe.

I knew everything now. Shane the elf had been hired by Dickie Celebratorio to trail Karl, the Traveling Santa. But Shane had made an error. He didn't know there were two Traveling Santas living at the same address. So when Alf Glockner left the building, Shane mistakenly followed Alf instead. Then Shane gave his report on Alf's routine to Dickie, who turned around and gave it to the killer, who followed Alf and shot him.

Of course, Alf wasn't blackmailing anyone! Killing Alf was a mistake—one the killer obviously figured out because he caught up with the right Santa, Karl Kovic, a week later. But the killer didn't have the chance to search Karl's apartment long enough to find the evidence. *I did!*

"Mom!" Joy called, her voice sounding a little odd. "Can you come down?"

I was halfway down the spiral staircase when I saw him—

"I'm sorry, Mom," Joy whispered. "I thought he was the delivery guy."

Chaz Chatsworth, costar of *The Chatsworth Way* and the featured performer in Karl Kovic's little flash-drive slideshow, stood behind my daughter. His left arm was wrapped around her throat in a choke hold; his right hand held a gun to her head. Joy's wrists were bound behind her back.

"My God . . ."

"I want what you took from Kovic's apartment," Chatsworth told me evenly.

Mr. Charm's signature snowy hair was hidden under a baseball cap. He wore a fake brown beard and mustache and tinted eyeglasses. His cheap sweatpants and sneakers were the color of night.

I stared in shock at the man. *Ten minutes until Mike gets*

here. Maybe forty seconds have passed since I hung up. Nine minutes at least. An eternity—

"Did you hear me, Ms. Cosi?" Chatsworth drove the weapon into Joy's temple with enough force to make her cry out.

"You son of a bitch! Leave her *alone*."

"Do you want her to die?"

"No!"

"I *saw* you there last night," Chatsworth said. "Do you hear me? I *saw* you in Kovic's apartment."

I swallowed hard. This creep shot two men to death in cold blood. No matter what I said or did, I knew he was going to kill Joy and me, too. I had to stall—give Mike the time to get here—and the only bargaining chip I had was the flash drive in my pocket. The second Chatsworth got it, I knew he'd have no reason to keep my daughter and me alive.

"Yes, okay, I was there last night," I slowly admitted. I glanced at the wall clock; another minute gone, another minute for Mike to get here. "And I found Kovic's body . . . but I just called the police. That's all—"

"Don't lie to me," Chaz snapped. "I waited outside until the police came. When they didn't show right away, I knew you and that guy in the tux were searching for the pictures."

I remembered Shane Holliway and his dumb soap star act. "What pictures? I don't know what you mean—"

Chatsworth's arm tightened around Joy's throat.

"*Please*, don't hurt her," I said. "She has *nothing* to do with all this. She doesn't know anything. I'm the one who can help you. Just let her go—"

"Maybe I will, if you tell me something. Come on, Clare. Tell me something that will make me *happy*."

"It was the kitten! The man you saw—he took the cat from Kovic's apartment."

Chaz frowned. "The man in the tux was carrying a pet carrier *and* a cardboard box. I heard him tell the cab driver to take him to the Village Blend. I want the contents of that box or your daughter dies."

Yeah, I'll give you the contents of that box, asshole. "That box was full of cat crap!"

Chatsworth's nostrils flared as he tightened his choke hold on Joy. "Don't you know that six out of ten American men experience *anger* when a woman *lies* to them!"

He's losing it! He's choking her! "Okay, you win!" I shouted. "Here's what you came for!" As slowly as I could, I pulled Karl's secret flash drive out of my pocket and held it up.

"I want your computer, too," Chaz said. "And I'm pretty sure I'll find it upstairs with the little girl's help. Lights out now, Clare. I don't need you anymore."

"What are you going to do?" Joy screamed.

"Early-morning robbery, cute thing," Chaz replied. "Mother and daughter dead. A tragedy."

Joy struggled, but Chatsworth tightened his grip again, until she could hardly breathe, let alone fight.

My fists clenched. There was no time left. Nowhere near time for Mike to get here. I had to do something.

"Mom goes first," Chatsworth said. "So I can have a little fun with daughter before I put *her* lights out."

He slowly shifted the gun until I was staring down the barrel. *I'll die*, I decided, *that's what I'll do. I'll run at him, take the bullets, give my Joy a chance to get away—*

I was about to lunge when I heard the loud *boom!*

A gun went off, I was sure of it, but I wasn't shot—and then I realized *Chatsworth* was the one reeling, blood spurting from his shoulder.

But who shot him?!

The noise of falling glass caught my attention. I looked up to see a familiar silhouette through the cracked windowpane. *Mike!* I tore Joy away from Chatsworth's grip and pulled her to the ground, out of the line of fire.

Glass exploded inward as Mike Quinn came through the French doors, firing two more shots as he moved. Bullets ripped Chaz Chatsworth, twisting him around until his limp body crashed into a café table.

Quinn stood over the dead man, his weapon smoking but steady in both hands. His clothes were rumpled, a five o'clock shadow on his cheeks and chin. He kicked the gun away from Chatsworth's dead fingers and faced me.

"Are you okay?" he asked, his voice tight with emotion.

I helped Joy to her feet and nodded. "We're *both* okay. How did you get here so fast?"

"I never left," he told me. "I was sleeping in my car outside when your call woke me. I would have fired sooner, but I couldn't get a clear shot until he took the gun away from Joy's head."

Five minutes later, Emmanuel Franco climbed through the shattered window, followed by his partner, Charlie Hong. For a few silent seconds, we all stared down at the dead celebrity. Then Franco turned to me and asked—

"Who the hell is *he*?"

"It's a long story, detective," I said with a sigh. "And I'll be happy to start at the beginning. But first I'm going to need a really big cup of coffee."

EPILOGUE

~~~~~~~~~~~~~~~~~~~~~~~~~~~~~~~~~~~~

"**LOOK** up."

Mike Quinn's whisper tickled my ear as I began pulling two new shots behind the espresso bar. I glanced toward the ceiling to find a small bunch of green herbs dangling above my head.

"What is that?"

"Mistletoe."

I laughed. "Mike, that is *not* mistletoe."

"No?"

I sniffed the flat-leaf bouquet. "It's Italian parsley!"

"Really?" Quinn pointed across the Blend's crowded main floor. "Your former mother-in-law assured me it was mistletoe."

Madame, looking stunning tonight in a jade and burgundy ensemble, gave us a little wave. I shook my finger at her. She laughed, then turned to rejoin Otto, Matt, and Breanne.

"So what does that mean?" Quinn complained. "Are you telling me I'm not getting a Christmas kiss out of this?"

"Not a mistletoe kiss, no. Now shoo, Detective, and let me work . . ."

It was Christmas Eve and the Village Blend was packed with Santas—*Traveling* Santas. After the crime-scene cleanup, I'd called Brother Dom and suggested something that would cleanse the Blend's karma: a party for the men and women who'd been working so hard to bring the spirit of the holidays to the needy of the city.

Once Brother Dom and his crew finished their Christmas Eve rounds at the shelters, churches, and soup kitchens, I invited them here for Fa-la-la-la Lattes and an avalanche of cookies baked by my baristas.

Brother Dom was thrilled to accept the offer, as well as the check from Madame for his charity. But that wasn't the biggest donation. After finding out about Dexter Beatty's and Omar Linford's little scheme to cheat the city, I phoned Omar and *strongly* suggested he give back a little. Or even better, *a lot*.

Linford quickly—even happily—wrote the check for Brother Dom. He didn't even mind hearing from me again (a miracle, because I'd been responsible for having his son busted). It seemed the arrest finally put the fear of the DEA into Dwayne Linford. He stopped fighting his dad and agreed to enroll in college for that music degree. At last, Dwayne's nights of club hopping were finished (for a while, anyway) and for that, Omar was grateful.

With Chatsworth dead—and his DNA and fingerprints not only linking him to Alf's and Karl's murders, but also the Pilgrim's Daughter and Cora Arnold OD cases—you'd think Madame's friend Mr. Dewberry was finished, too. But Phyllis Chatsworth had just been handed the publicity bonanza of a lifetime.

Within days of her husband's death, she'd tearfully appeared on every major interview show in the country. Her instant prime-time special, *Phyllis: How to Survive the Unthinkable*, just got the green light for development into a new weekday talk show. Her executive producer? James Young.

Dickie Celebratorio (aka Richard Torio) was facing a

number of charges that *he* considered *unthinkable*. But the DA's office had solid testimony to back up their charges of accessory to murder, among others.

With the promise of immunity, Shane Holliway agreed to testify that Dickie had hired him to surveil Alf Glockner two days in a row before he was shot to death by Chaz Chatsworth (the recovered fingerprints on the gun confirmed Chaz as the killer). The TV talk show host had used Shane's lousy PI report to follow the wrong Santa.

And then there was Heidi Gilcrest, that pretty, young *Chatsworth Way* production assistant who always made sure Chaz got his junk food. She tearfully agreed to testify that whenever she and Chaz slept together, Dickie was the one who'd provided the recreational drugs—the very same drug that ended up killing Billie Billington and Cora Arnold.

Dickie was the one who'd provided the guns for Chaz, as well. Recovery of the second weapon provided that link. It seemed Madame was right again: Dickie was a guy who "helped" celebs. The fact that the "help" involved drugs, cover-ups, blackmail, and murder didn't appear to faze a man from the Bronx streets. But then, as Quinn had pointed out to me, this was the season of favors; and in Dickie's world, the bigger the favor owed, the better.

Of course, Dickie's lawyers were working overtime to broker a deal with the DA. But one thing was certain for the New Year: No matter how much or little time the man did behind bars, the amount of scandalous newsprint he was getting would render his days as the PR Party King over for good.

As for Shelly Glockner, she turned out to be innocent of all charges. The bank account numbers at the end of Linford's blackmail letter belonged to Karl Kovic and Karl alone. He really was a Man of a Thousand Schemes.

After I'd visited Shelly that day on Staten Island, she'd told Karl everything I'd said—but she had no idea Karl was going to dump me off the ferry or even that he was blackmailing her neighbor in her husband's name. I might have disbelieved her, but in the end Shelly handed the entire check for Alf's life insurance money over to her daughter.

"Your father and I always thought you'd inherit the restaurant," she confided to Vicki. "So we never saved for you. Never created a college fund. This is your fund now. Your father would have wanted it that way . . ."

Vicki was thrilled, of course. She was planning to enroll in Joy's old culinary school this fall. And I was happy to hear she was going to stay on at the Blend, too. One day soon, I might even trust her with a key to this place again.

And speaking of keys—I'd already handed the key to my duplex back to Detective Mike Quinn. For one thing, I didn't think my French doors could handle him coming in any other way. And for another, I firmly decided I wanted Mike in my life.

Like I'd told my daughter, who was talking a little too much to Emmanuel Franco this evening (the man actually exchanged his red, white, and blue do-rag for a red and green one), relationships were never easy. But I sincerely believed the best gift we could give or receive was the chance to love one another.

Which brings me to that passage in Charles Dickens's *A Christmas Carol*, the one that Brother Dom said had inspired Alf. I finally read it, and—thinking of my friend—my eyes failed to stay dry. Quinn even asked me about it late on Christmas Eve . . .

WHEN the Traveling Santa party finally wound down and the last guests sang out their good-nights, Joy headed upstairs, and Mike found me again.

After I flipped off the shop's lights, he pulled me into a quiet corner by the fireplace. Our lovely white pine tree was twinkling softly. The smells of mulled cider and fresh evergreen were in the air. And Gardner's music was still playing on the sound system—one of the many CDs he'd mixed especially for the party: jazz versions of holiday standards that even Dante and his roommates thought were cool.

"Hey, Cosi, didn't you say something the other night about *A Christmas Carol*?"

I nodded. "You had to get off the phone before I could tell you. Some issue at the precinct."

"There aren't any issues now, sweetheart. There's just you and me."

I touched his clean-shaven cheek and pretended that was true. But Leila Quinn said she wasn't through trying to get what she wanted. *She wants my love back, Clare.* That's what Mike had told me. And after all they'd shared together—two kids, a home, a history—I knew it was still possible, no matter what Mike said.

"So what was that Dickens passage about exactly?" Quinn asked. "The one that helped change Alf's life, give him a new perspective . . ."

"Well, the passage came at the end of the book's first chapter. Scrooge is visited by the ghost of his old business partner, Marley, who tells Scrooge to look out his bedroom window. Scrooge does and suddenly realizes there are ghosts like Marley everywhere; and they're all weighed down with long, heavy chains—chains made of links these souls forged in life from their days of continual greed and selfishness."

"Cheery."

"No, listen. The saddest spirit of all has a monstrous iron safe attached to his ankle. This ghost is bitterly crying. But he's not crying because of the heavy burden he can never throw off; he's crying because he's unable to help a wretched woman with a baby, shivering below him on a doorstep. 'The misery with them all,' Dickens wrote of these doomed spirits, 'was that they sought to interfere, for good, in human matters, and had lost the power forever . . .'"

Quinn was silent a long moment. "That is moving," he finally said. "But . . ."

"But what?"

"Is that what Alf was trying to do on that balcony the night he was killed? Interfere for good?"

"None of us are perfect, are we? Not even Santa Claus.

But Alf wasn't a Bad Santa, Mike, he was a good man. He took some relatively innocent celebrity photos for YouTube and Ben Tower because he wanted to repay a debt to his neighbor—and protect his wife and daughter from becoming responsible for that debt."

I shook my head. "I'm sure Chaz Chatsworth felt justified in shooting Alf in cold blood for the same reason. If Chaz had any doubts about killing Santa Claus, they probably evaporated when he saw Santa taking photos of his wife with James Young. I'm sure Chaz justified his killing as protecting his and his wife's way of making a living, protecting their television show."

Quinn's jaw tightened. "Except there's no justification for leaving two overdosed young women to die or threatening to kill you and Joy."

I nodded, still shuddering at the image of Chatsworth with that gun to my daughter's head.

"But I do agree with you about Alf," Quinn added. "There was no evidence that he was part of the blackmailing scheme against Chatsworth, Dickie, or Linford."

"I know Alf wasn't perfect. But I never doubted he was a good man. Whatever his faults, Mike, I'll always think the best of him. He did so much *good* before he died, so much to lift people up . . ."

"I can see why you admired him," Quinn said, meeting my eyes. "Striving to interfere, for good, in human matters is a quality worth admiring."

He gazed at me so long after that, I was beginning to think I had parsley stuck between my front teeth. "Mike?"

"I have the right stuff now, you know," he finally said.

"Excuse me? What stuff?"

He reached inside the jacket of his sports coat and brought out a leafy green bundle tied up with a red velvet ribbon.

"Mistletoe. *Authentic* mistletoe. This time *Joy* assured me, and I was thinking . . . After my holiday overtime is through and Joy's back at her job in France, I'll be getting Molly and Jeremy for two weekends in January."

"Right. I understand." I nodded, ready to be patient. "You'd like to visit with them alone."

"No, Clare. I was thinking this time you could join us. We could go ice skating or see a movie or drink frozen hot chocolate at Serendipity. What do you say? You think that's a good plan?"

"No, Mike. I think that's a *great* plan."

"We're on, then . . ."

"Oh yeah, we're on." I moved closer then. Much closer. Into the man's lap, actually. "So when exactly were you planning on using that mistletoe?"

"I was waiting."

"For what?"

He tapped his watch. "Midnight."

I glanced at the clock on the wall. Both hands had just reached twelve. It was officially—

"Merry Christmas, Clare."

"Merry Christmas, Mike."

Then the mistletoe was above my head and the gift of love, at last, was right in front of me.

Dear Editor: I am 8 years old . . . tell me
the truth; is there a Santa Claus?

—Virginia O'Hanlon,
115 West Ninety-fifth Street,
New York City

. . . Yes, VIRGINIA, there is a Santa Claus.
He exists as certainly as love and generosity
and devotion exist, and you know that they
abound and give to your life its highest beauty
and joy. Alas! How dreary would be the world
if there were no Santa Claus. . . There would
be no childlike faith then, no poetry, no
romance to make tolerable this existence . . .
No Santa Claus! Thank God! He lives, and he
lives forever. . . .

—Francis P. Church,
New York Sun, Sept. 21, 1897
Excerpted from one of the
most reprinted newspaper editorials in history.

AFTERWORD

❧❧❧❧❧❧❧❧❧❧❧❧❧❧❧❧❧❧

THE Traveling Santas may have been my own fictional invention for the plotline of this novel, but there are many worthy holiday charities that really do exist. Here are two I'd like to tell you about . . .

Operation Santa Claus

More than one hundred years ago, New York City postal clerks (in what was then known as the Money Order Division) dug into their own pockets to answer Santa's mail and purchase food and toys for children who faced the unhappiness of an empty Christmas stocking. Over the years, as the letters increased, the post office opened the program to the public.

Now Operation Santa Claus is an annual program sponsored by the New York Post Office. Letters addressed merely to "Santa Claus" are delivered to the Operation Santa section, where they are opened by postal employees and made available between December 2 and 24 for the public to answer. In recent years, the program has expanded to U.S.

post offices in California, Illinois, Pennsylvania, and Washington, D.C.

To find out more about the U.S. Post Office's Operation Santa Claus program and whether it's expanded to a city near you, contact your local post office with questions. To find the physical address and phone number of your local post office, visit www.usps.com.

The Salvation Army's Red Kettles

Until I wrote this book, I had no idea how or when the Salvation Army's street-corner collectors began ringing their Santa bells and collecting change in their ubiquitous red kettles—as sure a sign of the holiday season in New York as the lighting of Rockefeller Center's Christmas tree.

According to the Salvation Army, the red kettle's origin dates back to 1891 when one of their members named Joseph McFee was distraught because so many poor individuals in San Francisco were going hungry. He resolved to provide a free Christmas dinner for the poverty-stricken of the city, but where would he get the money to feed a thousand of the city's poorest people on Christmas Day?

McFee found the solution in a past memory of his days in Liverpool, England. He recalled people throwing change into a large iron kettle to help the poor. Because the pot had been placed near a landing where boats came in, McFee put a pot just like it at the Oakland Ferry Landing at the foot of Market Street. He soon had the money he needed.

Six years later, the kettle idea spread to Boston and New York, then to other cities around the United States, Europe, and beyond. These days, according to the Salvation Army, they assist more than four and a half million people during the Thanksgiving and Christmas holiday season.

The millions of dollars' worth of change they collect is used to aid needy families, seniors, and the homeless. Donations provide Christmas dinners, clothing, and toys for families in need. Volunteers distribute gifts to shut-ins in hospitals and nursing homes, and shelters are open for sit-down dinners.

Now that you know the red kettle's history and its role in helping so many in need, I hope you'll join me in being a "Secret Santa" every time you pass one.

RECIPES & TIPS
FROM THE VILLAGE BLEND

Visit Cleo Coyle's virtual Village Blend at
www.CoffeehouseMystery.com
for coffee tips, coffee talk, and bonus recipes for—
* Clare's Panettone-Inspired Coffee Cake
* Nonna's Traditional Italian *Struffoli*
(with step-by-step photos)
* Matteo's Italian-Style Fried Shrimp with
Garlic-Mayo Dip, and more . . .

As a holiday gift to my readers, I've expanded this section to serve as a handy little primer—essentially a mini-book—on coffeehouse terms and drinks, including recipes for making your own coffee syrups and Fa-la-la-la Lattes! In the second part of this section, you'll find additional holiday recipes courtesy of *Holiday Grind*'s cast.

(Photos for many of these recipes can be found at my Web site: www.CoffeehouseMystery.com.)

During my own Italian upbringing, food and drink were essential in celebrating the holidays. 'Tis the season for feasting. May you eat and drink with joy!

Happy Holidays!
Cleo Coyle

Coffeehouse Terms

~~~~~~~~~~~~~~~~~~~~~~~~~~~~~~~~~~

barista—A trained espresso bartender.

espresso—A concentrated coffee drink made by forcing a small amount of hot water under high pressure through a puck of finely ground coffee beans. Experimentation with creating an espresso machine began in the nineteenth century, but it wasn't until the early twentieth century that the Italian inventor Luigi Bezzera resolved early problems with the device and patented it. The Italian company La Pavoni began manufacturing a slightly upgraded version, and the drink began following Italian immigrants, who popularized it in each country they settled. Throughout the twentieth century, engineers continued to improve the device's design. The most significant improvement came in the 1940s from Giovanni Achille Gaggia. His lever-operated piston machine was able to consistently produce pressure high enough to create the signature *crema*—the creamy foam that today's espresso drinkers now *expect* to see. Gaggia essentially invented the modern-day espresso.

   Meanwhile, in 1933, a *home* method for making espresso coffee was invented by Alfonso Bialetti, an Italian engineer who ran his own metal and machine workshop. Although the result is not considered a "true" espresso with *crema*, Bialetti's Moka Express stovetop pot nevertheless produces a bold cup that Italians have enjoyed for generations.

espresso blend—A blend of coffees, often from different regions, especially for use in an espresso machine. There is no definitive espresso blend. Creating coffee blends is a culinary skill, and roastmasters create their own unique blends.

espresso roast—Coffee beans can be roasted from light to dark. Every level of roast is given a name—Vienna roast, for example, is a lighter roast than a French roast. Espresso roast is a distinctly dark style of roasting the coffee beans, typically applied to an espresso blend. (See my Guide to Roasting Terms later in this section.)

crema—The golden foam (also described as tan or reddish brown) that forms on top of a properly pulled espresso shot.

shot—A single serving of espresso, approximately 1 fluid ounce. Coffeehouse baristas often use shot glasses when mixing coffee drinks. They let the espresso extract down from the machine right into a shot glass, then pour the shots into larger cups or glasses into which other ingredients are mixed to create espresso drinks such as cappuccinos and lattes.

doppio—A double espresso or two straight shots of espresso. A *triple* is three shots; a *quad* is four.

pull—The reason you hear about a barista "pulling" an espresso shot is that on earlier espresso machines, the barista literally pulled a handle down to force the hot water through the coffee at a high pressure. Modern espresso machines are operated by pushing a button to start the extraction process, but the traditional term *pull* is still used.

ristretto—This is a more concentrated shot of espresso with a more intense flavor. The term comes from the pull of the shot being a "restricted" or shorter pull. Less water is used to make this espresso, and the coffee beans really should be ground finer. The amount of liquid in your cup will be slightly less than a regular espresso.

lungo—This is a weaker shot of espresso with less intense flavor. The term comes from the longer pull (*lungo* means "long" in Italian). More water is used to make this espresso, so there will be slightly more liquid in your cup than a regular espresso. In France, this drink is called *café allongé*. Be warned, this style can be slightly bitter. If you're really looking for a diluted espresso, I suggest you try an Americano!

demitasse—The small cup in which a straight espresso is served.

espresso Romano—An espresso served with a twist of lemon. This is the peel only and should not include the bitter white part of the skin. Do not put the twist in the espresso drink. Instead, rub the lemon around the rim of your cup to impart the bright lemon flavor. Ironically, although the espresso Romano is popular in North America, it is *not* popular in Italy; and, although the taste combination of coffee and lemon may seem incomprehensible to some, the best single-origin beans in the world (Ethiopian Yirgacheffe, for example) actually display notes of lemon flavor. (For instructions on how to make your own candied lemon and orange peel, an elegant holiday treat with after-dinner espresso or coffee, turn to page 364.)

espresso con panna—An espresso served with a dollop of whipped cream.

macchiato—An espresso macchiato is an espresso that is "marked" or stained (that's what *macchiato* means in Italian) with a small amount of foamed milk. Americans, however, are probably more familiar with the latte macchiato, which is the opposite—a steamed milk that is marked or stained with a bit of espresso. The biggest difference between a caffe latte and a latte macchiato is the method of making the drink. In a caffe latte, the espresso goes into the glass or cup first and the steamed milk is added. In a latte macchiato, the steamed milk is placed in the cup first and then "stained" by the addition of the espresso. A caramel macchiato, for example, would be made by placing vanilla syrup at the bottom of a cup, mixing in steamed milk, then adding the espresso (thus "staining" the milk), and finally topping the drink with caramel syrup—the heat of the espresso right under the caramel syrup will also help it melt down into the drink.

caffe freddo—A chilled espresso in a glass, sometimes served with ice and sweetened. In Italy the term *freddo* is sometimes used to mean coffee that is no longer hot—coffee that has simply gone cold. Note, however, that in Italy it is *blasphemy* to warm up cold coffee!

caffe Americano, Americano—The Italian answer to American-style drip coffee. An espresso diluted with hot water. It has a similar strength to drip coffee but a different flavor. The drink's origin dates back to World War II when American GIs stationed in Italy added hot water to their espressos to create a drink closer to the type of coffee they were used to back home.

Americano misto—An Americano with steamed milk added.

cappuccino, cappa, cap—An espresso drink made with straight espresso, steamed milk, and foamed milk spooned on top. Although baristas may vary their ratios of steamed milk to foamed milk, the most common ratio is one third espresso, one third steamed milk, and one third foamed milk. The basic thing to keep in mind when you order a cappuccino is that it has more foamed milk than a caffe latte and will give you a stronger espresso flavor than a caffe latte or latte.

cappuccino dry—Depending on the barista, a *dry* may mean a cappuccino with foam only or simply one with more foamed milk than steamed milk.

cappuccino wet—A cappuccino with more steamed milk and less foam.

caffe latte, latte—Mike's drink. An espresso drink made with straight espresso and steamed milk (about one third espresso to two thirds steamed milk). In Italy, a latte will have only steamed milk. In America, baristas often top the drink with a bit of foamed milk. The basic thing to keep in mind here is that the latte has more milk than a cappuccino, so the strong espresso taste will be more diluted. The latte is the most popular drink in American espresso bars and is often flavored and sweetened with coffee syrups. (See the Coffee Syrups section.)

microfoam—Latte nirvana. Microfoam refers to *properly* textured steamed milk. It is a thick, velvety potion of pourable microbubbles created by the expert use of an espresso machine steam wand. (See *latte art*.)

latte art—An artistic design or pattern, such as a heart or rosette, created by a skillful pouring of steamed milk into your cup. You may think this is just a cutesy flourish, but major props are due to any barista who can master the steam-wand creation of pourable *microfoam* (a texture required to create latte art). So if you are served a latte that features artwork floating on top, you can be assured of two things: Your latte milk has been *properly* prepared, and your barista rocks!

breve—A term used to indicate that you'd like your drink made with half-and-half instead of milk, such as a *latte breve* or a *cappuccino breve*.

mochaccino—A cappuccino with chocolate syrup added.

caffe mocha—A caffe latte with chocolate syrup added.

Fa-la-la-la Latte—A caffe latte that uses coffee syrups or flavorings that evoke memories of the holiday season, such as a Gingerbread Latte, Eggnog Latte, or Holiday Spice Latte. This term was *my own invention* for the purposes of this novel!

café au lait—The French version of a caffe latte, made with equal parts hot milk and freshly brewed, darkly roasted coffee, usually French roast.

caffe con leche—The Spanish version of caffe latte with equal parts scalded milk and a strong, freshly brewed coffee. Sugar is added according to taste.

frappe—A cold, frothy coffee drink usually made from blending espresso, milk, crushed ice, and sugar or sweet syrups that can give the drink a variety of flavors.

red eye—Mike's drink when he's on an all-night stakeout. A regular drip coffee with a shot of espresso dumped in. (I think of it as a much more sobering version of a boilermaker!)

unleaded—A slang term for a decaffeinated coffee.

half-caf—A cup of coffee that's a 50/50 mixture of regular and decaffeinated.

single-origin—A single-origin coffee is one that comes from a single region or farm, as opposed to a coffee "blend," which is a coffee that is created by a roaster or retailer who combines beans from more than one coffee-growing region. Ethiopian Yirgacheffe, for example, is a single-origin coffee that comes from the Yirgacheffe region of the African country of Ethiopia. It is a single-origin coffee. A roaster may decide to combine the Ethiopian Yirgacheffe with a coffee from Colombia and one from Sumatra to create a "blend."

regular—In New York City, a *regular* is a cup of coffee brewed in a drip machine with milk and sugar added.

steamer—This beverage has *no* espresso. It's simply a cup of milk that's steamed to warm the beverage and increase its volume. It can be flavored with whatever sweet syrups suit your fancy: hazelnut, caramel, orange, French vanilla, peppermint, toasted marshmallow, toffee nut, and so on. (See the Coffee Syrups section.)

GUIDE to ROASTING TERMS

When coffee beans arrive at a roaster, they are "green." The roaster then decides what style of roast will best bring out that particular bean's flavor. Here is a basic guide to the spectrum of roasts and the terms often applied to them. Some coffee roasters even mix together medium- and dark-roasted beans for a delightful combination of flavors.

Light

Cinnamon, New England, Half City

Light to Medium

American, City, Brown

Medium to Dark

Full City, Vienna (or Viennese), Velvet

Darkest

Espresso, French, Italian, Spanish

Tips For Being Your Own Barista

∽∽∽∽∽∽∽∽∽∽∽∽∽

HOW TO MAKE ESPRESSO WITHOUT A MACHINE

See photos of this process at www.CoffeehouseMystery.com

In *On What Grounds* and *Murder Most Frothy*, Clare uses a small stovetop Moka Express pot to make herself a strong jolt of espresso-style coffee. Because affordable home espresso machines (remember, I said *affordable*!) cannot reproduce the kind of pressure that a professional, restaurant-quality machine can, I also use a stovetop Moka pot to make my espresso-style coffee at home. (Note to purists: I said espresso-*style*! I fully realize there's no *crema*!)

The beautiful, eight-sided Moka Express pot is the same sort of inexpensive stovetop espresso maker that members of my Italian family have used for generations. The taste experience you'll have with the stovetop pot is deliciously intense. Although not the same as a machine-made espresso (again, there won't be any *crema*), the stovetop version produces a rich, satisfyingly bold jolt of java. This is also an excellent way to make strong shots of coffee if you're planning to mix them with steamed or frothed milk and syrups to make caffe latte, café au lait, or cappuccino—or if you have a culinary recipe that calls for adding espresso.

The traditional eight-sided Moka pots come in 1-, 3-, 6-, 9-, and 12-cup varieties. Note that a "cup" of stovetop espresso is not equal to a cup of regular drip coffee, which yields about 6 ounces of fluid. A "cup" of espresso made in a

Moka pot will give you an intense little 2-ounce jolt (¼ of a *measuring* cup of fluid).

The beans: As any chef will tell you when you begin a culinary endeavor, the end product reflects the quality of your ingredients. You can't make a decent cup of espresso with bad beans. So buy good-quality beans freshly roasted, and grind them fresh with a home grinder if you have one.

What beans? What roast? *Espresso* refers to the *method* of making the coffee and not the coffee itself. The dark "espresso roasts" are certainly a traditional way to go for that bold, dark, caramelized flavor with hints of bittersweet chocolate, and you'll find them wherever a variety of coffees are sold.

But you may find that a lighter roast is more enjoyable, giving you citrus, berry, or floral notes, depending on the coffee's origin. Experiment with different types of coffees, blends, and roasts to see what flavors, bodies, and aromas appeal to your particular taste buds!

The stovetop method: Using a stovetop espresso maker is fairly simple. After a few tries, you'll get the hang of the timing, so don't stress over a few trial-run mistakes.

Step 1—Unscrew the top and bottom chambers. Remove the little basket (A) out of the bottom chamber and fill the bottom chamber with fresh, cold water. (Filtered is best.) You want to fill it just up to the base of the little steam valve (B). Don't go over the valve.

Step 2—Grind the beans finely. You want the consistency of fine sand. Don't grind them *too* finely—you don't want powder—or you'll make the beans bitter. Conversely, *do not* use coffee that's been preground for a *drip* maker. The grind should be finer than a drip grind. If you don't have your own grinder, then look for a coffee that's been preground especially for making espresso.

Step 3—Measure the grinds *loosely* into your stovetop basket (A). For each cup, the measure is 1 to 3 level teaspoons of finely ground coffee—using the teaspoon from your measuring set. I use 2 level teaspoons per cup, which comes out to 6 level teaspoons total for a 3-cup Moka pot; 12 level teaspoons for a 6-cup pot, and so on. If you like your espresso milder, then add less coffee; if you like a stronger taste, add more. Don't tamp the grounds in—just pile it up into a pyramid in the basket. *NOTE:* You should not try to make *less* coffee than the pot holds. If you have a 3-cup espresso pot, then you must make 3 cups every time—not 1 and not 5. If you have a 6-cup maker, you must make 6 cups, and so on.

Step 4—Tightly screw the upper pot down onto the lower one, making sure no coffee grounds are sitting on the rim to prevent a tight seal. Put the pot on the stove over low to medium heat. (If you make your espresso over heat that's too high, you may overextract your espresso and turn it bitter. As with many things in life, you shouldn't try to rush the process!)

Step 5—The entire brewing cycle takes between three and six minutes, depending on the size of your pot. The water will heat up in the lower chamber, producing steam. Because steam occupies more space than water, it builds pressure and forces the hot water up through the puck of coffee grinds in your filter. You will hear your espresso gurgling up through the pot's "fountain" (C) and into the upper chamber. When you hear the gurgling slow, watch for steam puffing out of the pot's spout, then check the upper chamber. If it's filled with coffee, then you're finished! Remove from the heat and pour into prewarmed cups. (To prewarm my cup, I simply use hot tap water. Fill the cup; let sit a minute; discard the water; wipe dry; and you're good to go!)

HOW TO CREATE LATTE AND CAPPUCCINO FROTH
WITHOUT AN ESPRESSO MACHINE STEAM WAND

No, it is not the same as professional, coffeehouse-quality foamed milk, and I wouldn't even *try* to pour latte art with it. For true microfoam nirvana, you should visit your local barista! To have some fun at home, however, my stovetop method allows you to create a *rustic* version of a coffeehouse cappuccino and latte in your own kitchen.

If you're looking for something *higher*-tech, you can now find machines designed solely to heat and froth your milk. Just type "automatic milk frother" into an Internet search or shopping engine, and you'll get a variety of affordable models to begin considering. In the meantime, here's a low-tech solution for creating foam at home!

Step 1—Fill a medium-size saucepan about ⅓ full with water. Place the pan over high heat until the water begins to boil. Turn the heat down to medium and allow the water to simmer.

Step 2—Select a heatproof mixing bowl from your cupboard that is large enough to sit on top of the saucepan. (You are creating a double boiler.) Make sure the simmering water beneath the bowl is not touching the bowl's bottom. Pour fresh, cold milk into the bowl and allow it to warm over the boiling water for *one* minute, no longer! How much milk? About ⅔ cup per serving.

Step 3—With an oven mitt on one hand to hold the hot bowl and a handheld electric mixer in the other, tip the bowl enough to tilt all of the milk into one deep, concentrated pool and then whip it. (Whip it good! Use the *fastest* speed available on your mixer and simply hold the mixing beaters in the center of the milk pool—do not move the mixer around.) In a matter of *seconds*, you'll see the warmed white fluid froth up. Whip the milk 20–90 seconds, depending on how much foam you'd like to create, and you're done! Do not over whip the milk. You won't be able to foam up every molecule of milk with this method, and if you whip it too much, you'll just begin breaking down the foam you've created.

Troubleshooting: To make this rustic frothing method foolproof, keep these four suggestions in mind. (1) Never try to re-froth milk that's been whipped and has fallen. It won't work. You must always start with cold, fresh, undisturbed milk. Pour it straight from the fridge to your measuring cup to the bowl. That's it. (2) Don't try to start whipping at a low speed and increase it. Whip it like crazy from the start, using the highest speed possible on your blender—if there's not enough immediate, vigorous whipping action, the milk won't properly foam up. (3) If you want to infuse spices or flavorings into your latte or cappuccino, then stir them into your hot espresso shot. Do *not* add syrups, flavorings, or ground spices into the milk before trying to froth it. (4) Finally, do not allow the milk to warm much longer than a few minutes over the boiling water. Steaming milk properly brings out its sweetness. If the milk is overheated, however, your latte will have a terrible scorched taste instead of a sweet one. That's why my rustic frothing method is done double boiler style instead of in a pan sitting directly on the stove burner. It's the best way to control the heat and prevent your milk from scorching.

MAKING A RUSTIC CAPPUCCINO

For one serving, start with 2/3 cup of cold, fresh milk. Follow my directions for frothing the milk. After 60–90 seconds of whipping, when much of the milk in the mixing bowl has grown into a thick cloud of rustic foam dense enough to scoop with a spoon, you're ready to create your cappuccino.

Step 1—Pour 1–2 shots of hot espresso (1 shot = 2 tablespoons) into an 8-ounce mug. The number of shots depends on how strong a coffee flavor you'd like in your drink.

Step 2—Stir in 1–2 teaspoons sugar, if desired. Or, if you'd like a flavored cappuccino, this is the time to stir in syrups or other flavorings.

Step 3—Carefully tip the mixing bowl and allow a bit of the steamed milk fluid to pour into the espresso. (Use a spoon to hold back the gobs of foam as you pour.) Finally, spoon the remaining thick foam into your mug—or as much as you can fit!

MAKING A RUSTIC LATTE

A latte is similar to a cappuccino. The difference is in the amount of foam—a cappuccino has much more foamed milk than a latte. For one serving of a latte, start with 2/3 cup of cold, fresh milk, right from the fridge. Follow my directions for frothing the milk. Do not whip the milk more than 20–30 seconds. At that point, about half of the milk in the bowl should still be fluid and half foamy. Now you're ready to make your latte. Simply follow the directions for my Basic Caffe Latte recipe on page 311.

Note on type of milk: In Italy, the use of full-fat whole milk is the standard. If you order a cappuccino with skim milk, they'll look at you like you're crazy. Why? *La dolce vita*— "the sweet life"—is the philosophy. It means you should savor the joy of living. If you're going to have a cappuccino, have it with the *better*-tasting milk and drink with joy. If you want to limit the fat and calories in your drink, however, by all means use 1% or skim milk for most of the recipes in this book.

COFFEE DRINK RECIPES

∾∾∾∾∾∾∾∾∾∾∾∾∾∾∾∾∾∾∾∾∾

Espresso Variations

In Italy, ending a meal with a freshly made demitasse of espresso is not only common, it's also thought to aid digestion of the meal. Here are some ideas for serving espresso as an after-dinner experience in your home.

ESPRESSO ROMANO "SWEET"

"Sweet" is my own term for this way of serving espresso that I've seen in some Italian-American homes. Rub the edge of your cup with a lemon wedge, then dip the dampened edge in sugar and sip the espresso through the sweet, lemony rim.

ESPRESSO WITH CANDIED ORANGE PEEL

Simply serve the espresso with the candied citrus peel on the side of the demitasse saucer. See my recipe on page 364 for instructions on how to make your own candied orange, lemon, or grapefruit peels.

ESPRESSO AMERICANO

Pour 1 shot of hot espresso into an 8-ounce mug. Fill the rest of the mug with hot water.

ESPRESSO WITH SAMBUCA

Serve the demitasse of espresso with a shot of Sambuca on the side. Sambuca is an Italian liqueur with an anise flavor—and Italians believe that anise aids digestion after a meal. Traditionally it is served in a shot glass with roasted coffee beans floating on top. The beans can be ignored as ornamental, or you can chew them to increase the anise flavor of the liqueur. Three coffee beans is traditional good luck, standing for health, happiness, and prosperity. So when you serve your guests, count accordingly!

CAFFE CORRETTO ("CORRECTED COFFEE")

Add ½ teaspoon of brandy or grappa (Italian brandy) to 1 shot of hot espresso.

ESPRESSO AMARETTO

Add 1 teaspoon of amaretto to 1 shot of hot espresso. Especially delicious served with Dante's Christmas Fruitcake Cookies and Mike Quinn's Cherry Cordial Fudge. (See recipes for these goodies and more in the following section.)

ESPRESSO ANISETTE

Add 1 teaspoon of anisette liquor to 1 shot of hot espresso. Serve with a lemon twist.

ESPRESSO KAHLUA

Add 1 teaspoon of Kahlua to 1 shot of hot espresso. Top with a bit of milk foam.

ESPRESSO WHISKEY

Add ½ teaspoon of Irish whiskey to 1 shot of hot espresso. Top with a bit of whipped cream.

ESPRESSO RUM

Add 1 teaspoon of dark rum to 1 shot of hot espresso. Top with whipped cream and a dash of ground cinnamon.

ESPRESSO COCONUT RUM

Add 1 teaspoon of Malibu rum to 1 shot of hot espresso. Malibu rum is made in Barbados with natural coconut extract. Top with a bit of whipped cream and a garnish of lightly toasted flaked coconut. A spirited accompaniment to Clare's "Bar-ista" Special Macaroons. (See recipe on page 339.)

COFFEE SYRUPS

~~~~~~~~~~~~~~~~~~~~~~~~~~~~~~~~~~

FLAVORED syrups date back to antiquity, when honey was used as a preservative for fresh fruit juices so that flavored drinks could be enjoyed all year long. As time went on, syrups evolved into flavors such as mint, orange, lemon, and almond and became a popular way to mix a refreshing drink. These days in Europe, flavored syrups are added to sparkling water to make classic "Italian sodas," while in North America, they are more commonly found as a way to flavor a coffeehouse latte or cappuccino.

The flavored latte revolution is actually a very recent one. As the story goes, a coffee industry veteran named "Brandy" Brandenburger noticed bottles of Torani brand syrup behind a counter in San Francisco's Caffe Trieste. These bottles were being used to create Italian sodas, but Brandy decided to bring home a bottle and experiment with espresso and steamed milk, and voila! The first flavored caffe latte was born! By the 1990s, adding syrups to espressos, lattes, and cappuccinos was an idea that had spread across the United States.

These days, there are a dizzying array of syrup flavors to choose from—not just vanilla, chocolate, caramel, and hazelnut, but also butter rum, carrot cake, chocolate chip, maple spice, eggnog, English toffee, pistachio, piña colada, roasted chestnut, tiramisu, toasted marshmallow, and many, *many* more! The possibilities for flavor combinations alone can make your head spin—and your mouth water.

As far as what brand of syrup to buy, coffeehouse pros will usually advise you to look for quality syrups that use pure cane sugar as the sweetening agent. Here are three great brand names to get you started. Go to their Web sites to learn more about the flavors they offer and where to purchase them. These sites are great. They even offer recipes! (Note: If any company does not sell its syrups directly to you from its Web site, just look for the link on the site where it suggests online retailers that *do* sell to the public.)

Torani—This is the oldest American brand of gourmet syrup, started in 1925 by Italian immigrants in San Francisco. www.torani.com

Monin—Monin was founded in France in 1912. Enjoyed for nearly a century by Europeans, it came to the American market in the early 1990s. www.monin.com

DaVinci Gourmet—This respected brand was launched in Seattle in 1989. www.davincigourmet.com

Tips for Using Gourmet Coffee Syrups

No need to add sugar—I love this. When you add a syrup to a drink (whether it's a latte, a steamer, or a cold sparkling water), you're automatically sweetening it, so there's no need to add more sugar. One tablespoon of syrup equals about 1½ teaspoons of sugar *and* it brings plenty of flavor to the party, too, not just sweetness. (Sugar-free syrups are also available.)

Italian sodas—Just as the Europeans do, you can mix syrup flavors with sparkling water to create your own Italian sodas at home.

Cremosa—A cremosa is an Italian soda with a little cream, milk, or half-and-half added.

Steamer—A steamer is a latte *without* the espresso, and it's great for kids or for someone who likes the idea of a delicious, warm latte but doesn't want any caffeine. Simply warm some milk in a saucepan and add the syrup as a jazzy alternative to hot cocoa. A gingerbread-caramel steamer, chocolate-chestnut steamer, or eggnog–butter rum steamer, for example, would be delicious to serve around the holidays. Just look for those syrup flavors among the brands on the market.

Desserts and baking—You can drizzle gourmet coffee syrup over ice cream or fruit (poached pears, caramelized bananas, glazed peaches, fresh strawberries). You can even add them to a favorite recipe for a slightly different flavor profile. For instance, you might add 1 tablespoon of hazelnut syrup to your chocolate chip cookie recipe; 2 tablespoons of rum syrup to a yellow cake mix; or 1–2 tablespoons English toffee syrup to your favorite brownie recipe.

Syrups with "spirit"—Gourmet syrups are nonalcoholic, even the rum and crème de menthe flavors are alcohol free! But if you'd like to be your own bartender and make your own version of a liqueur, just combine any flavored coffee syrup with vodka in a 1:1 ratio. One ounce of cherry syrup and 1 ounce of vodka, for example, will give you 2 ounces of cherry liqueur. You can serve these in a decorative shot glass with after-dinner coffee, or add espresso and steamed milk for a "spirited" caffe latte.

Using a Syrup Pump—A syrup bar can be a lot of fun, especially for parties where guests can experiment with mixing flavors. If you like the idea of setting up your own coffeehouse-style syrup bar—for coffee drinks, cold drinks, or Italian ices—then consider purchasing pumps to dispense the syrup. These plastic pumps are inexpensive and reusable. (Just remember that every syrup company offers its own pump to fit its own bottles—some Web sites sell them with the syrups and some under the heading Accessories.) As far as measure, a syrup pump will give you ¼ ounce per pump (¼ ounce = ½ tablespoon or 1½ teaspoons). Coffeehouse baristas use pumps regularly, which is why they memorize drink recipes by number of "pumps" per cup. Tastes vary and some syrups carry much stronger flavor profiles than others, but a good rule of thumb is to use about 1 pump of syrup for every 4 ounces of other liquid (coffee, carbonated water, milk, etc). So for an 8 ounce drink, you'd add 2 pumps of syrup (1 tablespoon). For a 12 ounce drink, you'd add 3 pumps of syrup (1½ tablespoons); and so on.

CAFFE LATTE RECIPES

∼∽∼∽∼∽∼∽∼∽∼∽∼∽∼∽∼∽∼∽

Basic Caffe Latte

Step 1—For one serving, start with ²/₃ cup of cold, fresh milk, right from the fridge. Heat the milk using an espresso machine steam wand or my rustic stovetop method for creating cappuccino and latte froth (page 300).

Step 2—Into an 8-ounce mug, pour 1–2 shots of hot espresso, depending on how strong a coffee flavor you'd like in your latte. Remember that 1 shot = 2 tablespoons.

Step 3—Stir in your favorite flavored syrup—1–2 table-spoons (or 2–4 pumps from a syrup bottle), adding more or less, depending on the strength of the particular syrup and your own taste. Stirring the syrup into the hot espresso helps infuse it into the drink. Or skip the syrup if you want a plain traditional latte.

Step 4—Carefully tilting your milk pitcher or bowl, pour the steamed milk into your 8-ounce mug, filling it nearly to the top. (Use a spoon to prevent any foamed milk from pouring out, too.) Stir the mug again to distribute the flavor.

Step 5—Spoon the remaining foamed milk onto your drink. Serve plain or, depending on the syrup flavors you may have added, garnish with any number of finishers: whipped cream, a dusting of sweetened cocoa powder, a sprinkling of ground cinnamon or nutmeg, white or dark chocolate shavings, or even rainbow or chocolate jimmies (aka sprinkles).

NOTE: If you don't have an espresso machine or a stovetop Moka pot, simply brew up some dark-roasted coffee at double strength to use in my latte recipes.

Latte Variations

CAFFE MOCHA

Use my Basic Caffe Latte recipe, adding 1–2 tablespoons of chocolate syrup in Step 2. If you don't have bottled chocolate syrup, try one of my Homemade Chocolate Syrups (page 313).

CAFFE CARAMELLA

Use my Basic Caffe Latte recipe, adding 1–2 tablespoons of caramel syrup in Step 2. Try my Homemade Caramel Syrup (page 315).

CHOCOLATE-CARAMEL LATTE

Use my Basic Caffe Latte recipe, adding 1–2 tablespoons of my Homemade Chocolate-Caramel Sauce in Step 2 (page 316).

TURTLE LATTE

Use my Basic Caffee Latte recipe. In Step 2, add ½ tablespoon (1½ teaspoons) of my Homemade Chocolate-Caramel Sauce and ½ tablespoon of hazelnut syrup or a nut-flavored liqueur (such as Frangelico or amaretto). Top this latte with whipped cream, a drizzle of chocolate-caramel sauce, and chocolate jimmies or shavings.

APPLE PIE LATTE

Pour 1 shot of hot espresso into an 8-ounce mug. Stir in 1–2 tablespoons of my Homemade Apple Cider Syrup (page 317). Fill the rest of the mug with steamed milk, created with an espresso machine steam wand or my rustic stovetop method (page 300). Stir again to distribute the flavors. Top with a cloud of foamed milk and a drizzle of my Homemade Apple Cider Syrup.

RASPBERRY TRUFFLE LATTE

Pour 1 shot of hot espresso into an 8-ounce mug. Stir in ½ tablespoon (1½ teaspoons) of my Homemade Dark Chocolate Syrup (recipe follows) and ½ tablespoon of raspberry syrup. (You can make your own raspberry syrup by using my Easy Homemade Fruit Syrup recipe, which also follows.) Fill the rest of the mug with steamed milk, created with an espresso machine steam wand or my rustic stovetop method (page 300). Stir again to distribute the flavors. Top with a dollop of whipped cream and chocolate shavings. Try serving with fresh raspberries on the side!

Homemade Dark Chocolate Syrup

Makes about 1 cup

1½ cups granulated sugar
1 cup unsweetened Dutch cocoa powder, sifted
⅛ teaspoon salt
1¼ cups water
2 teaspoons vanilla extract

Step 1—In a bowl, combine the sugar, cocoa powder, and salt (but *not* the vanilla). Add the water and whisk well until thoroughly blended. Pour into a saucepan and place over medium heat. Stir frequently until the mixture comes to a rolling boil; continue stirring and boiling the mixture for a full 7 minutes. (You're watching for the syrup to reduce and thicken. It will also darken a bit.) If the mixture threatens to boil over, just reduce the heat a bit and keep stirring.

Step 2—After 7 full minutes, remove from heat. Allow to cool a minute and stir in vanilla. Transfer to a bowl and place in refrigerator. When completely chilled, remove any skin from the top and strain through a fine-mesh sieve. I recommend storing this syrup in a standard plastic squeeze bottle in refrigerator. Once chilled, this syrup may firm up on you. Just reheat the bottle in microwave for 30 to 60 seconds or set plastic bottle in a warm-water bath for a few minutes.

HELPFUL HINT: Chef's say stirring in a continuous circle is not the best way to mix ingredients. Instead, stir in a figure eight, an S-shape, and a circle. In other words, vary the way you stir the pot to make sure the ingredients are blended well.

Homemade Milk Chocolate Syrup

Makes about 1½ cups

1 cup granulated sugar
½ cup unsweetened Dutch cocoa powder, sifted
⅛ teaspoon salt
1 cup whole milk

½ cup light corn syrup
½ cup heavy cream
½ teaspoon vanilla extract

In a saucepan, combine the sugar, cocoa powder, salt, milk, corn syrup, and cream. Stir over medium heat until the sugar dissolves and you have a smooth mixture. Keep stirring until the mixture boils, then keep it boiling for 7 minutes, stirring frequently. After 7 minutes, remove from the heat, let the mixture cool for a minute and then stir in the vanilla. Before storing, allow the syrup to come to room temperature. I recommend storing in a standard plastic squeeze bottle in refrigerator. Once chilled, this syrup may firm up on you. Just reheat bottle in microwave for 30–60 seconds or set bottle in a warm-water bath for a few minutes.

Homemade Caramel Syrup

Makes about 2 cups

1 cup heavy cream
½ cup whole milk
1 cup light corn syrup
½ cup granulated sugar
½ cup light brown sugar, packed
¼ teaspoon salt
2 tablespoons butter
½ teaspoon pure vanilla extract

In a nonstick pan, combine the cream, whole milk, corn syrup, sugars, and salt. Stir over medium heat until smooth and blended. Bring to a roiling boil and maintain for 8–10 minutes. Keep stirring—do not let it burn! After 10 minutes, stir in butter; continue heating and stirring for another 3 minutes until butter is completely melted. Remove from heat. Let stand a minute, then stir in vanilla. Serve warm in your latte or try drizzling over ice cream, baked apples, or pie. Let syrup come to room temperature before pouring into a standard plastic squeeze bottle and storing in refrigerator. Once chilled, syrup will firm up a bit. To use right out of fridge, simply reheat plastic bottle in microwave for 30–60 seconds or set bottle in a warm-water bath for a few minutes.

Homemade Chocolate-Caramel Sauce

Makes about 2 cups

Use all of the ingredients in the Homemade Caramel Syrup recipe, plus:
2 tablespoons (¼ stick) butter
½ cup unsweetened cocoa powder, sifted

Step 1—Follow the directions for previous caramel syrup recipe. When caramel syrup has finished simmering and recipe asks you to add butter, increase amount by 2 tablespoons—for a total of 4 tablespoons added to caramel syrup mixture. Stir until butter is melted and then stir in the sifted unsweetened cocoa powder. (Make sure cocoa is sifted or you'll be battling lumps.)

Step 2—Remove chocolate-caramel sauce from heat and stir in ¼ teaspoon vanilla—as per previous caramel syrup recipe. If your hot sauce is still lumpy, transfer to heatproof mixing bowl and whisk until completely smooth. Let sauce cool to room temperature before pouring into a plastic squeeze bottle and storing in fridge. Once chilled, the sauce will firm up quite a bit (like a hot fudge sauce). To use right out of fridge, simply reheat plastic bottle in microwave for 60-90 seconds or set bottle in a warm-water bath for a few minutes.

Homemade Apple Cider Syrup

Makes about 2 cups

> 2 cups apple cider
> 2 cups light brown sugar
> ½ teaspoon ground cinnamon
> ¼ teaspoon ground nutmeg
> 2 tablespoons butter
> ¼ teaspoon vanilla extract

Combine apple cider, light brown sugar, cinnamon, and nutmeg in a nonstick saucepan. Over medium-high heat, bring mixture to a boil, stirring frequently. After mixture comes to a boil, reduce heat to medium-low and simmer for 20 minutes, stirring every so often to prevent sticking or burning. The mixture will reduce and become thicker. Now add butter and stir continuously until completely melted. Remove pan from heat. After a minute, stir in vanilla. Syrup will thicken as it cools.

Serve in your latte or try this delicious Apple Cider Syrup over ice cream or even pancakes, waffles, and French toast.

The best way to store homemade syrups is in a plastic squeeze bottle. To reheat fast, place bottle in microwave for 30 to 60 seconds or set in a warm-water bath for a few minutes.

Easy Homemade Fruit Syrup

Makes about 2 cups

2 cups water
1½ cups granulated sugar
1 cup of your favorite flavor of jam, jelly, or fruit preserves

Flavor suggestions: Raspberry, strawberry, peach, apricot, orange, blueberry, mango, mint.

In a *nonstick* saucepan, stir together water and sugar with your favorite jam, jelly, or preserves. Bring to a boil over medium-high heat, stirring often to prevent burning or sticking. Reduce heat and simmer for 20 minutes, stirring frequently. After 20 minutes, mixture should be slightly reduced and thicker. Remove from heat and strain through a fine-mesh sieve. (Strain a second time if needed.) Allow to cool to room temperature in a bowl and remove any skin that forms. Transfer syrup to a plastic squeeze bottle and store in refrigerator. To re-warm syrup, simply place the plastic bottle in the microwave for 30-60 seconds or set bottle in a warm-water bath.

NOTE: If using an "all-fruit" preserve—the kind sweetened with fruit juice or concentrate instead of corn syrup—add about 10 minutes to the simmering process. The corn syrup in standard jellies and preserves is what helps the mixture thicken. If your jelly or jam does not have corn syrup in it (check the ingredient label), you'll simply have to boil this mixture down a bit longer for the same result.

Fa-la-la-la Lattes

~~~~~~

Unless otherwise indicated, the recipes that follow are for single servings.

Gingersnap Latte

1 shot hot espresso or strong coffee
1 tablespoon Homemade Gingersnap Syrup
⅔ cup cold milk

Pour the espresso into an 8-ounce mug. Stir in gingersnap syrup. Fill the rest of the mug with steamed milk. (Use an espresso machine steam wand or my rustic stovetop method on page 300.) Top with a cloud of foamed milk and a criss-crossing drizzle of gingersnap syrup.

Homemade Gingersnap Syrup

Makes about 1½ cups syrup

2 cups water
1½ cups granulated sugar
2 tablespoons ground ginger
½ teaspoon ground cinnamon
¼ teaspoon vanilla extract

In a nonstick saucepan, combine the water, sugar, ginger, and cinnamon. Over medium-high heat, bring the mixture to a boil, stirring frequently to prevent burning. After the mixture comes to a boil, reduce heat to medium-low and continue simmering for 15–20 minutes, stirring every so often to prevent sticking or burning. The mixture will reduce and become slightly thicker. Remove pan from heat. After mixture cools a minute, stir in vanilla. Serve warm in your latte or try it over ice cream! The best way to store homemade syrups is in a plastic squeeze bottle. To reheat fast, place bottle in microwave for 30–60 seconds or set in a warm-water bath for a few minutes.

Pumpkin Spice Latte

2 teaspoons canned pumpkin
¼ teaspoon pumpkin pie spice (see note)
1 tablespoon vanilla syrup (or ¼ teaspoon vanilla extract and 1½
teaspoons granulated sugar)
1 shot hot espresso or strong coffee

⅔ cup cold milk
Cinnamon stick

Step 1—In an 8-ounce mug combine canned pumpkin, pumpkin pie spice, and vanilla syrup (or vanilla extract and sugar).

Step 2—Pour the *hot* espresso into the mug. Stir well to blend the flavors.

Step 3—Froth up the milk using an espresso machine steam wand or my rustic stovetop method (page 300). Using a spoon to hold back the foam in your pitcher or bowl, pour the steamed milk fluid into the hot espresso. Add a cinnamon stick and stir to mix the flavors. Top with foamed milk.

NOTE: Pumpkin pie spice can be found in most grocery store spice sections. If you don't have it or can't find it, you can make your own. Simply mix the following ground spices to get 1 teaspoon of pumpkin pie spice: ½ teaspoon cinnamon, ¼ teaspoon ginger, ⅛ teaspoon ground allspice or ground cloves, and ⅛ teaspoon ground nutmeg.

Eggnog Latte

½ cup cold eggnog
¼ cup cold milk
1 shot hot espresso or strong coffee
Pinch ground nutmeg

Step 1—Combine the eggnog with the milk. Steam the liquid mixture using an espresso machine steam wand or my rustic stovetop method (page 300). Note that eggnog will scorch faster than milk, so watch the steaming process closely.

Step 2—Pour the espresso into your mug. Fill the mug with the steamed eggnog mixture. Top the drink with a bit of foamed eggnog mixture. Garnish with ground nutmeg.

White Chocolate "Snowflake" Latte

½ cup milk
¼ cup white chocolate, chopped, or white chocolate chips
¼ teaspoon vanilla extract
1–2 shots hot espresso or strong coffee
Whipped cream (optional)

Step 1—Combine milk and white chocolate in a heatproof bowl and place over a saucepan about ⅓ full of boiling water. (The water level should be under the bowl but not touching it.) Stir constantly until chocolate is melted.

Step 2—Using a whisk or handheld electric beater, whip in the vanilla. Continue to whip about a minute until the warm mixture is loosely frothy.

Step 3—Pour the espresso into a large mug. Add the steamed white chocolate milk and stir to blend the flavors. You can top with whipped cream, but I serve it without. (This drink is absolute heaven. It tastes like a rich, warm coffee-infused milkshake! Enjoy!)

Candy Cane Latte

⅔ cup cold milk
1 shot hot espresso or strong coffee
1 candy cane
½ tablespoon kirsch (cherry liqueur) or cherry syrup
½ tablespoon crème de menthe liqueur or peppermint syrup
Whipped cream
Finely crushed candy canes (optional)

Step 1—Froth the milk using an espresso machine steam wand or my rustic stovetop method (page 300).

Step 2—Pour the espresso into an 8-ounce mug and use the candy cane to stir in the kirsch and crème de menthe.

Step 3—Fill the rest of the mug, nearly to the top, with steamed milk and stir a second time with the candy cane to distribute the flavors. Top the drink with whipped cream and a sprinkling of finely crushed candy canes. Leave the whole candy cane in the mug for a festive serving touch!

Orange-Spice Yule Latte

⅔ cup cold milk
½ tablespoon orange syrup (see note) or Grand Marnier liqueur
½ tablespoon amaretto syrup or liqueur
Pinch of allspice
1 shot hot espresso or strong coffee
Cinnamon stick
Whipped cream

Step 1—Froth the milk using an espresso machine steam wand or the rustic stovetop method (page 300).

Step 2—Measure out the flavored syrups or liqueurs into an 8-ounce mug. Add the allspice, pour in the shot of hot espresso, and stir well with the cinnamon stick to distribute the flavors.

Step 3—Fill the rest of the mug, nearly to the top, with steamed milk and stir a second time with the cinnamon stick to mix the flavorings through the drink. Leave the cinnamon stick in the mug to continue adding spiced flavor. Top the drink with whipped cream.

NOTE: You can either use bottled orange syrup or follow the Easy Homemade Fruit Syrup recipe (page 318), using orange marmalade to create your syrup. You can also use the orange bar syrup that's created as a byproduct of making the homemade candied orange peels (page 364).

Esther's Jelly Doughnut Chanukah Latte

⅔ cup cold milk
1 tablespoon Homemade Caramel Syrup (see note)
1 tablespoon Homemade Raspberry Syrup (see note)
2 shots of hot espresso or strong coffee
Powdered sugar for garnish

Step 1—Steam the milk using an espresso machine steam wand or my stovetop method (page 300).

Step 2—Measure homemade raspberry and caramel syrups into an 8-ounce mug, add the hot espresso and stir.

Step 3—Fill the rest of the mug, nearly to the top, with steamed milk (using a spoon to hold back the foam in your pitcher or bowl) and stir a second time to distribute the flavors through the milk. Top the drink with a cloud of foamed milk; garnish with crisscrossing drizzles of homemade raspberry and caramel syrups and a light dusting of powdered sugar. (It really does taste like a jelly doughnut!)

NOTE: To make your own raspberry and caramel syrups, see Easy Homemade Fruit Syrup and Homemade Caramel Syrup recipes (pages 318 and 315).

Holiday Recipes

❧❧❧❧❧❧❧❧❧❧❧❧❧❧❧❧❧❧

Clare's Old-Fashioned Sugar Cookies

At the start of the holiday season, Clare Cosi mixes up a big batch of this sugar cookie dough and keeps it in the fridge, wrapped tightly in plastic. When she's ready to make a sheet pan full of cookies, she breaks off a piece of dough about the size of an orange, rolls it out, and bakes up a panful so she can serve freshly baked cookies to guests with their after-dinner coffee.

Makes 48–60 cookies, depending on the size of your cookie cutters and how thin or thick you prefer to roll your dough.

6 cups all-purpose flour
4 teaspoons baking powder
2 teaspoons salt
2 cups (4 sticks) unsalted butter
2 cups granulated sugar
4 eggs, room temperature!
3 teaspoons vanilla extract

Step 1—Make your dough: Sift together the flour, baking powder, and salt. In a separate bowl, cream the butter and sugar. Beat in the room temperature eggs and vanilla. Gradually add the dry ingredients to the wet ingredients until a smooth dough forms. (Do not overwork dough or your cookies will be tough.) Lightly pat the dough into a big ball, wrap snugly in plastic, and chill for at least 3 hours or overnight.

Step 2—Roll your dough: First, preheat the oven to 350°F. Break off an orange-sized ball of dough, place it on a flat surface that's been rubbed with flour, and (if you know what you're doing) roll away! For a thin, crisp cookie—which Clare recommends—roll the dough between ¼ and ⅛ inch thick. If you prefer a thicker cookie, roll the dough ½ inch thick.

WARNING: If you skipped the chilling of the dough as suggested in Step 1, it may be too warm to work with and will stick to everything. So chill it, baby! When you take it out of the fridge, it will be firm. If it's too firm, let it warm until it becomes pliable. If you start having trouble rolling out the dough, then read the following suggestions to prevent sticking, tearing, or the toughening of your cookies by adding too much dusting flour!

Parchment paper solution: A good way to prevent dough from sticking is to roll the dough out between two flour-dusted sheets of parchment paper. The best method for rolling, by the way, is to roll in one direction, then turn the dough (paper and all) clockwise to the right and roll again. Keep turning the dough and rolling, turning the dough and rolling, until it's nice and thin. Before removing the paper, slide the sheet of rolled-out dough (paper and all) onto a flat pan and place the whole thing in the fridge to chill for ten to fifteen minutes. This will firm up the butter in the dough and make it less sticky so you can easily peel away the top sheet of paper without chunks of dough sticking to it.

Step 3—Cut your dough: Once the dough is all rolled out, cut the dough into shapes with cookie cutters. Place the cookies carefully on a sheet pan covered in parchment paper or silicon sheets. (If you have neither, use cooking spray to keep the cookies from sticking.) Ball up any remaining dough pieces and either place them back with the remaining dough in your fridge or roll them out all over again to cut more cookies.

Step 4—Bake: Bake for 10–15 minutes. Oven temperatures vary, so watch your cookies and don't let them overcook or they'll be tough instead of tender! Determine the best time for baking based on your own particular oven and your cookie's size and thickness.

Step 5—Decorate: While your freshly baked cookies are still on the sheet pan, brush them with Sugar Cookie Glaze and sprinkle with colored sugar.

SUGAR COOKIE GLAZE

½ cup powdered sugar
2 tablespoons milk
¼ teaspoon vanilla extract
Few drops food coloring

Combine the sugar, milk, and vanilla in a bowl and whisk until smooth. Clare makes three bowls of this glaze: one with red food coloring, one with green, and one she leaves as a clear glaze with no coloring. After creatively "painting" her holiday cookies, she sprinkles them with colored sugar.

Clare's Mini Red and Green Holiday Biscotti

See photos of this recipe at www.CoffeehouseMystery.com

This is a mini version of the cookies that Clare baked for Mike Quinn the morning after she found Alf's body; when she asked her baker to reproduce batches to sell in the Village Blend pastry case, they sold out in record time! Chopped pistachios are what give this festive cookie its hint of green, and dried cranberries provide the cheerful red accent. Dipping the top edges in melted white chocolate bestows holiday richness while mimicking a kiss of winter snow. Clare's addition of ground cinnamon is unconventional for biscotti, but the hint of holiday spice strikes a surprisingly harmonious chord with this combination of flavors. The melted butter imparts a pleasant taste, too; and while the addition of shortening to any biscotti recipe reduces its shelf life, these cookies look and taste so good, they disappear quickly anyway!

Makes 36–40 mini biscotti

1 cup dried cranberries, or "Craisins"

1 cup pistachios (I use dry roasted, salted pistachios from the snack food aisle and remove shells by hand.)

2 large eggs

1 egg yolk (save egg white for glaze)

⅔ cup granulated sugar

2 teaspoons vanilla extract

½ cup unsalted butter (1 stick), melted and cooled

2¼ cups all-purpose flour

1 teaspoon baking powder

1 teaspoon ground cinnamon

2 cups white chocolate, chopped into small pieces or use chips

Step 1—Prepare Red and Green Goodies: Place dried cranberries in a bowl and cover with hot tap water to plump up. Let sit for at least 15 minutes but no longer than an hour. Drain well before adding to recipe. For pistachios: Remove shells, measure out 1 cup's worth, then roughly chop. Clare simply places nuts in a plastic bag and bangs away with a ladle or meat hammer. (If using a food processor or spice grinder, be careful. You want roughly chopped pistachios not green powder.)

Step 2—Make dough: Using an electric mixer, beat eggs, egg yolk, and sugar for 2 full minutes. Add vanilla and melted (and cooled) butter and beat for another full minute. In a separate bowl, whisk together flour, baking powder, and ground cinnamon. Now marry your wet and dry ingredients, mixing only enough to form dough. Fold in drained, dried cranberries and roughly chopped pistachios. (At this stage, Clare dusts her hands with flour and uses her fingers to fold in the goodies, making sure they're evenly incorporated. Just take care not to overwork the dough.)

Step 3—Form logs and glaze: Divide dough into two equal portions. On a floured surface, use floured fingers to form each portion into a round log measuring 12-inches long and no more than 1-inch in diameter. Place both logs onto a baking sheet covered with parchment paper or silicon sheets to prevent sticking. Press down lightly to flatten a bit. These skinny logs will spread out more during baking so be sure they're well separated. Using a pastry brush, glaze the unbaked logs with the reserved egg white (just whip it up a bit with a fork before brushing). Now sprinkle both logs with granulated sugar. The glaze will help brown the logs and hold them together when you slice them.

Step 4—Bake and slice: Bake in a preheated 350°F oven for 25 to 35 minutes (depending on your oven). Logs are finished baking when they are light golden brown, firm to the touch, and cracking a bit on the surface. Remove from oven, transfer off the hot baking sheet, and let cool completely. Wait at least 1 hour (3 is better!) and slice up like a loaf of bread. Ideally, cookies should be about ¾ of an inch in thickness. Each log will yield 18 to 20 mini-biscotti, depending on how thick or thin you slice them. For tips on preventing crumbling, see CLARE'S CRUMBLE ALERT at the end of the recipe.

Step 5—Second baking: In Italian the term "biscotti" actually means baked again. So turn the sliced mini-cookies onto their sides and bake again, in 350°F oven, for 8 minutes on one side, then carefully (don't burn your fingers!) turn over and bake another 7 minutes on the other side. You want your cookies to dry out and toast a bit on the surface.

Step 6—Dip in White Chocolate: Let your biscotti cool completely and then dip the top edges of each cookie with melted white chocolate. (Melting chocolate is easy but tricky. See melting instructions at the end of this recipe.) Set your freshly chocolate-dipped cookies on flat plates covered with wax or parchment paper for easy clean-up. (Do not use paper towels. They'll stick to the chocolate!) Wait until chocolate hardens before moving again. To speed up this process, I pop the plates in the freezer for 5 minutes (just be sure to use the wax or parchment paper or some may freeze to the plate). Then fire up the coffee maker or espresso machine and enjoy!

CLARE'S CRUMBLE ALERT: Here are four tips to help prevent mini-biscotti from crumbling: (1) Let your logs cool completely, 3-4 hours is best. You can even allow the cooling logs to rest overnight. (2) Use a sharp, non-serrated knife. (3) Press straight down. No sawing. (4) Don't try to slice cookies any thinner than ½ inch (¾ of an inch is ideal). Inevitably, a cookie or two will break apart. No worries, a few usually do (and you wanted to taste them anyway, didn't you?). In the end, remember what Nonna Cosi always said: "Good is better than perfect."

HOW TO MELT CHOCOLATE

WARNING: Make sure your bowls, pans, and utensils are completely dry before you begin. Even a few drops of water can make the chocolate seize up!

Easy microwave method: Place chopped chocolate pieces or chocolate chips in a *dry* microwave-safe bowl and warm on medium power for *only* 30 seconds. (Why? Because you are trying to prevent scorching, which will ruin the taste of your chocolate!) Now take the bowl out of the microwave and stir it with a *dry* rubber spatula. Continue warming, 30 seconds at a time, stopping to stir each time. As the chocolate gets closer to melting completely, shorten the interval to 15 seconds, continuing to stir until the chocolate is *just* melted. Because of their milk solids, white chocolate and milk chocolate are more sensitive to scorching than dark, so be careful not to overheat.

Stovetop method: Place chopped chocolate pieces or chocolate chips in the *dry* top of a double boiler with hot water in the pan beneath. If you don't have a double boiler, create your own by placing a *dry*, heatproof glass or metal bowl over a saucepan with hot water in it. The fit between your larger bowl and smaller saucepan beneath it should be snug and *not* loose. *WARNING:* The water you use should be hot but *not* boiling or simmering; neither should it be touching the container holding the chocolate. While your white chocolate melts, stir *constantly* with a *dry* rubber spatula. Remove from the heat as *soon* as the chocolate is melted. Do not allow it to scorch!

Clare's Golden Gingerbread-Maple Muffins with Warm Holiday-Spice Glaze

To bring the taste of home-baked holiday spices to her coffeehouse customers, Clare created these light, moist, gingery muffins for the Village Blend's pastry case. You'll notice there is no sugar in the muffin part of this recipe. The sweetness comes from the pure maple syrup, which is an important ingredient to get right. Pure maple syrup is not the same thing as "pancake syrup." Pancake syrup is usually just maple-flavored corn syrup. Be sure to use real maple syrup for this recipe or the texture of your muffins will be dry instead of moist and buttery, and the taste will be less appealing, too. When in doubt, check the label. As Clare puts it: "Pure maple syrup will list only one ingredient—maple syrup!"

Makes 12 muffins

1 cup raisins

2 extra large eggs, room temperature

1 cup pure maple syrup (do not substitute pancake syrup)

1 tablespoon molasses (unsulphured, not blackstrap)

1 cup sour cream

⅓ cup milk

½ cup (1 stick) butter, melted

2⅓ cups all-purpose flour, sifted

1½ teaspoons ground ginger

½ teaspoon allspice (see note)

1 teaspoon baking soda

3 teaspoons baking powder

½ teaspoon salt

Step 1—Make the batter: First, preheat the oven to 350°F. Place your raisins in a bowl and cover with hot tap water for 15 minutes to plump. Drain the water and set the raisins aside. Using a whisk or electric mixer, whip up the (room temperature) eggs for two minutes, until they double in volume, then beat in real maple syrup, molasses, sour cream, milk, and melted butter. In a second bowl, stir together the flour, ginger, allspice, baking soda, baking powder, and salt. Now blend your dry ingredients into your wet ones, fold in raisins, and mix the batter just enough until blended (do not overmix at this stage or your muffins will be tough).

Step 2—Bake the muffins: Spray the tops of your standard muffin pans with a nonstick cooking spray to prevent big muffin tops from sticking. Line 12 muffin cups with paper or foil liners. Fill each cup with the thick batter. (You may think there's too much batter for 12 standard muffin cups, but it's the right amount.) Don't be afraid to heap the batter high, dividing it evenly among the cups until all the batter is used up. Filling the cups this much will create big, coffee-house-style muffin tops. Bake for 25 to 35 minutes at 350°F.

They're done when a wooden skewer or knife inserted in the center of a test muffin comes out clean.

Step 3—Dust or glaze: Muffin tops will spread out during baking and fuse together. Use a knife to carefully separate them. Then remove the muffins from the pan as soon as they are cool enough to handle (about 5 minutes). Do not leave the muffins in the hot pan to cool or the bottoms will steam and become tough! You can pretty up these muffins with a light dusting of powdered sugar (shake the sugar through a fine-mesh sieve) or you can glaze the tops with the Warm Holiday-Spice Glaze below. Let cool completely before glazing.

Warm Holiday-Spice Glaze

2 tablespoons pure maple syrup, not pancake syrup
2 tablespoons butter
2 tablespoons water
½ teaspoon allspice
1¼ cup powdered sugar

Warm pure maple syrup, butter, water, and allspice in a saucepan over medium heat, stirring constantly until butter melts. Gradually stir in powdered sugar. Keep stirring and heating, simmering for a few minutes, until mixture is smoothly blended. This is a thin glaze that will appear almost transparent on the muffins. Using a pastry brush, generously coat the top of your cooled muffins while the glaze is still warm. If glaze hardens up in pan, reheat and stir. Serve glazed muffins immediately or let the glaze cool first. Glaze will harden in 20 to 30 minutes.

NOTE: Sure, it *sounds* like a combination of spices, but allspice is actually one spice that mimics the flavors of cinnamon, nutmeg, and cloves. Because the cost of buying spices can be pricey—*especially* ground cloves—allspice is not only a delicious alternative, it's a clever way to keep your holiday baking within your budget. The pea-sized allspice berry comes from the evergreen pimiento tree, by the way. Although the tree is grown in the West Indies and South America, Dexter's island of Jamaica provides most of the world's supply!

Clare's "Bar-ista" Special Macaroons

As Clare noted in one of her old In the Kitchen with Clare columns: Your basic coconut macaroon is simply a cookie made with lots of flaked coconut that's mixed into a paste and baked. One way to do this is with sweetened condensed milk and egg whites. Another way is to combine a 14-ounce package of sweetened flaked coconut (5⅓ cups) with ⅔ cup granulated sugar, 6 tablespoons flour, 1½ teaspoons vanilla extract, and ¼ teaspoon salt. Fold in 4 egg whites that have been lightly beaten with a fork and mix well. Create cookies by packing the coconut batter into the rounded tablespoon (from your measuring spoon set) and dropping onto a cookie sheet that's been lined with parchment paper or well greased to prevent sticking. Using your fingers, mold each cookie into a little pyramid. The triangular shape actually helps the cookie to brown on the outside for a slightly crispy bite while remaining soft and chewy on the inside. Bake at 350°F for 15 to 20 minutes or until the edges of cookie are golden brown. Do not over bake or inside won't give you the proper chewy consistency. (Makes about 30 cookies.)

Clare's "*Bar*-ista Special" Macaroon recipe puts the basic macaroon on top of a bar cookie that's quick and easy to make and sell out of the coffeehouse pastry case.

Makes 16 bars or 36 bite-sized squares

For the cookie crust:

> 6 tablespoons unsalted butter, softened to room temperature
> ½ cup light brown sugar, packed
> 1 cup all-purpose flour
> ¼ teaspoon baking soda
> ¼ teaspoon salt
> 2 teaspoons vanilla extract
> 2 egg yolks, room temperature (save whites for topping)

For the macaroon topping:

> 2 cups flaked sweetened coconut, not shredded
> 2/3 cup sweetened condensed milk
> 2 egg whites
> 1 tablespoon granulated sugar
> 2/3 cup semisweet chocolate chips

Step 1—Make cookie crust: First, preheat the oven to 325°F. Using an electric mixer, blend all of the cookie crust ingredients together. Using your fingers, press the dough into a 9-inch square pan that's been greased or sprayed with nonstick cooking spray. Bake for 10–12 minutes. No more! You want the cookie crust to set but *not* brown. Leave the oven at 325°F for Step 3.

Step 2—Make macaroon topping: In a small bowl, mix the coconut with the condensed milk. Let stand to soak. In a larger bowl, beat the egg whites until you see soft mounds. Keep beating while adding the sugar. When stiff peaks begin to form, fold in the milk-soaked coconut. Finally, stir in the chocolate chips and spread the topping on the cookie crust.

Step 3—Bake macaroons: Bake for 25–30 minutes. Cool and cut into 16 bars or 36 bite-sized squares.

Nonna Cosi's Linguine with White Clam Sauce

As with many Italian families, Clare Cosi grew up with the holiday tradition of eating "seven fishes" on the night before Christmas. Italian cooks take this tradition very seriously, coming up with many different fish dishes to serve. Clare's grandmother almost always served this one. The clam sauce is so easy to make that Clare got into the habit of keeping cans of clams, packages of pasta, and Wondra flour in her pantry so she could throw together a quick, delicious meal without much notice—just the way she did for Mike Quinn the night she was arrested. Of course, Clare's Nonna didn't have "packages" of linguine. She always made her pasta from scratch. Those were the days!

Makes 4–6 servings

For the white clam sauce:

½ cup scallions (green onions), minced
4 garlic cloves, minced
4 tablespoons chopped fresh parsley
24-ounces of canned minced clams
4 tablespoons (½ stick) butter
4 tablespoons Wondra flour (see note)
1½ cups whole milk
¼ teaspoon salt
Freshly ground black or white pepper

For the pasta:

5 quarts water
1½ tablespoons (5 teaspoons) salt
Splash olive oil
1 pound linguine (or pasta of your choice)

Step 1—Prepare ingredients: Put the pasta water over *low* heat and then mince the scallions and garlic and chop the parsley. Drain your canned clams, reserving the clam juice. (You'll get about 2 cups.)

Step 2—Make the sauce: Melt the butter in a large skillet over low heat. Do not allow the butter to brown or burn! Add minced scallions and garlic. Sauté until the scallions are transparent, 5–7 minutes. Stir in the flour until all of the liquid is absorbed. With the heat still on low, add the milk, stirring constantly to keep from forming lumps (whisk if you need to). Add your minced clams and half of the reserved clam juice (1 cup). Stir in your parsley, salt, and pepper.

Step 3—Thicken the sauce: Turn up the heat to medium and continue stirring. In about 3-5 minutes, you'll see the sauce begin to simmer. Continue stirring and simmering on medium heat for another 5 minutes, or until sauce thickens. When done, remove from heat, cover, and allow to stand about 10 minutes, letting flavors continue to blend while you cook your pasta.

Step 4—Cook the pasta: Turn the heat to high under the pasta water pot that you put on to boil in Step 1. As bubbles begin to appear, add the salt and a splash of olive oil to keep the pasta from sticking together. When the water is at a roiling boil, add your pasta and stir the pot every so often to prevent sticking. Cook until tender—about 9-10 minutes, depending on your pasta. (Check the package instructions if you're using premade pasta. Check your recipe if you're using homemade.)

Step 5—Finish and serve: Drain the pasta, then return it to the original pot (now drained of water). Add the sauce and stir until well blended. Serve immediately with suggested garnishes (see note).

NOTE ON FLOUR: You can substitute regular flour in this recipe, but Wondra is a great product to have in your cupboard. This superfine flour helps thicken sauces and gravies with a minimum amount of lumps. Look for its blue cardboard canister in the same grocery store aisle that shelves all-purpose flour. (A handy, foolproof recipe for making a basic white sauce can be found right on the canister's label, too.)

NOTE ON GARNISHES: A number of garnishes will work well with this dish. Try freshly ground black or white pepper, lemon zest, and/or sea salt. In lieu of salt—and contrary to those who say seafood should not be paired with cheese—I find a strong, aged cheese like Pecorino Romano lends a delicious, piquant note when freshly grated over this dish!

Gardner's No-Bake Mocha Rum Balls

Because Gardner's memories of the holidays always included Caribbean rum (thanks to his auntie), he contributed this deliciously decadent recipe. Sophisticated yet easy (and fun) to make, these treats blend the flavors of chocolate and dark rum with another ingredient Jamaica has long been proud of exporting—coffee.

Makes about 48 cookies

*4 ounces semisweet chocolate, chopped into small pieces,
or 2/3 cup semisweet chocolate chips*

4 ounces milk chocolate, chopped into small pieces,
or ²/₃ cup milk chocolate chips
½ cup (1 stick) butter, softened to room temperature and cut into
small pieces
3¹/₃ cups powdered sugar
1 tablespoon instant coffee crystals
1 tablespoon dark rum or 1½ teaspoons rum extract
1 tablespoon espresso or strong coffee
¼ teaspoon salt
One or more of the following finishers: chocolate jimmies; toasted
coconut; toasted almonds, pecans, hazelnuts, or another favorite nut
(see note on toasting nuts)

Step 1—Melt the chocolate: Melting chocolate is very easy, but also tricky. If you do it wrong, the chocolate can seize up on you and become coarse and grainy. If the chocolate scorches, the flavor will suffer. Avoid these disasters by following Clare's directions for properly melting chocolate (page 335).

Step 2—Mix the dough: To avoid problems mixing the dough, you'll want to keep the bowl of melted chocolate warm. If you used a microwave to melt the chocolate, then simply transfer the bowl to sit snugly over a saucepan with hot water in it. (The water should not be touching the bowl.) The pan of water can sit on your stovetop with the burner turned very low. Just don't let the water boil or you'll risk scorching the chocolate and ruining the taste of the cookies. To make the dough, work quickly: Stir in the softened butter pieces. After they have completely melted, stir in 2 cups of the powdered sugar. Dissolve the instant coffee crystals into the dark rum and espresso, and then stir into the chocolate mixture. Finally, mix in the salt and the rest of your powdered sugar (the remaining 1¹/₃ cups). If you're having trouble getting the final bit of sugar to melt into the dough, you probably allowed the bowl to cool off too much. Just turn up the heat under the saucepan of water and keep stirring until all of the sugar is incorporated.

Step 3—Roll the balls: When the dough is smooth and all ingredients are well incorporated, begin making your cookies. This pliable dough should be warm yet cool enough to touch. (If it's too warm, turn down the heat under your saucepan of water and keep mixing with a spatula until it's cool enough to work with.) Using your hands, roll the mocha mixture into balls. These are very rich cookies so keep them small, no more than 1-inch in diameter. Between every few cookies, use a spatula to remix the dough, bringing up the warmer dough from the bottom of the bowl and folding it into the top layer. Troubleshooting: As you work, if you see liquid forming on the surface of the dough, then your dough is separating: Turn down the heat beneath your pan of water and fold the dough again, remixing with a rubber spatula until it's smooth and dry and pliable once more. On the other hand, if you're having trouble getting the garnish (below) to stick to your mocha balls, then your dough is too cool! Turn up the heat and make sure the dough is warm and sticky enough to allow the finishers to adhere to the surface.

Step 4—Garnish with flare: The brown balls themselves won't look too impressive until you finish them. Immediately after you roll each ball, transfer it to a shallow bowl and coat with one of the following finishers: chocolate jimmies, toasted almonds ground finely in a food processor or spice grinder, toasted coconut. Gardner suggests dividing up your cookies and giving guests a variety of these flavor combinations.

Step 5—Serve or store: Place finished mocha balls on a flat surface and allow them to set. This will take one to two hours. Serve or store in an airtight container. Warning: Do not place mocha balls in fridge or freezer before cookies set on their own or you'll end up with a cookie texture that's grainy instead of smooth. For best results, simply allow cookies to remain in a cool, dry area of your kitchen until they've hardened enough to handle without changing shape. For a polished presentation, especially on dessert trays or party tables, nestle each mocha ball in its own fluted paper liner. (I use the mini muffin cup liners sold in the baking supplies aisle of my grocery.)

NOTE: To toast nuts or coconut, preheat oven to 350°F, spread nuts or flaked or shredded coconut (sweetened or unsweetened) in a single layer on cookie sheet and heat for 10 minutes. Stir a few times during this process to ensure even toasting.

Dexter's Flourless Chocolate Jamaican Rum Cake with Warm Coffee-Rum Sauce

See photos of this recipe at www.CoffeehouseMystery.com

A slice of fudgy heaven with hints of rum and coffee. Just as good, if not better, when served the day after baking. Of course, Dexter wants you to purchase dark Jamaican rum for this recipe, but any good dark rum will work; and (don't tell him I told you, but . . .) here's a good rule of thumb to remember for rum-flavored baking: If you'd rather not use alcoholic rum, you can always substitute rum extract by following this ratio:

1 tablespoon dark rum = 1½ teaspoons rum extract
1 tablespoon light rum = ½ teaspoon rum extract

Makes 1 sinfully fudgy single-layer cake (serves 8)

Butter
Granulated sugar
5 extra large eggs, room temperature!
1 teaspoon vanilla extract

2 teaspoons baking powder
¼ teaspoon salt
1 tablespoon instant coffee crystals
2 tablespoons espresso or coffee brewed at double strength
2 tablespoons dark rum or 3 teaspoons of rum extract
4 teaspoons cornstarch
2 cups powdered sugar
8 ounces semisweet chocolate, chopped into small pieces, or 1⅓
cups semisweet chocolate chips
1 cup heavy cream
Coffee-Rum Sauce, optional

Step 1—Prepare your 9-inch single layer cake pan: First, preheat the oven to 350°F. This cake is truly amazing, but you'll be heartbroken if it sticks to your pan. The absolute foolproof method to prevent sticking is: (1) Generously butter the sides of the pan and dust with a bit of granulated sugar (dumping out excess). The sugar will give your cake its caramelized crust. (2) Cut a sheet of parchment paper to fit into the bottom of your pan. (If you've never used parchment paper, look for it where wax paper and plastic wrap are sold.)

Step 2—Make your cake batter: Whip up room temperature eggs using an electric mixer. Continue beating 2 to 3 minutes until the eggs double in volume. Now mix in vanilla, baking powder, and salt. Dissolve your instant coffee crystals into your espresso (or double-strength coffee) and dark rum, and add these ingredients to your eggs. To make sure the cornstarch blends in smoothly and does not clump, stir it into your powdered sugar first and then add these ingredients to the egg mixture. Continue whipping with your mixer for another minute or two, making sure the mixture is light and frothy. Set aside as you melt the chocolate.

Step 3—Add melted chocolate: Melt your chocolate. Very easy to do but just as easy to ruin—take care to follow Clare's directions and warnings on page 335 (How to Melt Chocolate). Now slowly pour the melted chocolate into your egg mixture while continuing to beat with mixer. (You don't want the warm chocolate to cook your eggs!) Set aside for a minute while you whip your cream.

Step 4—Whip your cream: In a separate chilled bowl, beat your cold heavy cream with an electric mixer until stiff. Using a spoon or spatula, fold your freshly whipped cream into your chocolate batter.

Step 5—Bake: Pour finished batter into your prepared 9-inch layer cake pan. In the process of rising, the cake may slosh a bit of batter over the sides of the pan. To prevent spillage in your oven, simply place a sheet pan on the rack beneath your cake pan. Bake for one hour. Remove the cake from the oven and let it cool completely. No kidding. Let that cake cool on a rack at least 40 minutes before removing or you'll risk it breaking!

Step 6—Cool and plate: As the cake cools, you'll see it fall and that's okay. The finished cake should be dense and fudgy and only about 1 inch high. Don't worry about any cracks on the cake's top, either, because nobody will see them! After cooling at least 40 minutes, run a butter knife around edges of your cake pan.) Place your serving plate over the top of the cake and gently invert (like pineapple upside-down cake). Now gently peel away the parchment paper to reveal a perfect, level cake top. (See, I told you!) Leave cake inverted this way on the serving plate. Dust lightly with powdered sugar for a wonderfully rustic presentation.

Step 7—Serve or store: To serve, cut the cake into slices. Whipped cream or vanilla ice cream make delicious accompaniments for this baby. For a delicious and decadent finish, make the Coffee-Rum Sauce (recipe follows). Pool the sauce on the dessert plate and place your slice of Chocolate Rum cake right on top of the sauce, or scoop ice cream beside or on top of the cake and drizzle the warm sauce over both. This cake is even better the second and third day! To store, make sure it's completely cool, then wrap in plastic, and store in a cool, dry area of your kitchen.

COFFEE-RUM SAUCE

Makes 1 cup sauce

¼ cup freshly brewed coffee
3 tablespoons butter
2 tablespoons dark rum or 3 teaspoons rum extract
1½ cups powdered sugar

In a small saucepan, warm brewed coffee over *low* heat (do not boil). Add butter, stirring until completely melted. Finally, stir in rum and powdered sugar. At no time should this mixture be allowed to boil. When sugar is completely dissolved, the sauce is ready to serve. Pool the sauce warm on each dessert plate and place a slice of rum cake right on top of sauce. This sauce is also delicious over ice cream! If you don't have the time to make Dexter's Flourless Chocolate Rum Cake, simply buy a pound cake from the bakery, place a scoop of vanilla ice cream on top of each slice, and generously pour the warm Coffee-Rum Sauce over it all.

Esther's Roasted Garlic
and Herb Latkes

(POTATO PANCAKES)

Latkes or potato pancakes are Esther's favorite Chanukah food. The Jewish custom of eating foods fried or baked in oil comes from the original miracle of the Chanukah menorah, which involved the discovery of a small flask of oil that lasted many more days than it should have—which is why the "Festival of Lights" is eight days long and is marked each night by the lighting of a new candle! Here's Esther's own unique spin on her mom's traditional latke recipe, which adds the pungent flavor of roasted garlic as well as the aromatic notes of rosemary and scallion. You can even try experimenting with this recipe, replacing the fresh rosemary with a favorite herb of your choice. Serve the pancakes plain or with sour cream on the side. Yum!

Makes 2 servings or about nine 3- to 4-inch latkes; for family-size meals, you'll want to double, triple, or quadruple this recipe and have *two* frying pans working at the same time!

10 garlic cloves, roasted and smashed
(see note)
¾ cup onions (2 to 3 medium size onions), finely grated
2 tablespoons scallions, finely chopped
1 tablespoon minced fresh rosemary (optional) or
½ teaspoon dried rosemary
2 teaspoons salt
1½ pounds Idaho baking potatoes (about 3 medium russet potatoes)
1 large egg, beaten with a fork
Canola or light olive oil
Sour cream (optional)

Step 1—Prepare aromatics: First, preheat the oven to 250°F. In a large bowl, combine the garlic with the onions, scallions, rosemary, and salt.

Step 2—Grate potatoes: Do not peel your potatoes. Grate by hand with a simple box grater, or use a food processor. Add the grated potatoes to the bowl of aromatics and stir well.

Step 3—Press out moisture: Place the potato mixture in a large sieve and press down to strain out moisture. Esther notes that getting rid of excess moisture will help you create latkes that are crisp and golden brown. Now return the mixture to the bowl and stir in the egg to finish your latke mixture. Cook immediately.

Step 4—Fry pancakes: Place a heavy frying pan over medium heat and add oil, at least ½ inch deep. As Esther says, "Don't freak over the amount of oil. It's the *temperature* of the oil that makes for greasy latkes, not the *amount* of oil. Besides, the *mitzvah* is the oil!" When the oil is hot enough, begin cooking. (See note at the end of recipe on judging when oil is hot enough.) Pack potato mixture into a ¼ cup measuring cup. Turn out onto a plate in a little mound. Do this four times. Place the four mounds in quick succession into the hot oil and immediately flatten each mound into a 3- to 4-inch pancake. (Flattening is important or you may have latkes that are cooked on the edges but raw in the middle!) Cook each pancake for about 3 minutes on the first side, until the bottom is golden brown. Now flip and cook the other side 1–3 minutes until it's golden brown, too. Do not flip more than once, but Esther suggests lightly pressing the pancakes a few times with your spatula during the cooking process to make sure the centers cook. Drain in a single layer on paper towels. Keep finished latkes warm in the 250°F oven while you're cooking the rest of the batter. Serve warm with sour cream!

NOTE: If your oil is too hot, you'll burn the latkes. If your oil is too cool, your latkes will be greasy. Test the oil with a drop of water. When it dances or bounces on top of the oil, it's ready. If the oil begins to smoke, it's too hot! Also keep in mind that if you crowd the pan with too many latkes, the oil temperature will drop dramatically, so don't fry too many at once—for big batches, have two pans going at the same time.

HOW TO ROAST GARLIC

Using a whole head: Cut the top off the head (the pointed end), then wrap in aluminum foil and bake at 350°F for 30–40 minutes, until the garlic is soft. Remove from the oven. *Let the foil-wrapped garlic cool down enough to handle.* Pop the warm, roasted garlic pieces out of their skin and you're good to go. Roasted garlic is delicious and good for you! Try spreading it on slices of a French baguette or Italian bread, or mashing it and mixing it into your mashed potatoes!

Using prepeeled cloves from a jar or green market: Place your peeled cloves into a small ovenproof dish, drizzle with a bit of oil (olive is best), and add a splash of water. Cover with foil, place in the oven, and bake as described for a whole head.

Dante's Christmas Fruitcake Cookies with Snow-White Glaze

As a fine arts painter, Dante appreciates the jewel-toned colors of the traditional holiday fruitcake, but he never tasted a fruitcake he actually liked. This is his solution—yummy, buttery, refrigerator cookies with chopped candied fruit peeking through the batter like stained glass windows in a brown brick church. Like a hot cross bun, the simple snow-white glaze cross finishes off each treat, reminding us all of the reason for the season.

Makes 2 to 3 dozen refrigerator cookies, depending on how you slice them

> ½ cup (1 stick) butter, softened to room temperature
> ⅓ cup light brown sugar, firmly packed
> ¼ cup granulated sugar
> 1 egg, beaten with a fork
> ¼ cup sour cream
> ½ teaspoon orange extract or 1½ teaspoons Grand Marnier
> ½ teaspoon vanilla extract
> ½ teaspoon lemon zest, freshly grated
> 2 cups all-purpose flour
> 1 teaspoon baking powder
> ¼ teaspoon baking soda
> ½ teaspoon salt
> ¼ teaspoon allspice
> ¼ teaspoon nutmeg
> 1½ cups candied fruit, finely chopped and drained of any liquid
> (see note)
> ¼ cup pecans, chopped (optional)

Step 1—Make your dough: Using an electric mixer, cream the butter and the sugars. Add the eggs, sour cream, orange extract, vanilla, and lemon zest, and blend well. Add the flour, baking powder, baking soda, salt, allspice, and nutmeg.

Step 2—Fold in your goodies: Using a large spoon or spatula, fold in the chopped fruit and (optional) pecans.

Step 3—Form your log and chill: Dust your hands with flour. Dump your dough onto a nice big sheet of wax paper. Form the dough into a long log about 1 foot in length and

2 inches in diameter. Wrap the log up tightly in the wax paper and chill well in refrigerator—at least 3 full hours. (Overnight is even better. You can even make the dough in advance of baking and keep in the fridge for a day or two.)

Step 4—Bake, cool, and glaze: First, preheat the oven to 375°F. When ready to bake, unwrap your well-chilled log and make uniform slices between ¼ and ½ inch in thickness. Slicing tip: use a sharp, smooth knife (one that is not serrated) and press straight down, no sawing. Place cookies on a lined or greased cookie sheet and bake for 9–13 minutes. Cool completely and serve plain or drizzle a cross, like a hot cross bun, over each cookie with the easy Snow-White Glaze (recipe follows).

NOTE ON CANDIED FRUIT: Around the holidays, containers of ready-made candied "fruit and peel" are usually easy to find in grocery stores. (Always drain these well before using.) Like any homemade goodies, however, the quality of the final product is reflected in the quality of your ingredients. That's why, like Dante, I always create my own candied fruit mix for these cookies. I start with jarred maraschino cherries (be sure to drain and chop before adding). To the cherries, I add chopped golden raisins and candied pineapple, bought at my local grocery store. Finally, I add candied orange peels, which I make myself at home—you can, too, just follow my recipe (page 364). It's easy to create your own unique mix based on what appeals to you. Here are more suggestions: candied citron; candied papaya; dried blueberries, figs, dates, currants, cranberries, prunes; or any of your own favorite dried or candied fruits or peels. If you've got a really picky crowd to bake for or finicky kids and don't think a fruit mix will fly, just drain and finely chop 1½ cups of maraschino cherries. Most people love these sweet cherries on their ice cream sundaes and should enjoy finding the same flavor in these buttery sweet cookies.

SNOW-WHITE GLAZE

1 cup powdered sugar, sifted
2 tablespoons milk

Whisk together both ingredients and drizzle glaze in the shape of a cross (like a hot cross bun) over cooled Christmas Fruitcake Cookies. Let dry 20 minutes, then serve or store in an airtight container.

Tucker's Gingersnaps
with Whiskey-Lemon Glaze

Tucker's ex–Hollywood actress mom did love her bourbon. According to Tuck, this gingersnap recipe was something her southern family baked for years around the holidays. The whiskey-lemon glaze, however, was his mother's own "spirited" version of the more traditional royal icing!

Makes 36–48 cookies

2½ cups cake flour (see note)
½ teaspoon salt
¼ teaspoon baking soda
2 teaspoons ground ginger
½ cup (1 stick) unsalted butter, softened to room temperature
⅔ cup light brown sugar, packed
¼ cup molasses (unsulphured, not blackstrap)
⅓ cup milk

Step 1—Assemble dry ingredients: First, preheat the oven to 350°F. In a bowl, sift together the flour, salt, baking soda, and ginger. Set aside.

Step 2—Make dough: Using an electric mixer, cream the butter and sugar; add the molasses and milk, and blend again. While continuing to beat at a low speed, slowly add in your dry ingredients, blending just enough to make a smooth dough. Do not overbeat at this stage or your cookies will be tough.

Step 3—Wrap and chill: The dough will be very sticky. Wrap in plastic and refrigerate for at least 1 hour, overnight is fine, too. (You can also make the dough a day or two in advance and store it in the fridge.)

Step 4—Roll dough: Using a rolling pin, roll out the re-frigerated dough on a flour-dusted board or between sheets of flour-dusted parchment paper. For tips on rolling out dough, see the recipe for Clare's Old-Fashioned Sugar Cookies (page 330). The biggest issue you'll have is with the dough's stickiness. Adding flour to your board and rolling pin will help. If using the parchment paper method, slip the flat sheets of paper (with the rolled-out dough between them) into the freezer for 10 minutes. Once the rolled-out dough is well chilled, it will firm up and separate more easily from the paper. The thinner you roll your gingersnap cookies, the crispier they'll bake. Tucker suggests ⅛ inch, but you may prefer ¼ inch or thicker for a softer cookie. Experiment with what appeals to you.

Step 5—Cut cookies: Use your favorite shaped cookie cutter or a small biscuit cutter, or even the round rim of a juice glass. When you lift the snaps onto the baking sheet, be careful since they're thin and soft. (Try slipping a metal spatula or pie server under the cutout cookie dough. Or bake the cookies right on the parchment paper where you rolled it.)

Step 6—Bake and glaze: Your baking sheet should be greased, sprayed with non-stick cooking spray, or lined with parchment or silicon sheets to prevent sticking. Bake for 8–10 minutes. Cool on a rack and brush with Whiskey-Lemon Glaze (recipe follows).

NOTE ON CAKE FLOUR: I strongly recommend using cake flour for this recipe for the best results. Cake flour is milled finer and lighter than regular, all-purpose flour and will give you a more tender cookie. If you've never bought cake flour before, look for it in boxes (not sacks) in the grocery store aisle where all-purpose flour is sold. If I still haven't convinced you to use cake flour, and you want to use all-purpose flour for this recipe, then make sure to reduce the amount of flour by ¼ cup. In other words replace 2½ cups cake flour with 2¼ cups of all-purpose flour.

WHISKEY-LEMON GLAZE

1 cup powdered sugar
2 tablespoons fresh lemon juice
1 tablespoon whiskey

Too easy. Just place the sugar in a mixing bowl and whisk in the lemon juice and whiskey until smooth. Brush onto your freshly baked gingersnap cookies—but allow cookies to cool before glazing!

Tucker's Supremely Easy
Candy Cane Brownies

1 package of your favorite brownie mix
1 cup pecans, chopped
1 cup chocolate chips

Prepare the brownie batter according to package directions. Fold the pecans and chocolate chips into the batter. Bake according to the package directions. Cool, frost with Candy Cane Frosting (recipe follows), and cut.

CANDY CANE FROSTING

Makes 1¾ cups frosting—enough to frost a 9 × 13-inch pan of brownies (also fun to use on birthday cakes and cupcakes)

4 tablespoons (½ stick) butter, softened to room temperature
1–2 tablespoons milk
1½ cups powdered sugar
¼ teaspoon peppermint extract or 1 tablespoon peppermint schnapps
¼ cup candy canes, finely crushed (see note)

Using an electric mixer, beat the butter until it's light and fluffy. Stop the mixer! Add the milk, sugar, and peppermint extract. Fire up that mixer again—at a *low* speed—and blend until the sugar is fully dissolved (about 1 minute). Add the crushed candy canes and beat at a higher speed until the frosting is light and fluffy (about 1 minute more). If the frosting is too stiff, add 1 tablespoon of milk. Frost your brownies, cut, and enjoy!

NOTE: To make finely crushed candy canes, simply place your store-bought candy canes in a plastic storage bag and bang the heck out of them with the back of a ladle or meat hammer. An instant holiday stress reliever, too.

Mike Quinn's Chocolate Cherry Cordials

See photos of this recipe at www.CoffeehouseMystery.com

Yes, this is the recipe Mike made for Clare. Mike's mom gave him the recipe for this candy with helpful, handwritten notes. She made it almost every year at Christmas for family and friends.

30 maraschino cherries with stems (one 10-ounce jar has about 30 cherries)
¼ cup amaretto or other liqueur (optional)
4 tablespoons butter
4 tablespoons light corn syrup
1⅓ cups powdered sugar
3 cups chocolate chips (see note)

NOTE: If you would like to use blocks of chocolate instead of chips, you'll need 18 ounces, chopped into small, uniform pieces to ensure even melting. You can use milk, dark, or white chocolate for this recipe, depending on your preference. Or divide the total amount of chocolate into thirds and make a variety of chocolate cherry cordials: 1 cup of melted chocolate chips will cover 10–12 cherries.

Helpful hint on chocolate conversion:
6 ounces of block chocolate = 1 cup chips

Recipe notes from Mike's mom: There are four simple steps to making this candy. Step 1 is *getting the liqueur flavor into your cherries*, which you need to do the day *before* you make this candy. If you don't want your cherries to have any alcohol infused in them, you can skip the first step. Step 2 is *creating the sugar coating* around the cherry. Step 3 is *dipping the candy-coated cherry* in chocolate. Step 4 is *letting the finished chocolate-dipped candy set in the fridge for 1–2 weeks* so the sugar coating around the cherry has time to liquefy inside the chocolate shell, giving you the sweet liquid around the cherry center. So keep the timing in mind if you are planning to serve this candy for a special occasion. In other words, be sure to start well in advance!

Step 1—(Optional) Infuse cherries with liqueur flavor: Drain the liquid from one 10-ounce jar of maraschino cherries, reserving the juice. If the reserved cherry juice measures less than ¾ cup, add water to make ¾ cup of liquid. In a saucepan, bring the cherry liquid to a boil. Remove from the heat and let cool for 2 minutes before stirring in ¼ cup of any *one* of the following: amaretto (almond-flavored liqueur), Frangelico (hazelnut-flavored liqueur), white crème de cacao (clear chocolate-flavored liqueur), OR kirsch (cherry-flavored liqueur). Add the cherries and stir. Once the mixture has reached room temperature, transfer the cherries and the liquid to a bowl, cover tightly, and store in the refrigerator overnight or even longer if you're in no hurry. You can allow them to sit for a few days or even a week. (*NOTE:* Liqueurs work best to create "spirited" cherries because of their high sugar content. Sweet wines and champagnes will also work, but stay away from hard alcohols like rum, whiskey, gin, and vodka—they're strong, but they won't give you a pleasant taste.)

Step 2—Create sugar coating: In a saucepan over low heat, melt the butter and stir in the corn syrup. Add the sugar and continue stirring until it's completely dissolved. Remove pan from heat and transfer the thick white mixture to a bowl. Let cool for a full 15 minutes, stirring occasionally to keep smooth. Use your fingers to mold about a teaspoonful of the white doughy mixture around each cherry. Be generous and make sure the entire cherry is covered, sealing it up to the stem. Place the finished cherries (stem-side up) on plates lined with wax or parchment paper. Chill in the fridge until firm—at least 3 hours.

Step 3—Briefly freeze cherries: To prevent the white sugar coating from melting off your cherries during this process, transfer the cherries from the fridge to the freezer for at least 10 minutes before you begin enrobing them in warm chocolate.

Step 4—Melt chocolate: You'll need a heatproof bowl and a rubber spatula. Make sure both are completely dry. (Even a few drops of water can ruin the texture.) Place chocolate chips or pieces into the bowl and set the bowl over a saucepan with water. Turn heat to low and stir chocolate with your dry rubber spatula until it's completely melted and smooth. Make sure the chocolate *stays* melted during the coating process or you'll have trouble working with it. Just keep the heat on low beneath the pan and every so often, stir the melted chocolate. (Do not let the water boil or touch the bowl's bottom or you'll risk scorching the chocolate and ruining its taste.) For advice on properly melting chocolate, see How to Melt Chocolate instructions on page 335.

Step 5—Cover cherries with chocolate: Work in small batches, taking only five or six cherries out of the freezer at a time, keeping the rest chilled until it's their turn. Do not *dip* the cherries. If you do, the sugar coating may melt right off into the bowl of hot chocolate! Instead, hold each cherry by its stem over the melted chocolate. Using a rubber spatula (spoons won't work, the chocolate sticks too much), drip gobs of the melted chocolate down over the cherry, gently turning the cherry by its stem until it's completely covered. As the chocolate drips off, pat the bottom with more chocolate to make sure the cherry is completely coated. For the candy to be successful, you need to seal up the entire cherry with chocolate, from the bottom to the cherry stem. Allow excess chocolate to drip off each cherry and then place them on a baking sheet lined with wax or parchment paper. Once the chocolate shells around the cherries have cooled and firmed up, transfer to a tightly covered container and store in the fridge for 1 week.

Step 6—Taste test: After 1 week in the fridge, the sugar coating around each cherry will break down and liquefy. Do a taste test to gauge when the cherry cordials are ready to serve. When you bite through the crisp chocolate shell, you should have a sweet semi-liquid center around your cherry. If you don't, give it another 2 days and test again until your candy is ready to serve. (It can take up to 2 weeks.)

Mike Quinn's Cherry Cordial Fudge

As a holiday tradition, Mike Quinn's mother would infuse maraschino cherries with liqueur for her Chocolate Cherry Cordials (see the preceding recipe). What cherries were left over ended up in this quick and easy holiday fudge.

Makes about 2½ pounds of fudge

6 tablespoons unsalted butter
2½ cups granulated sugar
½ teaspoon salt
5 ounce can evaporated milk
7½ ounce jar marshmallow fluff

2 cups semisweet chocolate chips or 12-ounces of
block chocolate, chopped
1½ teaspoon pure vanilla extract
⅔ cup maraschino cherries, drained, dried, and chopped (see note)

NOTE ON CHERRIES: For ⅔ cup, you'll need about 25 cherries. (There are about 30 cherries in one 10-ounce jar of maraschino cherries.) To infuse the cherries with liqueur, simply follow Step 1 in previous recipe for Mike Quinn's Chocolate Cherry Cordials. Just make sure that you drain the cherries well and dry *completely* on paper towels. You don't want excess liquid messing up your fudge!

Step 1—Combine ingredients: In a large *nonstick* saucepan, melt butter (do not let brown or burn). Add the sugar, salt, evaporated milk, and marshmallow fluff. Warm mixture over low heat, stirring until blended.

Step 2—Boil the candy: Bring to a boil over moderate heat. This will take 5–7 minutes. Be careful not to mistake escaping bubbles (from the air in the marshmallow fluff) for a real boil. Continue to boil slowly, stirring constantly, for 5 minutes. (This entire step will take about 10 minutes.)

Step 3—Add the flavor: Stir in the chocolate chips or pieces until completely melted. Remove from the heat and stir in the vanilla. Finally, fold in the cherries, making sure (whether they are "spirited" or not) that they're drained of all liquid and dried on paper towels. Now stir again for two minutes until the mixture is completely smooth. This final stirring is important. Be sure to stir for a *full* two minutes.

Step 4—Pour and set: Transfer to a 9 × 9-inch pan that's been buttered or lined with parchment paper to prevent fudge from sticking. Even out the mixture with a dry rubber spatula and allow fudge to cool, uncovered, for *at least* 2½–3 hours before cutting. DO NOT place the pan in the refrigerator or freezer to speed up the hardening process, or the sugar in the fudge may crystallize and the final texture will be grainy instead of smooth. Simply let your pan sit at room temperature until completely firm. (Also, be sure to keep uncovered. If you put plastic or foil over the pan, the heat will condense liquid into the fudge and ruin it.) After 6–8 hours (or overnight), the fudge will be hard enough to store safely in the fridge without worry of crystallization. Or simply store the fudge in an airtight container in a cool, dry area of your kitchen.

HELPFUL HINT: Mike's mom could never get her sons to wait more than 2½ hours to start gobbling up the fudge. If you live in a cold, dry climate, this shouldn't be a problem. But if you're living in a warm or humid climate, the center of the pan may still be a little soft after such a short time, so take care in removing the fudge squares. A smart way to serve fudge that's still a little soft—or to give your fudge as a gift—is to place each fudge square in its own little, fluted paper holder. No need to scout out bakery supply stores for pretty paper holders, Mike's mom recommends using fluted cupcake pan liners sold in most grocery store.

How to Make Candied Orange Peels

See photos of this recipe at www.CoffeehouseMystery.com

These sweet little strips of crystallized citrus can be a festive addition to after-dinner coffee trays, especially around the holidays. They're also great flavor enhancers for recipes. Just chop up the strips and add ¼ cup to a favorite cookie, cake, or muffin recipe. Making your own candied peels also gives you a fantastic byproduct. If you follow this recipe, you'll end up with 2 cups of incredible, citrus-infused syrup that can be used to sweeten iced tea or mix your holiday bar drinks.

The unused fruit can be stored in the freezer in small plastic bags and used to make smoothies. Candied citrus is also delicious with chocolate. Try giving your guests a variety of chocolate experiences to choose from in the serving bowl by dipping some strips in milk chocolate and others in dark or white chocolate. You can even offer different degrees of the chocolate-citrus taste combination—just the tip of the candied strip, half of the strip, or the entire strip.

Makes 70–90 sugared citrus-peel strips

7 average size or 5 very large oranges, navels work best (see note)
6½ cups granulated sugar
Optional holiday flavor ideas: 2 cinnamon sticks or 2 vanilla beans or 2 whole cloves.

Recipe Variation: This recipe will also work with 10 lemons or 5 grapefruit. Always look for citrus with thick skins.

Step 1—Cut and peel: Rinse and dry your fruit, and cut into quarters or eighths. Now gently separate the citrus skins from the fruit inside, taking care not to tear or rip skin. The easiest way to do this is with your fingers, as if you were peeling the fruit to eat it. Make sure to keep the white pith attached to the skin. The final citrus peels should include the white pith. (See my suggestions at the end of this recipe for what to do with the unused fruit.)

Step 2—Boil out the bitterness: Place your citrus peel sections into a large saucepan and cover with cold water. Bring to a boil, turn the heat down, and simmer for 20 minutes. Drain and repeat. (Boiling two times removes bitterness.)

Step 3—Cook in simple syrup: In a saucepan (*nonstick* is best), stir 4½ cups of the sugar into 3 cups of cold water. (If using a flavor enhancer like cinnamon sticks, vanilla beans, or cloves, then add to the pot now.) Bring to a boil. Add your citrus peels and turn the heat down to medium. Simmer the peels uncovered for 1 hour. When cooking is done, gently remove citrus strips from saucepan and drain. *Keep the liquid! See note below on citrus-flavored bar syrup.* Handle your peels with care at this stage. They are still wet and soft, so they can rip easily. (They'll firm up as they dry.)

Step 4—Cut into strips and roll in sugar: When peels are cool enough to handle, use kitchen sheers to cut them into strips about ¼ inch thick. Roll the strips in the remaining 2 cups of sugar. Use more sugar if you need it.

Step 5—Dry the strips: Preheat the oven to 180°F. Spread the sugar-coated strips in a single layer on cookie sheets. Bake for 60–90 minutes. (*Do not* try to speed up the drying process by turning up the heat! Keep oven temperature low or you will melt the sugar! Do not leave in oven longer than 90 minutes for the same reason.) Remove from oven and transfer strips to a rack or paper towels to cool to room temperature (another hour at least, but you can allow to dry overnight if you wish). Once completely cool and *completely dry*, store in an airtight container. (If you store these while they're still damp, they'll become soggy and the sugar will begin to melt off. If that happens, simply re-roll in sugar and allow to dry at room temperature overnight before storing again.)

DIPPING IN CHOCOLATE: If you are going to chocolate dip part or all of your citrus strips, make sure they are completely dry first. For advice on properly melting chocolate, see How to Melt Chocolate instruction on page 335.

CITRUS-INFUSED BAR SYRUP: A fantastic byproduct of this recipe is the drained liquid leftover from boiling the peels. Do not discard this liquid. This is a citrus-infused simple syrup that can be used to sweeten iced tea or mix bar drinks. Simply allow the liquid to cool to room temperature, and then transfer it to an airtight container and store in the refrigerator. For mixing into bar drinks, here's one suggestion: 1 part citrus-infused syrup to 4 parts club soda or seltzer. Serve over ice for a virgin drink or splash in some of your favorite alcohol: I like amaretto, but you can always add something stronger, such as vodka, gin, or (Gardner's favorite) Caribbean rum!

UNUSED CITRUS FRUIT: The other byproduct of this recipe are sections of unused citrus fruit. Don't let these go to waste. You can either drop them in a blender for a quick, delicious pint of fresh fruit juice. Or seal them in a plastic bag and store them in the freezer. Whenever you're in the mood for a fruit smoothie, remove some of the frozen citrus sections and drop them in a blender with a sliced up banana, a bit of milk, and a few ice cubes (strawberries or blueberries are a great, healthy addition, too). Blend on high until smooth, pour into a chilled glass, and enjoy!

**Don't Miss the Next
Coffeehouse Mystery . . .**

ROAST MORTEM

Available in hardcover from Berkley Prime Crime!

Clare Cosi has perfected the pulling of steaming hot espressos. But can she keep New York's Bravest from getting burned?

After local firefighters pull Clare out of a blazing café, she happily comes to their rescue by teaching them how to operate their newly donated espresso machine. But soon more coffeehouses are torched around the city and firefighters begin to die in suspicious ways.

Believing the two events are related, Clare investigates, staking out a five-borough bake sale and sniffing out clues in the pizza ovens of Brooklyn. Then her detective boyfriend, Mike Quinn, is pulled into the fire of a false accusation and Clare is desperate to put out the flames. But will she be able to come to Mike's rescue before someone tries to extinguish her?

**For more information about
the Coffeehouse Mysteries,
visit the author's Web site at
www.CoffeehouseMystery.com.**